VEIL ONLINE
Book 2

An Epic LitRPG Series

Written by John Cressman

ISBN: 978-0-9844087-7-1 (Paperback)
ISBN: 978-0-9844087-8-8 (Hardcover)
ISBN: 978-0-9844087-6-4 (Amazon Kindle)
ISBN: 978-1-7351302-9-3 (Audiobook)

Any references to historical events, real people, or real places are used fictitiously. Names, characters, and places are products of the author's twisted imagination.

Front cover image by May Dawney from maydawney.com.
Book design by Rebecka Yaeger of Becka's Best Author Services.

Printed by Maverick-Gage Publishing in conjunction with IngramSpark, in the United States of America.

First printing edition 2020.

Maverick-Gage Publishing
Allentown, PA
info@maverick-gage.com
www.maverick-gage.com

John Elijah Cressman
www.johnecressman.com

VEIL Online

Chapter 1

"I said, I found your body," Charlena repeated. The red-headed elf had finally shown up in the Dwarvish Fork Inn just as they were finishing dinner and suddenly announced she had found Jace's body in the real world.

"Wha-" Jace said in shock. He tried to sort through the maelstrom of emotions he was feeling. When he'd first woken up in the game, he'd assumed he was dead and had been uploaded into VEIL Online as his last will and testament had stipulated. It had been a surprise, but he quickly realized other things were amiss.

Waking up in a non-player character (NPC) monster body hadn't been part of the plan. He had expected to wake up in Mordred, his vampyre assassin character that he had spent years building up. Not only that, the money from his life insurance policy should have been transferred into the game, giving him a comfortable "after life" in the game.

Instead, he'd been inside one monster body after another as he was killed by players. Each time he died, he'd end up inside a different monster, able to control it but not communicate with anyone except other monsters.

Luckily, being a junior programmer, he'd managed to hack the system and changed himself back into a player but only as a human character, the most basic race in the game with no special features or abilities.

He'd met Charlena, who was a real life person playing the game, and together they'd made it to the capital where he could find an old and now hidden way of contacting support inside the game. Inside the Royal Palace was a secret room that contained a *Help Desk* that would allow him to communicate to support and get this situation resolved.

Along the way, Charlena had found out that he had no death certificate and thought he was alive. Now, she was saying she had just found what she thought was his body. He had no idea what to feel. Should he shout for joy or cry? He didn't feel like either of those. Jace just felt… numb.

Was it possible that he really was alive and stuck in a coma inside a medical VR pod? He knew hospitals had them. He'd seen commercials on the vid streams about them. They were meant for long term use and took care of a body's biological functions while keeping the brain active.

So much had happened, so quickly, he didn't really know what to think or feel about this latest development. Part of him thought of all the things he'd thought he missed out on. Now he'd get a true second chance.

Another part of him held back. He'd had so many things happen to him in such a short time span, he didn't want to get his hopes up. Not yet. He had to know. Jace had to be certain before he really released the floodgate of emotions that would go with truly being alive.

"Thomas Jefferson University Hospital," she said, snapping Jace back to the conversation.

He noticed that Charlena was looking a little green and seemed to be swaying on her feet.

"Are you okay?" he asked her.

"Too much celebrating last night," she told him. He knew she'd gone out drinking with her friends in the real world. She must have really over done it.

"So," interjected Diana. "You found our savior's body. He's alive?"

Diana had been in the same situation as Jace, trapped inside an NPC monster body until Jace had helped free her by showing her how to hack the system and convert herself into a player. Surprisingly, Charlena had heard of her. Her real name was Anika Holden, but she was a romance novelist who used the pen name Diana Stewart.

"Truly?" Mika asked, smiling.

Like Diana, Mika had died and been uploaded into the game. She was Japanese and had been flying back from inheriting her grandmother's estate in Tokyo when the plane had crashed. She'd been trapped inside a monster body as well until Jace freed her.

Charlena nodded and Jace could see it was taking some effort for her to stay upright. He stood up and helped her sit down in his chair. He would have offered her the chair next to him, but it was currently occupied by his familiar, an orange tabby cat he'd named Luna, after his sister.

Luna stirred slightly when Charlena sat down and opened one eye. After seemingly finding nothing interesting worth waking up over, she closed her eyes and went back to sleep.

After sitting, Charlena looked up at him gratefully but still looked a little green. "Thanks."

"This is very good," Mika said smiling. "You are alive."

Charlena nodded. "I just need to go ID the body."

"ID my body?" he asked.

Charlena let her head fall into her hands. When her voice came out it was muffled. "I guess I forgot that part. There's a John Doe that matches you. Well, what happened to you. John Doe brought in the same day, car accident and coma patient."

"Darling," Diana said. "You're not even sure it's him yet?"

Charlena let out an exasperated breath, her head still in her hands. "It's the same things that happened to Jace, on the same day in the same way.

And there's no death certificate for him. It's got to be him."

Was he this John Doe? He did agree with Charlena that it seemed remarkably coincidental that another auto victim would come in the same day in a coma. Jace didn't believe in those types of coincidences.

He felt the excitement finally getting some confirmation that he was actually alive not really dead. Even though Charlena had told him earlier that he might be alive, he hadn't really believed it. Things just never seemed to work out that way for him. As Damian said, if Jace didn't have bad luck, he'd have no luck.

"Yes," Mika said, looking at Jace. "You are a good person. You should be alive."

Jace was sure that wasn't the way it worked. Just because you were a good person, didn't mean things always worked out for you. He'd learned that at an early age when his parents and his sister were killed in a car accident on the day of his high school graduation.

No, life wasn't fair. The good guys didn't always win, and the bad guys didn't always get punished. That was life. He'd learned to accept it. But he did hope he was alive. Especially since that would mean he might possibly have a real relationship with Charlena.

"I have an appointment for Friday to go identify. We'll know for certain then," Charlena murmured.

"You know I don't look like this right? I'm much skinnier and my jaw isn't quite as um… heroic…." Jace felt a little embarrassed to point it out but he knew it needed to be said. The game generated an avatar for you based on your DNA. Basically, it created your ideal body in peak athletic shape. If you chose a player race that wasn't human, it would apply that race's template to the body but usually the person was recognizable unless they chose one of the more monstrous races like half-dragon.

Charlena looked up, forcing a smile through her obvious discomfort. "You know I'm not really an elf in real life, right?" She winked at him. "I know you look different too, but I'll recognize you."

Jace put a hand on her shoulder. "Thanks for coming in and telling us. Why don't you log out and feel better? We'll meet you here later?"

Charlena gave him a thankful smile. "Okay. I'll be back tomorrow." Without any further ado, her avatar faded away.

"Poor thing," Diana commented. "I remembered my party days. Or should I say, I remember I had party days. The details are a bit sketchy."

Jace turned away from the spot where Charlena had been and back to the two women in front of him. "So, about our plan to get inside the Royal Palace."

"We have a plan?" Diana asked with a raised eyebrow.

Jace rolled his eyes. "No, I mean we need to make a plan."

"Yes," Mika agreed. "We need to make a plan."

"Darling," Diana cooed. "I know you have feelings for him, but you don't have to parrot everything he says."

Mika quickly lowered her head but not before Jace saw the color in her cheeks. It also surprised him. He had no idea that Mika had any feelings for him. After all, their initial meeting was short, and she'd been a yeti at the time. Tonight was the first time he'd seen her since then.

The revelation made him feel awkward. After all, Charlena and he were… well, he wasn't sure what they were, other than the fact they'd shared some kisses. He liked Charlena and he was attracted to her but then again, he was attracted to Mika too. Jace was even attracted to Diana but knowing she was in her 90s, or had been, made it very weird.

He tried to push those thoughts out of his mind and get back to the plan. After all, they were all stuck like this until they could get the game maker, WorldCog, to fix them. And the only way that was going to happen was for them to contact support directly. That meant getting to the *Help Desk*.

Diana looked over at Mika, who still had her head bowed. "Oh darling," she said, her voice now tender. "I'm sorry if I embarrassed you. The way you wore your heart out there on your sleeve, I didn't realize you were trying to hide it."

"So, back to the plan," Jace cleared his throat. "Our goal is to get to the *Help Desk*. That's inside the Royal Palace, which is inside the Noble District. The *Help Desk* is hidden. We can address that when we get inside the palace. We can't get inside the palace until we get inside the Noble District."

Jace had planned assaults on strongholds and castles before and was usually pretty good at it but this was unlike anything he'd ever pulled off. The first rule to assaulting a stronghold seemed to be applicable here to: gather information.

"If you're both willing to help," he said and waited for nods of confirmation. "Good. Since you're both willing to help, I suggest gathering all of the information we can about the Noble District and the palace."

He turned to Mika, who had finally raised her head. "Mika, can you find out about the Noble District? Find out who goes in, who goes out, do they need papers, passwords. That sort of thing. Gather as much information as you can."

"Diana..." he started but she interrupted.

"Find out everything I can about the Royal Palace," she interjected. "Darling boy, I've written a few intrigue novels in my day. I'll do my best to find out everything there is to know about that place."

Jace couldn't help but crack a smile. She was certainly a feisty old woman. And confident. But then again, she had more life experience than Jace, Mika, and Charlena put together. Plus, she was a famous author. She had every reason to be confident. The only thing she really lacked was experience in the game.

"I will do my best," Mika said, not quite making eye contact with him.

"I know you will." He smiled at her, trying to make her feel at ease. Jace was all too familiar with being embarrassed in front of someone you were attracted to. Heck, that was pretty much the story of his real life dating experience.

"We should also get a room," he told them.

"Dear boy," Diana purred. "I thought you'd never ask."

Mika blushed and Jace just rolled his eyes but couldn't help but feel a little excitement. Diana seemed to be an incorrigible flirt but Jace admitted it was nice having an attractive woman flirt with him. Even if she was old enough to be his... grandmother?

He'd never really thought about age before in the game. Everyone's virtual body was generated to appear 25 years old. Other than a few friends in college, he'd rarely known the people he associated with in game or how old they were. And most of the time it didn't matter. But thinking of this attractive, raven-haired young woman having the mind of a 90-something-year-old was very strange.

"To use as a base of operations," he continued. "That way we have a place to meet, no matter what time of day it is. I'm sure you've all noticed by now that we don't sleep."

They two women nodded.

"And like real life, the shops, inns and taverns have a schedule. The NPCs go to sleep just like real people which means we need a place to regroup," he said. "This seems like a good place, plus I'm hoping one more person joins us."

He had freed another player, Duglas Morgan. He had been a day trader who had been uploaded. Duglas had been in the body of a goblin when they'd met and Jace had shown him how to hack his way into a human body. Like the others, he'd told Duglas to meet here but so far there was no sign of him.

"How are you two on gold?" he asked them.

"I spent my last gold on this lovely outfit," Diana said, leaning forward so Jace got an unobstructed view of the plunging neckline and her ample bosom. "Wouldn't you say it was worth it?"

Jace cleared his throat and only lingered for a moment before looking over to Mika. "I have 32 gold."

He nodded. "I have a little over a hundred left, so I'll pay for the room but we're going to need to earn some more money. Not only will we need to maintain a room, we'll also need supplies, bribes and who knows what else to get into the palace."

Diana sat back against her chair and crossed her arms over her breasts. "And how do you suggest we earn money?"

Jace smiled. "Quests!"

Chapter 2

"Yes," Mika agreed.

"Quests?" Diana said disdainfully but then brightened. "How about I make money my own way?"

Jace raised an eyebrow. "And how's that?"

Diana stretched sublimely, displaying her large assets. "Let's say my real body never looked this good and it's been a VERY long time since I was able to use what I have to get what I want."

Mika's almond eyes went wide, and she flushed crimson. "You would trade… for money?"

Diana gave her a dismissive gesture. "We're consenting adults. And if they want to help a girl out, who am I to say no."

Jace shook his head at the wanton ex-author. That type of thing wasn't unheard of in the game and most people didn't find it offensive since it was all virtual. "If that's what you want to do, good luck. Just be careful."

"I am the vision of caution, young man," she replied confidently.

"Mika?" He turned to the girl.

The Japanese girl's face went red and she shook her head. "I will do quests."

Jace smiled and winked at her. "Me too."

This caused her to blush even redder and Diana laughed melodiously. "You youngsters are so adorable."

"Whitecliff is a capital city," he told them. "It will have quests of all levels. Just be very careful about what quests you accept. Make sure they're of a level you can handle. Guild quests should be good since they scale to your level."

Mika nodded. "I will be careful."

The older woman stood from the table and winked at Jace. "I'm going to ply my trade and see what trouble I can get into. I'll meet you here."

"Hold on," Jace stood as well, disturbing Luna again. "Let's get the room first and then we'll agree to meet back tomorrow morning, but it will at least give us a place to return to."

"That is a good idea," Mika agreed.

"Smart and cute," Diana said, running a finger along his jaw. "My kind of man."

Jace shuddered despite himself. The woman literally oozed sexuality but he had the impression that it was all some act. He wondered if this was the real

Diana or if she were roleplaying one of the characters from her books.

The three of them, plus Luna who had finally finished napping, found the dwarven innkeeper and requested a large room. The stocky, gray-bearded dwarf, who Jace's HUD identified as Vaddatum Barrelshield, eyed the three of them. "How many beds?"

Diana spoke up before Jace could answer. "Just one. A very large bed."

The dwarf looked surprised briefly and then glanced from the two beautiful women to Jace and gave him an appreciative nod. "Very well. Three keys?"

"Four actually," Jace said, feeling slightly embarrassed. "We have another woman joining us."

Vaddatum raised an eyebrow and glanced over the three of them again before nodding. "Four keys it is. How many nights will you be staying?"

"Let's start off with a week," he told the dwarf. "But we may need to stay longer."

The dwarf coughed, trying to suppress a grin. "All... uh... four of you... staying a week?"

Jace nodded. "Yes, maybe longer."

"Excellent, good sir. That will be 20 gold a night for the room, so 140 gold for the week for our honeymoon suite, it's the largest room we have with the um… largest bed," the man shot a glance at Diana who just winked, while Mika tried to disappear behind Jace. "Payable in advance."

Jace handed the dwarf the gold, leaving him with 4 gold to his name. Barely enough to buy breakfast in the morning. He'd need to earn some serious money and soon.

You receive 4 keys from Vaddatum.

He handed out the keys to the girls and stashed his and Charlena's in his inventory. "I'll see you both back here for breakfast tomorrow."

"Ta ta!" Diana blew him a kiss, while Mika just nodded to him and hurried away.

Jace needed to find the thieves guild here in Whitecliff. The problem was, he had no idea where to look. This was the capital of Zushor, the human kingdom. It would have the heaviest guard population of nearly any city in the game. That meant the thieves guild would be hidden well, though possibly in plain sight.

He needed to find it. And the sooner the better so he could do some quests and make some money. He needed to find another Rogue and he had an idea of where to find one.

He left the Dwarvish Fork Inn and headed towards the docks. For some reason, Jace noticed that docks tended to attract Rogues. He guessed it was the ships. Ships meant cargo, cargo meant money and money meant Rogues.

The city was large, and it took him a half hour to get to the docks. When he finally did reach them, he realized that they spanned nearly the entire length of the city. It was an impressive sight. As he walked the length of the docks, he kept a wary eye out for Rogues.

Jace's vigilance was rewarded before he'd walked halfway down their length. Movement along the periphery of his vision attracted his gaze. He saw a female halfling pick a dock worker's pocket as the man carried a large barrel from one of the ships.

Jace smiled and brought up his HUD to examine halfling.

Name: Justina Pockets
Race: Halfling
Class: Scout
Level: 1

The thief was a player, though by her level she was a new player. Still, she might know where the guild was, so it was worth trying to talk to her.

He looked back to see the halfling cross the street and duck into the alley. Jace rushed after her, hoping she knew where the thieves guild was in the capital. As he reached the entrance to the alley, he peered in, realizing how dark it was outside the range of the oil lamps.

He mentally toggled on his *Cat-Vision*, an ability he gained from having a cat familiar, so he could see in the dark. With his enhanced vision, Jace looked down the alley but didn't see her. Had she already left the alley? He walked in a few feet when the little halfling stepped out from behind a barrel that seemed too small to hide her.

It was the same halfling he'd seen before but close up, he was able to see more details. The first thing he noticed was the halfling's spiky black hair, tipped in red. It wasn't exactly period, but players could generally customize their characters however they saw fit - within reason.

Her garb was a similar anachronism. She wore tight, black leather pants and a form-fighting, low cut sleeveless leather shirt. She wore high leather boots and matching leather bracelets. Around her neck she wore a spiked leather choker. Her make-up was all blacks and dark reds, giving her a very goth/punk look.

What really got Jace's attention were the two throwing knives she held, poised to throw at him. Just like elves got bows as a bonus skill, halflings received thrown weapons as a bonus skill.

"Reach for the stars ya filthy copper," said the punk halfling.

Jace wasn't really worried. Despite her bravado, they weren't in the player versus player (PvP) area, so she couldn't just attack him outright. They were also in the same faction. That meant, she'd need to duel him, and he'd have to accept the duel request. He guessed she was roleplaying, so he decided to play along. Maybe he could get on her good side.

"I ain't no copper," he said. He had recognized the slang from old vidstreams, a copper was old slang for a police officer. He idly wondered if she was a fan of the retro vidstreams like him. He thought for a second before he remembered some other old slang. "We're in the same line of work dollface."

She tried looking menacing for a moment, but he saw the corners of her mouth curve up as she fought to control a smile. Apparently, she hadn't expected him to play along. "The big guy has some moxy, I'll give you that."

"Alright, ya big palooka," she said as she lowered her throwing knives. "What do you want from Justina?"

He thought it interesting that she talked in third person, but some people did when referring to their character. He guessed they needed that separation between who they were and who their character was. Or she was crazy.

At the thought of crazy people, he suddenly remembered another player he'd encountered who had been trapped in a monster body. He'd called himself Big Cheese and had gone completely insane. Instead of letting Jace help him, the crazy goblin had killed him.

Remembering Justina, he asked, "Do you know where the thieves guild quest starts?"

She eyed him. "The Hideout, huh? I ain't no rat, see. But, if a certain person was to go to a certain place near the docks and do a certain thing to some certain people's pockets, a certain thing might happen to him. Capiche?"

"Um… no…" he muttered, not understanding her at all. He did enjoy retro vidstreams and books, but this was one genre he wasn't familiar with.

She gave an exasperated sigh and her voice changed from an old time gangster accent to a more modern accent. "Geez! Go down the docks, pick a few pockets and then leave the dock area. When you do, someone will show up and offer you the starter quest. Got it?"

He nodded. "Yes."

She seemed to catch sight of Luna then and her eyes opened wide. "Is that a cat? Oh my god, you have a cat! How'd you get a cat? Can I get one?"

Before Jace could answer, the halfling had rushed forward and grabbed Luna. Luna started to protest but the little halfling was stroking her fur and giving her scratches and the little cat began to purr.

After a few minutes of petting Luna, she put Luna back on the ground and looked up at Jace. "Where did you get your cat? Is it a prestige pet?"

Jace shook his head. "She's my familiar."

"Your familiar?" the halfling looked at him skeptically. "Wait, you're a wizard? And you're looking for the thieves guild?"

"Mage actually. I'm multi-class," he explained. "I've got some levels of Rogue."

"Rogue? Not Scout?" she looked confused. "Mage and Rogue? Are you hardcore or something?"

Hardcore players were those who only believed in only playing the race and classes from the original game, before WorldCog introduced the premium races. That meant only human and only the base classes: Fighter, Rogue, Mage and Priest. Coincidentally, that was the only race and classes Jace had available. He guessed he was involuntarily hardcore.

"Something like that," he said.

"To each his own," she shrugged. "Not this little girl. I was born to be a halfling."

"Thanks for your help," he told her.

"Sure, thing goon," she said, reverting back to the gangster accent. She looked around conspiratorially. "Now get your ugly mug out here before coppers come along and drag me to the big house in bracelets."

With that, she whirled, skipped to the end of the alley and disappeared around the corner. Jace watched the strange little thief go and shrugged. She was odd, but definitely not the most unusual person he'd met.

At least she'd been helpful. If he understood her correctly, he just needed to go down to the docks and pick a few pockets and then leave the dock area and that should trigger the starter quest. Seemed easy enough but then again, it was a starter quest. It was supposed to be easy.

"Time to pick some pockets," he told Luna.

Chapter 3

Justina had given him what he needed. He knew from experience that some of the most rewarding quests were the class guild quests. Of those, the thieves guild quests were the best in his opinion since they offered the best rewards. They also offered the most risk, but he'd deal with that.

But first he needed to actually join the guild. Each guild had its own starter quest for membership. Some were as easy as walking into the guild and talking to the guildmaster. Unfortunately, the thieves guild starter quests were never that easy.

If he were back in the real world, he would have just looked up the quest details on the internet. There were sites devoted to all aspects of VEIL Online. Unfortunately, that wasn't an option at the moment. If Charlena was on, he could have asked her, but she was sleeping off her night of frivolity.

Jace reached the dock area and almost turned back. The smell of rotting fish was overwhelming to his maxed out sensory feedback. It made him want to gag and he wished he could turn down his sensory level like regular people.

Trying to breathe through his mouth, he entered *Stealth. Pickpocket* wasn't one of the skills he was able to train in yet, so he needed to pick a very easy mark or two, or he'd risk getting arrested or fined. Neither of which he could afford.

Jace crept around the dock area, but the hour was growing late and most of the workers were heading off to the taverns. The only people out were a few sailors here and there either returning from or heading off to a tavern and the few guards who patrolled the docks.

He crept up further down the docks, trying to find a lone sailor that he could attempt to *Pickpocket* but there were none to be found. The sailors were moving in groups, probably because they knew there were safety in numbers.

Frustrated, Jace turned to check out the other end of the docks when a sound caught his ears and he paused to listen. It sounded like yelling. Or was it really bad singing? Sensing he may have found his marks, he followed the sound several berths down to a long stretch of dock that ran between two ships.

As he looked down the expanse of the dock, he realized the yelling really was singing. Then Jace amended himself, it was *supposed* to be singing but it was like really bad karaoke. With his enhanced *Cat-Vision*, he was able to make out two figures leaning against some crates at the very end of the dock.

The pair seemed to be very drunk and Jace decided they would be perfect. He made sure no one was around and then crept down the dock towards his marks.

Getting closer, Jace recognized them as dock workers, probably recently off duty. One was a short, fat dwarf and the other taller, skinny human. The two were passing a bottle between them and belching out the lyrics to a song loudly and quite out of tune.

"What do you do with a drunken halfling?

What do you do with a drunken halfling?

What do you do with a drunken halfling?

So early in the mornin'!"

The pair were sprawled out against a stack of crates, which actually made the perfect spot to hide behind and try to pick their pockets. Jace slowly maneuvered behind the crates as the two finished another stanza.

"First you spin him, then you dunk him.

First you spin him, then you dunk him.

First you spin him, then you dunk him.

Early in the morning."

There was a pause in the song while one of the dock workers hiccupped loudly. Being careful to stay hidden, Jace inched his way around one of the crates, towards the skinny human as the inebriated duo resumed their song.

"What do you do with a drunken halfling?

What do you do with a drunken halfling?

What do you do with a drunken halfling?

So early in the mornin'!"

Jace moved within inches of the oblivious worker and waited. The next time the worker leaned over to grab the bottle, he deftly reached into the skinny man's pocket and grabbed the first thing he found.

Pickpocket successful.
You have stolen 1 gold piece.
Your Pickpocket skill has increased by 1.

Smiling, brought the coin back to his side and put it into his inventory. That was a success, in more ways than one. He got a gold piece and a skill up. Jace moved his hand back into position and waited again, while the two drunks bellowed more lyrics.

"What do you do with a drunken halfling?

What do you do with a drunken halfling?

What do you do with a drunken halfling?

So early in the mornin'!"

Once more the skinny drunk leaned over to get the bottle and Jace's hand snaked into his pocket. He pulled his hand out and this time he held a knife.

Pickpocket successful.
You have stolen an item.

Your Pickpocket skill has increased by 1.
You receive bundle of pipeweed.

Jace shrugged and tossed it into his inventory. He didn't smoke in-game or out but maybe he could sell it. Besides, he'd gotten another skill rank and that made it worth it. He got back into position for one more attempt. He remembered that there was a limit to how many times you could *Pickpocket* an NPC but couldn't remember what the number was.

"Next you dress him, then you feed him!

Next you dress him, then you feed him!

Next you dress him, then you feed him!

So early in the morning!"

Making another *Pickpocket* attempt when the time was right, Jace was rewarded with a folded piece of paper and another skill up. He slipped the paper into his inventory and made a mental note to read it later.

Not wanting to press his luck, he crept around the crates behind the dwarf. He repeated the same thing he had before on the dwarf, slipping his hand in the fat worker's pocket when he leaned over to grab the bottle.

Pickpocket successful.
You have stolen 1 gold piece.
Your Pickpocket skill has increased by 1.

He stashed the coin in his inventory and reset his position as, yet another chorus of the song continued.

"What do you do with a drunken halfling?

What do you do with a drunken halfling?

What do you do with a drunken halfling?

So early in the mornin'!"

Once again, he waited and reached into the dwarf's pocket, but the dwarf shifted, and he felt his hand rub against the dwarf's leg.

Pickpocket unsuccessful.
Target alerted.
Your Pickpocket skill has increased by 1.

Jace swore silently. He'd pushed his luck too far and now he might need to make a run for it. As he thought it, the dwarf stopped in the middle of taking a swig of whatever was in the bottle and looked down at Jace's hand, inside his pocket.

"Is that your hand in me pocket, laddy?" the dwarf slurred.

Jace said the first thing that came to his mind and snatching his hand back, he blurted out, "No."

No? He actually said no. He wanted to face palm himself. Really eloquent, he chided himself. But then he remembered his *Bluff* skill. Had that come into play here?

The dwarf eyed him suspiciously. "Then what (hiccup), what do you be doin'?"

That was even more interesting. The dwarf wasn't attacking him. Did that mean his *Bluff* worked? Or was the dwarf just too drunk to raise the alarm. Possibly both.

He noticed the dwarf still waited for him to answer. Thinking quickly, he produced a coin in his fingers from his inventory. "I thought such a hard working dwarf like yourself deserved a drink, so I wanted to give you this gold so you could buy yourself some more… um… whatever it is you're drinking."

The dwarf eyed the coin suspiciously for a moment, then smiled a broken smile as he clumsily snatched the coin from his fingers. "Thank you kindly, stranger."

You gain +1 faction with Kostell the Dock Worker

"You're welcome," Jace said.

The dwarf suddenly looked up at him. "Wait just one (hiccup) minute! How do you be knowin' (hiccup) I'm so hard workin'? Do I know ya?"

Thinking quickly, he examined the dwarf and skinny human in his HUD to get their names. Jace put a shocked looked on his face. "How do I know you? Why, everyone has heard of hard working Abutt and Kostell, the hardest working two on the docks!"

The dwarf sat up a little straighter, and hit Abutt in the chest with his hand, sloshing some alcohol out of his bottle. "Hey Abutt," he called out louder that he needed to, "you hear that laddy, we be famous."

Abutt didn't respond but seemed fixated on the bottle of booze the dwarf was still sloshing around.

Jace stood up and started to walk away, making sure there were no guards in sight. Behind him he heard the two break into another verse of the song, but he quickened his pace before he could hear all of the words.

He was nearly out of the dock area when he heard someone call out to him from the shadows, "Psst. Hey you. Come here."

He looked over to where the voice had come from. Halfway out of the shadows was a short, thin human dressed in dark leather armor and leather hood. He motioned for Jace to come closer.

Fearing a trap, Jace readied his weapons as he cautiously approached the figure. He was about to bring the man up in his HUD when the man spoke.

The man held his hands up. "Easy friend, I just want to talk. I couldn't help but notice the certain skillful way you relieved those two fellows of a few coins, not to mention fast-talking yourself out of trouble once you got caught."

Jace lowered his weapons, but still kept them in his hand. If the halfling Rogue had been right, this was the thieves guild starter quest. He decided to play the role a bit.

"I don't know what you're talking about," he replied to the dark clad figure.

The shadowy figure smiled. "Sure you don't buddy. Sure you don't. The thing is, my organization is always looking for talented individuals who are looking to earn some extra coin. Are you interested?"

Jace took his hands off his weapons and crossed his arms. He put a curious look on his face. "I'm always interested in making some coin."

He took the opportunity to check out the newcomer in his HUD.

Name: Webley the Snake (Hero)
Race: Human
Level: 75
Profession: Thief

Webley was level 75, which meant he could kill Jace without even breaking a sweat. It also meant he might be the guild leader or at least a high-ranking member. If so, he was much more powerful than Drakkar had been. Then again, Crossroads was a small town, and this was the capital.

The thief's smile grew wider. "Excellent. Go to the corner to Helm and Green Street. You'll see a grate in one of the alleys. Open it up and drop down. Follow the passage north until you come to a large metal door. We'll be waiting for you in the room beyond."

Webley the Snake has offered you the quest, "Find the Thieves Guild"

Reward: +50 faction with Whitecliff Thieves Guild, Variable.
Accept quest? (Yes or No)

Smiling, Jace accepted the quest. He'd gotten exactly what he was looking for.

Webley matched his smile. "Good. I'll expect to see you soon. Oh, and this offer is only good for the next hour."

Quest "Find the Thieves Guild" Updated.
Time Limit: 1:00 hour

With that, the man moved back into the shadows and in a second had disappeared completely, leaving Jace alone. Looking at the timer ticking down, Jace turned to Luna. "Geez, no pressure."

Luna stared back. "Yes."

Chapter 4

Jace had no idea where to find Helm and Green. Whitecliff was the largest city he'd ever been in and it could take all night to search the city for a specific intersection. Even then, he may not find it. He would need to ask for directions.

Looking around, he couldn't find any guards. Jace smirked. Just like in real life, there was never a guard when you needed one. He backtracked to the docks and found the roving patrols.

The guards stopped and eyed him warily as he approached. The pair were dressed in matching chain mail armor over which they wore navy tabards. The tabards bore the symbol of Whitecliff, the twin griffons facing outward.

"Can we help you?" asked the first guard. The man was taller and broader than Jace with a trimmed black beard that was just starting to show some gray. Jace noticed he kept his hand near the long sword he wore at his belt.

Jace smiled and showed his empty hands. "I'm trying to find Helm and Green Street."

The other guard, a shorter, skinny fellow with a much younger face, spoke up before the older one could answer. "And what business do you have in the Luxury District at this time of the night?"

The other guard shot him an annoyed glance but then turned back to Jace expectantly. Thinking quickly, he came up with the best lie he could think of on short notice. "I'm supposed to meet a girl there. She's gorgeous. Slender figure, short dark hair, gorgeous almond eyes." Jace put a note of desperation in his voice. "I was supposed to meet her 15 minutes ago, but I got lost. Please!"

The younger guard gave him a sly grin. "Sounds like quite a looker."

The older man elbowed the other guard and straightened up. "Helm and Green are in the Luxury District."

The man gave Jace directions that he did his best to memorize them before thanking the guards and hurrying away. As he followed the directions, he realized they were taking him back near the entrance, to the west of the main gate.

He passed a few patrols that gave him suspicious glances, but they didn't stop him. Jace navigated the guard's directions for nearly a half hour before finally reaching his destination, a well maintained, cobbled street in the heart of the Luxury District. If this was where the thieves guild was located, it was a huge step up from the dilapidated building used by the Crossroads guild.

Jace looked around. This was the Luxury District, an affluent area that contained upscale shops which catered to lesser nobility and wealthy merchants. It also catered to players who enjoyed frivolous items that didn't necessarily affect the game.

Many of the game's role-players saved up or transferred in real money to buy virtual luxury items like gowns, high quality outfits, non-magical jewelry, costumes, and other items that didn't affect game play. Being practical by nature and necessity, Jace eschewed those sorts of superfluous items. He preferred to stick to the armor and weapons that actually helped him in the game.

He didn't see the grate at the intersection, so he checked the alleys nearby. He found a grate down the second alleyway he looked down and walked over to it. The grate was locked with a large, old style padlock. He tugged on it, but it was extremely sturdy. There was no way he was going to break it, either with brute force or with his weapon.

Being that this was a thieves guild quest, the solution to opening the padlock was obvious, as were the many scratches from previous lockpicking attempts. Judging by the sheer number of scratches around the keyhole, he guessed many players had picked this lock before him.

"Keep an eye out," he told Luna as he bent down and retrieved his picks.

Glancing around to make sure no one was watching, he crouched down next to the lock and produced the lockpick and tension rod from his inventory. Picking locks in the game was exactly like picking them in real life. The developers had designed it that way. The only thing skill did was limit what level of lock you could attempt. Otherwise, it was all player skill.

Since he had played his vampyre assassin previously, Mordred, he'd taught himself how to pick most locks by watching vidstreams. After all, you could learn how to do almost anything on the internet nowadays. But, with this avatar, his skill was still low enough that he could break a lock pick if he wasn't careful.

Focusing on the lock and feeling the tumblers, Jace set his tension rod and with a few twists and a pop, the lock snapped open. He smiled as he saw the system message. He'd done some lock picking in the village and should be nearly at the maximum rank for his level.

Your Lock Pick skill has increased by 1.

Glancing around again to make sure no guards were going to see, he removed and lock and opened the grate. He peered down into the drain hole it had been covering. With his *Cat-Vision,* he could see the bottom about ten feet below. It appeared that the floor was moving, but he realized it was water running along the floor. At least, he hoped that was water.

Jace didn't have a choice if he wanted to continue with the thieves guild quest and ten feet was an easy drop. He looked at Luna. "Ready for a swim?"

"No!" Luna looked at him aghast. "Bad water!"

"If you don't come down, I've got to leave you up here," he told her.

In response, the cat walked over to a barrel next to the alley wall and hopped up. She sat back on her haunches, wrapped her tail around herself and stared off into the distance.

Chuckling, Jace rolled his eyes. "I take it you're staying up here?"

Luna ignored him and continued to stare at nothing.

"Fine," he laughed and turn back to the grate. He lowered himself down the hole using his arms, finally letting go and dropping lightly to the ground while the grate slammed shut above. Instantly, he received a message.

Your Find Trap skill has increased by 1.

He froze in place and looked around carefully. Chances are, if this was the path to the thieves guild, then there were traps all about. He scanned the floor, the walls and even the roof. He didn't see anything suspicious.

Cautiously, he looked up and down the passage he was in. He remembered Webley had told him to go north, so he faced north. At least, he hoped it was north. Once again, he scrutinized the passage before him. He could see a door further down the passage and assumed that was the door the thief had mentioned.

As he moved his gaze closer to him, a thin line around ankle height seemed to flash briefly and then glowed lightly.

Your Find Trap skill has increased by 1.

He bent down and gingerly ran his finger along the thin line. It was loose. He knew from experience with his assassin that a loose line was a tripwire that could be cut. Pulling out his dagger, he gently cut the wire. He braced for something bad to happen, but after nothing changed for several seconds, he stood up

Your Disarm Trap skill has increased by 1.

Jace started taking a tentative step forward but right before he set his foot down, the stone he was about to step on lit up. It was another trap.

Your Find Trap skill has increased by 1.

He stopped immediately and retracted his foot, placing it gingerly in its original resting place. Carefully, he bent down and inspected the glowing stone. He saw no wires, so it was most likely a pressure plate.

Jace looked out onto the passage directly in front of him and saw more stones lit up. He received several more skill ranks and chuckled. If only skill ranks were this easy at higher levels. But that's how VEIL worked. Lower levels were easy but became progressively more difficult.

From his experience, he guessed these rocks were all pressure plates. He wasn't sure what they did, but he was sure he didn't want to find out. He mentally plotted a course through the glowing rocks and then carefully navigated through them, checking each stone before he placed his foot on it.

He stopped as he cleared the pressure plates and looked at the passage immediately in front of him. It was flat and much smoother than the cobblestones in the rest of the passage. In fact, it was unnaturally flat and smooth.

Bending down again, he caught sight of a small seam between the rough area and the smooth surface. As he stared at it, the entire smooth area in front of him glowed.

Your Find Trap skill has increased by 1.

The whole thing was a trap. But what kind? Was it a pressure plate? It seemed large for a pressure plate, probably a good 10 feet long. And what did it do? A trap door? An elevator trap?

Jace quickly glanced up at the ceiling. He had suddenly imagined the whole area shooting upward as soon as he stepped on it and squishing him against the ceiling. There were no blood splatters on the ceiling, so he didn't think that was it. He looked back up. Unless they cleaned it each time. He shook his head. That probably wasn't it.

He looked around at the walls for holes that might shoot out spikes, poisoned darts, fire, acid or any number of equally lethal things but found no holes that he could see and nothing lit up on either side of the wall. In fact, if anything, he would say that the walls on either side of the trap were rougher than the rest of the wall with stones that seemed to protrude out even further than the other parts of the wall.

Since he wasn't making any progress in figuring out what sort of trap it was, Jace flatted himself against one wall in case spears or darts shot from the far wall and with his toe, he pressed down on the flat area.

To Jace's surprise, the flat area sank down but nothing else happened. He waited a bit longer to see if there was some sort of delayed trigger. After several moments, he stepped out from the side and looked at the huge plate. He pushed down on with the toe of his boot again and it smoothly and effortlessly tilted downward. As it did, the opposite side tipped upward.

Jace kept his weight on his back foot and pushed hard with his front foot and watched as the whole 10 feet long section easily and silently tilted down. It was a revolving section of floor, almost like the old style see-saws they still had at some parks. The problem was, it was 10-foot-long and would tilt either way, dropping him below. He could only imagine what lay below: spikes, water, acid. Who knew with devious developers? It could be killer bunny rabbits at the bottom of the pit for all he knew.

He looked beyond the tilting trap and saw a door another 15 feet down the passage. Was that the door Webley had mentioned? If so, he was so close.

But how could he get past the tilting trap. It was too far to try a standing long jump. A running long jump was out of question because of the pressure plates behind him. He had rope but nothing to anchor it to.

He looked at the side of the passage again. They were really rough - probably as rough as that stone wall in the bandit fortress he'd climbed as Mordred. Could he climb across?

Reaching out, Jace tested the rocks. They were sturdy and large enough to use as handholds. It might work. But if he fell, he'd hit the plate and slide right into whatever doom waited below.

Should he risk it? If he died in some pit trap, would he be able to retrieve his corpse? Was it worth it?

Chapter 5

Jace stood there at the trapdoor for several minutes, weighing the risks and rewards before finally deciding to try it. He psyched himself up, knowing this could be a very gruesome death. Without giving himself time to reconsider, he pulled himself onto the right-side wall.

He used the hand and foot holds to keep himself close to the wall. Slowly, he moved his left hand over to the next hold towards the far end of the trap, followed by his left foot. With those holds secure, he moved his other hand and foot in the same direction. It was slow going but not particularly difficult and he made it to the middle with no issues.

Then, as he moved his left hand and foot to the next foot hold, there was an odd sound down near the rock his left foot was on. His foot slid off the foot hold, forcing him to quickly grip more tightly with his hands and try to move the weight to his right foot. He tried to find the rock again with his left foot, but it was gone.

Where it had been just a second ago, he felt a rough indented spot. Had the rock broke under his weight? He stretched his left foot further to the left to find the next rock. It was a little awkward, but he managed to find it. Gingerly, Jace started putting some of his weight on the foot. A little bit of weight. Then a little more. This one seemed to hold, so he relaxed a bit and put the weight on his toes in this uncomfortable position to give his arms a rest.

After a minute, he decided to push on. He still had five feet to go. He moved his left hand to a new stone and gripping it tightly, started to move his weight to it when it suddenly exploded in a shower of chalky bits. This time, he almost fell. His body started to sway backwards but he quickly pushed up with his toes and pulled with his right arm until he was flush against the wall again.

Your Find Trap skill has increased by 1.

That's right, he could get a skill up by blundering into the trap as well. He brought his left hand to his face and sniffed. Darn it! It WAS chalk. With alarm, he realized that some of the stones were fake and made of chalk. It was a trap within a trap. Or in this case, a trap next to a trap. This just got a bit more interesting.

Bringing his left arm to a lower rock, he tried to put some weight on it and like the previous one, it too exploded into chalky bits. Frustrated, he tried another rock a little higher than was comfortable and this time, it held. He held his precarious position and let his body rest as much as it could under these circumstances.

His muscles ached and even though he realized he didn't really have muscles; the game sure did a very good job of emulating fatigued muscles. He checked his *Stamina* and realized it was draining quickly. He needed to get off this wall and fairly fast. If he ran out of *Stamina* while still on the wall...

Carefully feeling each and every foot and hand hold, he slowly made his way to the end of the area. He had a few more close calls, but since he was ready for them, none were as bad as the first two. His *Stamina* was nearly gone.

When he got to the edge of the smoothed floor, where the floor once again became stones, he very carefully looked the area over as well as he could from his perch on the wall and then tested the area with his leading foot before finally dismounting on the floor.

With his *Stamina* a few seconds away from nothing, he stepped off and started to sit down to rest. As he bent to sit, he stopped as a thin light lit up again right in front of him at ankle height.

Your Find Trap skill has increased by 1.

Another tripwire. That was diabolical. If he had tried to jump and made it, he would have tripped the wire for sure. He moved his finger very gently over the wire and realized it was pulled taunt. If the wire was broken and the tension released, whatever trap awaited would be sprung.

Examining the area on the other side of the tripwire, he made sure the area was clear of traps. Then, he carefully stepped over the tripwire and searched the area on the other side.

Nothing seemed to be amiss, so he collapsed in a heap. He stayed there for several minutes, letting his *Stamina* regenerate.

The course had been strenuous both mentally and physically and he'd been seconds from a certain death. But now it was almost over. Or was it? Jace looked toward his goal. The door was just a dozen or so feet away, so he would need to be careful and certainly get food and rest after this.

Suddenly he wondered if this might be the part where most people relaxed, with the goal so close. Any sadistic developer worth his salt would put the worst traps in the last stretch, hoping to catch the unwary.

With an effort, Jace stood and carefully examined everything around him. He didn't find anything. He moved a little closer and examined everything again. Still nothing.

As he got closer to the door, his tension grew. There had to be something else. The last part of it couldn't be that easy.

Then he found something. It was a barely visible crack along the edge of the stones on the left wall. Oddly, Jace received no skill up and the crack didn't glow like other traps he had found. He followed the crack from bottom to top, then over and then down again. Roughly the shape of a small door. It was a secret door!

He turned his head to the back to the large door that had been his goal since he dropped down in the sewer and then back at the secret door and then back to the large door. Should he just to the big door? There were several locks on the door that could take some time to pick.

He looked at his quest timer. Five minutes left. Finish the quest or see what's behind the secret door. Curiosity got the best of him. The other door could wait. He wanted to see what lay behind the secret door he had just found. Maybe it was treasure!

Jace needed to find the trigger mechanism for trigger mechanism for the door. He tried pushing, but the door didn't budge. He found a handhold and pulled with the same result. That meant it was latched. He started feeling around the area until his fingers found a smaller brick that felt differently than the others. He pushed it and heard an audible click and the secret door swung outward slightly.

Jace quickly grabbed the edge of the door and pulled it open. It opened into a passage to his right, that ran parallel to the corridor he was in and past the other door. Cautiously, he entered the passage and looked down it.

It only went about ten feet, which was a few feet beyond the door he was supposed to get into. He crept quietly to the end of the passage, carefully looking for traps the entire way. When he reached the other end of the short passage and hadn't found any traps, he relaxed slightly.

There was obviously another door here, that led back to the original corridor he had been in, but past the door. Was this a way to bypass all the locks on the other door? That would be nice.

He saw the door had a latch on this side and reached for it. He stopped his hand inches from the door handle. This seemed too easy. Was this the moment when people relaxed? Was this the final test? He checked his timer. Three minutes left.

He moved to the side of the door and retrieved his tin knife. Using the blade, he carefully lifted the latch. He heard the soft ping of something hitting metal.

Looking around to the back of the knife, Jace saw that a long, thick needle protruded from the door and had been stopped by the metal of the knife's blade. With his *Cat-Vision*, he could tell the blade was coated with something, poison no doubt.

Your Find Trap skill has increased by 1.

Jace continued lifting the latch with the knife blade, the door made an audible click and started to swing outward. Once the door was open and he checked for any tripwires in the doorway, he peaked out.

The passage was similar to the one he had just left, except the floor was dry. It was about 60 feet long with torches every 10 foot on alternating sides. At the end was a large wooden door.

He looked back towards the door only to find a wall. There was no door on this site. That meant the door on the other side was a fake door. There was actually no way to get through it. The door he'd seen early was a decoy. He smirked. Kudos to the developers on that one.

He crept out of the door and seeing that it had a latch on the outside as well, let the door shut. He examined the area around him but found no traps. He moved forward a foot and bent over, with the intention of searching the area in front of him when the door at the end of the passage opened and a head poked out. Jace recognized it as Webley the Snake.

"You made it with," Webley said and produced a small hourglass. "A few grains left. Well done..."

The thief opened the door further, revealing a well-lit room beyond. "Come on, we haven't got all night."

Reluctantly, Jace stood up and began walking towards Webley, but keeping a wary eye on the floor and walls. He made it to the door and the thief beckoned him inside.

"Not exactly the trusting sort," he said as Jace walked past him into the room. Webley slapped him on the back and shut the door behind them. "A man after my own heart."

He stepped around Jace and flourished his hands, "Welcome to the thieves guild. You passed our little test in the nick of time. Very good. Most don't pass at all. But you did. With flying colors and that calls for a little something extra."

Unable to think of anything to say, Jace nodded at the man's words.

"Right you are," Webley continued. "First, I want to officially offer you a place in the guild. Do you accept?"

"Yes," Jace replied. That was why he'd gone through all of this, after all.

"Excellent," Webley told him. "Now, since you are a member and you passed our little test in the time frame allotted, I want to present you with this."

Webley produced a black leather jerkin from a bag at his waist that was much too small to contain it. A bag of holding, Jace guessed. He handed the jerkin to Jace. "Wear it with pride. Just, not in front of the guards."

You receive Thieves Guild Jerkin.
You have completed the quest, "Find the Thieves Guild"
You gain 500 experience. Experience to next level 470.
You gain +50 faction with Whitecliff Thieves Guild
You gain +25 Webley the Snake

As Jace was gawking at the amount of experience he'd received, Webley gestured to him for him to follow. "Time to meet the crew!"

Chapter 6

As they went through the wooden door, Webley turned to him, "I forgot to ask. You didn't get poisoned by the needle trap in the door handle, did you?"

"No," he told the thief.

The room they entered was well lit with torches and sparsely furnished with only a small table with a few chairs, currently occupied by two men and a halfling playing cards. There was a painting of an armored knight on white horse hanging on the wall. It seemed almost out of place in the otherwise sparse room.

Webley caught his eye and said with a broad grin, "That's from the Duke's personal collection. I nicked it myself."

"This room is where we greet new recruits, like yourself," he continued, moving towards a door on the far end of the room. "This is Grub, Gridon and Aland." None of the players looked up from their cards. "By the way, that is not the entrance you'll normally use. Unless you feel like going through the gauntlet again."

Jace nodded his acknowledgment and continued to follow the thief. He was glad he didn't have to go through that again.

Webley led him through the door into a noisy circular chamber. Lining the walls, were indoor merchant stands. Jace knew what this was immediately, the Black Market. They were the places where you could find stolen goods, poisons, and other things that the authorities had outlawed.

People were packed in like sardines and his HUD showed him that most of them were players of various levels.

"I know, tight squeeze," Webley remarked. "And this is an off night."

"We have our merchants here," the guildmaster pointed out. "They can fence anything you acquire that might have a little heat on it. You can import anything you wish from central or western Alaes," he said with a sly smile, "for a small finder's fee of course. After all, we have expenses."

Webley continued to walk as he talked, leading Jace through the crowd to another door on the far side of the room. The door opened into a long, rectangular room with tables and a bar near the far end. It looked and smelled like a seedy dive bar.

There was a single open door on the far end of the long room. On the left hand side, there were three doorways, one of which was behind the bar and judging from the smoke wafting out, led to the kitchen. Other than the stone ceiling and floor, it looked like any other in-game tavern he'd been in.

Looking around, Jace spied a number of shady looking characters populating the place. They sat at the small tables or at the bar, eating, drinking, or playing cards. There were also a number of scantily clad women of varying races near the far doorways, as well as a few shirtless men. He didn't have to ask what their profession was.

"This here's the Lucky Coin Inn. It's a place you can kick back between jobs. Food's better topside, but if you've got heat on you, this'll be the only place the guards won't find you. Plus, you can always try your hand at Skulls and Crowns or Knucklebones."

Jace knew Skulls and Crowns was a card game and Knucklebones was a dice game. He never really got into games within games so hadn't bothered to learn the rules. He did know that the two games had become so popular in the game that people now held tournaments in the real world.

As they neared the middle door, he nodded towards it. "The Lucky Coin has some rooms for rent. Again, not as nice as the ones above, but if you have heat and need a place to stay, it beats sleeping in the sewer or under the docks. Just make sure you bar your door before you fall asleep. No killing, that's the rule. But other than that, I generally leave 'disagreements' up to your crew to work out between yourselves."

They got close to the bar and a burly bartender bellowed out, "Hey Webley, fresh meat?"

Things in the underground tavern got quiet suddenly and almost every head turned to look him over. He was uneasy under all the scrutiny. The thieves stared only briefly, apparently sizing him up, before going back to whatever they were doing before.

"Yeah Olin," Webley yelled back. "Just showing him the lay of the land."

"Welcome kid," the large man said, waving a hand holding a dirty dishrag.

"Thanks," Jace responded. "Good to be here."

They walked to the far end of the room and Jace saw a sunken in the right corner that had a dirt floor and some shabby fencing around it. "What's that?"

Webley smiled. "That's the arena. Occasionally, one of the members has a disagreement with one of the other members and we let them settle in there. And, of course, there's always betting on the winner."

Webley led him through the far door and into the next room. Unlike the previous two large rooms, this was tiny in comparison. It was a square with a large metal door on the right wall that was guarded by two burly panda-kin.

Panda-kin were one of the neutral races. They were large and looked like tall, anthropomorphic pandas. The panda-kin were more beast-like than some of the other kin, which made them excellent fighters. They might look cute, but Jace knew they could be vicious killers.

"Old Thom and Gerry over there keep watch over our vault, as well as the entrances," Webley said. "I would suggest not trying to get through them."

As if to emphasize his point, one of them made a fist and cracked his knuckles loudly.

"And this here is the main entrance you'll use, it leads up to the Fainting Unicorn," said Webley, pointing to a stairway leading up. Then he gestured to a metal door near it. "While this tunnel leads to a sewer grate on the west side of town, in case you need to enter or leave the city when the heat's on you."

"We don't have many rules," the thief said sternly, "but this one is important: Do not ever lead the guards to either entrance. If you do, we WILL find out and the assassin's guild will have a new contract, get it?"

Jace nodded. "I get it."

Webley the Snake grinned. "And by the way, I'm the guildmaster. I'll be the one handing out assignments. When you're ready for one, let me know. We'll start you off easy, but every one's expected to pull their weight around here."

"Right, thanks!" Jace told the thief.

"Good," he said. "When you need to find me, I'll usually be in the Lucky Coin," the thief said. "If I'm not, I'm up in the Fainting Unicorn common room, but we don't conduct business up there, got it?"

"Got it," Jace replied.

"Good luck thief," Webley told him. "Try to stay out of the dungeons."

You are now a member of the Whitecliff Thieves Guild.

And with that, Webley turned and headed back to the Lucky Coin. Jace was now an official member of the thieves guild and could start doing their quests. He turned around and followed Webley back into the tavern. He needed to make some gold.

The guildmaster went to an empty table and slid into one of the chairs. Without looking, he gestured for Jace to join him.

Jace sat in the chair across to him. "I'd like to get started right away."

Webley looked him over. "Well, you're new… but you did make it through the gauntlet, so maybe I have a thing or two for you."

"I'll take whatever you have," he told the guildmaster.

"Very good," the guildmaster smiled. "I have two jobs. You can take either or both, but they both need to be completed before tomorrow morning. If you agree to both and can't pull them off or only pull off one, you'll be looked down upon in the guild."

In other words, Jace thought, I'll lose faction with the thieves guild. Just great. "What are the jobs?"

"Good. Right to business," he said approvingly. "The first job is a simple burglary. Colin Hackett has a house down on Wall Street, just south of the Temple district. It's a big green house with yellow trim. Hard to miss. Colin owns a silver statue of Chykela and one of our clients would like it as her own. Break in, grab the statuette and get out. Anything else you find is all yours."

Webley continued, "The second job is a little trickier. One of the merchants near the West Market, a one Myles Murrily, has been petitioning the guard to increase patrols around the markets to protect them from thieves. Obviously, this would affect us, so we need to eliminate the threat. What I want you to do is take these vials of Deadnettle and place them in his bottom desk drawer in his shop the Jolly Raven Book Shop, preferably where he won't immediately find them. We'll then drop an anonymous tip to the guard, they'll find the Deadnettle and that will be that."

Deadnettle was a rare, expensive, and very deadly herb. It was used almost exclusively by assassins. He knew, because he'd used it when he was playing Mordred, his vampyre assassin. It really increased his damage per second (DPS).

Because of its deadly properties, Deadnettle was outlawed in all major good faction cities and a fair number of the neutral ones. That also meant, if he was caught with it, he would spend weeks in jail. And since he couldn't logout or create a new character, he would actually serve time in jail.

One the other hand, NPCs couldn't access a player's inventory except in very special situations - like their body decaying. He couldn't be patted down or frisked by the guard so he should be safe. He hoped.

The fact was, he needed the money. But even more importantly, he needed to build up faction in the guild if he wanted to ask for help getting in the Still, he needed to build up his faction with the thieves guild, so he might as well start now. He looked Webley in the eye and said, "I'll take them both."

Webley grinned broadly. "I thought you might."

Webley the Snake has offered you the quest, "Love's Likeness"
Reward: +25 faction with Whitecliff Thieves Guild, 25 gold, 1 piece of Thieves Guild Armor.
Accept quest? (Yes or No)

Webley the Snake has offered you the quest, "Silence the Squeaky Wheel"
Reward: +25 faction with Whitecliff Thieves Guild, 25 gold, 1 piece of Thieves Guild Armor.
Accept quest? (Yes or No)

Jace accepted both quests. "I'd better get going."

"Remember," Webley said as Jace stood up. "Both need to be done by morning."

Quest "Love's Likeness" Updated.
Time Limit: 5:00 hours

Quest "Silence the Squeaky Wheel" Updated.
Time Limit: 5:00 hours

Chapter 7

Jace left the guild through the Fainting Unicorn Tavern and quickly found Luna curled up on the same barrel. Unsurprisingly, she was sleeping.

"Time to go," he told her mentally.

Luna opened up a single eye and glared at him for a long moment. Then she stood up and stretched and hopped down to follow him.

His first job was the simple snatch job. He just needed to break into a house and take a statuette. That sounded easy. Of course, he had no idea where the Temple District was. He asked a guard, claiming that he needed to get to the temple quickly because he'd just cheated on his wife with a cat-kin and needed to repent. After some snickering, the guards gave him directions.

He and Luna followed the directions and found the Temple District at the far end of the city. Once Jace got closer, it was easy to spot. The large stone temples stood out among the two-and-three-story Tudor homes and shops.

Jace went south and found Wall Street. He also figured out why it was called Wall Street. It actually bordered the city wall itself. He looked up and could make out guards walking and standing on the wall.

That complicated things. The last thing he wanted was a guard looking down at the wrong time and seeing him.

He walked by the row of homes until he passed the big green house with yellow trim. With the muted colors of the other houses, it really stood out. Jace continued past the house, turned the corner, and entered the alleyway.

Entering *Stealth*, Jace crept down the alley to the back of the green house. The alleyway was shielded from the eyes of the guards, but it paid to be cautious. When he reached the house, he stopped and turned to his familiar.

"Keep an eye out," he told Luna. "Warn me of anyone coming to this door or any guards who turn down this alley."

Luna looked bored. "Yes."

"If I do this job," he told her. "I will get enough money to buy you fish for breakfast."

"Fish?!" she asked excitedly.

"But if we get caught, no fish," he told her.

"Yes," she said with more enthusiasm. Luna was highly food motivated it seemed.

Jace made another check of the alleyway and then bent down and brought out his picks. The lock was no more difficult than the padlock on the grate had been and soon it clicked open. Making a final check of the alley, he slid the door open and slipped inside.

With his *Cat-Vision*, he could see that he was in some sort of pantry. There were many boxes stacked around the room, some open and some closed but he didn't have time to rifle through them all. He was on a timetable.

He moved out of the pantry, through a kitchen and into a dining room. Off the dining room was what he guessed passed as a living room or sitting room. From his vantage point, he could see a small alcove. In the alcove was a statue of a beautiful naked woman carved from ivory.

He'd seen statues of Chykela, the goddess of love and beauty, and seen her image in various establishments, so he recognized the statuette instantly. It was what he was here to steal.

Crossing the floor, he stopped in front of it and reached out to take it. As he did, he caught the glimmer of a glowing line which was connected to the back of the statuette.

Your Find Trap skill has increased by 1.

It was a thin wire and if he needed any hint at what it was for, his *Find Traps* rank up just told him. It was some sort of trap. Jace followed the wire to the wall, then up to the top of the alcove where it ended in a small bell. A simple alarm trap that would ring the bell if anyone moved the statue. He used a dagger to cut the thin wire, allowing him to retrieve the statuette and put it in his inventory.

He had what he had come for, but he wasn't done. Creeping around the house, Jace found a locked strongbox in a closet on the first floor. Part of him felt guilty for stealing, but as he reminded himself, it's just a game.

This lock was only slightly more difficult than the door lock and soon he had it opened. Jace double checked the strongbox for any traps and then opened it. Inside, he found a large pouch of coins, several pieces of jewelry and a carved ivory pipe. He took it all and stashed it in his inventory.

Then he closed the lid and relocked the strongbox. The owner would probably check everything when he noticed the statuette missing but there was no reason to be too obvious.

Next, he quietly sneaked up the stairs and checked the three upstairs rooms. One was a study with nothing of value he could readily steal except some expensive looking bottles of alcohol. On a whim, he grabbed them all and tossed them into his inventory.

The next room was a washroom where he liberated an ivory comb. The final room was a bedroom where two humans slept in the bed. As quiet as he could, Jace crept around the room. He'd "tossed" many houses as Mordred and had an idea of where to look. First, he moved to the taller dresser that had a small jewelry box on top.

The jewelry box was unlocked, and he pocketed several expensive looking pieces of jewelry. Next, he checked the other dresser. He found a silver chain and a silver ring inset with an onyx. He took both and then silently checked the closets. Finding nothing else of interest, he moved out of the room.

Jace went back downstairs and stopped at the door. "Any guards?"

"No," came Luna's reply and he slipped out of the house. He didn't bother relocking the door. All of the quiet creeping around had eaten up the better part of an hour and he needed to get to his next job as quickly as possible, but he still needed to play it cool.

He walked as casually as he could, so as not to attract any undue attention from the guards. The West Market was his next destination and Jace already had a rough idea where it was located.

Half an hour later, he arrived at the West Market. It was a large open area that might once have been a park, but which was now filled with stalls, tents and tables. While normally bustling during the day, it was empty at this late hour.

Jace scanned the buildings that enclosed the market and spotted his target. One of the shops had a sign above the window with a raven wearing glasses and reading a book. The sign said Jolly Raven Book Shop.

Slipping into the alley behind the shop, he once again set Luna to guard while he picked the lock to the backdoor and slipped inside. The room he entered was obviously a storage room for the store as it contained crates of books, stacks of books and more books on shelves.

There was a door on the far end of the room which Jace assumed led to the store. On the right wall was a set of stairs that lead up what must be the living quarters over the store. Jace carefully navigated the mess and slowly, stealthily made his way up the steps.

At the top of the steps was a long hallway that ran the length of the hallway. The left side of the hallway had windows that let in the light of the double moons. The right wall held three doorways.

As quiet as a mouse, Jace crept to the first doorway and peered in. It was a bedroom. On a four post bed against the wall was a large, pudgy man. The man was snoring loudly and Jace let him be and moved to the next room.

This room appeared to be another storage room, as it was filled with crates which also contained more books. While knowledge might be power, Jace had no desire to sort through a few hundred books to find the pearls among swine.

Slipping to the next door, Jace found what he was looking for. It was the man's study. The room had wall to wall bookshelves and a large wooden desk in the middle. The desk had two chairs on the far side of the desk for visitors and one larger, more comfortable leather-bound chair behind the desk.

Quietly making his way into the room, he went to the desk and pulled open the bottom drawer. It contained a stack of papers, a magnifying glass, and a few bottles of ink. He retrieved the vials of Deadnettle and placed them behind the ink bottles and gingerly closed the drawer again. Mission accomplished.

He almost turned to go but he couldn't resist and riffled through the other drawers. He found a small bag of coins in one of the drawers and a small, locked box in another drawer. The box was wooden, and the top was carved to resemble a Plautia, the goddess of the moons.

Curious, Jace checked the box for traps and, finding none, picked the lock. Inside the box was a large silver moon pendant. He pocketed it and started to close the box but hesitated. He opened the drawer with the vials of Deadnettle, took them out and placed them in the box before relocking it. That seemed like a better hiding place for a guilty person.

He looked at the quest timer still counting down and decided to get back to the guild. He reset everything the way it had been and then, after checking with Luna, left the building and stepped out of the alley as if nothing was wrong. Just a man taking his cat for a walk.

Taking a slightly roundabout way, Jace returned to the Fainting Unicorn to turn in his quests. He'd made over 100 gold just from the two money pouches he'd swiped. Once he sold the jewelry and other items, he hoped he'd break 200. Not bad for a night's work.

Jace reached the Unicorn and ducked in the back door. He found the catch that opened the secret door and went down the steps. He waved to Thom and Gerry and then slipped into the Lucky Coin to find Webley.

Chapter 8

The common room was bustling, and it took him a minute to find the guildmaster. Webley was alone at a table, working on what appeared to be some sort of ledger. He and Luna walked over and waited for the guildmaster to acknowledge him.

"Word on the street is, tomorrow the guards will be summoned to a certain man's house after someone reported seeing him buy vials of Deadnettle from a merchant ship," Webley said without looking up. "Will they find incriminating evidence?"

"Yes," Jace responded. "Even though the man cleverly hid the vials in a locked wooden box in his desk."

The guildmaster nodded and scribbled something in his ledger. "I'm sure some helpful citizen may mention this to the guard."

"Rumor also has it that the guards will be called to another man's house tomorrow after he notices that one of his prized statues is missing," said Webley. "Have you heard whether or not that rumor is true?"

"I have indeed heard that same rumor," Jace responded in kind. "And I believe it to be true. Of course, he may be missing a few other things as well."

The corners of the guildmaster curved upward but continued to write, still not looking up. "By the way, if you have any artistic pieces, like say, statuettes, that are weighing you down. Thom is a very strong half-orc and would be glad to hold it for you - for safe keeping. After that, you should get some rest. Tomorrow night will be here before you know it."

Smirking at the double talk and charade, Jace walked back outside the Lucky Coin. As much as he didn't like hardcore roleplaying, he did enjoy it from time to time.

Walking over to the two panda-kin, Jace retrieved the statue from his inventory and handed it to Thom. "The boss told me to give this to you, he said you'd like it."

Thom grunted what could be some sort of reply and took the statute. He turned around and started fiddling with the locks on the metal door.

Gerry looked over and smiled. "Oh, that's Thom, a great admirer of art."

Thom pulled the door open a crack and slipped inside. He reappeared a moment later without the statuette. After shutting and relocked the door, he resumed his stoic posture until he noticed Luna nearby.

Grinning, he stepped forward, bent down and scratched Luna's chin. "Nice kitty!"

Jace gawked down at the stoic panda-kin and Gerry rolled his eyes at the other panda's uncharacteristic show of emotion. Luna just soaked up the affection for a few minutes until Thom stood up and resumed his post. Once again, his deadpan expression matched the other panda-kin.

Jace turned to leave and nearly ran into Webley, who had managed to sneak up on him. The guildmaster carried a small sack and handed it to Jace. "Well done tonight. Now, go pawn your items and then come back tomorrow night and we might have some more work for you."

You have completed the quest, "Love's Likeness"
You gain 250 experience. Experience to next level 220.
You gain +25 faction with Whitecliff Thieves Guild

You have completed the quest, "Silence the Squeaky Wheel"
You gain 250 experience. Experience to next level 1970.
You gain +25 faction with Whitecliff Thieves Guild

You have gained a level.
You are now level 6 in Rogue.
You gain 8 health.
You gain 4 mana.

You receive Thieves Guild Bracers.
You receive Thieves Guild Boots.
You receive 50 gold.

Jace smiled as he saw his level increase. Early levels were easy, but it still felt good to be increasing. He'd need the skills, health and mana if he wanted to get to the *Help Desk*. That plus the faction he was earning with the guild.

He thanked the guildmaster and took the bag from him. Jace stashed it in his inventory, nodded to Webley and went to the Black Market. He'd examine the armor later but if it was anything like the jerkin, it would be an improvement over what he currently wore…

In the Black Market, Jace went to the first stall and started bargaining with the man over the price for the items he'd stolen. He was pleasantly surprised to see that he gained the *Haggle* skill.

You have gained a new skill: Haggle

The *Haggle* skill was useful for getting the best price from NPCs on goods and other items. The higher your skill, generally the less you paid. He hadn't had the opportunity to practice in Sinking Springs or Crossroads, but now it looked like he'd be using it often.

After a bit of haggling and several rank ups, he ended up getting another 100 gold for the items. Together with the money he'd got from the quest and the money he'd stolen, that was just over 250 gold in one day. Jace smiled. Who said crime didn't pay?

"Fish?" Luna said as they were walking back into Lucky Coin.

Jace looked down at her. "You did do a good job tonight."

"Yes," she said expectantly.

"And I did promise you some fish," he said, drawing it out.

"Yes," Luna said more urgently.

Jace smiled at his little familiar. "Ok, we'll order fish. But we have to go meet the girls. It's Sunday, so maybe Charlena will be on shortly."

With Luna happily trotting after him, Jace left the thieves guild through the Fainting Unicorn. He considered buying some breakfast there at the Unicorn, but dawn was breaking, and he'd promised the girls he'd meet them for breakfast back at the Dwarvish Fork.

The sun was halfway over the eastern horizon by the time Jace reached the inn. Going inside, the inn was just opening for breakfast but Jace saw the two girls already sitting at a table. They both looked a little worse for wear.

Walking up to the table, Jace slid into the chair opposite the girls. "Good morning ladies! How did the…"

Jace trailed off as he saw their expressions and general appearance. They both looked tired and disheveled. "What happened to you two?"

The two girls looked at each other and then back at Jace. Diana spoke up first. "Let me tell you. I tried using my feminine charms on the players here but not even in my wildest novel was I asked to do some of the things I was asked to do! You gamers are animals!"

Jace suppressed a smirk. In a fantasy world full of everything from vampyres to cat-kin, the sexual appetites of players had been, how could he put it, expanded. He wasn't surprised at what she'd encountered. He did feel bad for the woman. She seemed to have lost much of her bravado and he could only guess what she had gone through.

He looked at Mika. "How about you?"

Mika raised her chin. "I have completed two quests for the priest guild and earned 50 gold."

"Good job," he told her and received a smile. He'd also done two quests and received 25 gold each. That must be the standard rate at their level. Luckily, Jace's profession allowed him to earn a little extra.

Jace looked back at Diana. "Did you make any money?"

For the first time since he'd met her, Diana looked ashamed. "No."

Jace smiled over at her, remembering inside that youthful, raven-haired body, was the mind of a 90-something-year-old woman. He put a hand over hers and smiled. "It's okay. I made a little extra."

Diana gave him a grateful smile. "You really are a dearie."

"I don't suppose either of you learned anything about the Noble District or the palace?" he asked them and they both shook their heads.

"I asked around where I could," Diana offered. "But NPCs don't seem to be affected by feminine wiles."

"I was too busy trying to finish the quests," Mika said, bowed head.

"Me either." Jace leaned back in his chair. "Though I'm trying to build up my faction with the thieves guild to see if I can get them to help us get it. But I'm wondering if we're going about this the wrong way."

The two women looked over at him. Somehow, maybe because he'd helped them become human, he'd become the defacto leader. He'd been a group leader before, and the role was familiar to him. But now the stakes were higher. Much higher.

"Maybe we should be working together instead of breaking apart to work on our own personal quests," he told them.

"Hey, you all," Charlena said cheerfully as she bounded over to their table.

"Glad to see you feeling better." Jace stood up and kissed her. Out of the corner of his eye he saw Mika look away. He remembered what Diana had said about Mika liking him. But he couldn't deal with that right now.

Charlena blushed. "Sorry about yesterday. I drank way too much Friday night. That's the last time I'm going to do that though."

Jace gestured for her to sit down but saw that Luna was in her seat. The cat just looked over to him, then looked back at the table. "Fish."

Jace laughed and Mika giggled. He looked over to her. "You understood her?"

"Yes," she tried to stifle a laugh. "Luna would like fish."

Jace cocked an eyebrow and looked at Diana. "You too?"

"I heard her say fish if that's what you mean," she told him.

"Interesting," he said and picked up Luna. Charlena sat in her chair and then Jace sat back down with Luna on his lap. "It looks like you can understand monsters too."

"So, it's just me who can't understand," Charlena pouted.

A dwarven barmaid came over and took their breakfast order. Jace ordered his own plus salmon and eggs for Luna.

"We were just discussing working together," he told Charlena after the barmaid left.

"That sounds good," Charlena said. "Doing what?"

"Doing some quests," he told them. "If we join the adventurers guild, we can get some group quests that will give us more experience and more money, plus the chance for some real loot. Let's face it, the higher level we are when we attempt this, the better. And no matter what way we do it, we're going to need more money."

"I would like that," said Mika.

"It's got to be better than what I had to deal with last night," Diana agreed.

Charlena looked over at him. "Group quests sound fun."

Jace scanned his friends with his HUD.

Almedha Pressalor
Race: Elf
Class: Scout
Level: 4

Raajoget
Race: Human
Class: Priest
Level: 3

Mizzlethain-galliegarde

Race: Human
Class: Mage
Level: 2

Apparently, Mika had kept her yeti name of Raajoget, and Diana had kept her mechanical spider name of Mizzlethain-galliegarde. Jace no longer felt so bad with his kobold name.

Jace also saw that Diana was only a level 2 Mage. Because Jace had just hit 6th level, he was now 4 levels higher than she was. She would get no experience if they grouped. She couldn't even gain quest completions. That complicated things.

"What is it?" asked Charlena.

"Diana is too low," he told them. "I hit 6th level last night so I'm too high to group with her and get any experience. Diana, you'll need to do some solo quests and gain a level before we can group."

Diana made a face. "Do I have to?"

Jace nodded. "You need to hit level 3 before we can group together."

Diana pouted. "Can't I be like… the team mascot or something?"

"The higher level you get," he told her. "The more powerful you become and the more you can help us. Right now, it's just us four. We need to stick together if we're going to get in there and get WorldCog to set things right."

"Fine. Fine," the older woman said. "Where should I go to get some quests?"

Thinking back to when he'd been a newbie vampyre, he tried to remember where he'd found the easiest quests. "Try your guild or the guards at the gate. Usually there are some beginning quests in one of those two areas."

"What are we going to do?" asked Charlena.

"We're going to learn all we can about the Noble District and the Royal Palace," he told her.

Chapter 9

Diana had complained about having to do quests but had eventually left to go find the mages guild. Hopefully, she'd be okay. Normally, the first few quests for a guild were non-combat quests. If not, Jace had told her to come back and either Charlena or Mika would help her.

Meanwhile, the rest of them spent the morning asking around about the Noble District and how to get in. They talked to different people without success until Mika finally suggested following people who were leaving the district and asking them.

They'd done exactly that and found out some interesting facts. Unfortunately, what they learned wasn't promising.

The first thing learned was that the Royal Guard were responsible for security in the Noble District. Entry was only by a pass from the office of the captain of the Royal Guard. Jace had immediately thought about forging a pass - after all, that's what they always did in the vidstreams. Then, another person they questioned had informed them of how the mages guild had enchanted the passes, binding it to a particular person. So much for forging them.

They also learned that other than guards and workers with passes, they normally only allowed nobles in - which seemed obvious considering the name of the district. Local nobles presented signet rings that were likewise enchanted for just them and acted as passes.

Jace knew it was possible to buy a noble title, but that cost millions of gold. Plus, the title was mostly for show. Other than allowing a player to have a house in the Noble District and attend the various balls and parties, it really had no other game function. It was a waste of money in Jace's eyes.

Visiting nobles and dignitaries were given temporary passes by the Royal Guard themselves. But they were escorted to, from and during their visit to the Noble District by royal guards. And the guards who served in the Noble District also had bound passes in the form of necklaces stamped with the seal of the Noble District guards.

After finding out about the passes, Jace had walked around the perimeter of the Noble District. The more he looked, the more impossible the task seemed. The district was a city within a city and completely walled off from the rest of Whitecliff. The walls that surrounded it were over 30 feet tall with no easy handholds or footholds like he'd found in the bandit fortress.

Not only were the walls tall, but they were also manned. Jace could see guards stationed every 100 feet. Although they looked relaxed, they also looked alert. Given the sheer height and lack of handholds,

Jace wasn't even sure if Mordred would have been able to scale it. Jace certainly had no chance.

Somehow, he needed to find another way in. That meant he would need the help of the thieves guild. If anyone knew a secret way in, it would be them. It was more important than ever that he build up his faction with them. He'd need to do more quests. As many as he could.

"I'm going to have to gain more faction with the thieves guild," he told Charlena and Mika. "And hope they know a way in."

"I can join too," offered Charlena.

Jace considered that. "All of the jobs they have given me are at night. I'm not sure you'd have time to do more than one a night before you needed to log."

Charlena made a face. "Well, that's not fair!"

"No one ever said the game was fair," he shrugged. "The original designers tried to make it as 'realistic' as possible. I guess they figured thieving jobs were done at night. Or the game AI adapted to that pattern. Sometimes it's hard to know which."

"It still stinks," Charlena told him.

"I know," he said. "But there should be a scout's guild in the city. You could join that."

"But they're not going to know a secret way into the palace," she replied.

Jace had to agree. From what he remembered of the scout's guild, it dealt more with exploration of things outside the cities. It was highly doubtful they'd know or care about a secret way to anything in the city.

"I can join the thieves guild if it would help," Mika spoke up. She'd been silent for most of the walk, only responding to direct questions. "I can switch to Rogue, like you."

Jace smiled at her. "Thanks Mika but honestly, I don't know if having two people with thieves guild faction would be any better. It's all about getting a high faction as quick as possible. Plus, if we're going to do the adventurers guild quests, we're going to need a healer."

The girl nodded. "I understand. But I must switch to fighter. I wish to use a katana and that requires the two-handed weapon skill. I can switch back later."

Jace raised an eyebrow. "A katana?"

She gave him a defiant look. "Yes. I wish to use a katana. I have studied kendo since I was a girl. Now, I wish to use a real katana."

"You can do whatever you wish Mika," he told her. "Plus, even as a fighter, you'll have access to your priest spells."

She gave a nod and then went back to staring ahead. "Yes, I do not mind healing. But I want to fight too!"

Jace smiled. "Good, because I think we might have to pick up a little slack from Diana."

They all had a chuckle at that. The older woman didn't really seem to understand the game or its mechanics. Doubtless, she'd thought she would be a game socialite.

Thinking about it, Jace realized that may have been exactly what she'd planned. After all, the woman had millions of dollars. She could have afforded a title and then spent the rest of eternity doing nothing but attending parties and gossiping with the NPCs and player nobility.

Jace shuddered. What a boring existence. For him, there were always new things to explore. New quests to do. That's what had made the game so fun. Sitting around gossiping was not his idea of the perfect eternity. But maybe it was for Diana.

They checked in at the Dwarvish Fork at lunch, but there was no sign of Diana. He hadn't intended to order lunch, but a certain little orange tabby cat had insisted. In fact, the cat stubbornly refused to leave the place until she had fish.

Ignoring the amused looks of the cat, he ordered some lunch for himself and the girls did likewise. As the dwarven barmaid dropped off their order, Charlena spoke up. "So, what are you going to do when you wake up?"

Jace started when he realized she was talking to him. "Wake up?"

"From your coma," she retorted.

"Assuming it's me," Jace told her. The fact that he might be alive had been weighing on his mind since she told him yesterday evening. He was both excited and frightened of the prospect. He felt like he'd just started to come to terms with being dead only to keep having pieces of hope dangled in front of him.

"It's gotta be you," she told him.

Jace only nodded. It did seem like too much of a coincidence. He really could be alive. And that frightened him almost as much as being dead. What if he were in a coma? What if he never woke up? Or worse, woke up but had serious issues.

He pushed the morbid thoughts from his mind. He couldn't deal with them. Not yet. He wasn't going to get himself worked up until he knew for certain. Right now, he needed to focus into getting to the *Help Desk* so they could fix him and the others.

"You should eat chocolate cake," Mika offered in an uncharacteristic outburst. "That's what I would do if I was dead and then came back to life! Eat chocolate cake!"

"You know," Jace couldn't help but laugh. "Maybe I'll do just that!"

She grinned and went back to eating her food.

Charlena smiled at him suggestively. "I'm sure we can think of something for you to do when you wake up."

Jace blushed but also felt excitement. He'd entertained notions of what it would be like when they met in the real world. Mostly he'd felt nervousness. Would she even like the real him, assuming his body was fully functional after the accident?

He noticed suddenly Mika became much more interested in her food at Charlena's comment and remembered Diana saying that Mika had feelings for him. For some reason, that made him feel even more awkward.

Jace wished he could be more confident with women, like the vidstream stars. They always knew the right thing to do and say. Then again, if he had a screenwriter, he would know the right things to say and do.

At that moment, he caught sight of Diana, coming into the inn. She sauntered over to their table and slid into the seat next to Jace once he picked up Luna. He took that time to see her progress.

Mizzlethain-galliegarde
Race: Human
Class: Mage
Level: 3

"If I ever have to deliver another packet of herbs," she said as she sat down. "Or retrieve another borrowed dusty tome from a Mage who forgot to return it, it will be too soon."

Jace smiled. Beginner quests were boring but usually had multiple purposes, like giving the player a lay of the land. He remembered his own beginner quests back in Sinking Springs. He'd had to find a lost dog, fetch stones from a lake and all sorts of other mundane things.

Then Jace remembered that Sinking Springs had been destroyed by the dragon and his heart grew heavy. Even though they were all just NPCs, they had been very real to him.

"It's not that serious," Diana said to him, probably mistaking his sullen expression as a reaction to her statement. "But I did learn of some serious news from the mages guild person."

The rest of the team looked up at Diana expectantly and after a pause, the woman continued. "It seems there's a black dragon wiping out entire towns at a time. It's become such a problem that the king has turned to the mages guild for help."

Jace, Mika and Charlena exchanged looks and Diana picked up on the inside knowledge. "Do you all feel like sharing?"

"The player's a dragon," Jace told her. He hadn't mentioned it to Diana before because he hadn't thought it was relevant. He hadn't realized the dragon was rampaging around the country destroying other towns.

"Oh dear," the woman responded. Diana looked thoughtful for a moment. "I wonder if that's related to that extremely irate - and if rude, I might add - gentleman I tried to entertain last night."

Jace raised an eyebrow and the other girls stopped eating and turned to her.

"Now," Diana said, raising her palms. "I don't pretend to understand all this game talk, but he said something about a raid against a dragon and losing his body and some sword or another because the dragon dissolved their bodies."

If he understood her, Diana was telling him that a raid had already been called, most likely by the adventurers guild. Players had tried to raid the dragon but died - no surprise there. Not only that, it had dissolved their corpses so they couldn't retrieve them.

Whoever was inside the dragon was exploiting all of his or her game knowledge to… To what? What was the dragon's purpose? Were they trying to get WorldCog's attention? That made sense. Do something so disruptive that it could get the company's attention and force them to take a look at them. Jace thought he might even do something like that.

Another possibility was that the player enjoyed being a dragon and didn't want to be killed and thrust into a different, much weaker, monster body. After being killed so many times, Jace could understand that too. Much better to be the apex predator than the prey.

Jace thought of another possibility, but he hoped it wasn't the case. He remembered Big Cheese, the player in a goblin chief body who had killed him. The player had gone insane from all the monster jumping. If someone like that had control of a dragon body, who knew what they would do. They could bring the entire game down, just to watch it burn.

Chapter 10

"So, what does this mean for us?" Diana asked.

"That's a good question," Jace replied, this mind whirling at the possibilities. "It might not mean anything. Even if the dragon wanted to take on Whitecliff, there are so many high-level NPCs here, he probably couldn't do it."

"Probably?" Charlena asked, her face worried.

Jace shrugged. "There's a big difference between 40 players of high-level and a few hundred NPCs of high-level. Plus, you've got the main temples here. Don't discount that. The gods and goddess have appeared in the world before. Any one of them can probably bring down a dragon.

"Will the dragon acting differently get WorldCog's attention?" asked Mika. "Maybe there is no reason for us to attempt to get into the palace."

"No," Jace shook his head. "I used to work for them. I'm sure, even now, they're going through the monster AI code with a fine-toothed comb. The problem is, the issue doesn't lie there. It lies in player consciousnesses being used in place of AIs. It would take them months or years to figure that out."

"Won't the players complain if they lose their bodies?" Charlena wondered.

Again, Jace shook his head. "It's not as bad for high-level characters. Most of their items are soul bound, so they respawn with the person. All they'd really lose is any potions or non-bound items they were carrying, plus any gold they were stupid enough to have on their body. It's more of an annoyance for them."

"Last year," he told them. "There was a red dragon who had settled inside a volcano. During the battle, quite a few people were knocked into the lava and lost their bodies. They whined and complained but WorldCog didn't do anything. You play at your own risk."

The table was quiet for a few minutes before Diana spoke up. "Well, as asked, I did run a bunch of tedious errands and got myself up to level 3. So, can we go do whatever it is that we're going to do together?"

"Yes," Mika said. "But first I must change to fighter and get a katana!"

Diana raised an eyebrow but said nothing.

"All right, let's go," he told them. "To the adventurers guild!"

They left the inn and hailed a passing guard for directions. It was located inside the Merchant District, to the south. To the east of the park. Jace had remembered seeing the park on his way to the docks last night was able to lead them to it.

Once they were at Merchant District, they found the adventurers guild on the eastern side of the park, closer to the docks. It was a large tower which rose above the smaller Tudor buildings near it, standing out in its simplicity and intimidation factor.

Jace took note that the Central Market was just south to them by the sounds and the smells. If it were like the street markets in the other cities he'd been in, they sold almost anything you could imagine. He hoped they could find a katana for Mika there.

"Are you members of the guild?" said a middle-aged warrior in plate armor as they walked in. The man sat behind a large oak desk as they walked into the adventurers guild. He had shoulder length graying hair and a large mustache. His face had a large scar that ran from the upper left of his face, across his nose and down to the right side of his chin.

"No," Jace answered for the group. "But we'd like to join."

The man smiled, making his scar stand out even more. "Good! We can always use fresh meat!"

Jace didn't know how to respond to that so he just smiled.

"Do you wish to register as a band or a company?" he asked.

From his previous experience, Jace knew a band was a group of four players and a company was a raid of forty. Ignoring the puzzled looks on his companions' faces, he answered. "A band."

The man had taken out a parchment and was scribbling something on it with his feather quill. "I see. And who is the leader of your band?"

The girls were all looking at Jace, so he took the hint. It did make sense considering he had the most experience in the game. "I am. Ja… Dedrurrurth."

"Dedrurrurth," the man repeated, writing it down on the parchment. "And what is the name of your band?"

Jace turned to the girls. "What do we want to call ourselves? We have to give our group a name when we join the guild."

The girls looked at each other and then at Jace, then back to each other.

"Uh… the dragon slayers?" offered Mika.

"I'm sorry," the man cut in. "That name is taken."

"It has to be unique?" Charlena sighed.

"How about the Formidable Four!" Diana said.

"I'm sorry," the man repeated. "That name if taken."

"The Fantastic Four?" Charlena said.

"The Furious Four!"

"I'm sorry," the man said again, like a broken record. "Those names are taken."

They spent fifteen minutes thinking of names, only to have them be taken. Considering how many people played the game, and how many groups must have been formed, Jace wasn't all that surprised. He vaguely remembered having a similar problem when he'd formed a group years ago.

"Friends of Luna," Charlena offered.

"That name is available," the man said.

Jace cringed. "Can't we think of something else?"

They turned and looked at Luna, who was sitting behind them. The little cat had its tail wrapped around herself and her little chin was raised. "Yes."

Rolling his eyes, Jace waited for any objections and when he received none he nodded to the man. "Friends of Luna."

"Very good," the man said in his bored, monotone voice.

"That will be 50 gold a piece to join the guild," the man told them. "And another 50 gold to register your name with the guild and 50 gold to register it with the guard."

The girls all looked at him and he sighed and pulled out his gold. "How much do you guys have?"

He knew it was more gold than he had, especially after paying for the room. He definitely needed to do more thieves guild jobs tonight and hope there was a chance to earn some extra money.

Mika handed over all 50 of her gold without complaint, even though Jace knew she'd been planning to buy a katana. Charlena gave him another 50 gold and he took the rest out of his own gold.

He pushed the gold over the man and waited while he finished scribbling something on the parchment. It took the man a minute to finish his writing and then he took out some wax and a seal and affixed the guild's seal to the parchment. Rolling it up, he handed it to Jace.

"This is your copy of your band's charter," he told them. "Keep it with you while on guild business. This is especially true when operating within the city. If you lose it, it is 25 gold to replace it. If you need to add or remove a member, it is 25 gold plus their annual dues, which is 50 gold.

As Mordred, such small sums wouldn't have concerned him, but right now it was nearly every penny they had. Hopefully, it would pay off quickly.

"As guild members," the man continued. "You may check the board any time, day or night, to see if there are any jobs. Once you take a job from the board, you have 24 hours to complete it before another band can take it. If another band does take it, the first one to return with the job complete gets the reward."

Jace nodded. This was all stuff he knew. It wasn't a big deal with the smaller quests. With raids, it meant the first group who got the raid had 24-hour exclusive rights to it. In VEIL, that was huge. Guilds usually had a member standing by the board 24 hours a day to wait for new raids to come in. Then it was just a fight to see who would grab it first.

"Thank you," Jace said and motioned his companions outside. In the courtyard, they had passed a large board that Jace had noticed earlier. The thing had to be ten feet long and six feet high and it was covered in parchments.

The board also had about 30 players standing around it. They varied in level but Jace could see many of them were level 95 and above. Those were probably the raiders.

Jace gestured to the board. "Start looking for a quest we can do. If you stare at them, some of them will be outlined in green, others in yellow and rest in red. Or, and the white ones. The red ones are higher than the highest level member. Yellow ones will be higher than the average level of the group but still in the same or lower than the highest level member. And greens are ones where the level is equal to or lower than the average level in the group. White ones are too low for us and we won't get any experience."

The three girls looked at him blankly and Jace sighed. "Look for yellow or green ones. Call it out if you find one."

The three girls nodded and the four of them immediately began rifling through the various pieces of parchment. Most of them were red. Jace wasn't surprised. Most people would solo through the first 10 levels within a week or two and then start joining groups. Because of this, most group quests started at level 10 and went up. The raids were all level 90+.

"Found one!" said Mika, holding up a piece of yellow tingled paper. "A yellow one!"

She handed the parchment to Jace who looked at it.

Dear guild members,

The city sewer guild has recently reported that some of their members have gone missing while inspecting the sewers.

They have hired the Adventurers Guild to find and eliminate the cause of the disappearances.

Signed,

Guildmaster Leofsige Blackwoode

As the group leader, only Jace could accept the quest. Tentatively he viewed the text of the quest.

The Adventurers Guild has offered your group the quest, "Alligators in the Sewer"
Reward: +25 faction with Whitecliff Adventurers Guild, +25 faction with Whitecliff Guard.
Level: 5
Accept quest? (Yes or No)

Jace read over the quest twice. It looked like exactly what they needed. He accepted and then received a new message.

**Quest "Alligators in the Sewer" Updated.
Exclusive Time Limit: 24:00 hours**

"We have a quest," Jace told them. "And we have 24 hours to complete it before someone else can grab it."

"Are we really going into a sewer?" Diana asked, her face a mask of disgust.

The game designers had made the choice to exclude normal body elimination functions except for vomiting, which certain poisons, diseases and spells caused you to do. But there was not the normal bodily waste elimination. Despite this, they'd included sewers in all the major cities as a way for the criminal element to get around.

In fact, Jace had used them many times to get from one part of the city to the other during jobs for the Assassins Guild when he was playing Mordred. He smiled. "That's one nice thing about the sewers. There's just water down there."

"And alligators," Mika offered.

Chapter 11

Several hours later, Jace and his companions trudged through the sewers. While what he said earlier was true, about it only containing water, Jace had forgotten that the developers did include the sewer smell. He assumed they either wanted it to at least smell authentic or they were just sadists.

Charlena had been able to mostly ignore it by turning down her sensory input. Jace guessed he'd done the same as Mordred, which is why he hadn't remembered it. Unfortunately, for Jace, Mika and Diana, that wasn't an option. They were stuck at full sensory input and got to enjoy the full effect of the sewer smell.

"Can we just give up already?" Diana asked, her nose and mouth now covered with some cloth she'd purchased. "We've been down here for hours and we haven't seen a single alligator."

Jace shared her frustration. When they first opened the sewers, they immediately ran into the smell and Diana forced them to go to the market and, after borrowing some gold from Charlena, bought a cloth to cover her nose and mouth.

As it happened, Jace had to get some cloth as well to make a sling to carry Luna. They discovered the water was knee level and if he didn't carry her, she would have been swimming the entire time. His familiar had made her feeling VERY clear on how she felt about swimming, so he'd suggested the sling.

Next, when they'd all climbed down into the sewers, Diana and Mika realized it was too dark to see for normal human eyes. Charlena was fine with her elven sight and Jace could use *Cat-Vision,* but the other two girls were, literally, in the dark.

That's when he learned Diana had also chosen a cat familiar too but hadn't summoned it because it was too painful. They had tried in vain to convince her to summon it, but Mika had presented a different solution. One of the spells she had was called Moonlight and created a globe of pale light the two girls could see by. So, they'd used her spell to light the way through the sewer.

Once they started exploring, they quickly learned that the sewers were a vast labyrinth that stretched beneath the entire city. They quickly ran across some large rats, which they dispatched with ease but no alligators. Now, hours had passed and still no sign of the creatures they were here to kill.

"What do you say?" Diana asked again.

Jace considered her request. He had to admit, he was tempted to give up. But if they did, they would have wasted all that time and even if they came back tomorrow, another group could have grabbed the quest and completed it. He really wanted to finish this quest, if for no other reason than he didn't want to feel like he had wasted everyone's time.

He looked beyond the glove of light and thought he caught movement again. He'd seen it several times now and had started to wonder if perhaps the alligators were repulsed by the light. Maybe they were scaring the creatures off with the very thing they were using to find them.

"Let's try something," he offered. "And if it doesn't work, we call it quits for the day and maybe try again tomorrow morning."

"I can't," Charlena said apologetically. "I start my summer job tomorrow. I've been meaning to tell you but just didn't get a chance."

Jace turned to the elf. "Summer job?"

Charlena looked embarrassed. "Yes, I have student loans, but I use the money from my summer job to pay for my incidentals. I start tomorrow, 10am-6pm. So, I'll be logging in later starting tomorrow."

Jace tried to keep his face impassive but inside he was disappointed. He knew she'd just taken her finals and had assumed she would be on summer break and could log in most of the day and they could do things as a group. Now it looked like that wouldn't be the case.

"Where are you working?" Diana asked her.

Charlena smiled. "I'm working at Johnny's Bistro as a waitress. It's a nice place near campus that my friends and I hang out at sometimes."

Diana nodded. "I remember working as a waitress when I was younger." The older woman seemed to lapse into nostalgia and didn't offer any details. Quietly, Jace heard her mutter. "So long ago."

"No problem," Jace said, forcing a smile. Jace knew it was a problem. It would be more difficult for them to level together without Charlena. And he wasn't sure how well he could depend on Diana to level up herself.

"What was your idea?" Charlena said, obviously trying to change the subject. She was a smart girl and she most likely knew it was problematic. That was probably why she'd been waiting to tell him.

Jace gestured to the sphere of light. "I wonder if we're scaring them off with the light."

The others looked around but Charlena nodded. "Are you seeing things moving too?"

Nodding, Jace looked down to Luna. "You still can't smell anything, right?"

"No," came a muffled meow from inside the sling and not for the first time, Jace felt sorry for the little cat with its superior olfactory senses. Jace was barely suppressing a gag reflex as it was. He couldn't imagine his nose being as sensitive as his familiar's.

"Can you hear things moving?" he asked her.

"Yes," came the muffled reply after a few seconds of twitching ears.

He peered into the dark but the light he was in was throwing his vision off. He guessed it was similar with Charlena. If they wanted to be able to see fully, they needed to get outside of the globe.

"Diana and Mika," he addressed the two light dependent members. "I want you to stay here and be ready. Charlena and I will go off in opposite directions. If we encounter any alligators, we'll attack them and then pull them back here."

"Won't the light just scare them off again?" Diana asked.

"Once we attack, they'll follow us," Jace told them. "It's just the way they're programmed. They may be avoiding the light but during combat, they'll ignore it."

He hoped. Jace hadn't run into this exact scenario before but he did have plenty of experience pulling enemies. It should work the way he described unless the creatures had a strong aversion to light, like true vampires. And he hoped they weren't dealing with vampyric alligators.

Walking over to Charlena, he took off the sling he was using to carry Luna and handed it to her. She looked at it without understanding.

"Take Luna," he told her. "If you pull an alligator, she can send me a message, so I know not to pull one. And vice versa."

"But I can't understand her," Charlena protested.

Jace smiled and scratched Luna behind the ears, causing her to start purring. "She'll get your attention if I send her a mental message. Right?"

The cat didn't take its head out from the sling, but he heard her response. "Yes."

Charlena shrugged and took the sling. She slung it diagonally across her shoulders as Jace had done. "I'm ready."

"Alright," he told them. "The plan is, Charlena and I go out into the dark, see if there are any alligators lurking out there and if so, we pull it in. When it gets here, wait for me to *Taunt* it before you do damage but once I do, take it down as quickly as possible."

The girls muttered their understanding of the plan. After giving Charlena the signal to proceed, Jace moved off in the opposite direction. He stepped out of the light and paused to let his eyes adjust. It took almost a full minute but then shapes began to take shape and Jace swallowed.

Staring back at him from the darkness were four alligators. They were submerged fifteen or twenty feet away just staring at Jace with those reptilian eyes. Jace wondered if the gators had been here the entire time, following them. That was an unsettling thought since they hadn't known they were nearby.

Out of habit, he scanned them in his HUD.

Sewer Gator
Level: 5

"Alligator!" came a voice in his head. It was Luna. Charlena must have pulled one of the alligators. Jace turned to start back and saw the gators behind him surge forward.

"Alligator! Alligator! Alligator!" came the voice and Jace cursed aloud. The alligators were linked! Pulling one of them had aggroed the ones around him, like a swarm.

"Incoming!" He yelled and ran back to the group. He looked behind him to see the gators closing the distance quickly. He activated his *Air Armor* to increase his *Defense*. Now that his *Air Magic* skill was maxed, the spell gave him a total of 3 *Defense*. Combined with his armor, buckler and abilities, his *Defense* jumped up to 10.

Entering the globe of light, he could see Charlena moving towards the other two. He also saw four alligators coming into the sphere, swimming after her. One of them had an arrow in its head.

Jace made it to the group right before the first gator reached Charlena. The ones following him were only a few feet from him and he shouted out his *Taunt*. "Get over here!"

As the ability washed over the seven alligators, they immediately switched their focus to Jace.

Sewer Gator bites YOU for 0 damage.
Sewer Gator bites YOU for 0 damage.
Sewer Gator bites YOU for 1 damage.
Sewer Gator bites YOU for 0 damage.
Sewer Gator bites YOU for 0 damage.

Sewer Gator bites YOU for 0 damage.
Sewer Gator bites YOU for 0 damage.

Jace winced as one of the alligator's bites got through his armor, driving its large teeth into his thigh. Charlena fired an arrow at one, while Mika slammed one with his mace and Diana just stood there open-mouthed, staring down at the alligators.

You stab Sewer Gator for 4 damage.
You stab Sewer Gator for 1 damage.
Sewer Gator is Poisoned.

Jace had aimed at the same one Charlena had shot twice but his strikes barely penetrated the alligator's hide. His damage was disappointing, and he knew the creatures must have thick skin that acted as armor.

"Everyone," Jace grimaced. "Focus on a single target. Kill it then move on to the next one."

Mika nodded and switched her focus. Diana seemed to snap out of her stupor and began casting a spell. Unfortunately, the gators were faster.

Sewer Gator bites YOU for 0 damage.
Sewer Gator bites YOU for 0 damage.
Sewer Gator bites YOU for 0 damage.
Sewer Gator bites YOU for 0 damage.
Sewer Gator bites YOU for 0 damage.
Sewer Gator bites YOU for 0 damage.
Sewer Gator bites YOU for 0 damage.

Poison hits Sewer Gator for 3 damage.

This time, the gators didn't break through his *Defense* and their jaws slid off his legs. Jace stabbed back at the same gator's head, hitting it twice

You stab Sewer Gator for 5 damage.
You stab Sewer Gator for 1 damage.
Sewer Gator is Poisoned.
Almedha Pressalor shoots Sewer Gator for 6 damage.
Raajoget crushes Sewer Gator for 3 damage.
Mizzlethain-galliegarde burns Sewer Gator with Flame Bolt for 4 fire damage.

Jace was momentarily confused by the system messages until he remembered that Mika's character name was Raajoget and Diana was Mizzlethain-galliegarde. At least they were all on the same target.

Sewer Gator bites YOU for 0 damage.
Sewer Gator bites YOU for 0 damage.
Sewer Gator bites YOU for 0 damage.
Sewer Gator bites YOU for 0 damage.
Sewer Gator bites YOU for 0 damage.
Sewer Gator bites YOU for 0 damage.
Sewer Gator bites YOU for 0 damage.

Poison hits Sewer Gator for 3 damage.

Once again, Jace's *Defense* saved him from taking any damage. The synergy of his class abilities and spells were working out well, but these were also only the minions. Jace knew that somewhere down here in the sewer was a group level monster that was going to be much tougher.

One by one, he and his companions killed off the alligators. Jace received a few more bites from lucky hits but all in all, it was better than he had expected. He actually felt like a real tank.

The alligators dropped only hides, which Jace threw into his inventory. He was hoping he could sell them to a vendor or possibly on the Player Auction House.

"Are we done?" asked Diana. The older woman had done well, despite her early hesitation, Jace had to admit. She cast her spells and then continued hitting the alligators with blasts from her wand. The wand did less damage than a dagger, but the damage wasn't stopped by armor of *Defense*.

Jace shook his head and looked at his *Stamina*. It had taken a long time to finally finish all of the alligators and the sheer number of blows had worn him down. "No, somewhere down here there is an alligator boss. We have to kill it to get credit for the quest."

Chapter 12

They trudged through the sewers for another hour, using their tactic to attract more alligators and then kill them. Each of the girls eventually gained a level. Charlena was now level 6, while Diana and Mika both hit level 4.

Upon hitting 4th level, Mika switched to fighter so she could use two-handed weapons and wield a katana. Jace wished she wouldn't have switched. Having played more groups than any of the others, he knew the importance of a talented healer. But they were still low level and if she switched back, he doubted they'd have a problem. Besides, he might be their leader, but he couldn't tell them what to do.

After the first hour, the alligators became sparser and he and Charlena had to roam further from the group to find and pull them. Jace was stalking through the water when he heard what sounded like voices ahead. Curious who else might be down in the sewer, Jace quietly crept toward the voice.

It took him a few minutes to find the source of the voices because it echoed through the sewers. As he drew closer, he caught part of the exchange.

"Listen Tiebaut…" a man's voice said. The voice was coarse and somewhat familiar, but with the echo, Jace couldn't place it.

"Lord Tiebaut..." corrected another man. This voice was more refined and carried an air of superiority about it.

"Listen, Lord Tiebaut," the first man resumed, his voice dripping with honey. "I have the package and if you want it, you must deal with me now."

"Do you have the tiara with you?" the refined voice asked.

"Package," the other man corrected.

"Yes, yes," the refined man said with obvious frustration. "You thieves and you're little code words."

Jace spotted a light coming from a tunnel and slowed down as he approached to make as little noise as possible. He entered *Stealth*, but he wasn't sure if it would work while he was in this much water.

"I told you," the first man said. "I'm not with the guild. Not anymore. I'm… independent."

"Yes, yes," the second man said. "I get it. With the reward I'm offering, it's certainly enough for you to jump ship." The man laughed. "Pun intended."

"Yes, Lord Tiebaut, very funny," the first man said.

Jace turned the corner and saw a raised area in the sewer. It appeared to be a junction room where several sewer tunnels intersected. Jace could make out four men in the room. Two of the men were close to each other, they appeared to be the ones who were talking. The other two men were further back and were holding torches.

"When do you make the exchange and where?" asked the refined voice. Jace could now see it belonged to one of the closer men, the one who was facing him. The man was too far away to view in his HUD, but he'd already identified himself as Lord Tiebaut.

The lord looked around the sewer junction. "And please don't say this dreadful place again."

"We can meet in front of the Royal Palace, if that's more to your preference," the other man said. Jace couldn't see the second man's face since his back was to Jace, but he wore a long coat and tricorn hat, like a pirate. Jace even saw a saber at his side. He was the man whose voice sounded familiar.

"Listen Captain," Tiebaut spat. "I am paying you a lot of money and I expect a little respect."

"Your gold has my respect," the captain replied. "But if it makes you feel better, I will meet you on Tideday, at the large blue warehouse on the corner of Mackerel and Anchor Street in the Docks District."

"Two days?! Why not tomorrow? And you expect me to go to the docks?" the lord asked incredulously. "Me?"

"Why not the docks? You met here in a sewer," the other man said nonchalantly. "As far as the waiting until Tideday, I need to deal with your former… partner."

"I see. You really think you can deal with the guild? Never mind, best if I don't know," Tiebaut said in annoyance. "Fine! What time on Tideday?"

"Noon," replied the captain. "Don't be late."

Jace sensed the conversation was ending and didn't want to run into any of them when they left. Both were too far to examine in his HUD and for all he knew, they were level 100. It was time to leave.

He had just retraced his steps back to a side tunnel when he saw light coming towards him. Jace quickly ducked into the side tunnel and quietly began backing away. He saw the pirate walk by, holding one of torches, and disappear down the tunnel. Jace crept back to the main tunnel and followed the light for a dozen yards to make sure it was gone.

It had been an odd exchange. Obviously, Tiebaut wanted the package and this Captain fellow had it. And apparently the lord was willing to pay a good amount of gold for it. And what was this guild they were talking to? A merchant guild? A craft guild?

Jace was still thinking about the meeting he'd overheard when he turned a corner and came face to face with the largest alligator he'd ever seen. It was even bigger than the one he'd killed for the saurian tribe.

"Found the boss gator!" Jace sent to Luna. "Bring the girls! Quick!"

The alligator was still a dozen paces away and Jace barely got off his *Air Armor* spell before the thing crashed into him.

Sewer Gator Bull bites YOU for 5 damage.

The gigantic thing snapped its enormous jaws around Jace's leg, causing him to cry out in pain. He didn't hesitate and jabbed both his weapons down at the huge gator's head.

You stab Sewer Gator Bull for 1 damage.
You stab Sewer Gator Bull for 0 damage.

Both his blows glanced off the beast's scaly head, his dagger not even making a scratch.

Sewer Gator Bull uses Trip Attack.

The huge alligator twisted its head and pulled Jace's leg out from under him, causing him to fall back into the water. The gator then opened its mouth to release his leg and sank its teeth into his thigh but didn't get as good a grip as the previous time.

Sewer Gator Bull bites YOU for 1 damage.

Unable to do much from his prone position, Jace scrambled to his feet. This gave the alligator another chance to attack him.

Sewer Gator Bull bites YOU for 4 damage.

Jace cried out again as the large teeth sank into his knee. He *Feinted* and stabbed down at the gator's head.

You critically stab Sewer Gator Bull for 8 damage.
You critically stab Sewer Gator Bull for 2 damage.

Sewer Gator Bull is Poisoned.

That time, his blades had found an opening near the eyes and the thing jerked its head. Unfortunately, that was exactly what he didn't need.

Sewer Gator Bull uses Trip Attack.

Once again, the thing pulled him off his feet like he was a rag doll. And to the alligator, he probably was. This thing had to be 15 feet long and weigh close to 1,000 pounds, if he had to guess. If the others didn't get here soon, it was going to eat him.

Once again, Jace scrambled to his feet, giving the thing another opportunity to snap at him.

Poison hits Sewer Gator Bull for 3 damage.
Sewer Gator Bull bites YOU for 6 damage.

Jace tried another *Feint* and attack combo, trying to inflict more damage on the great beast.

You critically stab Sewer Gator Bull for 0 damage.
You critically stab Sewer Gator Bull for 0 damage.

Both blows were deflected by the alligators thick, bony scales and Jace let out a frustrated snarl at having wasted the mana on a *Feint*. The gator didn't seem to care and let go of its grip and snapped at him again.

Poison hits Sewer Gator Bull for 3 damage.
Sewer Gator Bull bites YOU for 0 damage.

That time, Jace managed to deflect the alligator with his buckler, but just barely. He tried aiming for its open mouth with his blades, but the thing snapped its jaws shut.

You stab Sewer Gator Bull for 0 damage.
You stab Sewer Gator Bull for 0 damage.

The bull gator lunged at Jace again, nearly bowling him over but wasn't able to get its jaws around him before he danced away.

Poison hits Sewer Gator Bull for 3 damage.
Sewer Gator Bull bites YOU for 0 damage.

He saw light coming down the tunnel and hoped it was his friends and not that strange captain from the meeting. He tried stabbing it again.

You stab Sewer Gator Bull for 5 damage.
You stab Sewer Gator Bull for 0 damage.

His dagger glanced off its scales, but his rapier found a softer spot and did some damage, but the huge alligator seemed to pay it no attention.

Just then, a *Flame Bolt* flew past time and hit the creature in the head, followed by an arrow that bounced off the thing's snout.

Mizzlethain-galliegarde burns Sewer Gator with Flame Bolt for 5 fire damage.
Almedha Pressalor shoots Sewer Gator for 0 damage.

The gator didn't seem to like the fire and flinched away briefly before snapping at Jace again and barely missing his leg.

Sewer Gator Bull bites YOU for 0 damage.

Jace wanted to try and turn the gator away from his companions but there was simply not enough room in the tunnel to go around it.

Mika came splashing up to stand next to him. "We shall kill this beast together!"

Raajoget crushes Sewer Gator for 1 damage.

Unfortunately, her mace bounced off the thick skin, barely doing any damage.

"I could use some healing," he told her. "If you get the chance."

"Yes," she said and stepped back as Jace tried stabbing at the thing's nose.

You stab Sewer Gator Bull for 0 damage.
You stab Sewer Gator Bull for 0 damage.

Once again, his blows bounced harmlessly off the creature, even as another *Flame Bolt* and arrow whizzed past.

Mizzlethain-galliegarde burns Sewer Gator with Flame Bolt for 7 fire damage.
Almedha Pressalor shoots Sewer Gator for 0 damage.

Once again Charlena's arrow bounced off the things bony scales and he heard her make a frustrated noise.

Suddenly the alligator started to push past Jace and Mika, towards Diana. The older woman let out a terrified scream before Jace could use his *Taunt*. "Come get some!"

The gator stopped its advance and snapped at Jace, locking its jaws around his leg again. He barely stifled a scream at the intense pain as the teeth ground against his bones.

Sewer Gator Bull bites YOU for 6 damage.

Jace barely stifled a scream at the intense pain as the teeth ground against his bones. Jace was almost at half health and it looked like they had barely made a dent in this thing's health.

Raajoget heals YOU for 8 health.

Suddenly warm golden healing light bathed him, and he felt some of his wounds mending. That was right before the alligator jerked its head, sending him crashing to the water.

Sewer Gator Bull uses Trip Attack.

Jace was really tired of being thrown down into the water by this thing and promised to make a pair of boots out of its hide once they killed it. Once again, he tried getting back up to his feet, giving the alligator ample opportunity to snap at him.

Sewer Gator Bull bites YOU for 0 damage.

It bit down on him, but his *Air Armor* seemed to deflect the teeth and save him from any damage. Then his companions attacked, giving him a chance to make his own attacks.

Mizzlethain-galliegarde burns Sewer Gator with Flame Bolt for 6 fire damage.
Almedha Pressalor shoots Sewer Gator for 0 damage.
Raajoget crushes Sewer Gator for 1 damage.

You stab Sewer Gator Bull for 5 damage.
You stab Sewer Gator Bull for 1 damage.
Sewer Gator Bull is Poisoned.

"Are you kidding me?" Charlena yelled in frustration as another of her arrows bounced harmlessly off the thing's scales.

Jace's own hits had made it through the tough scales finally but did a paltry amount of damage to the great beast. Unfortunately, they must have done enough total damage to kick off one of its special abilities.

Sewer Gator becomes Frenzied.
Sewer Gator Bull bites YOU for 0 damage.
Sewer Gator Bull bites YOU for 1 damage.

Poison hits Sewer Gator Bull for 3 damage.

The alligator bull had suddenly become much faster and was attacking twice as often.

"It's some sort of haste effect," he called out. "You might want to throw me another heal, just in case."

Mizzlethain-galliegarde burns Sewer Gator with Flame Bolt for 8 fire damage.
Almedha Pressalor shoots Sewer Gator for 5 damage.
Raajoget crushes Sewer Gator for 0 damage.

"Finally!" Charlena shouted as her arrow finally found a soft spot in the gator's armor.

"Out of mana!" yelled Diana. "Switching to my wand, such as it is!"

Jace tried to get his own attacks in but once again his dagger did no damage.

You stab Sewer Gator Bull for 3 damage.
You stab Sewer Gator Bull for 0 damage.

Then the gator snapped again at him as if trying to bite his leg off.

Sewer Gator Bull bites YOU for 5 damage.
Sewer Gator Bull bites YOU for 0 damage.
Poison hits Sewer Gator Bull for 3 damage.

Then the gator snapped again at him as if trying to bite his leg off. While it attacked, a magical bolt from Diana's wand went sailing past, as did another of Charlena's arrows.

Mizzlethain-galliegarde shoots Sewer Gator for 2 magic damage.
Almedha Pressalor shoots Sewer Gator for 1 damage.

Jace heard Mika's sing-song voice uttering the words of the healing spell and then he felt the healing magic flood over him.

Raajoget heals YOU for 5 health.

And then the alligator decided to attack again.

Sewer Gator Bull bites YOU for 2 damage.
Sewer Gator Bull bites YOU for 4 damage.
Poison hits Sewer Gator Bull for 3 damage.

Once again, the creature's teeth bit into him, but he pushed through the pain to try and launch a counterattack, which was only partially successful.

You stab Sewer Gator Bull for 3 damage.
You stab Sewer Gator Bull for 0 damage.

His dagger failed to find a soft spot and skidded off the armored head. The girls followed up with their own attacks with some success.

Mizzlethain-galliegarde shoots Sewer Gator for 1 magic damage.
Almedha Pressalor shoots Sewer Gator for 3 damage.
Raajoget crushes Sewer Gator for 2 damage.

Sewer Gator Bull is no longer Frenzied.

The alligator's special ability seemed to run out and it slowed to its former pace, and Jace felt himself relax. They'd weathered its special ability - this time. Given that this was only a level 5 boss, it probably only had one special ability and it would either kick off once more at 25% or twice more at 50% and 25%.

He just had to hope they could keep going that long and that he could stay alive.

Chapter 13

His group continued to beat down on the giant alligator while Jace took small hits here and there, while delivering his own small hits in return. Their accumulated damage continued to whittle down the creature's health and eventually its *Frenzy* ability activated again.

Sewer Gator becomes Frenzied.

Once again, the creature's attack rate increased and Jace hoped he could stay alive. He had been keeping a mental tally of the damage they had done, and he guessed the ability kicked off at 75% health and then again at 25% health. At least, he hoped they had gotten it down to 25%. That meant this was the last time it would use a special ability.

Diana had been out of mana for a while and was limited to only her wand. Mika was out of mana as well, so there would be no more healing. He had a healing potion, but other than that, he was on his own. Charlena had circled around behind the alligator to take advantage of her *Precise Shot* ability, which was the ranged version of *Backstab*.

Jace looked at his own stats. He had 22 health left and only 4 mana. He'd had to use two more taunts to keep the gator's attention and he would have to use another one shortly.

Sewer Gator Bull bites YOU for 1 damage.
Sewer Gator Bull bites YOU for 0 damage.

Jace took another small hit and tried to stab the thing in return but once again, his weapons found no soft spot.

You stab Sewer Gator Bull for 0 damage.
You stab Sewer Gator Bull for 0 damage.

The girls joined in with attacks of their own.

Mizzlethain-galliegarde shoots Sewer Gator for 2 magic damage.
Raajoget crushes Sewer Gator for 2 damage.
Almedha Pressalor Precisely shoots Sewer Gator for 0 damage.

He heard Charlena curse as her arrow once again bounced off the thick hide. Jace tried to catch a glance of her but keeping an eye on the frenzied gator was consuming all of his attention.

Sewer Gator Bull bites YOU for 6 damage.
Sewer Gator Bull bites YOU for 0 damage.

The creature's last round of attacks brought him down to 16 health and they were barely scratching the thing. Jace got ready to use his health potion.

You stab Sewer Gator Bull for 0 damage.
You stab Sewer Gator Bull for 0 damage.

Jace's weapons once again failed to penetrate the alligator, and he silently swore. He really hated being a noob. He checked his *Stamina* and saw it was around 10%. Very soon, he'd have to stop attacking and focus solely on defense.

Mizzlethain-galliegarde shoots Sewer Gator for 2 magic damage.
Raajoget crushes Sewer Gator for 3 damage.
Almedha Pressalor Precisely shoots Sewer Gator for 7 damage.

At least the girl's attacks were doing more damage than he was. Then again, he was playing the role of the tank. He wasn't supposed to be the main damage dealer. But that just felt wrong after years of playing Mordred.

His mental counter was ticking down, and he prepared to use his *Taunt* for the last time without having to tap into Luna's mana. He spared a glance over to where Luna's head was bobbing. The poor cat had fallen out of the sling and was now just trying to keep its soaked head above water by doggy-paddling to stay afloat. Or was it called kitty-paddling when a cat did it?

Sewer Gator Bull bites YOU for 0 damage.
Sewer Gator Bull bites YOU for 0 damage.

The gator's attacks did no damage and Jace saw his opportunity. First, used his *Taunt* to keep the gator locked on him. "Fight me!"

Next, he produced the potion from his inventory and drank it down.

You use Cloudy Crimson Potion.
Cloudy Crimson Potion restores 10 health.

Jace shook his head at how little health the potion restored. It was a far cry from the Supreme Incandescent Potions he'd had as Mordred.

Mizzlethain-galliegarde shoots Sewer Gator for 2 magic damage.
Raajoget crushes Sewer Gator for 1 damage.
Almedha Pressalor Precisely shoots Sewer Gator for 5 damage.

His companions got in their attacks and thankfully their attacks were more effective.

"I'm getting really low on *Stamina*," Charlena yelled. "This fight has dragged on too long."

"Me too," Diana and Mika agreed at nearly the same time.

"Same here," Jace confirmed. "I've got a few more hits but then I have to save everything for my *Defense*."

Once again *Stamina* was becoming an issue for him. He rarely, if ever, had run out of *Stamina* as Mordred, but then again, he was mostly soloing or in higher level groups. But these marathon fights were where it normally became an issue.

Sewer Gator Bull bites YOU for 0 damage.
Sewer Gator Bull bites YOU for 0 damage.

The alligator seemed to be feeling it too, though he was sure this giant beast had plenty of *Stamina*. Plus, as a boss, it's stats were even higher than a normal monster's stats would be. Jace lunged out for the last time. After this, it would all be defense.

You stab Sewer Gator Bull for 0 damage.
You stab Sewer Gator Bull for 0 damage.

He frowned and cursed the random number generator. He couldn't even manage to do damage on his last hit.

Mizzlethain-galliegarde shoots Sewer Gator for 1 magic damage.
Raajoget crushes Sewer Gator for 1 damage.
Almedha Pressalor Precisely shoots Sewer Gator for 10 damage.

Jace was glad to see the girls were still doing damage, even if just a little. Charlena's damage had increased since she'd moved behind it, even though she'd been out of the fight for a few minutes to find a tunnel that led behind the monster.

Sewer Gator Bull bites YOU for 4 damage.
Sewer Gator Bull bites YOU for 5 damage.

As if sensing its end, the great alligator snapped twice at Jace, landing two hits, and almost completely undoing the healing potion he'd just used.

Angry, he almost lashed out at the thing but remembered he needed to conserve his *Stamina*. If he fell over right now, they'd all die. It was time to go full tank mode.

Mizzlethain-galliegarde shoots Sewer Gator for 1 magic damage.
Raajoget crushes Sewer Gator for 3 damage.
Almedha Pressalor Precisely shoots Sewer Gator for 6 damage.

More solid hits from his teammates and Jace wondered how much more health this boss had. By his calculations, they should be close to finishing it off. But maybe he'd miscalculated.

Sewer Gator Bull bites YOU for 5 damage.
Sewer Gator Bull bites YOU for 4 damage.

The alligator once again tore into Jace's legs causing him the grind his teeth to stop from crying out. He also saw his health had dropped down all the way down to 8. Another series of hits like the last two and he'd be done for. Screw *Stamina*, he needed to go all offense.

Jace needed something that would help end this fight quickly. The only thing that the creature's hide couldn't deflect was magic. Luckily, he could cast spells, but it would mean using mana from Luna.

He glanced over to the water-logged cat once more. If he died, all that mana would be wasted anyway. Jace set his jaw and cast his spell. "*Minima fulmen ignem!*"

You burn Sewer Gator Bull with Flame Bolt for 5 fire damage.
Your Fire Magic skill has increased by 1.
Sewer Gator Bull dies.
You gain 1000 experience.

You have gained a level.
You are now level 7 in Rogue.
You gain 8 health.
You gain 4 mana.

The fiery missile hit the creature in its open mouth, burning its sensitive skin. The alligator shuddered and then dropped lifeless to the ground. Jace saw that he had gained a new level and guessed the girls had too.

The girls cheered as the thing fell over, Diana grabbing Mika in a quick hug that the normally stoic girl returned. Charlena came bounding over the gator's corpse and jumped into Jace's arms.

"We did it!" she exclaimed.

Jace returned her hug and saw, out of the corner of his eye, his soaked familiar climb onto the alligator's head and begin shaking itself off. It caught him looking and glared daggers at him.

"I know. I know," he sent to her. "Extra fish tonight."

"Yes," the cat huffed, shaking water from her water-logged body. "Much extra!"

Jace looted the giant alligator corpse and was disappointed to receive only a superb quality alligator skin and a sewer gator bull eye, which was obviously the quest item. He was sure they could sell it for some extra money, but it was disappointing to get nothing else.

"That's it?" Diana asked. "We sit here for fifteen minutes, beating down a gigantic crocodile and all we get is a hide and an eyeball?"

"Alligator," Mika corrected.

Diana gave her a look and Mika just smiled in return.

Jace agreed with them. There should have been more loot. He remembered the extra treasure he'd found on the Spider Queen, back in the forest. It hadn't been on her body but actually in her spider web themselves, on mummified corpses. Perhaps there was a lair somewhere nearby.

"There may be more loot," he told them. "If so, it's probably in some sort of lair or nest nearby. Probably a large room or deep water where the alligator would have rested."

His comment got the girls excited and they spread out and searched the area for the creature's loot. Luckily, it didn't take long. Mika found a large pool where several pipes drained into. There were bits of floating debris in the room, but nothing that looked like loot.

"No loot though," Mika frowned, once they had all met in the room.

"Oh dearies," Diana said. "Don't you know, alligators and crocodiles like to stuff their victims underwater so they can come back and munch on them. I researched them for a romance novel set in the amazon but ended up changing the setting to Egypt and the Nile river instead."

"Was that's Pharaoh's Heart?" Charlena asked enthusiastically. "I loved that one!"

Jace had nearly forgotten that Diana was a successful writer and that Charlena was one of her fans. In this case, the old writer proved to be on the money.

The girls had unanimously volunteered him to dive under the murky water and search for bodies. Having no choice, he stripped off his armor and submerged himself in the dark waters. And he had found a number of partially eaten, bloated corpses stuffed into cracks it looked like the gator might have made with its massive tail.

After checking them all, he swam back over to them to show the girls what he had found.

Ring of Arcane Energy
Type: Ring
Level: 5
Wt: .2 lbs
Special: Wearer can store up to 4 mana in this ring
Description: This ring was given to the son of a rich nobleman who had been accepted into the Mages Guild. It was lost, along with the son, when he disappeared during a night of carousing.

Guardsman's Hauberk
Type: Chest Armor
Level: 5
Armor: 3 + 1 (Masterwork) + 1 (Sturdy)

Wt: 10 lbs
Description: By the faded guard emblem on the chest, this chain mail shirt probably belonged to a high ranking guardsman before his ill-fated trip to the sewer.

Ardmore's Bane
Type: Long sword
Level: 5
Damage: 10 + 1 (Sharp)
Wt: 4 lbs
Special: When unsheathed, this sword radiates light in a 30 ft radius.
Description: This weapon was enchanted for a wealthy merchant named Ardmore, who was rumored to be deathly afraid of the dark. Unfortunately, it made him a beacon for thugs when he ventured out one dark, stormy night.

Jace had also found 2 potions of healing, which the group insisted he keep, and 37 gold, which he divided among them. They talked it over for several minutes before deciding to give the ring to Diana. She was a Mage after all and would benefit the most from extra mana.

The hauberk went to Mika. It was better than the armor she wore and although Jace would have benefited too, it was only marginally better than his thieves guild jerkin and would make it harder for him to be stealthy.

For the moment, Jace told Mika to keep the long sword as well. At least until she was able to buy a katana. Jace could put it to good use, but the light casting qualities would cramp his *Stealth* when he was doing thieves guild jobs.

"Now can we get out of this dismal place?" Diana asked when they had distributed the loot.

"Yes," agreed Luna, who was still licking herself clean.

Chapter 14

The group found their way back to the surface. It was dark out and Jace realized they had been down in the sewers much longer than he had originally guessed. They went straight to the adventurers guild.

When they arrived, they all went inside and presented the paper and the eyeball to the person behind the desk. The man they'd spoken to early was gone. In his place was a grizzled old dwarf with an eyepatch over his left eye.

"What's this?" the dwarf demanded.

"We killed the giant alligator in the sewers," Jace told him. He examined the dwarf in his HUD.

Throdgrug Greydigger
Level: 50

Throdgrug looked down at the paper and then at the alligator eyeball that still lay on the desk. The dwarf gently picked up the alligator eye and brought up to his own good eye. He tilted it one way and then another, apparently examining it. Then, without warning, he popped it into his mouth and bit down. A popping sound came from inside his mouth and he smiled and began chewing.

A chorus of "ewws" came from behind him and even Jace had to admit he felt a little squeamish at the site of the dwarf chewing the eye.

"Eyes good!" came Luna's meow from a nearby chair she had appropriated.

"Any eyes we find that aren't used for quests," he reassured the cat, "you can have."

"Yes!" the little cat agreed.

The dwarf chewed for several minutes before signing his name on the paper. He reached into one of the drawers in the desk and retrieved four small pouches of gold. Tossing them onto the desk, he nodded. "There you go. Thanks for your service."

And just like that, the quest was complete.

You have completed the quest, "Alligators in the Sewer"
You gain 750 experience. Experience to next level 1,170.
You gain +25 faction with Whitecliff Adventurers Guild
You gain +25 faction with Whitecliff

Each of them collected their money, which was 50 gold each and Mika announced she was now 3rd level in Fighter. Two more levels and she could switch back to Priest.

"Is this enough money for a katana?" Mika asked, her eyes hopeful.

"I don't know," Jace shrugged. "We can go check out the weapon shops and find out."

Charlena looked out at the window and frowned. "Sorry, I need to get going. I work tomorrow and I need to be there early for orientation." She leaned over to Jace and gave him a quick kiss. "I'll log tomorrow night after work."

"See you then," he said but she had already faded away.

"Did someone say something about shopping?" Diana asked.

***

Two hours later, they were leaving the Central Market and heading back to the inn. Mika had found a katana for her level, but it was 200 gold since it was an exotic weapon. Jace had spent fifteen minutes *Haggling* with the weapon merchant and managed to get the price down to 150 gold. They'd pooled their money so that she could buy the two-handed weapon, which she now carried like a treasure.

The market had been good to Jace too. He ranked his *Haggle* skill to 10 and received the *Silver-Tongued* ability which gave him a permanent 2% discount on goods from NPC merchants. It wasn't much now, but at rank 100 it became a 25% discount. And that was significant at the later levels.

Jace had also managed to get his *Pickpocket* skill up to 10 by picking a few pockets as he bumped into people. He'd only earned a few gold, but he'd gotten the *Sleight of Hand* ability, which allowed him to do the opposite of pickpocketing, by placing an item in someone's pocket. It didn't seem particularly useful, but maybe he'd need it on a thieves guild quest.

"You girls can head back to the inn if you want," he told them. "Or go do some of your class quests. I need to work on my faction with the thieves guild."

"You're not eating dinner?" Mika asked. He'd noticed she was getting more and more vocal the longer she was with them. Was she simply shy and it had taken her some time to warm up to them?

"Don't worry dear," Diana told her. "We'll see him tomorrow morning."

Mika looked at Jace, then back at Diana. "Yes. See you tomorrow, Jace."

The two of them walked away, leaving Jace alone with Luna. He looked down at the cat who glared at him. "I forgot your fish."

"You forgot," she huffed.

"I'll make it up to your tomorrow morning," he told her. "I promise."

Luna didn't say anything, but she did follow him when he headed north to the thieves guild. He found Webley in the Lucky Coin and the guildmaster waved him over.

"Sit down," the master thief gestured to the seat across from him.

Jace sat and the guildmaster nodded to the bartender who brought over two pints of mead and slapped them down on the table.

"Thanks," Jace muttered and took a sip of his mead.

The guildmaster took a long dawn from his own mug and set it down. "I'm hoping you're here for work."

"I am," Jace nodded.

"Good," Webley said. He smiled but it didn't reach his eyes. He looked worried about something.

"Something wrong?"

Webley narrowed his eyes. "What makes you ask that?"

Jace smiled. "Other than you look like you're carrying the weight of the world on your shoulders?"

Webley relaxed and took another chug of his mead. "That obvious huh? I used to be better at hiding it. Let's just say we have some bad business going on at the moment."

"Anything I can help with?"

"We just found out the Crossroads guild was wiped out," Webley told him. "Down to the last man. And the guildhouse, which I hear had just started going through some renovations, was burned to the ground. Word on the street is the new guildmaster, some vampyre named Mordred something-or-other, might have done it. It could also have been the guard who found out the location of the guild and wanted to make an example."

Jace went pale and Webley noticed it. He raised an eyebrow. "Something you want to tell me?"

Jace tried to think quickly. He wasn't about to tell Webley he'd defeated another guildmaster and taken the guild from him. There might be honor among thieves, but he wasn't taking a chance. He had been wondering why the guild hadn't sent any updates. Now he knew. It had been wiped out.

He realized the guildmaster was still waiting for an answer and his face had become hard. It was time to see how well his *Bluff* skill would work against a high-level NPC. "I was just in Crossroads."

The guildmaster signaled him to go on.

"I met some of the Rogues," he told the man. So far, it was all true. He thought he remembered reading or hearing that the key to a good lie is mixing as much truth as possible.

"They made me a member, but the town was too small for me," Jace continued. Technically that was true. It was too small to have a *Help Desk*. And he had been a guildmaster, but technically that was still a member.

"So, I came here. When I left, the guild was under that Mordred guy." Again, technically true. It was under Mordred because he was Mordred, sort of.

Webley stroked his chin and stared at Jace for longer than was comfortable. Finally, he spoke. "I believe you. That makes you very lucky that you left when you did."

Jace nodded his agreement and tried to keep his face blank. He knew who had destroyed the guild. The former guildmaster who he had challenged and would have beat but the scoundrel had backstabbed Charlena and run away, Dainard Drakkar. He considered telling Webley, but that would just raise too many questions.

"There's also another matter," the guildmaster said after taking another long draw from his mug. "A big guild score that went south, but that's nothing you need to worry about."

Webley looked thoughtful for a moment. "And then there's the princess' birthday on Weeksend. The little trollop turns eighteen and the king and Queen are throwing her a big party. It's going to be a huge festival throughout the city. So, plenty of business to be made. I just need to figure out what the best scores will be."

That was news to Jace. He didn't even know there was a princess, let alone that she was having a birthday. He had bigger things to worry about than a NPC's birthday.

The guildmaster finished up his mead, slammed the mug down on the table and whipped the foam from his mouth. "What you do need to worry about is making sure you get the jobs I have for you done."

Webley the Snake has offered you the quest, "Spice is the Spice of Life"
Reward: +25 faction with Whitecliff Thieves Guild, 25 gold, 1 piece of Thieves Guild Armor.
Accept quest? (Yes or No)

Webley the Snake has offered you the quest, "A Lady's Locket"
Reward: +25 faction with Whitecliff Thieves Guild, 25 gold, 1 piece of Thieves Guild Armor.
Accept quest? (Yes or No)

Jace left the guild shortly afterwards with two more jobs. They were very different from what he had done last night. This time at least, they were near each other, on down by the Docks and the other in the Merchant District.

A smuggler known to the guild had managed to smuggle some rare spices into the city on one of the ships that docked recently and was planning to sell them to an exclusive inn up in the Noble District. The problem was, he hadn't paid the guild "tax" and was trying to circumvent them.

Webley wanted Jace to teach him a lesson. His job was to sneak into the man's house, find the herbs and mix in some powdered anise. The herb would completely spoil the flavor of the spice and give the man a very bad reputation. Not to mention the inn he sold it to would be furious and switch back to the guild connections to get the rare herbs.

His second job was a little different. He was to break into a house and steal an engraved locket, then break into another house and plant it where it would be found to make it appear the wife of a wealthy merchant was having an affair. Jace wasn't sure what that would lead to, but it probably meant more profit for the guild.

"What do you think," he asked Luna. "Finish up our jobs and then go buy some fish?"

Luna gave him an excited look. "Yes! Fish!"

The two of them hurried towards the Docks.

Chapter 15

Jace and Luna found the smuggler's house without much problem. Webley had told him it was right next to a tavern called the Drowned Fish. He'd found the tavern easy enough and immediately saw there was only one house on the same street. The other buildings were all shops.

He circled around the block, checking things out and marking his escape route if he was discovered. This person wasn't just some fat merchant. He was a smuggler. It was possible he could be a high-level Rogue himself. Jace would need to be careful.

Ducking into the alley behind the tavern, he crept up on to the back of the smuggler's house and looked around. The coast was clear and Jace bent down to pick the lock when the lock and the outline of the door began to glow.

Your Find Trap skill has increased by 1.

Freezing, Jace examined the door and the lock with only his eyes. He moved his head around to get a better view but couldn't figure out what type of trap the person was using. He guessed the door lock was trapped with some sort of poison needle, but the door was a complete mystery.

Checking to make sure no one was looking, Jace eased himself back away from the door and considered his options. He looked at the back of the house and saw several windows on the second floor. Would they be trapped too?

He looked down at Luna, who was sniffing the alleyway, "Stay here and keep watch."

"Yes," she responded and began cleaning herself.

Shrugging, he looked for a handhold and began climbing up the building, towards the second floor windows. There was no climbing skill in the game. Instead, it was one of those things that relied purely on the player's own skill and the avatar's *Brawn* and *Stamina*.

As Mordred, he'd fallen to his death more than once as he had attempted dangerous climbs. That wouldn't be the case here since it was only two stories and he had the *Safefall* ability. The worst that would happen is he might take a few points of damage and make a racket and draw the attention of the neighborhood.

Carefully, he climbed up the back of the building. Although the front was Tudor style, the back was flat with crisscrossed boards that actually made climbing fairly easy. Within a couple of minutes, he reached the first of the second story windows.

He examined the window very closely and did not see any traps. At least, nothing that his *Find Traps* skill picked up. He peaked in the window and saw that they opened into a hallway and that the rooms were towards the front of the house. That was good.

Reaching towards the windows, he tried to push it open, but it didn't budge. Putting his head against the window, he peered down and looked inside. It was locked with a simple swivel lock. Luckily, he knew how to open this lock.

Bracing himself with his legs and leaning his body against the house, he produced his dagger from his inventory and slid the blade in between the two parts of the window and then moved it to the right. He met resistance as the blade met the lock. Continuing the pressure against the lock, he slowly rotated the lock so that the latch was no longer locking.

Jace put his dagger away. Once again, he tried pushing the window open and this time it slid open. He waited to see if he had set off any alarms, but nothing happened. Smiling, he slipped into the hallway.

He heard snoring from one of the rooms and peaked in. While the covers obscured most of the person, he could see the tiny form of gnome huddled in the middle of the bed. That gave Jace pause.

Gnomes were one of the good races. While they were tinkerers, they were also excellent alchemists and could even make a sort of bomb that they could hurl at enemies. Those same bombs could be used to make traps. He would need to be extra careful.

He backed away from the room and crept down the hall towards the other room when he barely managed to stop in time to avoid a thin wire stretched across the hallway chest level. He had caught the sight of the glow just before he'd run into it.

Your Find Trap skill has increased by 1.

As Jace backed away, he realized the gnome had set the wire high enough wear he would walk beneath it, but an elf, human or even a dwarf would trip it. Smiling at the gnome's ingenuity, he ducked under the wire and continued more slowly down the hallway.

The second room was some sort of laboratory and Jace became even more cautious. Who knew what a diabolical gnome could cook up? Bombs. Acid. Acid bombs! There were all sorts of things they could do. None of which would be good for a thief who blundered into them.

He searched the room but found nothing that looked or smelt like the spices he was looking for. Webley had told him it would be in a small jar and be rainbow colored. He'd seen nothing that resembled that description.

Jace moved downstairs and encountered another chest-high wire on the way down the stairs, which he had to duck under. He also discovered that the second step from the bottom was a pressure plate trap. Unsure what the trap would do, he stepped over it to the floor.

As he did, he received his 10th rank of *Find Traps* and earned the *Danger Sense* ability, which gave him a 2% chance to avoid triggering a trap. At this level, it was laughable, but the ability improved as his skill improved until at level 100, it was a 20% to avoid setting off a trap.

The downstairs was a mess of crates, wooden boxes, and other packages. He quietly searched through them but didn't find the spice. Had the gnome already sold it? If he had, Jace would fail the quest. He glanced around the room again, but nothing caught his eye.

Going back to the stairs, he started to go up the stairs when he looked back down at the trapped step. Something seemed off about it. As he stared at it, he realized it seemed more worn than the others. That seemed strange for a trapped stair. If anything, he'd think it would be less used.

Jace bent down and examined it more closely. He examined the top of the step and then the bottom of the step and discovered a small wire with a tiny hook fastened to the top of the step. He took out one of his picks and carefully removed the hook from the step.

Your Disarm Trap skill has increased by 1.

With the trap disarmed, he ran his hand over the step. The top of the step moved slightly, and he pushed up on the lip of the step revealing a small, secret compartment underneath. Inside, he found a purse of coins, some vials, and a small jar of rainbow powder.

He pulled open the stopper and poured in the vial that he'd received from Webley. Replacing the lid, he shook it up to mix the herbs in. He replaced the jar and looked longingly at the purse of gold. If he took it, the gnome would know someone had broken in. He might check the spice and that would ruin the message the guild was trying to send.

Jace debated for a minute on whether to take the purse but finally decided against it. He needed the money, but he needed the faction with the thieves guild more. As Webley had said, no one went over the wall without his say so. He needed to earn the faction to be on the guildmaster's good side when he finally asked.

Jace replaced the step and then very carefully put the hook back on the lip of the step. He saw a new system message and was excited to see he had earned a new rank up in *Trapsetting*. He hadn't been able to raise that skill since he'd made the ogre pit trap.

Going back upstairs, he slipped out the window, re-closed it and dropped to the cobblestones below. Motioning to Luna, the two of them slipped away into the darkness.

An hour and a half later, Jace was back in the Lucky Coin, sitting across from Webley. The second quest had been easy and Jace had even managed to pocket a few extra pieces of jewelry without making it look too obvious. Hopefully, they wouldn't notice until the locket was found.

Jace had left it hanging out of the pocket of the husband's jacket so that it should fall out as soon as it was moved. Hopefully, the wife would find it when it fell out. He certainly wouldn't want to be that guy.

He had waited his turn to speak with Webley and had ordered some fish from the bar and Luna was happily eating them in the chair next to him as he talked to the guildmaster and turned in the quests.

You have completed the quest, "Spice is the Spice of Life"
You gain 600 experience. Experience to next level 520.
+25 faction with Whitecliff Thieves Guild

You have gained a level.
You are now level 8 in Rogue.
You gain 8 health.
You gain 4 mana.

You have completed the quest, "A Lady's Locket"
You gain 600 experience. Experience to next level 1920.
+25 faction with Whitecliff Thieves Guild

He read the system message and smiled. Jace was now level 8 in Rogue. He was making good progress now that he had real quests to do. In a few days, he would hopefully be level 11 and have access to the next tier of weapons and armor.

Webley chuckled. "You're definitely a natural, kid. You got those done in record time. You certainly earned these."

The guildmaster slid over a purse of gold and a bundle of clothing.

You receive Thieves Guild Leggings.
You receive Thieves Guild Hood.

You receive 50 gold.

"Thanks," Jace said and slid the items into his inventory. Both pieces of armor would be nice improvements to the items he wore now. "Do you have anything else?"

"You really are a scrapper," Webley said and scratched his chin as he thought. "There might be another job you can do for me tonight. Or what's left of tonight."

"Sure, what –" Jace started to reply but Webley held up his hand.

"Wait until I tell you what it is," the guildmaster told him and Jace nodded.

"We need to send a message to someone," the master thief told him, "a reminder that we have a long reach. But there is some risk. The person we need to send the message to is in the Noble District."

Webley paused to let his words sink in but Jace's mind was already whirling through the possibilities. If they had a job in the Noble District, did that mean they had a way in? Maybe even a pass? Did they have a way into the palace as well?

"Do you have a way into the Noble District?" Jace asked him, barely able to contain his excitement.

Webley nodded. "You could say that. We have an inside guy. A guard. Tonight's his night on the wall so he will let you over, but it has to be tonight. He won't get this post for another two weeks, so it needs to be tonight."

Jace nodded, his excitement waning. If their inside man wouldn't have this post for another two weeks, that meant his window to get in was effectively closing for another two weeks. It was disappointing, but at least he knew they could get into the Noble District.

On impulse, Jace smiled at the guildmaster and tried to use his joking voice. "An inside guy to the Noble District. That's great. Do you have one for the palace too?"

The guildmaster held a smile but his eyes narrowed. "Why, planning to heist to royal jewels?"

"Is that something we can do?" Jace asked, genuinely interested. If it was possible, that meant they had a way in.

"You are a scrapper," the man burst out laughing. "A few days in the guild and you're ready to waltz into the Royal Palace and rob them blind! You've got spunk, I'll give you that."

The guildmaster learned forward and his face became deathly serious. When he spoke, his voice was barely above a whisper. "Now listen up. No big scores happen in this city without my say-so. We don't do jobs in the Royal Palace. Ever. That's too much heat. We rarely do jobs in the Noble District and when we do, we do it at the bequest of one of the other nobles. And no one goes over the wall without my say-so. Got it?"

Jace noticed some people around him had grown quiet and were suddenly doing their best to be interested in anything but the guildmaster. NPC or not, real or not, the man was intimidating when he wanted to be and Jace nodded. "Got it. No one over the wall without your say-so."

Webley continued to look at him for longer than was comfortable before sitting back in his chair and smiled. "Now, about tonight's job."

Chapter 16

The guildmaster had glared at the other thieves around them until they stood up and left, giving them some extra space. When there was at least one open table between them and the other patrons, Webley turned back to Jace.

"I told you earlier that we had a deal go south, right?" the guildmaster asked in a soft voice.

Jace nodded and Webley continued. "It appears a third party has intervened in our affairs and is now attempting to broker a deal between themselves and our benefactor. It appears that our benefactor may be going along with this breach of contract and we would like to know who this third party is so that we can - thank them properly."

The guildmaster waited for Jace to acknowledge him and then continued. "I would like you to go and snoop around his place tonight and see if you can find any hint of who this third party is."

"And this person is in the Noble District?" Jace asked him.

"Yes, so you'll be going over the wall but don't get any bright ideas," Webley warned him. "Go right to our benefactor's estate on Lion Street, it's the 3rd estate up from the Crown Inn. Our inside man, Bliant, will tell you how to get there."

The guildmaster fixed him with a hard stare. "Remember, you're just there to collect the information. On second thought, if you find something small but valuable, feel free to take it. I don't care what it is, and you can keep it, but let's make sure he knows we're still expecting him to adhere to his contract and that our reach extends into the Noble District."

Webley the Snake has offered you the quest, "A Noble Job"
Reward: +50 faction with Whitecliff Thieves Guild, 50 gold, 1 piece of Thieves Guild Armor.
Accept quest? (Yes or No)

Jace accepted the contract and started to rise but the guildmaster wasn't finished. "There's a time limit on this one. Our man will only be on the wall for two more hours. You have that long to get over the wall, get the information and then get back over. I'd get whatever supplies you need quickly and get to the wall on the south side, just across from the Peacock Clothiers in the Merchant District. Oh, and make sure you bring a rope."

Thanking the guildmaster, Jace and Luna quickly headed back to the Black Market to sell his loot from the early caper and buy some equipment.

Thirty minutes later, Jace was at the bottom of the wall section across from the flamboyant merchant shop called Peacock Clothiers. At Webley's suggestion, Jace had purchased a 50-foot rope with a padded grappling hook from the Black Market. He held the rope in his hands and looked up at the wall.

If his contact wasn't up there, Jace would need to get out of here very quickly. He was ready for that contingency. He'd already planned an escape route and he'd dug out his Infiltrator's Hat he'd gotten from the forest ogre.

The magical hat allowed him to alter his appearance to that of nearly any generic humanoid. He wore it now instead of his leather hood. If he was forced to flee, the ability to change his appearance would come in a lot handier than a few extra points of armor.

He glanced down at Luna, who was back in her sling so he could carry her up. "You ready?"

Luna gave him an annoyed look. He knew she wasn't overly fond of the sling but Jace had no other way to take her with him.

"I'll take that as a yes," he told her.

Reviewing his escape plan one more time, he slung the rope around several times before releasing it and sending it sailing over the top of the wall. The padded grappling hook made no sound as Jace pulled it until it caught on something.

After testing it several times to make sure it would hold, Jace began climbing up the knotted rope. He'd purposefully brought the knotted rope to make it easier on himself as he climbed. His virtual body could climb a regular rope, but the more the difficult climb, the more *Stamina* it would use. And he would need his *Stamina* if he got up top and their inside man wasn't there.

It took him several minutes to shinny up the rope. He was only a few feet from the top when a burly man's head in a chainmail coif peaked over. Jace froze and looked at the man and the man just stared back at him. "You coming up or what?"

Jace hoped that meant it was the guild's man and scrambled the rest of the way to the top. He started to get to his feet, but the man gestured for him to stay down. "Keep low and go down the side as quick as you can."

Nodding, Jace took the grapple where it was lodged and found a spot on to wedge it on the other side of the four-foot-thick wall. Once it was secure, he flung himself over the edge. Just before he started descending, the man grabbed his forearm. "You got a little over an hour to get back here. If my shift ends, you're out of luck and it ain't my fault. Got it!"

Nodding, Jace started to climb down the rope but stopped and called up to the man in a low voice. "Where's the Crown Inn?"

The man looked around to make sure no one else was around before leaning down. "Head north to King Street, then west to Lion Street. It's up there a ways."

Jace waited a second longer to see if the man would add anything else but the guard had already turned away. Descending to the found, he jiggled the rope until the grapple disengaged. As he did that, Luna wiggled out of the sling and hopped to the ground. She immediately began sniffing the area, which even his human nose could tell smelled much better than the rest of the city.

The pair made their way north and then west until they found the Crown Inn. The houses they had been passing weren't houses at all but more like small manor homes on pristinely manicured lawns. It was a stark difference from the cramped housing in the rest of the city. Just like in the real world, it was good to be rich in-game.

From the inn, he stalked through the well-manicured yards, moving as stealthily as possible to avoid the few roaming patrols he'd spotted. He went up one home, then another and finally stopped when he reached the third house. Third house from the Crown Inn. This was his target.

It was a small stone manor on a two-acre plot of land, similar to the other two he'd past. It was a smaller home than he'd been seeing but still sported three stories and was easily as large as most of the inns in the city proper. There were no lights so Jace moved to the house and the around to the backdoor.

It took him several minutes to pick the lock and he broke several picks doing it. This was obviously a higher level lock and his lower skill gave him a severe disadvantage. After a few minutes, his persistence and real world skill paid off and the lock clicked open.

He looked at Luna, sitting quietly near the door. "You know the routine. Let me know if anyone comes."

"Yes," she replied in a bored tone and Jace scratched her behind the ears. Then, quiet as a ghost, Jace slipped into the house and closed the door behind him.

He'd entered into a small foyer that immaculately organized. There was a doorway in front of him that opened into a dining room and an open door to his right. He went to the door and peeked in to see it led down to the basement. He heard snoring from below. Since he doubted whoever the lord of the manor was would be sleeping in the basement, Jace guessed there was at least one servant down there.

Jace crept through the open doorway into the dining room. It was well furnished, and the walls were adorned with paintings. To his left was an open door that led into a kitchen. To his right was a drawing or sitting room. Ahead of him the room opened into a large living or entertaining room with a large staircase. Off to either side of the living room were two other open rooms that looked like smaller living rooms. That was a lot of living rooms.

Jace didn't see where the noble might put any important information down on the second floor, so he carefully took the staircase to the second-floor landing. The landing was U-shaped, allowing for those upstairs to view the action going on downstairs. It also had numerous doors along the walls.

He started with the closest. The first door opened into a small bedroom. It was unoccupied and the bed was made so Jace closed the door and moved to the next door, the door in the middle of the hallway. This was actually a double door and Jace guessed it opened into the master bedroom. He was right and wrong.

The double door opened into a smaller room that appeared to be a dressing room, with dressers and walk-in closets that were open. There were clothes strewn on the floor, as if someone had undressed quickly or while drunk.

On the far side of the room, were two other double doors which had been left open, revealing a richly furnished bedroom, completely with a four post canopy bed. Jace couldn't see the figure, on the bed but he heard the snoring. He peaked in and saw a jewelry box on a dresser near the bed. Remembering the guildmaster's instruction to get something small and valuable, he crept over to the jewelry box.

The man continued storing loudly and Jace saw empty bottles on the floor. It appeared the man had drunk himself to sleep. Turning back to the jewelry box, Jace opened the top to reveal some gaudy rings. They looked valuable but he checked out the sides and bottom drawer. The sides contained some similarly gaudy necklaces, but he hit paydirt in the drawer.

There, thrown haphazardly in the drawer were two gnomish timepieces. They were special clockwork devices made by the gnomes to keep time in the game. They were very expensive and considered a status symbol among rich merchants, nobility and players alike. Basically, it was this world's equivalent of a Rolex wristwatch, just a bit more clunky. It was exactly the sort of thing that would send a message.

He slipped one of the timepieces into his inventory and then, unable to resist, slipped the other one in too. Best to send a VERY strong message he told himself, all the while grinning like a madman.

Jace moved to the other side of the room to see if there were any notes. The dresser on the other side held only empty bottles and overturned wine glasses. Jace turned to go but stopped dead in his tracks as he caught sight of the sleeping man's face. He recognized that face. It was the man from the sewers. It was Lord Tiebaut!

Things began to click into place for Jace. Lord Tiebaut was the one who had hired the thieves guild to steal the tiara. Jace remembered the other man in the sewer. The one Tiebaut had called Captain. Was that the person who had the tiara now? Was he the one who was trying to cut the guild out of their cut and sell the tiara to the noble directly?

Jace needed more information for Webley. He needed to know who this captain was. He was sure that was what the guildmaster wanted. But the information didn't appear to be in the bedroom.

Slipping out of the room, Jace went to the next room, which was also another smaller bedroom. He moved to the next door and was happy to find that it was a study. The walls were lined with expensive looking shelves, filled with books and tomes of all shapes and sizes. In the middle of the room was a large mahogany desk that had several large, comfortable looking leather chairs around it.

Moving to the desk, Jace looked only briefly before finding what appeared to be a date book. Paging through the book, Jace saw an entry for early that day.

Meet Captain D. in sewers.

Frowning, Jace picked up the book and thumbed through the last week or two of entries but found no other references to the captain. He went to put the book back on his desk, but a folded piece of paper slipped out and fell to the floor. Jace bent down and picked up the note, opening it up so he could read it.

Dear Lord Tiabaut,

I have relieved Captain Shardin of command and I now have the package you ordered. I wish to deal with you directly rather than dealing with the third party you originally dealt with. Meet me on Sunday in the sewer at the place I've drawn on the map. If you don't show, I will find another buyer.

Sincerely,

Captain DD

That wasn't much, but he hoped it would be enough for Webley. He had no idea who Captain DD was, but the person was in for a world of hurt once the guildmaster found them.

Replacing the date book, Jace went downstairs and out the backdoor. He looked up at the sky to try and gauge the time and realized, he no longer had to guess. He produced one of the timepieces and checked. It was 4:33. He had 27 minutes to make it back to the wall.

Not taking the time to re-lock the door, he hurried back across the manors to the wall. This time, it took him less time because he knew where he was going. He made it back with 8 minutes to spare. He retrieved his grapple, tossed it up and quickly climbed to the top.

The inside man was there but looked nervous. He pulled Jace up and not waiting for him to get the grapple, pulled up the rope himself. "Cutting it a bit close, aren't you? My replacement will be here any minute! Go!"

The man handed Jace the grapple and motioned him to the other side of the wall. Obediently, Jace wedged the grapple on the outside of the wall and then went over. He climbed down as quickly as possible and jumped the last 10 feet. No sooner had he done that, the grapple was tossed down after him and the guard disappeared over the ledge.

Checking the street around him, Jace gathered up his rope and then disappeared back into the shadows. It was time to turn in his quest.

Chapter 17

The sun was peeking above the ocean to the east as Jace reached the Fainting Unicorn and slipped down into the thieves guild. Webley was waiting for him at the same table and gestured for Jace to join him as soon as he walked into the Lucky Coin.

"Did you find anything?" the guildmaster asked the moment he sat down.

Jace pulled the folded note out of his inventory and passed it over to Webley. As he did, the quest completion message appeared in his HUD.

You have completed the quest, "A Noble Job"
You gain 800 experience. Experience to next level 1120.
+50 faction with Whitecliff Thieves Guild

The guildmaster took it and read through it several times before looking up. He reached down into the seat next to him, pulled out a bundle and passed it over to Jace. "Nicely done. Was there anything else?"

You receive Thieves Guild Cloak.
You receive 50 gold.

This was the moment he'd been dreading. Jace felt like he needed to tell Webley about the meeting in the sewers he'd witnessed but wasn't sure how the guildmaster would take it. It seemed far too coincidental that he'd blundered into their meeting. Add that to the fact that Jace was new to the guild, and he was afraid the guildmaster would think he was in league with this captain fellow.

Jace's main concern was that he would lose faction with the guild. It was rare that players were expelled from a guild, since that interfered with gameplay, but it still happened if the offense was grave enough. After all, the AI might be tweaked in the players favor but it still tried to run the NPCs realistically.

Taking a deep breath, Jace decided to just tell him and let the cards fall where they may. "I need to tell you something."

The guildmaster raised an eyebrow but said nothing.

"Earlier yesterday," Jace began. "I was with my group down in the sewers hunting alligators for the adventurers guild. When we were looking for the bos… the big alligator, I happened across a strange meeting that I didn't understand at the time. But given what I just discovered, it makes much more sense now."

Webley was listening intently and motioned for Jace to continue.

"I overheard a conversation between two men. One was referred to by name, Lord Tiebaut," Jace said.

Webley's brow furrowed as he leaned closer. When he spoke, his voice had an edge to it. "Go on."

Jace swallowed and continued. He really hoped he didn't lose faction. He'd need the guild's inside man if he wanted to get into the Noble District. "I saw his face clearly and recognized him tonight. The other man had his back turned but Tiebaut referred to him as Captain."

Webley nodded. "And you think it's the same Captain?"

"It has to be," Jace said. "The note says Sunday and there was an entry in his date book for today that mentioned meeting Captain D in the sewers. It can't be a coincidence."

The guildmaster sat back and stared hard at Jace. He could almost see the gears turning in the guildmaster's head. He was probably deciding whether he believed Jace was part of it. Finally, the man leaned forward.

"I'm glad you told me about that," the guildmaster said. Even as he spoke, Jace felt like the man was still deciding. Watching for him for some reaction. "Either it's the biggest coincidence I've seen, or you've got Dolorea's own luck. I just can't decide which."

Dolorea was the patron goddess of thieves, since she was associated with shadows, secrets, cats, and luck. It wasn't uncommon for thieves to wear her symbol, which was a cat's head, half white and half black. Some thieves guilds even had a shrine dedicated to her but Jace had seen no such shrine here.

Luna chose that exact moment to hop into the chair next to him. She looked between the two men and settled on Jace. "Fish?"

The guildmaster looked over to the cat, then to Jace and then back to the cat. The guildmaster snickered. "Goddess of cats, indeed. Maybe you do have Dolorea's own luck. I'll see what I can dig up on our mysterious Captain DD."

"I think he's a pirate," Jace blurted out, remembering the man's clothes. "At least, he looks like a pirate. Or at least a ship's captain."

Webley nodded. "That helps to narrow it down. There can't be that many ship's captains with the initials DD - assuming that is the name he's going under. I'll see you tomorrow night."

Jace stood up and left the guildmaster. It was time to meet his friends back at the Dwarvish Fork and see what they had done that night. But first, he needed to go to the Black Market and sell one of the gnomish clockwork watches. He considered selling both, but there was something to be said for being able to tell what time it was. Especially considering the that many quests were time sensitive. He could always sell it later.

The Black Market never slept so Jace knew it would be open. When he entered, Jace didn't see any other players in the room. It was all NPCs. Jace went to one of the vendors and set the gnomish timepiece on the counter. "How much can I get for this?"

The vendor's eyes opened wide. "Oh, such a treasure. I am afraid that I cannot buy something of this value. Not from someone with such a low reputation. Perhaps one of the other vendors."

His low reputation? Did that mean he didn't have the faction to sell it? That was a first. But then again, he had never stolen something this valuable at such a low level before.

Jace picked up the timepiece and moved to the next vendor. And then the next. And the next. None of them would buy it from him. Several said almost the same thing as the first vendor while others told him to come back when he'd earned more of a reputation.

Disappointed, he left the Black Market. Jace didn't know exactly how much they were worth, but it had to be at least ten thousand gold, maybe even more. And he couldn't sell it. Not yet.

When he arrived at the inn, Mika and Diana were already waiting for him. The first thing he noticed was that Mika now sported much newer looking armor. He guessed she'd completed some of the fighters guild quests and received the class armor.

That was a nice perk of doing the class quests. Unfortunately, you couldn't sell or trade the armor to other players, you could only sell it to NPC vendors and they never gave you much for the armor you earned from those quests. Still, it was decent armor that you could earn at low level.

"There's our lovely," cooed Diana when she saw him.

Jace grinned despite himself. He knew she was an unabashed flirt and that she didn't mean anything by it. He also knew she had been in her 90s when she died. But in her hourglass, raven-haired, 20-something body, it was easy to forget sometimes.

"Good morning," said a smiling Mika. "I have completed four quests for the fighter's guild and now have new armor!"

Jace returned her smile. "Good job!"

"And you are level 8," she said enthusiastically and Jace couldn't help but notice the difference between when he'd first met the girl to now. At first, she'd seemed shy and soft spoken - almost demure. Now, she seemed much more vibrant.

"Yes," he returned her smile. Like Charlena, she had a brilliant smile. But then again, they were all in their genetically perfect bodies, so it was no wonder that the girls all had amazing smiles. He took a moment to scan the two girls.

Raajoget
Race: Human
Class: Fighter
Level: 5

Mizzlethain-galliegarde
Race: Human
Class: Mage

Level: 5

Jace wanted to roll his eyes at the monster names the girls still carried. Like him, when they'd used his "cheat code" to turn human, they'd retained the name of the monster they'd been last. It was extremely annoying, and he had to remember that Raajoget was Mika and Mizzlethain-galliegarde was Diana.

"Great job to both of you!" he told them. "You're both level 5!"

The two girls looked pleased with themselves and Jace sat down across from them. The barmaid came over to them and he ordered a full halfling breakfast for himself and a fish for Luna.

"You getting anything?" he asked the two smiling women.

"I ate waffles," Mika announced with a huge grin. "With whipped cream!"

"We both did," Diana told him. "After all, food doesn't affect your figure, blood sugar or heart in the game so why not eat whatever you want?"

"Good point," Jace told her. He hadn't really thought of it that way, but she was right. Food in game wouldn't affect him in any way. Assuming Charlena was right, and he was in a coma, he was in some long term medical pod, being fed intravenously right now. Diana was right, he could eat whatever he wanted in the game. He changed his order to waffles.

"So, dearie," Diana said when the barmaid had left. "What's the plan today? Hopefully not more traipsing around the sewers. That place was wretched."

"At least it was just water," Mika cheerfully offered. Jace was once again amazed at how much fuller of life she seemed now.

"Charlena won't be on until much later," he told them. "So, we'll be a man, or woman as the case may be, short."

"We can handle it," Mika stated and patted her katana.

"I like the enthusiasm," Jace chuckled and Mika beamed.

Thinking about their options, it really only boiled down to two things they could do as a group at their level. They could either find some group quests or go out and fight some monsters. Despite Mika's assurance, he wasn't sure about the adventurers guild quests, since they'd barely survived yesterday with four people. That meant finding some monsters to kill. And that meant leaving the city.

He was about to tell the girls but at that moment, his waffles and Luna's fish came and the two of them dug into their food. The first bite was absolutely delicious. The waffles were tall and golden brown. They were topped with some type of whip cream and fresh strawberries. Jace made an involuntary sound of pleasure as the flavors hit him.

Then he noticed the women were both staring at him, making him suddenly self-conscious. He looked up just after shoveling another bite in. "Wha?"

"Waffles are good!" Mika declared with a grin.

Jace tried to smile without opening his mouth. When he spoke, his words were muffled. "Waffles good!"

Chapter 18

After breakfast, Jace led the girls to the main city gate. It was where he had first arrived by caravan. It seemed like weeks ago now, but in actuality had only been a few days. Not sleeping or logging off tended to make the days feel like they blended together.

As they approached the gate, they encountered more and more players. He saw dwarfs, halflings, gnomes, elves, fairies, nephilim, and werebears. There was a smattering of all of the good races. He wasn't surprised.

As a capital city, Whitecliff could be selected as a starting city for any of the good races, just like humans could select any of the other race's capitals to start in. Since the larger cities had the most quests, they were favorite starting cities. Had Jace started here in the capital, he'd most likely be twice his current level.

When they finally made it to the gate, Jace walked up to one of the guards. "Well met, good fellow."

The guard, a human around Jace's general build, but dressed in the armor and livery of a Whitecliff guardsman, eyed Jace suspiciously. "Well met, stranger."

Jace understood that by addressing him as 'stranger', the guard was essentially telling him that he had very little faction with the Whitecliff guards. That meant the guard wasn't likely to help them much but would provide basic information.

"Is there some way we can help the guard with any problems around here?" he asked the guard.

The guard's eyes darted down to the weapons Jace wore and then to the two girls with him, taking note of their weapons and armor. The man gestured to a different guard who wore more stripes than this guard. "Ask the Sergeant. He'll know."

Thanking the man, Jace walked over to the Sergeant and viewed the man in his HUD.

Name: Sergeant Wyot
Race: Human
Level: 50
Profession: Soldier

The sergeant was dressed similarly as the previous guard. He wore a chain mail hauberk and leggings under a white tabard embroidered with Whitecliff's blue and gold crest. Wyot was a level 50 soldier, which was the NPC equivalent of the fighter. He was someone Jace didn't want to mess with.

Like the previous guard, Wyot looked him up and down as he approached. "How may I help you, stranger?"

Jace smiled at the man, trying to appear friendly. "Is there anything we can do to help

Whitecliff? Any tasks that you might need help with or foes that need to be vanquished?"

Sergeant Wyot gave Jace and the girls an appraising glance. "I'm afraid the orcs to the west are beyond your skill."

"However," the guard paused and stroked his chin. "A colony of giant beetles was found just this morning. I was going to have some of my men look at it, but two more caravans are due in soon. The Guard will pay you 1 gold for each of the little buggers you kill. I'll give you a better reward if you find and kill the queen."

Sergeant Wyot has offered you the quest, "Eye of the Beetle" (Repeatable)
Reward: +5 faction with Whitecliff City Guard, 5 gold.
Accept quest? (Yes or No)

Sergeant Wyot has offered you the quest, "Queen Beetle Mania"
Reward: +50 faction with Whitecliff City Guard, 60 gold.
Level: 6
Accept quest? (Yes or No)

Like the adventurers guild quests, the Beetle Mania quest was level specific and wouldn't scale to their levels like the thieves guild quests. The Eye of the Beetle didn't have a level but was repeatable so the more beetles they killed the more they could earn. Jace accepted both quests and shared them with his team.

"We'll take care of it," he told the sergeant.

Wyot grunted. "We'll see. The beetles are to the north, just west of the cemetery. Oh, and be careful. You might get some young orcs out that way. They may be young, but they're bred as warriors."

Jace thanked the man and he and the girls started north towards the cemetery. They all knew where the cemetery was since they had all bound themselves to it when they'd first arrived. Now, whenever they died, they would respawn there.

Whitecliff was built on a cliff that sloped up and then dropped off into the ocean, providing the Royal Palace great defense from sea attacks. The terrain immediately around the city to the north and west was mostly grass-covered hills.

As they travelled up and down the hills to the cemetery, they would occasionally see the half-naked bodies of players who had been killed and had respawned. They were too far to see their level, but they were obviously being killed by something.

Finally, they crested one of the taller hills and spotted the cemetery. The group looked west towards where the sergeant had said they would find the beetles. And find the beetles they did. Even from what seemed a half a mile away, they could see large dark shapes dotting the western hills.

"Are those the beetles?" Diana asked, squinting to make out the details. "They must be huge if we can see them from here."

Jace looked to the western hills and couldn't help but agree. They had to be at least as large as a person for them to be seen from this distance. "They do look big."

"They will still die!" Mika said optimistically, her hand on her katana.

Jace smiled back at the enthusiastic girl. "Yes, they will! Come on!"

"Bugs?" came a small voice and Jace looked down to see Luna. His familiar had been quiet since they'd left the inn and he'd almost forgotten she was still with them.

"Very big bugs," he told her.

"Big bugs?"

"Yes, very big bugs. Bigger than that giant rat we killed."

"I killed," the orange tabby insisted.

Jace chuckled. The giant rat had been about to take a bite out of Jace, possibly killing him, when Luna had pouched on it. She'd only did 2 damage, but it was enough to finish it off. So technically, she got in the final blow that killed it. Apparently, she had a good memory.

"Yes," he agreed. "You killed."

The girls were watching the exchange with amusement and he remembered that, like him, they could communicate with monsters too. That meant they understood the cat as well as he did.

"Luna is a good hunter," Mika said and bending down, scratched the cat behind the ears.

His familiar accepted both the praise and the scratches. "Yes."

"Let's go see how big these bugs really are," Jace told them once Mika had stopped petting Luna.

They traversed two more hills before they heard a loud voice from behind them. Stopping, they turned to see a naked dwarf, except for his loincloth, running at them.

"Make way! Make way! Dwarf comin' through!" yelled the dwarf. This particular dwarf had a mop of unkempt red hair. His beard was red as well but had been braided. His chest and arms were a collection of what Jace thought might be Celtic tattoos. At least, they looked Celtic to him.

Jace guessed it was a player but scanned the dwarf to make sure as he ran past.

Thedrir Stronggut
Race: Dwarf
Class: Paladin
Level: 5

"For the honor of Graykeep!" the dwarf shouted and ran past them and disappeared over the next hill.

"That was odd," Diana commented when the dwarf disappeared from view. Mika nodded.

"Welcome to VEIL Online," he told them and continued on.

Cresting the next hill, they found where the beetles were. The things were as large as Jace had guessed. The things were as long as a man was tall, maybe five or six feet. But they were also wide, maybe three and a half or four feet wide. Their entire body was covered in incandescent black carapace that looked as tough as plate armor.

"Oh my," Diana gasped. "They are huge."

Beside him, he saw Mika nod. "And armored. Beetle shells are very tough!"

"It's an ugly planet, it's a bug planet," Jace grinned. The two girls looked at him in confusion and he sighed, wishing Charlena was here to get his reference to an old science fiction vidstream. "Nevermind."

Readying his weapons, he looked at them. "Let's go kill some beetles."

They came up the hill only to find a werebear player killing one of the beetles. In between blows with his two-handed axe he shouted over his shoulder. "Get lost. This is my area."

Jace rolled his eyes at the player but gestured for the girls to follow him as they walked several hills over. There they found the red-headed dwarf, Thedrir, battling two of the beetles with an axe and shield. He must have retrieved his body because in addition to his axe and shield, he was now clad in plate mail armor.

The dwarf was intent on the battle and didn't notice them. They walked around and tried to find an open spot.

His group walked another few hills over and found that this area was both free of players and the hill they were looking at had three beetles on it. Out of habit, he scanned them.

Hive Beetle
Level 5

Despite their large size, they seemed to be only level five solo monsters. They should be about the same difficulty as the sewer gators. But he knew sometimes level was deceiving and some creatures had special abilities that made them more powerful than other creatures of the same level.

"Let's pull one and see how easy they are to kill," he told them, and the girls nodded in agreement. "I'll pull it with my *Taunt*. I'll bring it over here and then spin it, so it's back is facing you. We don't know if these things have any special attacks but if it does, hopefully it's a frontal attack."

"These are solo mobs," he told them, using the game slang that mob, which meant monster or boss. "So, they shouldn't be too hard."

"Ready?" he asked.

"Ready as I'll ever be," Diana replied.

Mika tightened her grip on her katana, her face serious. "I am ready."

"Here we go," Jace said and turned to face the beetles. He targeted the closest one and shouted his *Taunt*. "Get over here!"

The beetle he'd targeted had been munching on some tall grass. It looked up at him and chittered angrily with mandibles that were as long as Jace's forearm. Then it charged it.

Jace had been expecting this. What he hadn't expected was that the other two nearby beetles clicked and hissed and charged him too.

"Oh great," he muttered as the three enormous insects bore down on him.

Chapter 19

"They're swarm mobs!" Jace announced as he heard Diana squeal. Swarm monsters generally did not display any tactics but if you attacked one, any nearby monsters of the same type would attack as well. So instead of pulling just the one beetle, all three had come.

Backpedaling, Jace tried to pull the incoming beetles further back so he wouldn't have to turn them. Instead, he'd let the girls circle around.

The creatures were closing fast. Just before they reached him, Jace cast his *Air Armor* spell to give himself more *Defense*. He had no idea how hard they would be, but those huge mandibles had him worried.

The transparent armor swirled about him just as the three beetles came within melee range. All three chittered and snapped at him with their razor sharp mandibles.

Hive Beetle bites YOU for 0 damage.
Hive Beetle bites YOU for 0 damage.
Hive Beetle bites YOU for 0 damage.

Jace felt the mandibles snap at him, but they slid off the *Air Armor*. He took a moment to look at his *Defense*. With his new pieces of thieves guild armor, the buckler, the bonus from his skill and the griffon necklace, his *Defense* was at 11. That meant he'd ignore the first 11 points of damage now. These beetles may not even be able to touch him.

The girls circled around and began to hit the beetles with all they had. He seen Diana's *Flame Bolt* flash out and hit the creature on its shell.

Mizzlethain-galliegarde burns Hive Beetle with Flame Bolt for 0 fire damage.

"What the -?" shouted Diana. "It didn't even scratch it!"

Jace saw the system message too. Her flame attack hadn't done anything. Jace considered their shiny carapace and guessed it must protect them against magic attacks as well as regular attacks. "The shell must be magic resistant! Try your wand!"

He heard Mika's battle cry and could just make out the rise and fall of the katana.

Raajoget slashes Hive Beetle for 0 damage.

"Their armor is very tough!" he heard Mika's voice.

Jace frowned. This was going to be a very long fight if they couldn't actually hurt the creatures. The thought had entered his mind when the beetles snapped at him again.

Hive Beetle bites YOU for 0 damage.
Hive Beetle bites YOU for 0 damage.

Hive Beetle bites YOU for 0 damage.

Again, the intimidating mandibles failed to pierce his armor. That was good, but they needed to do damage to kill it. He struck out with his rapier and dagger to see if he could damage the giant bugs.

You stab Hive Beetle for 0 damage.
You stab Hive Beetle for 0 damage.

His own weapons bounced off the armored carapace as well. Were these things that heavily armored or had they just had bad damage rolls?

Raajoget slashes Hive Beetle for 0 damage.
Mizzlethain-galliegarde shoots Hive Beetle for 0 magic damage.

"Uh," Diana commented. "This isn't working. I can't do anything to them."

Jace understood her frustration. They hadn't met anything yet that had magic defense. That had been an advantage for her. Even though she had done less damage, her damage had always penetrated the creature's defense. Now it wasn't.

"Keep trying," he yelled to her. "Switch back to your *Flame Bolts*."

Hive Beetle bites YOU for 0 damage.
Hive Beetle bites YOU for 0 damage.
Hive Beetle bites YOU for 0 damage.

The beetles attacked again but his *Defense* held. Once again, he stabbed at the creature in front of him with his rapier and dagger.

You stab Hive Beetle for 2 damage.
You stab Hive Beetle for 0 damage.

This time his dagger found a gap in the plating and the beetle hissed angrily.

Raajoget slashes Hive Beetle for 5 damage.
Mizzlethain-galliegarde burns Hive Beetle with Flame Bolt for 3 fire damage.

The girl's attacks got through this time. It was impossible to tell exactly how much armor the thing had but he guessed it had at least as much as the alligator boss they'd fought in the sewers. Only the beetle's carapace also had defense against magic. It was going to be a long fight.

His group continued their attacks for several minutes before finally bringing down the first beetle. From Jace's mental tally, these things had lower than normal health for a level 5 creature, but their armor seemed to make up for their low health.

"That was frustrating," Diana gasped as the last of the three beetles fell dead. It had taken them at least another ten minutes of constant blows to kill them but all three beetles now lay dead.

Jace was breathing hard, having used much of his *Stamina* in the fight. Judging by the way the girls were breathing, they were feeling the same.

"Yeah," he agreed. "That's some seriously armored shell for a low level monster."

He walked over to the bodies and looted them.

You receive Hive Beetle Eye.
You receive Hive Beetle Carapace.

"Beetle Carapace?" Mika questioned as she saw the loot message and Jace examined it.

Hive Beetle Carapace
Type: Crafting Item (Armorsmithing)
Level: 1
Wt: 4 lb
Description: Part of the carapace from a giant beetle. A craftsman can use this to create unique armor.

"It's a crafting item," Jace told the group. "If we had the *Armorsmithing* skill, it looks like we could use it to create some armor. Too bad none of us have the skill."

Mika looked thoughtful but didn't say anything else.

***

They spend the rest of the morning killing beetles. The fights were long and boring, but that's why players called it grinding. To gain levels, players should kill monsters hour after hour to gain experience and loot. Even Jace had been forced to grind many of Mordred's levels, not for hours, but for days or weeks at the higher levels.

It was mind-numbingly boring, but it did work. By noon, each of them had gained a level. Jace was now a level 9 Rogue. Mika had hit level 6 in Fighter and then switched back to Priest, while Diana had hit level 6 in Mage early on and was now almost level 7.

Tired from their last fight, the three of them were laying back on the hill, letting their *Stamina* regenerate. Luna was nearby stalking butterflies with the same level of intensity they'd had fighting the beetles.

"How many did we kill?" asked Diana.

"36," replied Mika before Jace could mentally count them.

"Is that all?" Diana groaned. "It seems like we should have wiped them out by now."

Jace was about to answer when they heard a scream. "Boss!"

Sitting up suddenly, Jace glanced around to find the source of the scream. Scrambling to his feet, he gestured to the others. "Come on! That might be a queen beetle."

Not waiting for the others, Jace scrambled to the top of the hill just as the rude were-bear player they'd seen earlier came bounding over the crest.

"Boss!" the rude player screamed as he ran past.

Before Jace could do anything else, an enormous beetle came clattering over the crest of the hill. The thing was twice as large as the ones they had been fighting with clicking mandibles that were as large as his arm.

It was only second behind the werebear and he considered whether he should help the rude player. Before he came to a decision, it was made for him. The werebear tripped going down the hill and the beetle was on him in an instant.

Jace watched as the creature bit into him several times before the werebear could regain his feet. The werebear did manage to finally regain his feet and then turned to run again but another bite from the enormous beetle and the werebear collapsed in a heap.

Immediately after the werebear died, the enormous beetle swiveled towards his group and hissed loudly. The thing snapped its mandibles and charged them. Jace barely had time to check out the thing in his HUD and cast his *Air Armor* spell before it was on them.

Hive Beetle Queen
Level 6

Jace thought the thing was coming for him, but Diana was a few steps closer. Before he realized he wasn't the target, the thing rushed the Mage and bit into her side with its gigantic mandibles.

Hive Beetle Queen bites Mizzlethain-galliegarde for 9 damage.

Diana screamed as her abdomen was punctured by the creature and Jace felt sorry for her. Like him, her sensory feedback level was permanently set at maximum. They felt pain as if it were actually happening.

"Fight me!" he *Taunted,* and the thing immediately spun and hissed. It snapped its mandibles at him menacingly and then attacked him.

As it did, Mika took a swipe at it with her sword.

Raajoget slashes Hive Beetle Queen for 6 damage.

The blow connected with the beetle's legs and did some damage but that didn't stop the queen. During the fight with the smaller beetles, Jace had swapped out his dagger for the longsword he carried. Now, he attacked with his longsword and rapier, slashing and stabbing the thing's head.

You stab Hive Beetle for 0 damage.
You slash Hive Beetle for 0 damage.

Like the smaller beetles, his weapons found no openings in the beetle's armor and simply slid off. Then the queen's mandibles closed on his arm and Jace flinched.

Hive Beetle Queen bites YOU for 0 damage.

His armor held and Jace unconsciously let out a breath. The thing was huge, but hopefully its hiss was worse than its bite.

"Grabthar's hammer!" he heard from behind him and he glanced back to see the red-headed dwarf. "I needed that thing for a darn quest!"

The dwarf probably had the same quest they had. His group would no doubt do more damage than he could, so they'd get credit for the kill and he'd have to wait for the next time a beetle queen spawned.

He looked at Charlena's empty spot in the group and made a quick decision. He targeted the dwarf and sent him a group invite.

The dwarf looked surprised for only a moment. Then he grinned broadly and Jace saw the system message.

Thedrir Stronggut has joined your group.

"It's clobberin' time!" Thedrir bellowed and charged the beetle.

"I got us some help for this fight," he yelled to the others.

Raajoget slashes Hive Beetle Queen for 7 damage.
Mizzlethain-galliegarde burns Hive Beetle Queen with Flame Bolt for 0 fire damage.
Thedrir Stronggut slashes Hive Beetle Queen for 0 damage.

The dwarf growled with frustration as his axe bounced off the queen's thick shell. "You want me to tank?"

"What's your *Defense*?" he asked the dwarf. If the dwarf did tank, Jace would be free to get behind it and backstab.

The queen didn't seem to care about the new addition and focused its attention and attacks at Jace.

Hive Beetle Queen bites YOU but you Block.

Seemingly moving of its own volition, his left arm moved to block the blow with his buckler.

"8 *Defense*," the dwarf said proudly. Jace realized that was actually a very good *Defense* score for a low-level player.

"Mine's 11," Jace replied and took a certain amount of joy in the dwarf's reaction.

"11! How the heck are you getting an 11 *Defense*?" the dwarf roared as he and the other members of his group got in their attacks.

**Raajoget slashes Hive Beetle Queen for 0 damage.
Mizzlethain-galliegarde burns Hive Beetle Queen with Flame Bolt for 0 fire damage.
Thedrir Stronggut slashes Hive Beetle Queen for 0 damage.**

This time, none of his companions' attacks hit and Jace got in his own attacks.

**You stab Hive Beetle for 0 damage.
You slash Hive Beetle for 0 damage.**

Jace ground his teeth in frustration. In some ways he felt almost overpowered, like his *Defense*, but in other ways he felt subpar.

"If you're going to tank," the dwarf yelled, taking a step back. "I'm going to go full DPS!"

From the corner of his eye, he saw the dwarf put away his one-handed axe and shield into his inventory. In the next instance, the dwarf was holding a larger, two-handed axe. "For the honor of Graykeep!"

Hive Beetle Queen bites YOU for 4 damage.

He had been glancing at the dwarf so the mandibles piercing his leg came as a surprise and he couldn't stifle the involuntary gasp of pain that came out. The pain shot from his leg, up his spine and into his head.

The dwarf looked his way and must have seen his Jace's face screwed up in pain. "Turn your input down idiot!"

"Can't," Jace said through clenched teeth.

He barely caught Thedrir muttering something and rolling his eyes. Then the dwarf raised his weapon to the sky. A glow infused the two-handed axe and the dwarf struck out at the same time as his other companions.

Raajoget slashes Hive Beetle Queen for 8 damage. Mizzlethain-galliegarde burns Hive Beetle Queen with Flame Bolt for 0 fire damage.

Thedrir Stronggut smites Hive Beetle Queen for 14 damage.

Jace recognized the move from other paladins. It was their *Smite* ability and did double damage, much like a Rogue's critical strike. Once again, he was reminded how subpar the base classes were compared to the premium classes. The Fighter class had no equivalent ability to *Smite* and instead was focused almost exclusively on *Defense* and tanking.

Clamping down on the pain, Jace struck out as hard as he could at the beetle, hoping to get some small amount of revenge for the burning in his leg.

You stab Hive Beetle for 0 damage.
You slash Hive Beetle for 0 damage.

Unfortunately, he was once again left disappointed as his weapons failed to penetrate the queen's carapace. That's when he noticed the creature's thorax shaking. They must have hit some threshold, probably 75% of health, and activated a special ability.

"Special attack!" he shouted. Having no idea what might be coming, he used some of his mana to pop his *Evade* ability even as he backpedaled away from the huge insect.

After only a moment, huge wings popped out from underneath the beetle queen's shell. Before he knew what was happening, the beetle leaped up and came straight down onto him.

Hive Beetle Queen uses Crushing Attack on YOU but you Evade.

One moment Jace was where the queen was going to land and the next thing he knew, he had rolled several feet backwards to avoid the blow.

The wings retracted back underneath the beetle queen's carapace and it seemed to resume its normal attack pattern.

Hive Beetle Queen bites YOU for 4 damage.

His companions had backed away several yards and now rushed back to attack. They continued to rain blow after blow on the queen until Jace saw the thing start to open and close its mandibles over and over again. Another special attack was coming.

Chapter 20

"Special attack!" Jace shouted. He realized they must have hit 50% of its health and it was going to use its special attack again. He used his *Evade* again and took several steps back.

He saw his companions moving away as well and he waited for the queen to jump at him again. Too late, he remembered that this wasn't what the queen had done before. Instead of bringing out its wings, the creature opened its mandibles wide.

Hive Beetle Queen uses Dissolving Spittle on YOU for 12 acid damage.

A spray of viscous green liquid shot from the open mandibles of the queen. An instant before it hit him, he realized this was an AoE (area of effect) attack. His *Evade* wasn't going to protect him!

The green liquid struck Jace in the chest and arms. Where it touched, fiery pain exploded and as his skin dissolved away. Unable to hold back, Jace screamed as he fell to his knees.

"Jace!" he heard Mika yell.

Thieves Guild Jerkin has been destroyed.
Thieves Guild Bracers have been destroyed.

Netherlight has been destroyed.
Longsword has been destroyed.

The unbearable pain wracked his body what seemed to be an eternity before it subsided in a golden glow. Jace opened his eyes to see that the acid had dissolved the blades of his weapons, along with most his bracers and jerkin.

Then he saw the queen looming over him as the thing resumed its normal attack, biting at his head. Somehow, his buckler had survived, and he managed to get it up to help ward off the attack.

Hive Beetle Queen bites YOU for 5 damage.

The queen's attack dug into his arm and he consciously clamped his mouth closed to stifle another scream. He stood up as the thing reared back and hissed.

Raajoget slashes Hive Beetle Queen for 6 damage.
Thedrir Stronggut smites Hive Beetle Queen for 8 damage.

He saw Mika and Thedrir resume their attacks, but Diana no longer attacked at all. She was out of mana and her wand attacks weren't doing any damage at all to the queen. She stood back behind the beetle staying out of the way of danger.

The rest of the fight was grueling for Jace. He was still reeling from losing not only two pieces of Thieves Guild armor, but also his two best weapons. The loss of Netherlight was especially painful for him. Not only was it the only real magical weapon he had possessed, it was something he'd carried with him since Crystalburrow. Now it was gone. Destroyed in an instant by the special attack of some random boss.

The loss of armor also meant his *Defense* dropped from 11 down to 10. It was still a formidable score, but it seemed like more and more of the queen's attacks got through and he could do nothing except soak up the damage.

Mika and Thedrir finally managed to get the giant insect down to 25% health and Jace breathed a huge sigh of relief when he saw the queen's thorax wiggling. That meant another crushing attack and he used up the last of his mana to pop his *Evade*.

This time, Jace had been right and the queen once again let her wings come out and was about to pounce on Jace. Before it did, he heard battle cries from Mika and the dwarf as they rushed in to attack the softer, exposed wings.

Raajoget slashes Hive Beetle Queen for 10 damage. Thedrir Stronggut smites Hive Beetle Queen for 16 damage.

Jace barely had time to see the messages before the queen pounced on him and his *Evade* moved him out of the way.

Hive Beetle Queen uses Crushing Attack on YOU but you Evade.

Raajoget slashes Hive Beetle Queen for 14 damage. Thedrir Stronggut smites Hive Beetle Queen for 15 damage.

Mizzlethain-galliegarde shoots Hive Beetle for 2 magic damage.

Jace saw his companions, even Diana, had attacked again before the queen had managed to retract its wings. Their attacks appeared to bypass the carapace's armor and do regular damage.

Once the queen's wings were hidden, their attacks went back to doing reduced damage as they hammered on the beetle's carapace. However, with the extra damage they'd done to the wings, it only took a few more minutes before the thing collapsed under their continued onslaught.

Raajoget slashes Hive Beetle Queen for 0 damage.
Thedrir Stronggut smites Hive Beetle Queen for 10 damage.
Hive Beetle Queen dies.
You gain 600 experience.

"Yeah!" the red-headed dwarf cheered when the beetle spasmed and dropped to the ground. "Take that you oversized insect!"

Jace backed up from the beetle and then closed his eyes and collapsed onto the ground. His *Stamina* had been getting low and that translated into a general feeling of fatigue. More than that, all of the pain he'd had to endure had exhausted him mentally.

"Are you okay?" Mika's voice asked.

Jace opened his eyes and forced a smile. "Just great."

He saw the dwarf lumber over to him. "That was some good tanking there… uh… Ded… um… Deadrur… ah, darnit… how do you say your name?"

"Call me Jace," he smiled, this time genuinely at the dwarf's attempts to pronounce his monster name.

"Jace," the dwarf nodded. "Much better. That was good tanking. But why the bloody hell do you have your sensory input turned up. Either that or you have the best acting skills I've seen."

Struggling to his feet, Jace shook his head. "Not acting. It's at full."

The dwarf's eye grew large and opened his mouth, then closed it, then opened it again and then closed it again. It was almost comically and if he'd been feeling better, Jace probably would have chuckled.

Finally, Thedrir seemed to find his voice. When he spoke, his voice was incredulous. "You took all those hits - even that acid - at 100%?!"

Jace nodded tiredly.

"Are you insane?" the dwarf asked. Thedrir looked around from Jace to the girls and seemed to come to some conclusion. "Ah… you're those hardcore players, right? That's why you're all human. I didn't know you guys played on 100%! That's brutal!"

He was too tired to argue or explain things to the dwarf, so he just shrugged. "Something like that."

The dwarf grinned. "Wicked. Well, I need to get logging soon but thanks for inviting me. It was nice meeting you ...ah... Jace and... ah...Ra..ra... Oh geez, do you all have such crazy names?"

Mika smiled at him. "I am Mika, and this is Diana."

The dwarf smiled broadly at the two girls. "A pleasure ladies. Good journeys!"

Thedrir Stronggut has left your group.

He started to go but then Thedrir stopped and turned around. "Oh, one thing… my brother's band - Dwarven Thunder - is playing on Friday night at Twisted Tankard Tavern, in the Merchant District. I run thc door so if you want to stop by, I'll get you in for free. It's a lot of fun - especially if you like Celtic music. Plus, it's your last chance to come. This is our final week here in Whitecliff."

From his inventory, the dwarf produced a hand drawn flyer on a piece of parchment. "Here you go! One of our flyers. A fan did all the artwork."

Jace took the flyer and saw that it contained a cartoon style sketch of four dwarves holding mugs and musical instruments riding a thunderbolt.

Jace handed it to Mika, who was trying to peek over his shoulder. "We'll see what we can do."

The dwarf grinned. "Music starts at 8pm pacific time and goes until they're too drunk to play!"

With that, Thedrir turned and hurried off back to the Whitecliff gates and they watched the dwarf disappear over the hill.

"He was nice," Mika said when he was out of sight.

"And kind of sexy," Diana added. Then after a moment, the woman added, "though a bit short for my taste."

There was a moment of silence as the companions looked at each other and then they all burst into laughter. Once the moment of humor passed, Jace moved back to the beetle queen's body and looted it.

You receive Hive Queen Beetle Eye.
You receive Hive Queen Beetle Carapace.
You receive Hive Queen Antenna.

Jace looked at the items. The eye and the carapace were familiar, but he wondered what the antenna was. Out of curiosity, he examined it.

Hive Queen Antenna
Type: Wand
Level: 5
Damage: 2 + 1 (Masterwork) + 1 (Arcane)
Wt: 1 lb
Special: Attacks add 2 acid damage.
Description: When a Mage channels magic through this antenna, it acts as an arcane masterwork wand. In addition, it maintains some of the corrosive properties of the queen beetle it came from.

Jace whistled. "Diana, this antenna has your name written all over it."

Confused, the raven-haired Mage walked over to him and made a face at the antenna in his hand. When he kept holding it out, she finally took the offered antenna. Once she had it, her eyes went glassy and then she smiled. "Oh, this is nice!"

"It looks like you'll be doing a lot more damage now," he told her, and she nodded as she held it out.

"What does it do?" Mika asked, now curious as well.

"Does 4 points of damage plus another 2 acid damage," Diana said.

"That is wonderful!" Mika exclaimed.

Happy that Diana had gotten an upgrade, she looked around. It was lunch time and he was still shaken from the acid burns.

"Let's turn in this quest," Jace told them. Then he looked down at the ruined armor he still wore and sighed. "And I need to get some new weapons and armor."

Turning to go, Jace suddenly felt a small hand on his arm and stopped. Mika was there smiling at him. In her hand, she held the magical longsword they'd found in the sewer gator's stash in her hands. "I have the katana, I do not need this."

Jace returned the smile and took the weapon. It was actually a better weapon than his rapier had been, but it was a slashing weapon and wouldn't work with his backstab ability. Not that he used his backstab ability that much at the moment. "Thanks Mika. Are you sure?"

The girl put her hand on the hilt of her katana and gave him a curt nod. "I am sure."

"Wait," Diana said, looking around. "Does the queen have some loot?"

Jace shook his head. "She's not a real boss, just a random spawn. She doesn't have a lair."

"Well that stinks," Diana frowned. "After all that, I'd expect mounds of gold and a few dozen gems."

"That would be nice," he agreed and then gestured for the girls to follow him. "Let's turn in the quest and at least get that reward."

They walked back to the city gates and found Sergeant Wyot. After turning in the first eye, he realized only the people turning in the eye received the reward. He quickly divided the remaining eyes among himself and the girls.

Each of them turned in a total of 12 eyes, giving them 60 faction, 60 gold and another 300 experience each. Then he turned in the queen quest and thankfully they all received the rewards.

You have completed the quest, "Queen Beetle Mania"
You gain 300 experience. Experience to next level 720.
You gain +50 faction with Whitecliff City Guard

He also handed each of them a small pouch containing another 60 gold.

"Thank you for your service to Whitecliff," the sergeant told them and then excused himself to get back to his duties.

"Now what?" Diana asked.

He motioned the girls off to the side, away from the ears of guards. "I need to go to the thieves guild and see if there's a way to get replacement armor. I don't think there is until I hit level 11, but it's worth a shot. Then I need to go buy a saber."

"May I have the carapaces we looted?" Mika asked suddenly. The girl was smiling and had a slightly mischievous look to her.

Jace gave her a quizzical look. "May I ask why?"

The girl maintained her smile but shook her head. "It's a surprise."

He looked over at Diana. "I assume you have no objections."

Diana sniffed. "Oh dearie, you have all the carapaces you want."

Shrugging, he traded all of the carapaces they'd found to her. "All yours."

Grinning like a Cheshire cat, Mika accepted them. She made to leave but stopped. "I will meet you at the inn later." With that she moved off and disappeared into the crowd.

"What about you?" he asked Diana.

"I'm going to go to the inn and have a nice meal, dear one. Or should I say, a nice dessert," she told him. "You go run along."

Jace waved goodbye and then, motioning for Luna to follow him, disappeared into the crowd as well.

Chapter 21

Jace decided to go to the thieves guild first. It was closer than the Central Market and he didn't particularly care for walking around with a gaping hole in his jerkin. Heading south, he entered the Luxury District and made his way to the Fainting Unicorn.

His mind was so preoccupied with losing his equipment to the acid attack that Jace almost missed the increased guard presence. Everywhere he looked, he saw city guardsmen. Not only that, but they looked tense. He thought they might try to hide it, but they were guards, not actors. It was as if they were waiting for something.

Alarm bells started going off in his head. This was like a scene from one of the vidstreams, where all the cops raid a drug lab or a… crime lord. Jace had a terrible feeling about this. The only thing he could think they might be here to raid would be the thieves guild.

Jace stopped walking, unsure if he should continue towards the Fainting Unicorn. His abrupt halt caught the attention of some nearby guards and he had to quickly improvise. Feigning interest, he moved to the window of one of the shops and pretended to be very interested in the goods displayed there.

Through the reflection in the glass, he saw the guards watch him for a few seconds longer before returning to watching the people on the street. Were they looking for someone in particular? Or just noting who came and went from the Fainting Unicorn.

The guards certainly weren't subtle, and he couldn't imagine the other thieves not noticing them. Maybe they'd already cleared out. Jace didn't know. But he knew that if Webley got caught, Jace would have no way into the Noble District. Only the guildmaster knew the inside man on the wall.

Darnit! This was risky. Almost too risky. If Jace got arrested, he'd be serving a real sentence in a real dungeon. He couldn't log out and he couldn't create a new character. For him, it would be just like in real life. For him, the imprisonment would be all too real.

As Jace debated, he could see more guards coming into the district and then duck into alleys, probably to avoid making their presence even more obvious. Whatever was going to happen was going to happen soon. He needed to make his decision now.

Swearing under his breath, Jace looked down at Luna. That cat was sitting next to him, curiously watching, and sniffing the people walking back and forth.

"I need you to go back to the inn," he told the cat mentally. "The girls can understand you. Tell them they might arrest me. Tell them I went to the thieves guild."

His familiar looked up at him, cocked her head and then replied. "Yes."

The cat took off at a trot, easily navigating in between the people on the street. Jace took a deep breath. Did he really want to do this? The answer was no, but he had no choice. He didn't know another way into the Noble District. He needed to warn Webley.

Jace turned from the shop and then cut down an alley. This alley was clear of guards and he quickly brought out his Infiltrator's Hat. The magical hat would allow him to change his appearance to something roughly his own size. He'd also learned that if he concentrated on specific things, he could also change individual aspects of his appearance, like his clothing.

Putting on the hat, Jace changed his appearance to that of an elf. There was a rippling in the air and when he looked down to see he now looked like a normal elf commoner. Disguised, he left the alley and started towards the Fainting Unicorn.

The inn was only a few blocks away but the number of guards visible increased the closer he got. Jace made it to the Unicorn and went in the front door. The common room was mostly bare, and the bartender gave him a bored glance as he came in. Either the man didn't know what was going on outside or he was a talented actor.

Not wasting any time, Jace walked to the back and ducked down the corridor that led to the secret passage. Checking the corridor, Jace activated the passage and ducked inside. He rushed down steps into the small room below.

Thom and Gerry weren't there guarding the vault door this time. Instead, a burly human and dwarf with a sour expression were in their place. Were they the dayshift?

Wasting no time, Jace went into the entrance to the Lucky Coin and threw open the door. There weren't many people in the bar but the ones that were there all turned to look at him. He ignored their stares and scanned the room for Webley.

He spotted the guildmaster at his usual table, writing in a ledger book. Jace rushed over to the table, causing the guildmaster to look up. Webley seemed to be annoyed with the interruption and looked as if he was about to say something.

"I think we're about to be raided," Jace blurted out as he released the magic of the hat and resumed his normal appearance.

That got the guildmaster's attention, and the man was instantly alert and wary. "Dedrurrurth! Nice trick. What makes you think we're about to be raided?"

"Coming here, I just passed what looks to me like the entire Whitecliff guard," Jace told him. "And right now, they're all here in the Luxury District. It looks as if they were surrounding the Unicorn."

The guildmaster seemed to take a second to absorb his words before the man leapt into action.

"Kelton, Cenric," he called out as he sprang to his feet, "go up top and check out his story."

Two men from a table near the door immediately left their chairs and ran out the door towards the stairs.

The guildmaster turned to the bar. "Ciaran, go down the drainpipe and make sure it's clear on the other side. You have ten minutes. If you're not back, I will assume it's watched."

"Tarsire," he said, turning a halfling sitting wide-eyed at one of the tables. "Go down the bolt hole and make sure it's clear."

Jace watched the halfling run to one of the doors near the bar and disappear inside the dark corridor. When he looked back, the guildmaster was looking at Jace, his face deadly serious. "This better not be some sick joke. Because I can assure you, I don't find it funny."

Jace was about to answer when one of the two men who had gone upstairs came running down, missing a step, and nearly falling. He caught himself and then barreled back into the Lucky Coin. "He's right! There are guards everywhere. Lots of them."

The guildmaster swore loudly. "You and Kelton stay up there as lookouts. The moment you see movement towards the inn, warn us and then seal up the stairs. Do it now!"

The man, Jace assumed it was Cenric, spun and ran back up the stairs.

Webley turned to the bartender and nodded his head towards the rooms. "Get the girls ready to move out."

The bartender bobbed his head, took off the apron he was wearing and ran over to the far door and threw it open. He disappeared into the hallway and began yelling.

"Dedrurrurth," the guildmaster was looking at Jace now. "Go to the market and tell them to pack up and be ready to move out."

Jace was momentarily confused until he realized the guildmaster was talking about the Black Market. Leaving Webley, Jace ran over to the far door and rushed into the large room that held the market.

Like most markets in the game, this one never slept. There were always people in the market, both vendors, NPCs and players. "We're about to get raided! Guildmaster says to pack everything up!"

The vendors immediately burst into action and began packing their wares. The NPCs began crowding out the door into the Lucky Coin and he saw several players log out.

"Don't log out here!" Jace shouted and several players turned his way. "If the guard takes this place over and you log back in, they'll catch you."

Several players considered his words and then left along with the NPCs, but he saw other players fade away. They were idiots. Or they just didn't care what happened to their character. Either way, Jace had tried to help them. Leaving behind the Black Market, Jace went back into the Lucky Coin.

The tavern was now filled with people from the Black Market, as well as people from the backrooms of the tavern. Webley was barking orders, trying to organize the people, when Tarsire returned.

"Quiet!" yelled the guildmaster and the noisy clamour died down quickly.

"Tarsire," Webley addressed the out of breath halfling. "Report."

"Bolt hole is clear," he said and almost immediately the crowd began murmuring.

"Listen up," Webley shouted. "Follow Tarsire to the bolthole. The tunnel will lead you to a safe house a few blocks away. When you get there, exit in one's and two's. Space your leaving and don't look suspicious. Meet in the old guildhouse tonight. Make sure you're not followed."

The crowd surged for the bolthole, pushing and shoving to try to get ahead of the others. The scene was erupting into chaos but Jace saw nothing that could stop it at this point. Everyone wanted to get out.

Webley shook his head at the scene but must have realized there was nothing he could do at this point.

"They're coming!" a frantic voice yelled. "They're coming!"

"Seal up the stairs!" Webley yelled. The guildmaster started moving around the crowd to the entrance and, not knowing what else to do, Jace followed him.

Kelton and Cenric had put a thick sheet of metal, as large as the door, in front of the stairs and were now placing iron bars in slots Jace hadn't noticed before, effectively barring the door.

"Light from the drainpipe," yelled the dwarven tough who had been guarding the vault. The dwarf squinted as he looked down the passage. "Wrodgar's Beard! It's the guard!"

"Close the grate!" yelled Welbey, and he moved back just as something heavy thudded into the door. The city guard was trying to break in.

"Lock the grain grate and get out of here," Webley said. "This place is lost."

Webley turned away just as the dwarf was slapping a huge padlock on the grate that covered the drain cover.

The crowd had diminished much and Jace guessed the bolthole was only wide enough to fit people single file. He didn't think there was no way they'd all make it out before the guards broke down the door.

It appeared Webley realized the same thing. "It doesn't look like we will make it out."

Jace's heart dropped as visions of prison life filled his head. He had no idea how long of a sentence he might get. Perhaps he should just fight the guards and let them kill him. At least then he'd respawn. He wouldn't have his equipment, but he wouldn't be in prison.

Jace smirked. He could go back to the area with all the traps and just die there. Jace thought about the trap area for a moment. It had a grate above it. Could they get out that way? Climb up the grate to the alleyway nearby?

"What about the trap area?" he asked Webley. "Can we get out that way?"

The guildmaster considered for a moment and then his face brightened. "You know, you might be right."

Welbey took one last look at the crowd still trying to get into the door. He seemed to consider something. All at once a resigned look came over his face, and he motioned to Jace. "Come on."

The two of them raced through what had once been the black market and then into the room beyond. Webley opened the door, and they emerged into the corridor that Jace remembered. It had been where he'd had to prove himself to get into the guild by getting through a gauntlet of traps. Now it looked as if he may have to do the entire thing in reverse.

Jace frowned at the course but the guildmaster didn't even hesitate. He strode forward quickly, stepped over the tripwire and onto the rotating pit trap beyond.

"Watch…" Jace started to warn him, but then the guildmaster disappeared into the pit. Too late, Jace finished, "…out."

Had the guildmaster forgotten about the pit? Was he dead? Or was he high enough level that could survive following onto or into whatever was at the bottom of the pit?

He had just started edging towards the pit when he heard a muffled voice. "You coming or what?"

Walking over to the pit, he heard the voice again. "I'm not going to wait all day. Step onto the pit!"

Jace realized he didn't have a choice. It was either risk death in the pit trap or wait to be arrested and spend who knew how long in the dungeons.

"Here goes nothing," he said and stepped onto the pit. The trap rotated remarkably smoothly and the next thing Jace knew he was falling as the pit opened up beneath him.

Out of reflex, Jace had closed his eyes, so it surprised him when he slammed into something soft. Jace checked his system messages. There were none. Nothing saying he took falling damage, acid damage, burn damage, impaling damage, or any damage at all.

He opened his eyes. He was lying on sacks of feathers with some feathers still airborne from his fall.

An impatient looking Webley was looking down at him.

"You want to wait for the guard, or do you want to get moving?" the guildmaster asked him.

Chapter 22

Jace looked around at the sacks of feathers, trying to understand what he was seeing. He looked up at the guildmaster and was about to ask what was going on, but Webley seemed to see the question written on his face.

"What? You don't think we have lethal traps in the test for new recruits?" the guildmaster chuckled. He offered a hand to Jace and pulled him to his feet. "If we did, the guild would consist of you, me and about 3 other Rogues."

"But…" Jace started but then stopped. It made sense. After all, players who wanted to get to the Black Market would need to go through the trial as well and most of them wouldn't be Rogues. "So, the other traps? The trip wires?"

"Just alarms," the guildmaster responded. Webley walked over to an odd-looking cluster of stones in the wall and pressed it in three places. The largest stone popped open revealing a hidden lever inside. Reaching in, he pulled the lever. "That'll lock the pit in place, so a clumsy guard doesn't figure out where we've gone."

As the guildmaster was locking the pit into place, Jace remembered how stressed and anxious he'd been when he'd done the thieves guild trial. He'd really thought the traps were deadly and that one wrong move and he would have died. Had he known, the whole experience would have been much less stressful.

He took the opportunity to look around at where they were and realized he was in the sewer again, but in some sort of raised junction room. It reminded him of the room where Tiebaut had met the captain.

Webley closed the hidden panel and it once again blended in with the other stones of the wall. "We're going to split up from here. There may be guards in the sewers too for all we know. Better they catch one of us than both of us."

Jace nodded. That seemed like a sound plan to him as well.

"I will ask you a favor," the guildmaster continued. "That magic that you use to change your appearance. Is it something you can give to me temporarily? My face is known and if any of the guards catch me, I doubt I'd be able to talk my way out of it. Not if they were bold enough to plan this raid."

Taking the hat from his head, Jace considered. Maybe now was the time for him to make sure he had a way into the Noble District when he needed it. "How about a favor for a favor?"

Webley hadn't been expecting that and he raised an eyebrow. "Go on."

"At some point," Jace started, "I will need to get into the Noble District. If I lend you my hat, maybe you can lend me the use of our inside man - no questions asked."

The guildmaster smirked. "A trip into the Noble District, no questions asked, huh?" He paused as if considering but the man's cocky grin told Jace he'd already decided. "It's a deal. But… one time only. If you want a second jaunt over the wall, you'll have to do me another favor. Deal?"

In response, Jace held out the hat. "Put on the hat. Then think of a race you want to be. It doesn't do specific people, but you can emulate just about any race that's roughly your size, give or take a few feet."

Smiling, the guildmaster placed the hat on his head. His shape flickered and standing in his place was a sourly looking dwarf. Then it changed again, and it was an elf. It flickered again and he was back to Webley. The guildmaster was smiling.

"Nice toy," Webley admitted. "You've earned your favor. I need to go open up the old guildhouse so we can resume business. But you can be darn sure I'll be posting lookouts. I'm not sure who ratted us out, but I will find the person responsible and they will pay."

The guildmaster's comment reminded Jace of something. "Where's the old guildhouse?"

The guildmaster nodded. "That's right. You're still fairly new. It's north of the merchant district. On Tarot Street, you'll find a closed tailor shop called the

Griffon Fabrics. Go to the side door and knock three times, then once, then twice."

"Griffon Fabrics," Jace repeated. "Three times, once then twice."

"You got it. See you there tonight." With that, Webley changed back into a dwarf, turned, and stomped away in the opposite direction.

****

Jace walked for nearly fifteen minutes before he felt confident enough that he was out of the Luxury District. He wasn't about to climb out anywhere near the thieves guild and risk being seen by a guard.

But fifteen minutes should have easily placed him outside the Luxury District. He found a grate with rungs in the wall beneath it. Climbing up, he peered through the grate to figure out where he was.

The grate appeared to be in an alleyway. He waited a couple of minutes to see if anyone walked nearby. When no one did, he braced himself against the wall and picked the lock keeping the grate closed.

Pushing the grate open, he slowly poked his head up and looked around. He had been right. He was in some sort of alleyway and there wasn't soul in sight. He quickly pulled himself up and then closed and re-locked the grate.

As casually as he could, Jace walked back to the street and after a minute he figured out he was just east of the Luxury District. He felt good that he'd made it out of the raid alive and un-incarcerated. He felt really good that he had found a way to get into the Noble District! That was a big piece of his plan.

When Jace finally entered the Dwarvish Fork, he saw Mika and Diana sitting at their normal table with their back to him. Luna was on the table and immediately meowed when she saw him. "Jace."

At the cat's meow, the two girls turned around and stared at him and he could tell they had been worried. Mika shot out of her chair and charged Jace. Before he knew it, she had thrown herself at him and wrapped him up in a fierce hug. "Jace Burton! You are not dead or arrested!"

After a moment, Jace returned the hug and then, noticing some of the other patrons looking over his way, whispered. "Let's keep the talk of being arrested quiet."

Mika took a step back and looking around, she seemed to get his meaning. Blushing, she apologized. "Sorry. I am just very happy to see you."

"We both are, dear one," said Diana, who had come over to him as well. She gave him a small hug that could have been a friendly hug or a hug that a mother would give a child. But before she released him, she slapped his butt in a very un-motherly way, making him blush.

"Now," she said as she stepped back. "How about we sit back down, and you regale us your tale."

They did just that. Sitting back down at their table, Jace related the events of the last hour. He told them about the raid, his escape, and the favor he'd coerced from the guildmaster. When he was done, he sat back and took a sip of the mead he'd ordered.

"So, now we have a way into the Noble District," Diana said. "What about the palace itself? Have you made any progress on that?"

"No," Jace shook his head. "But I'm going to press Webley again. I think he owes me for the warning and maybe I can get him to tell me a way in."

"You can do it," Mika said enthusiastically and Jace couldn't help but smile. He also thought back to the hug she'd given him and how nice it had felt to have her pressed up against him. Then he remembered Charlena and quickly pushed those thoughts out of his mind.

"Are you going to the new guildhouse tonight?" Diana asked him. "Do you think it's safe?"

"I need to go," Jace told her. "I never got a chance to ask him about armor."

At that, Mika nearly bounced in her seat with excitement. "No, you don't!"

He looked at her with curiosity. Had she somehow managed to find some Rogue armor? Was that even possible? He hoped she hadn't spent all of her money buying armor for him.

Suddenly she pulled out some sort of plate looking armor that had a strange, organic look to it. It took him a moment to realize what it was. "Is this… chitin armor?"

"Yes," Mika beamed. "I made it for you!"

Jace looked at her in shock. "How did you…."

"I have been working on my skills," Mika interrupted. "I used the beetle carapaces to create it. Do you like it?"

Jace took the offered breastplate and examined it.

Chitin Breastplate
Type: Chest Armor
Level: 1
Armor: 4 + 1 (Masterwork)
Wt: 2 lb
Special: Provides 2 acid defense.
Restrictions: Leather armor skill or Metal Armor Skill
Description: Light and flexible, this armor was made from the carapace of a large insect. It has the strength of plate armor but the flexibility of leather armor.
Created By: Raajoget

"Wow," was all Jace could say. "This is amazing."

"Put it on!" Mika grinned. "I want to see it."

Jace obediently equipped the armor. It felt a little different from his leather armor but as he bent and twisted, it was remarkably supple. "It feels great!"

Mika beamed and clapped her hands together. Then she pulled out several more pieces from her inventory and handed them to Jace. "Good! These are for you!"

The other pieces didn't look quite as nice as the breastplate and Jace examined one.

Chitin Gauntlets
Type: Hand Armor
Level: 1
Armor: 4
Wt: 2 lb
Restrictions: Leather armor skill or Metal Armor Skill
Description: Light and flexible, this armor was made from the carapace of a large insect. It has the strength of plate armor but the flexibility of leather armor.
Created By: Raajoget

"Only one is masterwork?" he asked.

Mika's smile faded and she looked down at the table. "My skill is not good enough to make masterwork yet."

"But the breastplate…" Jace started and then remembered the queen's carapace. "Is the breastplate made from the queen's carapace?"

Mika looked up and nodded. "It was the only piece that turned out as masterwork."

Jace smiled at the girl. "I didn't mean anything. I think this is great and I really appreciate it. This is an excellent replacement for my old armor."

She beamed again and Jace couldn't help but chuckled. "Maybe we need to kill some more beetles so you can make some for yourself."

At that, she grinned even wider. Her eyes went glassy for only a moment and her character was suddenly wearing a full suit of chitin armor. "I already did!"

"Get a room you two," Diana said, rolling her eyes.

Mika blushed a deep scarlet and Jace was sure he was blushing too.

"Sorry dear ones," she said in a mock apology. "Did I embarrass you?"

Chapter 23

Charlena had logged in a little after 6pm. She'd waved away Jace's question about how her first day at work had gone. She was tired but had insisted on catching up with what they had done.

When they were done, Charlena smiled. "So, you basically played exterminators?"

"For giant bugs!" Mika said.

"That queen battle didn't sound too good though," she looked at Jace. "Are you sure you're alright?"

"I'm fine," Jace assured her. "Luckily, wounds don't scar in the game."

"Thank God for that," Diana chimed in. "No scars and no aging. This place really is heaven. Except for the very large beetles who try to chew off your leg."

"So, now what?" Charlena asked. "We need to do something so I can catch up. You guys are getting too far ahead of me."

Charlena was right. Jace had been worried about that exact thing. Now that Charlena could only play a few hours a night, the rest of them would quickly overtake her level if they kept doing quests.

There were two solutions Jace could think of. Either Jace, Diana and Mika would need to stop doing things that gave them experience when Charlena wasn't on - or the three of them would need to switch classes.

Jace looked between the three girls and sighed. "We will need to work on other classes."

Mika nodded but Diana looked aghast. "What? Change classes? I'm still getting used to being a witch!"

Jace held up his hands in a placating gesture. "Diana, you can switch classes and still continue doing exactly what you're doing. The only difference would be, you'd have some new skills and abilities."

The older woman fell silent and leaned back in her chair. "I can stay just like this?"

Jace nodded. "Plus, you could get more spells if you choose by taking Priest."

"How ghastly," Diana said, her mouth curved into a look of disgust. "I'm certainly not the celibate type."

Jace chuckled, remembering the small statuette he'd stolen. "It's a fantasy game. There are lots of gods and goddesses. In fact, there's a goddess of love and I know her followers aren't celibate."

"Oh?" Diana perked up.

"Chykela," Jace told her. "Goddess of love and seduction."

"Well," Diana purred. "That sounds right up my alley."

Charlena gave them an apologetic look. "Sorry to make you all switch classes. Hopefully, I can catch up on the weekends."

Mika gave her a big smile. "No problem! I will change to Rogue and become a ninja! Samurai by day, ninja by night!"

Charlena looked to Jace. "What about you? Don't you already have three classes?"

Jace nodded. "I do but I can switch back to Mage. I only took 2 levels, so I have a ways to go yet."

He wasn't happy with the idea. Part of him really wanted to reach level 11. At that level, his skill cap would jump up another 10 points and he'd have access to the next tier of weapons and armor.

But he also knew the importance of staying within 3 levels of Charlena and his other group members. If he was more than 3 levels above a member of his group, they would not receive experience from any kills. That would cause the person to fall even further and further behind.

"I'll change now," he said reluctantly and brought up his character sheet. He went to his class and clicked on the change class button. He chose Mage but then hesitated. Was this what he really wanted? He knew it wasn't, but he also knew that if he wanted to keep grouping with Charlena, he had no choice. He confirmed his choice. His main class was now Mage.

"I cannot change yet," Mika told them. "I switched back to Priest. I must reach level 7 before I can switch again. When I do, I will become Rogue!"

Charlena smiled at Mika and they all looked at Diana.

"Fine! Fine!" she said, rolling her eyes. "I'll switch." The woman hesitated for a moment then looked awkward. "How do I do that?"

Jace talked her through the process and after a few times of explaining things a second or third time, Diana finally managed to change her class. When she was done, he examined them all.

Almedha Pressalor
Race: Elf
Class: Scout
Level: 6

Raajoget
Race: Human
Class: Priest
Level: 5

Mizzlethain-galliegarde
Race: Human
Class: Priest
Level: 1

"It looks like we're ready," Jace said. "Shall we go see what the adventurers guild has in store for us?"

The four of them went back to the adventurers guild. On the way there, Jace stopped off at the Central Market and picked up a saber. It set him back 50 gold, but he didn't really have a choice. He needed a hard hitting weapon to replace his rapier and the saber was the best piercing weapon he could get at his level.

Once they reached the guild, they found a quest called "Way of the Shaman." It was the only level 5 or level 6 quest they could find so they had very little choice unless they wanted to go back to killing beetles. At the moment, Jace had no desire to lose more equipment, so they accepted the quest.

Dear guild members,
The citizens to the south have been attacked by grolls over the past two weeks. One of Whitecliff's scouts have reported that these attacks are being encouraged by a new shaman who has taken power.

The army has been dispatched to deal with the recent dragon sighting and the city guard has offered to hire the Adventurers Guild to find and eliminate the grolls.

Signed,

Guildmaster Leofsige Blackwoode

The Adventurers Guild has offered you the quest, "Way of the Shaman"

**Reward: +25 faction with Whitecliff Adventurers
Guild, +25 faction with Whitecliff Guard.
Level: 6
Accept quest? (Yes or No)**

Jace waited for the exclusive timer message to appear but after several seconds, it hadn't appeared.

"Uh-oh," he told the girls. "It looks like we didn't get this first. We may be competing with someone else for this quest."

"Other players?" Charlena asked.

Jace nodded. "And they have at least a 24-hour head start on us."

***

It took them almost a half hour to get to the south gate. Once they did, it took another half hour to reach the farmhouses that had been attacked. No sooner than they reached the first house when they heard a howl and what sounded like laughter but Jace knew better. It was the grolls.

Grolls were hyena-men. The creatures were roughly bipedal but could run on all fours when they needed a burst of speed. When they did stand on two legs, they were six or seven feet tall with very long reaches. While grolls weren't particularly intelligent, they were cunning and loved to ambush their prey.

As if to punctuate his point, arrows suddenly rained down on them from the top of the farmhouse.

Broken Paw Groll shoots Raajoget for 0 damage.
Broken Paw Groll shoots Mizzlethain-galliegarde for 2 damage.
Broken Paw Groll shoots Mizzlethain-galliegarde for 3 damage.
Broken Paw Groll shoots Almedha Pressalor for 4 damage.
Broken Paw Groll shoots Almedha Pressalor for 10 damage.
Broken Paw Groll shoots YOU for 0 damage.

"Oh geez," screamed Diana. "I've been shot!"

Jace hadn't been using his *Air Armor*, but his chitin armor and buckler had been enough to deflect the arrows. He wasn't about to test his luck. "*Aeris Armatura!*"

As the air around him solidified, Jace sprinted for the house. The grolls saw Jace coming and loosed their next volley at him.

Broken Paw Groll shoots YOU for 0 damage.
Broken Paw Groll shoots YOU for 0 damage.
Broken Paw Groll shoots YOU for 0 damage.
Broken Paw Groll shoots YOU for 0 damage.
Broken Paw Groll shoots YOU for 0 damage.
Broken Paw Groll shoots YOU for 0 damage.

Jace got as close as he could and then yelled his *Taunt*. "Come get some!"

The grolls howled and focused their attention on him, just as he was expecting. The problem was, they were on top of the house and he needed to get them down. Jace peaked inside the house and after making sure there were no grolls waiting in ambush, he ducked inside.

The *Taunt* would force them to attack Jace and if they couldn't see him, they would come looking for him. He was hoping that meant they'd jump down, allowing his group to attack them.

"When they come down," Jace yelled out. "Focus on one and kill it, then move on to the next."

Jace heard grunts and more hyena laughter as the grolls jumped down, just as he expected. They ducked behind the wall and broke the windows so they could fire inside the house at Jace. Not what he was expecting, but it didn't matter. He could take the arrows and it would give the girls time to finish them off.

Raajoget slashes Broken Paw Groll for 9 damage.
Almedha Pressalor shoots Broken Paw Groll for 8 damage.
Mizzlethain-galliegarde burns Broken Paw Groll with Flame Bolt for 3 fire damage.

Jace saw which one they were attacking and rushed over to that window. Using his sword and saber, he slashed and stabbed at the thing through the window.

You stab Broken Paw Groll for 2 damage.
You slash Broken Paw Groll for 0 damage.

He only scored a glancing blow, but every little bit helped. The grolls attacked again, but like previously, none of their arrows could damage him with his high *Defense*.

Raajoget slashes Broken Paw Groll for 11 damage.
Almedha Pressalor shoots Broken Paw Groll for 4 damage.
Mizzlethain-galliegarde burns Broken Paw Groll with Flame Bolt for 4 fire damage.

You stab Broken Paw Groll for 0 damage.
You slash Broken Paw Groll for 0 damage.

Jace's attacks bounced off the creature's armor, which seemed to be some sort of wooden plates that had been sewn into leather. That was something new he hadn't seen before.

The grolls retaliated with more arrows but Jace deflected them all.

Raajoget slashes Broken Paw Groll for 10 damage.
Almedha Pressalor shoots Broken Paw Groll for 0 damage.
Mizzlethain-galliegarde burns Broken Paw Groll with Flame Bolt for 8 fire damage.

You stab Broken Paw Groll for 1 damage.
You slash Broken Paw Groll for 0 damage.
Broken Paw Groll dies.
You gain 60 experience.

The first groll fell and they moved onto the next one. They continued like that until the last one fell dead. The grolls weren't as armored as the beetles had been, but they had still taken a while to kill.

Jace went outside and searched the bodies. Since these were intelligent creatures, he'd expect to find some gold on them but there was nothing other than their shortbows.

"No loot?" Diana complained. "Really?"

Jace shrugged. "Sometimes they don't drop anything."

"Now what?" Charlena asked, looking around for more monsters.

Jace looked around. There was no sign of any other grolls. That meant they weren't done with the quest. They'd have to follow them back to their lair and attack them where they were strongest.

"Now," he told his group. "We track them back and kill that shaman."

Chapter 24

Using their *Tracking* skill, they followed the groll's trail for fifteen minutes. The longer they followed, the more Jace was experiencing an old familiar feeling. It was the feeling he received when there was another player around - one who had been put into a monster body through the software bug.

Finally, Jace turned to the others. "Mika, Diana, do you have a weird feeling in the back of your mind?"

Mika nodded. "It has been getting stronger."

"I thought it was just nerves," Diana admitted. "What is it?"

Jace spent a few minutes explaining the strange feeling he got whenever there was another player who had been affected by the bug.

"So, we can sense the people affected?" Diana asked. "How does that work?"

"I don't know exactly," Jace said. "If I had to guess, I'd say that the hack we used to turn human didn't change all of the code. We must still have code left over from being an AI and that creates some sort of resonance."

Diana looked at him blankly.

Jace let out an exasperated breath. "Okay, I don't really understand it either and I'm just guessing. All I know is that I can sense other players who are affected by the bug. And apparently you two can as well."

Charlena, who had been quiet during their explanation, suddenly cleared her throat. "I hate to be a party-pooper, but I only have another hour or so before I have to log."

"Right," Jace smiled. "We can talk about this later. Let's see if we can find this shaman. I have a feeling the shaman is the player."

Jace led them further into the forest to the edge of a large clearing. The clearing was around a hill. The grolls had cut down the trees on the hill and used them to build a small fort. Jace had only fought grolls a few times, but he'd never seen them make forts before. They usually made their lair in caves or they took over a weaker tribe's dwelling.

But the strange feeling he and the two girls experienced was definitely coming from the fort. He looked back at the girls, lowering his voice to a whisper. "The shaman has to be a player. Maybe we can talk to him and let him know there's a way to become human again."

"Do you think that will work?" Charlena asked. "Remember Big Cheese?"

Big Cheese had been a player in a goblin leader body who had gone completely insane and even though Jace had offered to help him become human again had ended up killing Jace instead. But that was just one person. He'd managed to free Diana, Mika and Duglas - wherever he was - maybe he could free this person.

"I need to at least try," Jace said.

One by one, the girls agreed. Jace put his weapons into his inventory so they weren't showing. He wanted to show them he wasn't a threat. At the same time, he didn't want to get turned into a pincushion, so he kept his buckler on and recast his *Air Armor* - just in case.

"Here goes nothing," he said and stepped out into the clearing. He'd only taken a few steps when the air was suddenly darkened with arrows. Jace reflexively held up his buckler though he knew the bonuses from the buckler applied regardless of whether or not he was actually holding it up.

Broken Paw Groll shoots YOU for 0 damage.
Broken Paw Groll shoots YOU for 0 damage.
Broken Paw Groll shoots YOU for 0 damage.
Broken Paw Groll shoots YOU for 0 damage.
Broken Paw Groll shoots YOU for 0 damage.
Broken Paw Groll shoots YOU for 0 damage.
Broken Paw Groll shoots YOU for 0 damage.
Broken Paw Groll shoots YOU for 0 damage.
Broken Paw Groll shoots YOU for 0 damage.
Broken Paw Groll shoots YOU for 0 damage.
Broken Paw Groll shoots YOU for 0 damage.
Broken Paw Groll shoots YOU for 0 damage.

Jace counted at least a dozen arrows but none of them penetrated his *Defense*. He held up his hands again and shouted. "I'm here to speak with your shaman."

There was a pause. Then a high pitched voice yelled back. "Shaman no want to speak with you!"

The shout was followed by hyena-like barking laughter and then they rained down another volley of arrows. The second volley was ineffectual as the last but that didn't stop the groll's laughter.

Jace was about to yell out another request to speak with the shaman when he heard a louder, more commanding voice. "Switch to melee weapons, charge!"

"We know a way to make you human!" Jace yelled but it was lost in the groll's warcry and laughter as a group of them rushed down the hill. He counted six grolls coming down the hill at him. Given the number of arrows that they'd fire at him, he knew there were at least six more up top.

Jace put himself in the shaman's place. Faced with standard player tactics, he'd give them some melee fodder and while they were focusing on them, fill them full of arrows. If it were Jace, he'd focus on the Healer first, then the Mage, and then Rogue and leave the Tank for last.

Keeping the archers back would prevent Jace from using his *Taunt* on them and allow them to target any of his group. But would the shaman player think that way? And what would the shaman do if Jace didn't follow his plan?

The charging grolls were almost on him. In an instant, Jace's weapons were equipped and sprang into his hands. Behind him, he heard the girls coming out of the foliage.

"Stay back in cover," he told them. "I'll pull them out of the clearing so the grolls up top can't get a clear shot."

The laughing grolls reached him and attacked. Most of them had one handed weapons but two of them had larger, two-handed weapons.

Broken Paw Groll slashes YOU for 0 damage.
Broken Paw Groll crushes YOU for 0 damage.
Broken Paw Groll stabs YOU for 0 damage.
Broken Paw Groll slashes YOU for 1 damage.
Broken Paw Groll slashes YOU for 0 damage.
Broken Paw Groll crushes YOU for 0 damage.

The groll with the two-handed sword managed to penetrate his *Defense*, but the rest of the blows glanced off his armor.

"Here doggies!" he yelled his *Taunt* and then backed into the dense foliage to where his companions waited.

Under the influence of his *Taunt*, the grolls followed him into the cover. Jace pointed at the grolls. "Take out the ones with the two handers first."

The girls sprang into action and within a minute, the groll with the two-handed sword was dead. His group slowly took out one groll after another, as Jace kept a wary eye on the groll fort. He had expected more grolls to come down but instead, he had seen the wood door shut.

Finally, the last of the grolls fell dead and the group allowed themselves a short respite to regain their mana and *Stamina*. Jace had barely taken any damage so he waved away Mika's healing and let his health regenerate normally.

"How many more do you think there are?" Mika asked as Jace's mana and health topped off.

"I'm not sure," Jace shrugged. "At least six more but they could have some in reserve. If it's a player, who knows what his tactics will be. He could purposefully not show his full hand to lure us in."

"That's scary," Diana said. "We could be walking into an ambush."

"Except we're expecting it," Jace said.

"How do we get into the fort?" Charlena asked, glancing up at the wooden structure. It was crude. Basically, just large logs driven into the dirt and tied together. It reminded Jace of the makeshift raft he and Charlena had built to navigate the river on their way to Whitecliff.

Jace stared at the fort and then looked around. As he did, a plan began to formulate. Smiling, he turned back to his group. "We burn it down!"

The plan was simple, but he hoped it would be effective. They all gathered a large bundle of dried sticks and kindling. Once they had a large enough bundle, Jace walked up the hill with it while the girls stayed back and continued collecting more.

It was at least fifty yards from the edge of the clearing to the wooden wall of the fort and the grolls peppered Jace with arrows the entire time. But as before, his *Defense* easily repelled the arrows.

When he made it to the fort wall, he dropped the bundle next to the wall and then stepped back. "I'm going to burn down the fort now! If you can hear me, I know a way for you to be human again!"

Jace waited for an answer but there was none. Casting his *Flame Bolt* spell, he ignited the dried bundle and watched as it caught fire. The flames quickly spread to the entire bundle and soon it was a roaring fire.

Jogging back down the hill, Jace picked up the next bundle the girls had prepared and then jogged up the hill. This time, there were no arrows and Jace was worried the grolls might have escaped.

"Luna," he called out to his familiar mentally. "Can you circle around and let me know if you see any grolls trying to get away?"

There was no response for a moment and then he heard her reply in his head. "Yes."

He caught sight of an orange blur racing around the bottom of the clearing and then his familiar disappeared around the hill.

Jace made another trip down and started back up, this time he saw more arrows fly at him, only these were different. They were flaming.

Broken Paw Groll shoots YOU for 0 damage + 1 points fire damage.
Broken Paw Groll shoots YOU for 0 damage + 2 points fire damage.
Broken Paw Groll shoots YOU for 0 damage + 2 points fire damage.
Broken Paw Groll shoots YOU for 0 damage + 1 points fire damage.
Broken Paw Groll shoots YOU for 0 damage + 1 points fire damage.
Broken Paw Groll shoots YOU for 0 damage + 1 points fire damage.

Jace flinched as the flaming arrows thudded into him. Even though they couldn't penetrate his *Defense*, he had no fire resistance and the flames burned him. He ran faster up the hill but took two more volleys of arrows as he did.

The shaman player was using the fire to his advantage. They also had a good understanding of the game since they realized that flaming arrows would bypass his normal *Defense*. Jace had to admit, it was clever thinking. They'd taken down almost a third of his health on the way up and if they did the same on the way down, he'd be in trouble.

He saw the grolls peaking over the top of the wall, aiming another volley of flaming arrows at him. Even though he knew he was about to take even more damage, Jace grinned. They'd just made a huge mistake. The grolls had moved in range of his *Taunt*.

Just as the grolls released their arrows, Jace yelled out his *Taunt*. "Here doggies! Come to papa!"

Chapter 25

Jace turned and ran as fast as he could down the hill, managing to get only one more volley before he reached the cover of the trees. He looked back at the fort and saw the grolls climbing over the fence to come after him.

"I was able to *Taunt* them! You all stay here, I'm going to move further back and draw them in," Jace told them. "Use the same tactic as before."

The girls nodded grimly and readied their weapons.

"Oh," Jace said as he noticed his health. "And can someone heal me please."

Mika was able to give him two heals before the grolls came close enough to fire at him. They still had their bows and had flaming arrows notched but Jace knew once they used those, they wouldn't be able to replenish them.

Broken Paw Groll shoots YOU for 0 damage + 2 points fire damage.
Broken Paw Groll shoots YOU for 0 damage + 2 points fire damage.
Broken Paw Groll shoots YOU for 0 damage + 1 points fire damage.

Broken Paw Groll shoots YOU for 0 damage + 1 points fire damage.
Broken Paw Groll shoots YOU for 0 damage + 2 points fire damage.
Broken Paw Groll shoots YOU for 0 damage + 1 points fire damage.

The grolls fired and the girls moved to attack. Focusing on one, then moving onto the next.

As they fought, Jace kept watch for the shaman. He wasn't sure what the player would do at this point or even if he had more troops up in the fort. Luckily, Luna was still in place to warn him if the grolls tried to outflank him. As long as she wasn't chasing butterflies.

One by one, his group killed the six grolls that had followed him down from the fort. As the last one fell, the group relaxed. Jace looked at his system messages and saw he'd gained a new level in Mage.

You have gained a level.
You are now level 3 in Mage.

"I just gained a level in Priest," Diana said.

Jace was about to congratulate her when Luna's voice popped into his head. "Wolfer running."

Swearing, Jace looked at the girls. "The shaman's making a run for it!"

He heard the girls follow him and sprinted as fast as he could around the hill. As he came around the side, he saw a groll that was larger than the others he had fought halfway down the hill. It was stopped, picking up something from the ground.

Jace changed his course to intercept the large groll and saw it pick up a large chest and start to run away.

"WAIT!" he yelled. "We know you're a player!"

The groll stopped in his tracks and looked over his shoulder. He set down the chest and brought out a crooked staff decorated tipped with what Jace guessed was a bear or large wolf skull.

"Stay back!" he warned, and then broke into hyena laughter. "Argh! I hate that!"

Jace came to a stop about twenty feet from the large groll and put his hands up in a peaceful gesture. "We just want to help you. What's your real name?"

The hyena-man narrowed its eyes but didn't speak.

"I'm Jace Burton," he said. "This is Diana. That's Mika. And the elf is Charlena."

"We were like you," Jace told him. "Except for Charlena. She's a regular player. But Diana, Mika and I were also trapped in monster bodies. Each time we died, we jumped to a different body."

Jace stopped talking and looked to the groll shaman, silently urging him to speak.

Finally, some of the tension eased out of the groll's face. "I am Yosyp Svyatoslav."

"And you died and woke up in a monster body?" Jace asked.

"Yes," the groll said ruefully. "I guess it's true. I am dead. I wasn't sure at first. Things weren't the way I was expecting. I have a 77th level troll Rager and I was expecting to be him."

"You're from the European server I take it?" Jace asked. He knew some of the other player continents had different premium races and different prestige classes than the America continent.

"Yes," said the groll. "But I do not think I am there any longer. All this is new to me."

Jace nodded. "This is the Americas continent."

Yosyp had another groll laughing fit. "Figures, I'm not even on the right continent. No troll. No money. Not even million dollar life insurance policy."

"We can tell you how to become human," Jace offered. "And stop body hopping."

"Human?" Yosyp asked glumly. "Not my troll?"

Jace shook his head. "Not right now. I'm trying to contact support to get them to fix this bug and restore us all. But until then, you'd be a human. And you'd stay human even when you die."

"That would be something at least," he started to say but broke into another laughing fit. "Sorry, I hate that! Anyway, the constant hopping and dying was annoying. Finally, I was a boss and I had minions. It was nice. I could actually defend myself. I killed two groups of players. I thought I'd kill you too. But you were smart. And lucky."

"We knew you were a player," Jace told him. "We can… sense… players in monster bodies. Once I knew that, I figured you'd try some non-standard tactics."

"Ah," grinned the groll, showing off his large canines. "That makes sense. The others just blundered right in and I took them out easily. Take out the Healer, then the Mage, and casually pick off the other two. Very easy."

"We are strong," Mika said. "And Jace is smart."

Jace looked back at Mika and she blushed. As he turned back to Yosyp, he caught Charlena glance at the other girl with an unreadable expression.

"So," the groll-player broke into a fit of hyena laughter. It passed and he continued. "How do you turn me human?"

"You hack the game," Jace told him and then explained the code, as well as how and when to type it in.

"So, I need to die. Then I put in the code?" he asked just before another fit of laughter. "And then the next body I wake up in will be human, yes? And no laughing!"

"Yes," Jace smiled. "At least, you won't laugh unless you want to. But your new spawn location appears to be completely random. If you can make it back here to Whitecliff, we can help you. We meet at the Dwarvish Fork every morning."

"Whitecliff. Dwarvish Fork," Yosyp repeated. "Got it."

The groll looked around and sighed. Or at least, it might have been a sigh on a human. Jace wasn't sure if it was the same on a groll. "I'll do it, if just to stop this stupid laughing. Do I need to kill myself or will you kill me?"

Jace shrugged. "It's up to you, but if we kill you, we get experience."

"And we need experience, darling," Diana chimed in.

"Fine, fine," Yosyp said. "Kill me and get it over with. And treasure is all here in the chest already. There is nothing left in the fort now."

"Thanks," Jace told him. He looked at his companions and then back to Yosyp. "Ready?"

"Ready as I'll ever be," the groll said and then broke into more laughter. "Ok! I am more than ready for that to stop! Kill me already!"

They proceed to attack him and Yosyp took the blows more stoically than Jace thought he could have. When they reached 75%, 50% and 25% of his health, they received system messages about his special abilities, but the shaman didn't use them.

After several minutes of them attacking the groll and many laughing outbursts, Diana finally struck the killing blow and Yosyp.

Broken Paw Shaman dies.
You gain 1200 experience.

The groll's body fell face down into the dirt and the staff fell from his hands. Jace and Charlena looked down at the body, waiting for the transformation that they knew should occur. While he did, he picked up the staff and saw that it was a quest item. Probably the item they'd need to turn in to the adventurers guild.

"Are we waiting for something?" Diana asked.

Right as she spoke, the body began to bubble and shift, shrinking down and losing the fur. The canine features disappeared, leaving a mostly naked man in place of the groll.

"Oh my," Diana said, covering her mouth with her hand. "That was worth waiting for."

Yosyp looked to be about six or six and a half feet tall, built like an athlete. He had a mane of dark brown hair that only partially obscured his face. The part of his face that wasn't obscured showed chiseled European features that Jace associated with some of the male models he'd seen advertising various products.

Jace noticed all the women were staring at Yosyp's body and cleared his throat. "Let's check the loot."

Mika blushed and looked at Jace, but the other two girls stared for a bit longer.

"He's like a Greek god," Diana said before finally dragging her eyes away and turning to Jace. "I'm sorry dear one, did you say something?"

Jace rolled his eyes and went over to the chest. The chest appeared to have been dropped and had broken open, so Jace just lifted the battered lid to look inside.

Ring of Armor
Type: Ring
Level: 5
Wt: .1 lb
Special: Provide +5 Armor
Description: Created for a noble knight of Whitecliff, the ring provided little protection when his horse threw a shoe and he broke his neck.

Chainmail Bikini of Moureva
Type: Chest Armor
Level: 5
Armor: 3 + 1 (Masterwork) + 1 (Sturdy)
Wt: 3 lb
Description: Created for a priestess of Moureva, this scant chainmail garment affords all the benefits of its less revealing counterparts.

Bloodstained Katana
Type: Two-Handed Sword
Level: 5
Damage: 14 + 1 (Sharp)
Wt: 4 lb
Special: Foes struck are affected with Bleed for 3 seconds.
Description: Commissioned for Prince Nicbomqeis, this katana disappeared when the young prince's ship was lost at sea in a fierce storm.

Jace held up the chainmail bikini in front of his chest and shook his head. "This is NOT for me."

The girls chuckled but Diana spoke up. "I can wear armor now, right? Because I'm a priest?"

"Yes," he replied.

"I think that's got me written all over it," Diana purred, reaching out for it.

"Any other takers?" Jace asked. Mika blushed and Charlena just shrugged, knowing she couldn't use it. He handed it to Diana. "All yours."

"Is that… a… katana?" Mika whispered as she saw the katana sticking out of the chest.

Jace took it out and handed it to her. "You and I are the only ones who can use it. Take it."

The katana was well made with a black and red scabbard, a gold guard, and a crimson wrapped handle. Mika pulled the sword slightly from the scabbard revealing a polished blade that looked extremely sharp. Her eyes didn't leave the sword as she spoke. "Thank you."

Jace smiled and then held up the ring. "Any objects to me keeping this? It's an armor ring."

No one did, so Jace slipped it on his finger. That done, he pulled the money into his inventory to see they'd gained 314 gold. Breaking it up, he handed each of just over 75 gold.

"Charlena," he turned to the elf. "How much more time do you have? Enough for us to turn in the quest?"

Charlena's eyes went glassy and then she bit her lip. "I'll probably be a little over but that's okay. Let's go!"

They alternated running and walking all the way back to Whitecliff and reached the adventurers guild at a little after 9pm. Jace half-expected it to be closed and was pleasantly surprised when the door opened.

Behind the desk was their old friend, Throdgrug Greydigger. The dwarf looked up from scribbling something on a piece of paper and blew out a breath. "You lot again. Now what do you want?"

Jace handed him the quest note and the staff. He was curious to see what the dwarf would do with the staff since he'd eaten the alligator eye. Thus, he was disappointed when the dwarf leaned the staff against the wall and reached into the drawer to bring out their reward.

"Not bad," he said. "We'll make real adventurers out of you yet," Throdgrug said and slid the pouches containing their rewards across the desk.

You have completed the quest, "Way of the Shaman"
You gain 800 experience. Experience to next level 1,880.
You gain +25 faction with Whitecliff Adventurers Guild.

They each took their reward and stashed it away in their inventories.

"Sorry guys," Charlena said. "But I have to go. On the bright side, I made it to level 7 and almost 8! See you all tomorrow!"

Jace thought she would lean in to kiss him like she normally did but she just faded away.

After Charlena had completely faded away, Mika turned to him. "I also made level 7."

"Does that mean you'll switch to Rogue?" he asked.

Mika gave him a huge grin. "I already have. Now I will be ninja."

Chapter 26

"I guess this means we're off to do our own thing again?" Diana said. "More solo quests?"

"Yes," Jace told the older woman. Then thinking about it, he smiled. "Don't forget, you're a priestess of the love goddess now. Who knows what the type of quests they might have for you…"

"Oh," Diana's eyes lit up. "You really think it might be something fun?"

"Only one way to find out," Jace shrugged.

"Well then, I'll see you two in the morning," Diana told them and started to go. She took a few steps and then stopped and looked back over her shoulder. "Don't do anything I wouldn't do."

Diana winked at them, turned, and sauntered away. In a moment, she had disappeared into the crowd.

Jace looked at Mika, who had blushed slightly at the comment. He met her eyes and grinned. "Like there's anything she wouldn't do."

They both shared a chuckle and then he motioned her to follow him. "Come on, I'll take you to the guild."

The two of them went north from the adventurers guild and looked for Tarot Street. Jace briefly considered asking for directions but considering what had happened to the previous thieves guild hideout, he changed his mind.

After close to twenty minutes of searching, they spotted Tarot Street and then found the Griffon Fabrics shop Webley had mentioned. They went around to the side door which Jace noticed had been reinforced and looked newer than the rest of the building. It also had a slot at eye level that could be slid open. Not something you'd normally find in a tailor shop.

Jace thought back to his conversation with Webley. Remembering the knock series, he knocked three times, then once, then twice. Having finished the knock sequence, he stepped back and waited.

The door slit slid open and a pair of large brown eyes that belonged to a panda-kin. From just the eyes, Jace couldn't tell if it were Thom or Gerry. The eyes took in Jace but then narrowed when they caught sight of Mika. "Who's she?"

"Fresh recruit," Jace told the panda-kin, who he thought sounded more like Thom.

Having played an assassin to level 95, Jace had plenty of experience with the thieves guild and he knew quite a bit about their ways. He knew of only one sure fire way to get her in. "I vouch for her."

Thom's eyes widened slightly. "You know what that means, right?"

Jace knew. In the guild, vouching for someone meant he was equally responsible for anything they did. If they screwed up, they both paid the consequence. If they did something that got them kicked out of the guild, they both got kicked out. Jace glanced over at the petite girl and nodded. "I do. I vouch for her."

"It's your head," Thom said and slid the slot closed. There was some noise behind the door, as if a bar was being drawn back and then some clicking sounds that Jace guessed was the lock. Finally, the door swung open. Jace glanced up and down the alley and, seeing no one, stepped inside with Mika trailing after him.

No sooner had the door shut than Jace heard a cry of "Panda!" from Mika. Before he could stop her, she had thrown herself at Thom and engulfed him in a hug. For a moment, no one moved.

Thom was unsure what to do about the cute little human hugging him. Gerry still seemed in shock and just staring at the two. Jace was trying to figure out a way to get Mika and himself out of the guild alive if Thom or Jerry decided to attack her.

Several seconds passed and then Gerry erupted into laughter. It was a deep, bellowing laughter that echoed through the place and Jace heard the noise in the other room stop. If he had to guess, no one had ever heard Gerry laugh before. The panda-kin pointed at Thom, still laughing. "Looks like you got a fan there Thom!"

Thom's hands were still up, as if he hadn't figured out what to do about her yet. Mika looked up at him with her big brown eyes and huge grin. "You're so fluffy! And cuddly!"

Gerry lost it at that point, bursting into even more laughter. He was laughing so hard he lost his balance and slid down the wall, trying to hold his belly. "So fluffy…. And…. cuddly!"

Thom glared at Gerry but then looked down at Mika, gave her a smile and briefly hugged her back. Then he gently untangled himself and stepped back from her.

Mika looked at Gerry, rolling on the floor and might have tried to give him a hug as well but at that moment a familiar voice cut in from the next room. "If you two are done having fun. Perhaps you could go back to guarding the door."

Jace turned to see the guildmaster in the doorway. The man's face was serious but Jace caught the corner of his mouth twitch, as if he were trying very hard to suppress a smile.

"Yes sir," Thom said and hurriedly locked and barred the door.

Gerry held up a hand, trying to bring his laughter under control. "Thom... is cuddly."

At that, the guildmaster didn't seem to be able to hold it back and his face broke into a grin. "I think that might be your new nickname Thom, Mr. Cuddles."

Thom looked aghast and Gerry, who had nearly had his laughing under control, erupted in another fit of uncontrollable laughter. "Mister… Cuddles…."

Webley's face went serious again and he glanced from Jace to Mika and then back to Jace. "You two, come with me."

The guildmaster led them through a large room which had probably been the shop's showroom at one point. Makeshift tables and crates now littered the room and Rogues sitting on stools and smaller wooden boxes. They went to the back of the room, then up a flight of stairs to the second floor and into what Jace guessed had been the master bedroom.

The room had been converted into a makeshift office with a sturdy oak desk. Webley moved around to the far end of the desk and sat down in a worn, leather bound chair and then looked meaningfully at the chairs on the opposite side of the desk.

Jace and Mika took the hint and sat down in the chairs. Before Jace could say anything, Mika burst out. "I'm sorry I hugged panda!"

The guildmaster kept his composure for only a moment before his face split in a grin. "I have to admit, I haven't seen Thom so lost for what to do or heard Gerry laugh like…" Webley stopped and looked thoughtful. "Come to think of it, I don't I've ever heard Gerry laugh at all. That almost makes your presence here worth it." He then cast a much more serious glance at Jace. "Almost."

The guildmaster leaned back, relaxed but his voice was terse when he addressed Jace. "Now is not the time for new recruits. Or new people." Webley favored Mika with a smile. "No offense dear."

Mika beamed at the guildmaster. "None taken. I want to become ninja!"

Webley cocked an eyebrow. "Ninja?"

Jace leaned forward. "I vouch for her."

That caught the guildmaster's attention, and he sat up suddenly. "You vouch for her? And you know what that means and what that entails?"

Jace nodded.

"What does it mean?" Mika asked.

"It means," he turned to Mika. "He takes full responsibility for everything you do. If you screw up, the punishment goes to both of you."

Mika glanced at Jace and then back at Webley. "I will not screw up."

Webley chuckled. "She's got spunk. I see why you like her. Fine. From this point forward, anything you do is a reflection on him. Got it?"

"Got it," Mika said with a smile.

Webley nodded at the enthusiastic girl and then turned to Jace. He reached into a desk drawer and pulled out the Infiltrator's Hat. "It came in handier than I thought. So, I owe you that favor."

Jace took the hat and stashed it back in his inventory. When looked up, his face had become hard again. "I heard from some of my contacts in the docks and some loose lipped sailors. Looks like Tiebaut is trying to go behind our backs and make a deal with the person who now has the princess' tiara."

Webley paused and Jace could see the anger clouding his face. To the guildmaster, someone breaking a contract seemed to be very serious and Jace remembered the sense of "honor" the mobsters from the vidstreams had.

"It also seems this mysterious Captain DD," Webley said through clenched teeth, "is the one who ratted us out to the guard. I'm still not sure exactly how he got his information, but my contact in the guard says he was the one."

"I plan to deal with both parties," Webley said, bringing his voice under control. He looked pointedly at Jace. "And you will help me."

"Me?" Jace muttered. Something this serious would warrant the guildmaster himself getting involved. Jace was just a newbie in the thieves guild.

The guildmaster seemed to guess what Jace was thinking. "You're probably wondering why I don't do something about it personally. Trust me, I would like nothing better. But, considering the recent…

changes in the guild… I can't leave the guild alone right now. For the moment, my place is here."

"Also, you helped me out of a bind," Webley said. "First the warning about the guild raid. Then with the hat of disguise. I'm inclined to trust you. So, I will give you a job. A very important job."

Jace sat up straighter and leaned forward in his chair. "What job?"

"Since I'm stuck in here," the guildmaster told him. "You're going to dish out a little payback for us."

Jace raised an eyebrow, and the guildmaster grinned. "One of my contacts found our wayward captain and where his ship is berthed." Webley paused, seemingly for dramatic effect. "You're going to steal back the tiara and frame our good friend, Sir Tiebaut."

Jace could scarcely believe his ears. "When? And don't you mean Lord Tiebaut?"

"He fancies himself a lord, but he's just a Baronet," Webley looked at him. "Tonight. We have word that he will be making a handoff sometime tomorrow, so we need to move now. Get to the *Wyvern's Tail* at dock 17. The sailor said the captain keeps it in his cabin, so you'll need to get in, get the tiara and get out. If you can cause some damage to send him a message, all the better. Got it?"

Jace nodded mutely, still trying to absorb what the guildmaster was saying.

"Once you have it, make your way back to the wall," Webley continued. "Our inside man is there. I called in a lot of favors to get him put on twice in a row. Go back to Tiebaut's house and stash the tiara somewhere where he won't find it. When you get back here, we'll make sure the guard gets a tip. Questions?"

Jace had a million questions. As he tried to sort them out, Mika raised her hand.

The guildmaster shook his head and smiled. "You have a question?"

"Yes!" Mika beamed. "Can I help?"

Webley chuckled and then looked thoughtful. "Normally, we don't like outside help. But he did vouch for you so I don't see why not."

Almost as soon as he said it, new quests appeared in his HUD and he saw they were group quests. He was still grouped with Mika, so he accepted them.

Webley the Snake has offered your group the quest, "Rescue the Princess' Tiara"
Reward: +100 faction with Whitecliff Thieves Guild, 100 gold.
Level: 9
Accept quest? (Yes or No)

Webley the Snake has offered your group the quest, "Turnabout is Fair Play"
Reward: +100 faction with Whitecliff Thieves Guild, 100 gold.
Level: 9

Accept quest? (Yes or No)

Jace accepted the quests. As soon as he did, Webley looked at them both. "Same rules as last time with the wall. You need to be back to our man on the wall before sunrise or you're on your own."

Chapter 27

Twenty minutes later Jace and Mika were heading to the docks with Luna trailing them. He couldn't believe it when the guildmaster had given him the quest. He was supposed to find the princess' tiara, steal it back, and do some damage to the captain in the process. Then, he was supposed to go back to the wall, get over it, stash the tiara somewhere in Tiebaut's house and then get back over the wall - all before sunrise.

"We are robbing a pirate?" Mika said.

Jace glanced over at the young woman and smiled. "That's the plan. We need to check out the area first."

Checking his gnomish timepiece, he saw that it was 12:14am. The twin moons were high in the sky and Jace knew he would need to hurry. They needed to finish both quests before daybreak or their man on the wall would be gone and they would be trapped in the Noble District. He snickered to himself. No pressure.

The two of them made it to the docks and walked south until they found dock 17. Moored there they found the *Wyvern's Tail.* Looking at it, it was much smaller than Jace had imagined based on the old pirate vidstreams he'd watched. In fact, he doubted it was more than 100 feet long.

263

The docks had plenty of crates and other cargo laying around and this dock was no exception, he steered Mika between some crates so they could get a better look at the ship without looking suspicious.

"Is that the ship?" she whispered as they ducked down.

He'd seen the name painted on the rear of the ship, just under the windows of what he guessed was the captain's cabin.

"The ship is dark. I can barely make out anything," she told him.

Jace nodded. It was dark and normally he'd be in the same situation. But with his *Cat-Vision*, it was almost like it was daytime. He reached down and scratched Luna behind the ears as he took in the ship.

The gangplank was down, that was good. At first he thought it might be deserted or that everyone was asleep but just as he had that thought, he glimpsed one of the pirates coming down the stairs from the upper deck of the ship's rear, he thought it was called the stern but wasn't sure.

The pirate looked like a man, but it had a long, fluffy tail and Jace could just make out triangular ears poking through a mop of unkempt hair. It had to be either a dog-kin or fox-kin. That meant it had good night-vision, like him.

As he watched, another pirate came down the steps from the front of the ship. Was that called the bow? He could never remember. The second pirate appeared to be human, which meant his night vision would be limited.

The two seemed to be mirroring each other, making a full circuit around the ship. They must be the night watch and as far as he could see, they were the only ones awake.

"There's two guards," he whispered to Mika. "One is human, the other is either fox or dog-kin."

"Careful," Mika said and moved close to his ear. "Fox-kin and dog-kin have keen noses. They can track by scent."

He felt her breath on his ear and couldn't suppress a little shiver. Suddenly his mind was thinking of other things, things that involved Mika, but he forced himself to think of the job.

Besides, he was with Charlena. Wasn't he? They hadn't made anything official, but they had kissed. Did that mean they were together? He wasn't sure and now wasn't the time to figure it out.

He glanced back at the ship and watched the guards. The two occasionally paused and Jace thought he even saw one of them light up a pipe for a few minutes before continuing his circuit around the deck.

"What are they doing?" Mika asked, still unable to make out any real details.

"They're just patrolling the deck," he replied. "Maybe I can hide and sneak up the gangplank while the dog-kin is on the far side."

Mika shook her head. "As soon as it came near you, it would scent you and know you were onboard."

Jace frowned. She was right. He remembered how good Luna's nose was and dogs had even better senses of smell than cats.

"If we had a distraction," he told her. "Something that will get the guard's attention."

"A bomb?" Mika asked hopefully.

Jace chuckled softly. "Even if we could find a bomb, that might be a bit much. We need something that would get the captain out of his cabin. Just for a few minutes."

"I could pretend to be a guard," she suggested. "And ask for their permit or whatever it is they need to dock."

"Not bad," he told her. But even though there were female guards, he doubted any were as petite as Mika. Plus, guards would work in pairs, maybe even more if boarding a ship. "I'm not sure if we could pull that off."

Mika seemed to think about the problem for a bit before coming up with another suggestion. "What about fireworks! Everyone loves fireworks!"

Jace was about to dismiss the idea but it didn't give him an idea. In all the pirate movies he'd ever watched, the sailors were always worried about the ships catching fire. If Jace just set the ship on fire, that would surely put them on alert. But, if he could make it look like an accident, say… a misfired firework, then they'd be more concerned with the fire than looking for a culprit.

Without thinking he leaned over and kissed her on the cheek. "You're a genius. Come on, let's go!"

Before he knew what was happening, Mika had grabbed him and pressed her lips to his. At first, he was stunned, but her lips were insistent, and he found himself returning her kiss. When they broke away, they were both breathless.

Mika looked away. "I'm sorry. I should not have done that."

Jace was speechless for a moment but he didn't have time to figure this new situation out. "We can talk about it later. We have a ship to break into."

He crept back out from behind the crates and ducked into a nearby alleyway. Behind him, he heard Mika's light footfalls but didn't trust himself to turn around. He'd really enjoyed that kiss and now he was feeling guilty because of Charlena.

He shook his head to clear it. Jace needed to stay sharp. His time was running out. He needed to focus. Keeping his mind on his task, he led them to the Central Market. Jace knew from experience the large markets were always open. Some vendors closed but most of them had someone manning their booth 24 hours a day.

Jace went from booth to booth as quickly as possible, looking for the items he needed. He bought several vials of oil from one vendor, gnomish firesticks from another and then a crossbow and bolts from yet another vendor. When he finally found the last item he was looking for, he swore.

Gnomish rockets were the game equivalent of fireworks. Unfortunately, because they were gnomish, they were also expensive. At 100 gold each, he could only afford 3 of them and that was too little.

"What is it?" Mika asked softly. They were the first words she'd said since she apologized for their kiss.

"I have a plan," he told her. "But I need more than 3 fireworks. Unfortunately, that's all the money I have."

Without a word, she pulled forth several pouches with money. "Here."

"No," he protested. It looked like all the money she had. "I can't..."

"It's my quest too," she said, thrusting the money at him. "We both win or we both lose."

Jace looked at her for a moment and then took the money. He counted it up. With the little bit he had left over plus the money from Mika, it would be enough for five more fireworks. He looked back at her. "Are you sure?"

She smiled and nodded. "I'm sure!"

Jace looked at her for a moment longer and then turned back to the vendor and bought eight of the fireworks. Once he paid for his purchase, he stuffed the items in his inventory.

"Okay," he said, "let's go back and make this work!"

They made their way back to the dock and then to their hiding spot behind the crates. Making sure to stay hidden, he began setting out the items he bought. First, he brought out the crossbow and bolt. Next, he brought out two of the vials of oil and some twine he'd been carrying around for some time. Finally, he brought out the gnomish rockets and firesticks.

Mika looked at the items array on the cobblestones and then looked at Jace. "These are part of your plan?"

Nodding, Jace took the vials of oil and, using the twine, he began attaching the flasks to the ends of the crossbow bolts. After the first one, Mika got the idea and attached the second one while he finished the first.

With the flasks attached to the crossbow bolts, he had set them and the crossbow aside and motioned Mika to lean in and explained his plan.

"You were right about the distraction," he whispered. "But we need something that will keep their attention. Here's what we can do. I'm going to sneak around to the back of the ship."

She started to object but he held up his hand. "I'm higher level and I have a higher *Defense*. If there's trouble, I'll have a better chance of making it out of there."

Mika didn't seem convinced and opened her mouth, but he continued. "And I need you here for the best part of the plan."

She closed her mouth and looked at him expectantly.

"When I send a signal to Luna," he continued. "I want you to fire off the first firework over the ships here. Wait about 10 seconds, then fire off the second one."

She looked down in confusion at the fireworks laid out. "How do I light them?"

Grinning Jace pointed to the small pile of sticks. "These are gnomish firesticks. They're basically matches. Strike them against the stone or even one of the crates and they will light instantly."

Mika looked at the firesticks and then nodded.

"When you get to the third one, I want you to fire it off and when it explodes, fire the first crossbow bolt at the front part of the ship. Hopefully, the sound of the rocket exploding will hide the noise of the crossbow."

He paused to make sure she understood, and she motioned him to continue.

"Okay, so same thing with the next rocket. Fire the rocket, then the crossbow as it explodes," he said. "The fire the fifth rocket at the same place as you shoot the oil. When the rocket hits, it should ignite the oil and that will set the ship on fire—at least for a little bit."

She grinned at that and motioned for him to continue.

"Then go back to firing the rest over the ships," he told her. "Hopefully, they'll think it was a misfire and that will buy me some time. In the meantime, I'll use my grapple to climb up the back of the ship. When I see the captain leave his quarters, I'll break in, grab the tiara and then get out."

Suddenly he remembered Webley's admonishment about causing some damage. He thought about what he could do and remembered he had a few extra oil flasks. Maybe he could them set the captain's cabin on fire.

"If I give the word to Luna to run," he told her. "You run. If they leave the ship and come after you, you run. Meet me in the Merchant District, near the wall, at a place called Peacock Clothiers."

Jace turned to Luna. "You relay my messages to her and her message to me. Can you do that?"

The cat, who had been quietly cleaning herself, looked up. "Yes."

He smiled and scratched his familiar's ears. "You do this and there's extra fish tomorrow."

The cat perked up at that suggestion. "Fish?"

"Yes," he told her. "You relay our messages and stay with Mika and you get extra fish."

"Yes," the cat meowed enthusiastically.

"What if the captain doesn't leave?" Mika asked.

Jace considered it and then spoke honestly. "Then we're totally screwed."

He smiled again. "Wait for my signal, then let them rip."

She gave him a thumbs sign and he moved off into the shadows, praying whoever was listening that his plan worked.

Chapter 28

It was early morning and the docks were deserted except an occasional sailor stumbling back from a night of drunken carousing and the occasional guard patrol. Moving from shadow to shadow and trusting his *Stealth* skill to keep him hidden from prying eyes, Jace made his way around to a small foreman's shed near the rear of the ship.

Looking up at the rear deck, he saw that it was taller than he originally thought. The upper deck was a good forty feet above the waterline and the captain's cabin was right below it. The extra height would translate into extra time climbing. He hoped he could make it in time.

Removing his padded grapple attached to the knotted rope, he untangled the rope and made sure it was ready for him to throw. Once it was ready, Jace checked the dock for any patrols or wandering sailors. Satisfied that the coast was clear, he crept to the edge of the dock near the stern of the *Wyvern's Tail*.

"Go!" Jace sent to Luna and began swinging the grapple.

From near Mika's hiding place, Jace heard a whoosh as the gnomish rocket soared into the sky. A second later, there was a boom as the rocket exploded into a green and orange light that seemed to drift slowly down before burning away into nothingness.

Jace waited for the second rocket to go off and released his grapple. It soared upward and over the railing of the top deck. He pulled on the rope until the grapple caught on the railing. He tested his weight on it to make sure it would hold.

Above him, the third rocket went off and he let himself swing over the water and begin scaling the rope. If the captain heard him or happened to look out the window, he'd be screwed. He continued climbing and stopped short of the captain's window as he heard the fourth rocket explode above him.

The next rocket whooshed and exploded much closer, it was immediately followed by shouts. "Captain! Captain! Fire!"

Risking a peek in the window, Jace saw the door opposite the window open. He watched as the figure stalked through the doorway and slammed the door behind him. He heard yelling and activity from the ship's deck but there was too much yelling to make out. Above him, another firework exploded, and he used his dagger to shatter the window.

With some difficulty, he managed to pull himself through the window and into the captain's cabin. He could still hear chaotic shouts and commotion out on the deck and those covered the sounds of his entry.

Standing inside the cabin, Jace scanned the room for any sign of the tiara. He didn't see anything that resembled it but did see a large chest. Rushing over the chest, he tried the latch but, unsurprising, found that it was locked.

He dropped down and was about to pick the lock when he saw the keyhole glow. He quickly looked over the rest of the chest for any signs of a trap. When he found none, he guessed it was a poison needle trap that would jab and poison anyone opening the lock without a key.

In another place and another time, Jace would have disarmed the trap and picked the lock. Right now, he didn't have time. He took out his dagger, wedged it between the lid and the base of the chest and twisted it, trying to break the lock. Instead, his dagger snapped off at the blade.

Silently, Jace swore. He brought out his saber, which was longer and thicker than the dagger and tried the same trick. The saber snapped too but so did the lock on the chest. Flipping open the lid, Jace saw a fancy round box that looked like a hat box. He opened it and saw that it contained the tiara. Replacing the lid of the box, he grabbed the entire box and stuffed it into the inventory.

You receive Princess Tiara.

Under the box was a sack with coins spilling out. Never one to waste an opportunity, Jace grabbed the sack as well and tossed into his inventory. There were several log books under the sack and he grabbed those as well. Maybe they would contain some information worth money to Webley.

You receive Bag of Holding.
You receive 732 gold.
You received Captain Logs.

With the chest empty, Jace turned to leave but remembered he needed to cause some damage. He took out one of the vials of oil and poured it on the chest and surrounding area. He took another vial and poured it on the opposite side of the room, where the bed was. He took the final vial and poured in on the rug in front of the door.

He once again turned to leave but saw the captain's saber and sword belt hanging on a peg next to the door. He looked back to his broken saber on the floor near the chest and decided he had just found a replacement. Jace grabbed the sword and went to pick it up when he received a pop-up message in his HUD.

Kraken's Claw is a Soulbound item.
Do you wish to permanently bind this item to your character? (Yes or No)
Warning: This action cannot be undone.

Jace paused at the message. Soulbound items were items that were locked to a character permanently. They could never be traded or sold. Not only that, unlike regular items, they didn't stay with a person's corpse. Instead, soulbound items respawned with you. They were extremely rare. Without giving it any thought, Jace chose Yes and bound the saber to him.

Kraken's Claw has been bound.
You received Kraken's Claw.

As much as he wanted to check out the Kraken's Claw, Jace knew he didn't have time. He moved back over to the window and took a last look around the room, making sure he didn't miss anything of value.

Just then, the door burst open. A man in bed clothes was in the doorway, his face partially in shadow from the light of the behind him. While he couldn't quite make out the man's features, there was something familiar about him.

The man scanned the room before settling on Jace. When he did, the man took a step forward and Jace was finally able to see his face clearly. They both recognized each other as their eyes locked.

"You!" they said simultaneously.

The man, whose voice Jace recognized as the voice from the sewer, identified this person as the captain who had been speaking with Tiebaut. But even more than that, Jace recognized the face. It was Dainard Drakkar, the guildmaster he had defeated in Crossroads. And Drakkar recognized him as well.

Drakkar's face screwed up in rage and he reached for the spot where his saber had hung until recently. When his hand closed on empty air, the captain turned to see that it was missing. When he turned back to Jace, his face was a mask of fury.

"Intruder in the captain quarters!" he bellowed and started towards Jace.

Jace had no intention of staying to face Drakkar or his men. He couldn't afford to die here since that wouldn't mean not only failing the quest but also losing his corpse and everything on it.

He prepared to jump out the window. Before he did, he needed to ignite the oil. Yet, he felt like he needed to say something clever before his exit. Nothing came to mind, so he started his *Flame Bolt* spell. "*Minima fulmen ignem!*"

As the flaming bolt left his hand, he remembered a very old vidstream he'd watched with his father about a cop who fought terrorists in a large building. As Jace jumped out of the window, he yelled "Yippee ki yay!"

Behind him the captain's cabin erupted into flames and Jace could hear Drakkar screaming. He doubted the man was dead but hoped he'd be distracted enough.

Jace plummeted towards the water and remembered to send the message to Luna. "Run! I'm out!"

Then he hit the water and disappeared under the surface. Opening his eyes, he felt the salty water stinging them. He could see the glow of the fire above him and swam underwater to the dock near the ship.

As Jace's head broke the surface, he heard cries and shouts from the ship. It was a mishmash of voices but Drakkar's voice rang above them all. "Find him! He's stolen the tiara and your pay!"

Even as he looked over at the ship, Jace could see men streaming down the gangplank. With effort, he pulled himself out of the water and onto the dock. As he did, a shout game from the ship. "There he is! Off the stern! Off the stern!"

Letting out a breath, Jace climbed to his feet and unequipped and re-equipped his gear. It was an old trick he'd learned. The original designers hadn't thought to store the state of the clothes, like dirty, wet, etc., when they went into a player's inventory. When a player put something into their inventory and then brought it out, it came out clean and dry.

"Kill him! Kill him!" came Drakkar's voice from the deck.

He saw the sailors from the ship streaming off the boat and heading his way. They were led by the dog-kin who probably had the best sight. He saw the dog-kin sniffing as he moved and remembered Mika saying they had a very good sense of smell.

That complicated things. He had intended to use the Infiltrator's Hat to change his appearance and elude capture but if the dog-kin could track him, that wouldn't work. As far as he knew, the hat only changed appearance and not scent.

Turning, Jace fled back towards the wall as fast as he could. Maybe he could get to the wall and climb it before they reached it. Maybe that would work!

Then Jace lost a step and nearly stumbled as he realized he hadn't retrieved his grappling hook. It was still hanging on the back of the *Wyvern's Tail*. He had no way to scale the wall now. He was completely screwed.

He glanced behind him to see the pirates closing on him. Not only was he screwed, but he didn't think he could outrun or lose his pursuers for long. They would catch up to him, kill him and take the tiara.

Desperately he thought of some place he could go to lose them, but the dog-kin's scent ability would make that impossible. They'd find no matter where he went or who he changed his appearance to look like.

He looked up at the wall and wished he had some way to leap up or climb up on his own. If he could get up the walls, the guards would repel the pirates. They'd probably arrest him, but he wouldn't die.

Suddenly, he had a crazy idea. It wasn't quite what Webley had wanted but it might just accomplish the same thing. But it was risky. Very risky.

Seeing the mob of angry pirates who pursued him, Jace realized he had no choice. Pouring on the speed, he races for the entrance to the Noble District.

Chapter 29

The Noble District was not only surrounded by a wall, but it was also built on an elevated part of the city, adding to the isolation of the nobles from the common folk. The only entrances into the Noble District, other than the thieves guild inside man, was by one of two gates. The first gate was in the west, near the north entrance. The second was just before the Merchant District.

That meant it was only a scant distance from the docks, relatively speaking. But when he was running at top speed from a group of furious pirates, it seemed leagues away. Glancing behind him, he could see that some of the men, especially the dog-kin, were gaining on him.

Jace checked on his *Stamina* and saw that it was rapidly depleting. He couldn't sustain this much speed for long. Then he caught sight of the southern bridge up ahead and felt a sense of relief. Just a few hundred yards and he'd be on the bridge.

Those few hundred yards seem to pass in slow motion. He kept glancing back, seeing the dog-kin getting closer and closer to him. Finally, he reached the bridge on his right and swerved onto it with the dog-kin right behind him.

He saw the two towers that guarded the entrance into the Noble District and also saw that the portcullis was down. If he reached the gate and the portcullis was down, the pirates would have him before the guards could raise it and react. But how could he convince them to raise it in time?

He remembered the Infiltrator's Hat and a desperate idea came to him. He remembered the inside man's uniform the best he could in his mind and then willed his clothes to change. He blurred slightly and then he was wearing the uniform of a royal guard. Praying his plan would, he called out!

"Open the gate! Open the gate!" he yelled as he got closer to the portcullis. "I'm on the king's business!"

It was both risky and somewhat foolhardy. Most cities had laws against impersonating guards. Those laws carried some stiff penalties. Jace could only imagine what the penalties for impersonating a royal guard would be. At the same time, he had a trump card. The princess' tiara.

Jace was almost at the gate and could see that it was still close. His heart sank. It hadn't worked. Most likely their human eyes couldn't even see his uniform in the dark. He called out one last time.

"Open the gate!" he yelled with as much authority as possible.

Whether the guards could finally see his uniform or if the tone of his voice convinced them, he wasn't sure, but he heard someone yelled to raise the gate and then the loud cranking sound of the portcullis being slowly raised.

The dog-kin was almost to him when he finally made it to the gate. The portcullis was only up a foot or two when he got to it. Willing himself to use every rank of his acrobatics skill, he dove forward and rolled underneath.

The dog-kin hadn't expected his move and slammed into the gate which immediately got the guards' attention. A half dozen guards filed out of the two guard houses with pikes and they headed right for the gate.

"The men pursuing me... are pirates!" Jace blurted out, trying to get his breath under control. "They are under... the command of... Captain Drakkar... of the Wyvern's Tail."

Jace was still breathing heavily and talking was difficult. "Dock 17... They are responsible for... stealing the princess' crown!"

That got the guards' attention. One guard, whose uniform had more stripes than the others, ordered his men to pursue the men and hold them for questioning. Then the man walked over to him and Jace viewed him in his HUD.

Name: Sergeant Tristram Randle
Race: Human
Level: 25
Profession: Soldier

The sergeant walked over to Jace and looked him over with a critical eye. His eyes took in Jace's uniform and his face grew suspicious. "Who are you? What's your commanding officer's name? And what's this about the princess' tiara."

Jace needed to speak with someone in authority. Someone who might be willing to make a deal with him for the information he had. That was his best chance of staying out of the dungeons.

"I need to speak to the captain," he told the sergeant. "Right now!"

The man laughed mirthlessly. "You expect me to wake up the captain of the guard, before first light? Are you mad?"

The sergeant motioned for some nearby guards and two men came and stood on either side of Jace. Their weapons were at their sides, but they could no doubt bring them to bear instantly.

"Now," said the sergeant. "Let me repeat my questions. Who are you? And who is your commanding officer? Or are you a guardsman at all?"

Jace stood to his full height and tried to summon up all the bluster he had. Hoping his bluff skill would help. "You need to wake up the captain. Tell him I know where the princess' crown is. Tell him it involves treason and possibly even a danger to his majesty."

That shook the sergeant and the guards who looked at one another. Apparently throwing around words like treason and threats to the king got people's attention - especially people sworn to protect the king.

The sergeant bit his lip as he considered what to do. Jace guessed he was weighing which option would get him in the least amount of trouble. Finally, the man decided. "I'll send for the captain. But I warn you, if you are lying, after you face his wrath - you'll face mine."

"Put him in the holding cell in the east tower until the captain gets here," he told the two guards on either side of Jace. Then he motioned to another man, still by the gate. "Corporeal, go summon the captain. Tell him it's concerning treason and a threat to the king's life."

"Yes sergeant," the guards responded and shoved Jace toward the closest tower. One guard opened the door while the other prodded him inside.

The tower was square and the room he entered took up the entire inner space of the tower. It had a table near the door with several simple wood chairs around it and stairs that lead up to a second floor. Under the stairs was a barred area that appeared to be the cell. It was maybe three feet deep and the entire length of the staircase. On the floor was what looked like woven mat.

Taking a large key from the wall, the first guard opened the cell door while the second guard kept a sharp eye on Jace and then prodded him inside. Once he was inside, the door was locked, and the key replaced back on the wall.

Jace had gone into the cell obediently. He could have used his *Vanish* skill to disappear, run up the stairs and then jump over the wall. He might even have made it. But he needed to stay if he were to put his plan into motion and finish his quests.

After Jace sat down on the thin mat in the cell, the two guards who had escorted took seats at the table. They leaned in and began talking, occasionally casting glances at their prisoner. He didn't mind.

Ignoring the guards, Jace sent a mental message to Luna. "I'm in the Noble District. Captured by guard. Tell the girls not to worry. Hopefully, I'll see them in the morning at the inn."

"Yes," Luna's reply came almost immediately.

Mentally kicking himself, he belatedly asked. "Are you and Mika okay?"

"Yes."

At least Mika was okay. Thinking of her made him think of their kiss and that both confused and excited him. He wasn't used to having one girl interested in him, let alone two girls. It was confusing and flattering and he had no idea what to do about it.

He also thought of Drakkar. How had the former guildmaster become the captain of a pirate ship? He'd defeated the man in a challenge just over a week ago in Crossroads. The scoundrel had broken the rules and killed Charlena before disappearing. Jace really hadn't given the man any more thought.

Now, Drakkar was back. Not only was he back, but he had somehow gotten his hands on the princess' crown. How had he managed that? Jace wondered if the answers were in the captain's logs, he'd found but that would have to wait. He didn't want to bring them out in front of the guards.

He mulled over the various possibilities he could think of for what seemed like hours. Some of his scenarios made more sense than others and, in the end,, he just gave up and waited for the captain. And he waited.

He waited long enough that Jace wondered if the captain would ever appear. Several times, he'd thought about checking the time, but he had slipped the gnomish timepiece into his inventory when they first put him in the cell. After all, he was about to accuse Tiebaut of treason. No reason to be seen wearing a timepiece that belonged to the man.

Finally, the door opened, and a man walked into the room. This man was dressed in polished plate mail armor that, although shiny, had been dented in many places. Over the plate armor, he wore a tabard with the royal crest. Around his waist, he wore a sword belt with a long sword hanging in a scabbard on his right hip. He was a knight.

The guards stood as the recent arrival stepped in and saluted him. "Sir Villiame!"

Sir Villiame dismissed them with a wave of his hands. "It's too early for formalities, men. I'm here to escort the prisoner to Captain Avolin."

Jace frowned at being called "prisoner." He hoped he wasn't really a prisoner and that he wasn't bound for the dungeons, but he'd known that was a possibility when he'd thought of this plan. He'd have to wait and see.

The guards unlocked the cell and motioned Jace out. One guard looked to Sir Villiame. "Do you want him shackled?"

The knight gave Jace a pointed look. "We're not going to need those, are we?"

Jace shook his head. He had no desire to be shackled. That would make escaping more complicated.

"Good, let's make this as civilized as possible," Sir Villiame smiled and motioned for him to go out the door. "This way, please."

He went out the door and found four other knights waiting for him. These men were dressed identically to Sir Villiame and took up positions on each side of Jace. But that wasn't all he noticed. The sun was peeking over the ocean to the east, turning the sky into a tapestry of oranges, reds, and pinks.

Sir Villiame moved to the front of the front of the procession and motioned them forward. "All right then, let's get this done with."

Jace had no choice but to follow the knights as they led him through Noble District to the east. It only took him a few minutes to realize where they were headed. The knights were leading to the castle.

He was going to the Royal Palace.

Chapter 30

Just as the Noble District was walled and elevated above the rest of Whitecliff, the Royal Palace was walled and elevated from the Noble District. Saying it was the Royal Palace was not accurate. It was more like a sprawling castle where the palace itself was just one part.

The castle only had one entrance that was accessible by a bridge. He was escorted over the bridge and through the open gates, into the castle itself. As he crossed through the gates, Jace realized just how large the castle really was. It was a miniature city and was bustling with activity.

The palace itself was what truly dominated the castle however. It was a large, squat building that looked very little like the old fairy tale castles. It was much more sprawling and lacked the high, round towers that one normally associated with fantasy castles. Whitecliff's castle was a more practical, easily defendable structure.

Looking at it, Jace realized the enormity of his task. Even when he finally figured out a way into the castle, it would take him days, maybe even a week, to search the entire castle. Would he really be able to avoid notice for an entire week?

Jace had to bring his mind back to his current situation. Following his escort, he soon found himself at the large stone building that was adjacent to the western wall. The building was nondescript except for several large banners which displayed the royal coat of arms that fluttered on its walls.

Two guards manning the double doors at the entrance reached over and opened them as Sir Villiame and his group approached. They didn't salute or otherwise speak but simply stood at the side of either door at attention. These weren't just common soldiers. They were the Royal Guard. And now Jace was entering their stronghold. If he didn't play his cards right, he might not be leaving.

That thought was still in his mind when his group halted in front of the large wooden door. Villiame knocked and after a moment a voice from inside answered. "Yes?"

The knight opened the door to reveal a large, sparsely decorated room with a large wooden desk that dominated the room. Behind the desk sat a gray haired man with a short, well-tended beard and piercing gray eyes. Like the knights with Jace, this man was clad in shiny but obviously used armor. There was nothing to distinguish him from the other knights except an undeniable air of command. Jace guessed this was the captain.

To the right of the captain was a gnomish wizard, dressed in robes. Jace guessed the robes were made of silk or some other expensive material but were plain except for the royal crest sewn into the right breast.

On the captain's left was a stern looking woman with glowing gold eyes. He recognized her as a nephilim, a playable race that had a divine spark. She was dressed in robes as well but judging by the large golden symbol of the god, Tholtar, he guessed she was a priestess. He remembered Tholtar was the god of truth, honor and duty and was favored by guardsmen.

To be sure, Jace checked them out in his HUD:

Captain Gabrien Avolin (Hero)
Race: Human
Level: 90
Profession: Paladin

Jirbavog Noomwagurt (Hero)
Race: Gnome
Level: 85
Profession: Paladin

High Priestess Cristene Richenza (Hero)
Race: Nephilim
Level: 90
Profession: Cleric

As he suspected, these were all very high level, boss NPCs. Even if Jace had wanted to try and escape, he'd have no chance against them. He had no choice but to stick with his original plan. The priestess did complicate things. Depending on which god or goddess they served, some priests had the ability to detect lies. Given that she was a cleric of Tholtar. God of truth, he guessed that was her main purpose here. He'd need to watch his words.

"Ah yes," the captain. "Our guest has finally arrived. Thank you Sir Villiame. You may leave him here and wait outside."

"Yes Sir," the knight said and then he and his fellow knights left the room, shutting the door as they went.

Looking at the three people on the opposite side of the room, Jace suddenly began to doubt the chances of his idea. He had been hoping that he'd have a few words with the captain, hand over the tiara, tell them about Tiebaut and then he'd be on his way. Now, he'd need to think quickly to stay out of the dungeons.

"Have a seat," the captain gestured to the chair opposite him.

Jace walked over and sat in the chair and looked at the faces of the people around him. Each of them had serious expressions.

The captain leaned forward and looked at some notes on his desk. "My report says you claim to be on, and I quote, 'the king's business.' You also said to one of our sergeants that, and I am paraphrasing this time, that you know where the princess' crown is and that there is treason and danger to his majesty."

"Possible danger," Jace corrected.

The captain seemed unphased by Jace's interruption and nodded. "Very well, possible danger to the king."

The captain looked Jace up and down. "You appear to be wearing the uniform of a royal guardsman and yet, I do not believe you are a guardsman. If I am wrong, simply tell me the name of your commanding officer and I will have them come in here right now and verify your identity."

Jace knew his ruse was up and willed the magic of his hat to return him to his normal appearance. None of the people across the desk showed even the slightest hint of surprise.

"That's better," the captain said. "So, who are you?"

"I am called Dedrurrurth," Jace replied, remembering to use his character name.

"And who are you Dedrurrurth?" the man asked, leaning towards him.

Thinking fast, Jace brought out his charter from the adventurers guild. "I'm a mercenary with the adventurers guild."

The captain glanced at the charter and then called out for Sir Villiame. "Sir Villiame, have one of your men get someone in authority from the adventurers guild and bring them here."

"Yes, Captain," the knight said and then left the room again.

"We'll know soon if that is legitimate," the man said and then narrowed his eyes. "In the meantime, do you actually know where the princess' tiara is? Or was that another ruse?"

Jace pulled out the round box that contained the princess' tiara. He set it on the desk and slid it towards the captain. "It's right there."

Captain Avolin glanced at the gnome. The wizard stared at the box intently for a moment and then looked back to the captain. "I sense no traps."

Nodding, the gray haired man reached over and removed the lid to reveal the tiara inside. He replaced the lid and then handed the box to the gnomish wizard. "Jirbavog, can you have this authenticated with the dwarves."

Taking the offered box, the gnome nodded. "Right away, Gabrien."

The gnome then cast a spell that Jace had seen many times before, a teleportation spell, and disappeared.

Captain Avolin looked back at Jace, his face impassive. "And how did you come by the princess' tiara."

"I stole it," Jace admitted and the captain raised an eyebrow. "From the pirates who I believe had originally taken it."

"Are these the same pirates that you claimed," the captain leaned forward and glanced down at the parchment on his desk. "Were under the command of a Captain Drakkar of the *Wyvern's Tail*?"

Jace nodded, impressed at the level of information that the man had been given. "Yes."

"And you stole it from these pirates?" Avolin asked.

"Yes," Jace answered and suddenly felt like Luna with her one word answers.

The captain nodded again. "Why did you steal it from them? Why didn't you tell the guard about it?"

He glanced at the cleric, who was just watching him and knew he needed to tell the truth. But that didn't mean he needed to tell the truth, the whole truth and nothing but the truth. At least, he hoped not. He wasn't about to say that he stole the crown because the guildmaster of the thieves guild told him to. Instead, he answered the second question.

"I didn't tell the guards because I wasn't sure who I could trust," Jace said. "There's a conspiracy."

The captain looked skeptical. "A conspiracy? Is this the treason you spoke of?"

"Yes," Jace nodded. "Lord… I mean, Sir Tiebaut arranged to have the tiara stolen."

Both the man's eyebrows went up at that. He looked at the priestess who nodded. "You are accusing Sir Tiebaut of being involved in this? What proof do you have?"

Jace was now walking on thin ice. He couldn't exactly tell the captain of the Royal Guard that he'd broken into Tiebaut's house and read his datebook. He needed to be careful what he said and how he said it since he was now sure that the priestess could detect lies. "I was hunting alligators in the sewer…"

Both the people in the room shot him curious looks at the mention of alligators in the sewer.

"It was a job for the adventurers guild," he explained. "Anyway, I was down there trying to find the bos… the bull gator… when I happened upon a meeting between Captain Drakkar and Sir Tiebaut. That's where I learned that Sir Tiebaut had ordered the thing stolen and it appeared that Captain Drakkar actually stole it from whoever Tiebaut originally hired and was renegotiating with him."

The captain once again looked to the high priestess and she nodded. At that the captain's brow furrowed. "Do you have any other proof?"

Briefly, he thought of the note he'd found requesting a meeting, but he'd given that to Webley. "No, I don't have any other proof."

"And why didn't you bring this matter to the guard?" the captain asked.

Gesturing to the captain, Jace replied. "Look at your reaction. No one would have believed my word over his. And I might have been thrown into the dungeon just for making such an accusation."

Everything he said was true. Jace simply neglected to mention that going to the guards had never been an option.

"I see," Avolin said. "There may be some validity to that. Even now, I cannot act on so little proof."

Jace's heart sank at those words. He'd been hoping to get Tiebaut arrested but it didn't look like that was going to happen. He tried to think of anything else he could say when suddenly the gnome appeared in the room.

The tiny wizard set the box on the desk. "I just came from the master crafter himself. He confirmed this is the tiara the king commissioned."

"Thank you, Jirbavog," he smiled. "The king will be pleased. Can you take this to the Royal Counsellor?"

"Wait," Jace said and everyone in the room looked at him. "Would you really like to apprehend Sir Tiebaut, the person who is behind the theft?"

Captain Avolin looked at Jace with a stern expression. "I thought you didn't have any other proof."

Jace smiled. He had suddenly remembered the conversation in the sewer. Tiebaut and Drakkar were supposed to meet tonight. Maybe they could do some sort of sting operation. "I don't. But I know how to get some. Arranging to have the princess' tiara stolen was treason, right?"

The captain nodded. "It is."

"I happen to know that Tiebaut is planning to meet Drakkar to pick up the tiara," Jace said.

"And how do you know about this meeting?" the captain asked, eyes narrowing.

"It was the last thing they said in the sewers," Jace replied. "That they were meeting on Tideday, today, at a warehouse." He thought back to the conversation. "A blue warehouse Mackerel and Anchor. Today at noon."

"And what are you hoping to accomplish," the captain asked, but his voice held a note of curiosity. "Drakkar's ship is gone. The pirates who chased you made it back to their ship and it set sail. He won't be making any meeting."

Jace smiled again. "But Sir Tiebaut doesn't know that. He'll still show up and I can pretend to be one of Drakkar's men, exchanging the tiara. When he does the exchange, your men can grab him. I assume finding him with the tiara would be proof enough, right?"

The captain leaned back in his chair as he considered Jace's plan. Slowly, a smile spread on his face. "That would work." Avolin looked to the priestess. "Would you accompany us to see the truth of the matter?"

"Of course, Captain Avolin," the woman nodded. "It would be my honor."

Captain Avolin turned back to Jace. "Your plan has some merit. If we were to apprehend Tiebaut with the crown, that would be sufficient proof. However, if you can get him to admit his guilt in front of the priestess, that would seal his fate."

"I can try," Jace told him.

The captain's face became stern again. "And what's in this for you?"

Jace glanced at the priestess again. He couldn't tell the real truth: that he wanted to finish a quest so the guildmaster would help him sneak into the Noble District and possibly the Royal Palace itself. Instead, he went with a simpler truth. "I'd really like to not end up in the dungeons."

At that the man chuckled. "I'll see what I can do about that. Now, let's get you ready for the meeting."

Chapter 31

Jace had been taken to another room and given a meal oatmeal and bread. The door had been locked, but Jace was just happy it wasn't a dungeon cell. He'd sent a message to Luna, letting her know he was okay and would hopefully be back there soon.

"Girls worried," was the cat's reply.

"I'll be back soon," he sent her and hoped he wasn't lying. He was about to do a sting operation on a noble and he was trusting the captain to keep his word that they'd let him go afterwards. If not, Jace had already decided he would attack the guards and force them to kill him rather than be stuck in prison. He'd lose all of his equipment but at least he'd be free.

He was kept in the office for hours before Sir Villiame appeared with the dwarf from the adventurers guild, Throdgrug Greydigger. He escorted the sourly dwarf in and pointed to Jace.

"Is he a member of your guild, good master dwarf?" the knight asked.

Throdgrug looked him up and down and then shook his head. "Never seen him before."

The knight gave Jace a disapproving look.

"Wait," Jace blurted out before the dwarf could leave. "We killed the gators that were in the sewer. We brought back the eye and you… uh… ate it."

The dwarf stopped and squinted at Jace and then nodded. "That's right. Yah, him and three women. Brought me an alligator eyeball from a bull gator." The dwarf patted his groin. "Keeps things working!"

The knight gave the dwarf an unreadable look, clearly unsure of how to take his words. Finally, he motioned for the dwarf to leave. "Thank you for your assistance in this matter, good master dwarf."

"Anytime," the dwarf said and then turned back to Jace. "If you get any more of those eyes, you let me know."

The door was shut and locked behind them and Jace was once again left alone for several hours.

At 11:00am, and Jace knew because he'd just stolen a peek at his gnomish timepiece, the knight returned. He motioned for Jace to follow him. "It's time."

He followed the knight out of the building and this time, only two other knights accompanied Jace and Sir Villiame. The four of them left the royal grounds, went back through the Noble District and across the bridge into the city proper.

From the bridge, they went east to the docks and then south to a blue warehouse. It was smaller than Jace had imagined, being only the size of a large inn.

The only real difference was that the warehouse was only one large, open room.

Villiame motioned Jace into the warehouse. The room was littered with old crates, most of which looked like they had been rummaged through long ago and stank of fish. He was sure Tiebaut would find this only slightly better than the sewers.

The knights who had come with him spread out and disappeared behind crates. Villiame walked with him to the center of the warehouse. "We'll be nearby so don't get any ideas of running off with the tiara."

Jace glanced around, looking for the tiara. "Speaking of which…"

Before he could finish his sentence, three figures shimmered into being nearby. It was the captain, the wizard, and the priest. Jace guessed they'd been hidden by a group invisibility spell. He'd used those himself when he was with a group who needed to infiltrate into enemy territory or just wanted to avoid unnecessary fights.

Captain Avolin came forward with the round box that contained the tiara and handed it to Jace. "And he's not the only one who will be around. Just stick to the plan and, if you can, get him to admit being behind it."

Accepting the box, Jace nodded. "I'll try."

Villiame moved off and disappeared behind some of the crates and the captain walked back over the gnome and priest. The wizard waved his hands and they all shimmered and vanished, leaving Jace seemingly alone.

It had taken almost half an hour to get here, which meant he had another half hour to wait. On the off chance that Tiebaut was early, Jace wanted to be ready. Using the magic of his hat, he willed the magic to change his appearance to what he'd seen Drakkar wearing in the sewers. It couldn't make him look like Drakkar, but he should be able to pass as his first mate.

A half an hour later, a man walked cautiously into the warehouse, looking around in disdain. He recognized the man as Tiebaut and saw that he carried a bundle under one arm.

Tiebaut spotted Jace and started toward him. Then the nobleman stopped and eyed Jace with suspicion. "Who are you? Where is Drakkar?"

"Lord Tiebaut?" he asked in his best pirate accent, remembering to call the man Lord instead of Sir.

"Yes? Who are you? Where is Drakkar?" the irate noble demanded.

Jace noticed the man had taken a step back and was afraid he would bolt. He needed to get the man's attention before he left. He knew of only one way to do that for sure. He reached down and pulled the lid off the box and tilted it towards Tiebaut.

"Captain said you wanted this little trinket," he told the man, trying to stay in character. "But if you don't, he said we could find another buyer."

"Wait. What?" Tiebaut said, his eyes drawn to the sparkling tiara. "That's it?"

"Aye," Jace replied. "Captain couldn't make it on account of a certain guild being after him for turning them into the guard."

Tiebaut snickered and seemed to relax. "Yes, I heard about that fiasco in the Luxury District. So, now Drakkar has the guild after him. Better him than me."

Jace saw an opening to talk about the guild and took it. "Drakkar said to warn you that they might be coming after you."

"Ha," the nobleman waved dismissively. "I didn't turn them in."

"No," Jace said. "On account that you hired them first to steal the tiara and then broke the contract."

"Bah," the nobleman scoffed. "That may be true, but the deal was for them to deliver it to me. The way I see it, they broke the contract by not delivering it to me and I had to seek, shall we say, a secondary supplier."

Jace chuckled. "Yeah, that be us."

The noble looked Jace up and down, not even hiding his disapproval. His voice became mocking. "Yes, that be you. Now, hand over the tiara!"

Still in character, Jace shook his head. "Money first, Drakkar's orders. No money, no tiara."

Tiebaut rolled his eyes and brought out the bundle under his arms and unwrapping it, revealed a small chest. "Fine. One million gold in Whitecliff trade bars."

Jace had to work hard to keep the look of shock off his face. A million gold was a fortune. He wondered if there was any way he could arrange to keep the money. Knowing his luck, he doubted it.

Setting the tiara on the ground in front of him and motioned for Tiebaut to do the same with his small chest.

With a look of annoyance, Tiebaut set the small chest on the ground and then looked to Jace. "Now what? Do we dance or something?"

Jace shook his head. "On the count of three, we kick them to each other."

The nobleman let out an exasperated breath. "Fine, fine! Whatever."

He counted down from three to one and then used his foot to slide the box with the tiara over to Tiebaut while the other man kicked the small chest to Jace. The nobleman bent down and picked it up and looked inside. "Finally!"

"Sir Tiebaut," said a commanding voice as Captain Avolin and the others suddenly shimmered into being nearby. "You are under arrest for treason against the crown."

That must have been the queue because Sir Villiame and his men, along with seven other knights Jace hadn't known about, popped out from behind crates and moved to surround Tiebaut.

"You cannot arrest me!" sputtered the red faced Tiebaut. "I am a lord."

"You are a Baronet who just admitted to hiring the thieves guild to steal the princess' crown and then making a deal with pirates to secure it," retorted the captain bluntly. "But you shall get your day in court. Unless the king decided to dispense justice himself."

At the mention of the king's justice, the would-be-lord went white. He became very quiet and didn't struggle when the guards gripped his arms.

"Take him to the tower," Captain Avolin directed and some of the knights escorted him away. Once the nobleman had been escorted out of the warehouse, the captain looked down at the small chest at Jace's feet. He looked at Sir Villiame and nodded at the chest. The knight came forward and picked up the chest.

"Sorry," Avolin said as he caught Jace looking longingly after the million gold. "That's evidence."

"I know," Jace said. For a brief moment, he'd hoped. He'd even considered grabbing it and using his *Vanish* ability to get away but guessed there was probably some sort of magical defense around the place at the moment.

"I have to admit," the captain said. "I didn't really think that would work. I thought Tiebaut would be too smart for so simple a plan."

Jace grinned. "It was the pirate accent that sold it."

The captain shrugged and then his face became hard. "Perhaps. Now, about our little deal."

Looking up, Jace suddenly felt worry in the pit of his stomach. Was the captain going to throw him into the dungeons after all? Had Jace misjudged the man?

"You are free to go with our thanks," the man said. "But… don't let me catch you impersonating a royal guardsman again."

Relieved, Jace bobbed his head up and down. "Definitely not!"

"Well then," the captain said and looked to the gnome. "I think we're done here. Jirbavog, can you do the honors."

The remaining knights, the captain, and the priestess all moved in close to the little gnome. The wizard waved his hands and then they all disappeared with a pop. When they did, Jace let out a sigh of relief. He'd done it.

Jace had stolen back the crown, gotten Drakkar and his ship banned from the city and had gotten Tiebaut to take the fall. He just hoped it would satisfy

Webley's quests. But before he went to the guild, he needed to check in with the girls.

Chapter 32

Mika and Diana were waiting for him outside the inn when he arrived, as was Luna. The two girls threw their arms around him and gave him hugs, one on each arm, while Luna walked in and out of his legs, rubbing against him.

Jace moved them into the inn. He ordered some waffles for them all and some fish for Luna with the money he'd stolen from Drakkar. Then, he spent the rest of the afternoon recounting the entire story. For Diana's sake, he started when he and Mika had gone to the thieves guild and ended with him helping to set up Sir Tiebaut.

In the process, he remembered the saber he'd taken from Drakkar and retrieved it from his inventory. Jace thought it looked more like cutlass than a saber, the type that was typically carried by pirates. Its basket style guard was engraved with the image of a tentacled sea monster and a gaping maul. Jace examined it in his HUD.

Kraken's Claw
Type: Saber
Level: (9)
Damage: (10) + (3) (Legendary) + (1) (Sharp)
Wt: 3 lb

Special: This item is Legendary and scales to the wielder's level. In addition to normal damage, blows from this weapon inflict an additional (3) Acid damage. This weapon also carries the Puncturing quality and ignores 1 Defense.
Description: Forged in the heart of a volcano, the smith who created this blade is rumored to have embedded it with a fragment of the soul from the legendary Kraken.
Soulbound: This item has been soulbound. It cannot be sold or traded and appears in the wielder's inventory when they respawn.

"Holy-" Jace began but couldn't continue. He had found a legendary weapon. Legendary gear were the rarest weapons in the game. They dropped from time to time in raids but otherwise you normally had more chance winning the lottery than finding one.

The main reason they were so rare and sought after was not only because they were powerful, but because they scaled to the wielder's level. As Jace gained levels, the saber would grow more powerful - all the way to level 100. Not only would its damage increase, but it may even grant additional special abilities.

"What?!" both girls demanded. "What is it?"

Jace held out the sword so they could examine it.

Diana just looked at it and shrugged. "Is that good?"

Mika had more experience and must have known what a legendary item was. Her eyes grew wide as she must have read the description. "You have a legendary weapon! This is very powerful!"

Jace and Mika took turns explaining the legendary weapons and the scaling properties of the weapon, as well as how soulbound items worked. When they finished the older woman seemed to grasp most of it.

"So," Diana said, "this is like Excalibur? It's basically some sort of super weapon?"

Shrugging Jace slipped the sword into its scabbard at his side. "Something like that. The higher level I become, the more powerful the saber will become."

"That does seem handy," Diana agreed.

"Very powerful," Mika added.

"Speaking of leveling up," Jace checked his timepiece. It was 5pm. They had another hour before Charlena would log in. "Mika, let's go turn in our quests and hope that we get credit for both of them. Diana, can you head to the adventurers guild, in case Charlena logs in early."

"The adventurers guild?" Diana gave him a quizzical look.

"Remember, that's where she logged off last night," he told her.

"Oh," Diana nodded. "That's right. After the groll shaman."

"While you're there, can you check out the board and see if there are any level 5, 6, or 7 quests we can do later?" he asked.

Diana gave him a wink. "Anything for you, dear one."

They all left the inn then and went to the Merchant District. Once there, Diana split off and went to the adventurers guild, while Jace and Mika went to the thieves guild.

They found the fabric shop again and, after doing the secret knock, the two of them were admitted in. This time, Mika did not hug either of the panda-kin but did give them a huge grin and a wave. Jace was surprised to see both of them wave back.

Inside, they found Webley at one of the tables. When he saw them, he nodded to the stairs and then followed them up. He slipped past them on the second floor and motioned them into his office. When they were all seated, he spoke.

"I half expected not to see you again," Webley started. "Word on the dock was that a group of pirates were seen chasing someone away from the ship."

"But then, I heard another rumor that someone had turned over the tiara to the guard," the guildmaster said with a pointed expression. "As you can imagine, that caused me no small amount of concern."

The guildmaster paused and looked between Jace Mika. "But then I heard that Sir Tiebaut had been arrested with the tiara in a warehouse down by the docks. Not only that, but Captain Drakkar and his ship are now persona non grata in Whitecliff."

"So, what I'd really like to know," Webley said, "is what in Dolorea's name is going on?"

Jace and Mika looked at each other and then Jace relayed the story. He also included the fact that Captain DD was actually Dainard Drakkar, the former guildmaster of Crossroads. It took him nearly half an hour to get through the entire tale but finally he got to the bit where he'd help set up Tiebaut.

"So," Webley said after taking a moment to digest everything. "You did retrieve the tiara and you ended up getting Tiebaut arrested. I'd say you more than satisfied my requests. It looks like I owe you both some gold."

At that point, the guildmaster turned to Mika. "And I'd like to officially welcome you to the guild. After that story, I'd be a fool not to have someone like you around. Besides, you two make a good team."

Mika looked over at Jace with a big grin. "Yes, we do!"

You have completed the quest, "Rescue the Princess' Tiara"
You gain 900 experience. Experience to next level 980.
You gain +100 faction with Whitecliff Thieves Guild

You have completed the quest, "Turnabout is Fair Play"
You gain 900 experience. Experience to next level 80.
You gain +100 faction with Whitecliff Thieves Guild

Jace saw the system message and grinned. He was only 80 experience away from level 4 in Mage.

Webley handed over a pouch of gold for each of them and slid two pieces of thieves guild armor to Mika.

"Thank you," she said and accepted the armor.

"I'm assuming you would both like some additional jobs?" he asked with a smile.

Mika and Jace both nodded.

"As it happens," he told them. "Rumors of the raid on the guild have caused some of our clients who pay for protection to get a little bold. We need to remind them that we are still here and that they need the protection of the guild."

Mika looked confused but Jace nodded. He'd seen enough vidstreams to know a protection racket when he heard it. He leaned over to Mika and whispered, "I'll explain it later."

"I want you to hit two businesses tonight and make off with whatever you can," he told them. "There's two of you so I want you to really clean them out. That should send a message to the others to keep paying."

The guildmaster explained the targets as a pawn shopped called Broken Mirror Pawn and a bookstore called the Dusty Tome. Immediately, Jace received the quests.

Webley the Snake has offered your group the quest, "Pawn Broke"
Reward: +50 faction with Whitecliff Thieves Guild, 50 gold.
Level: 3
Accept quest? (Yes or No)

Webley the Snake has offered your group the quest, "Overdue Books"
Reward: +50 faction with Whitecliff Thieves Guild, 50 gold.
Level: 3
Accept quest? (Yes or No)

Jace noticed the quests were now being given out at Mika's level, rather than his level. That was disappointing. He would have earned three times the experience had it been based on his level. Then he realized it might be better this way since they didn't want to outpace Charlena again.

Once they had their quests, the guildmaster wished them good luck and Jace and Mika left the guild. By then it was almost 6pm and they headed straight for the adventurers guild.

Charlena was logged in by the time Jace and Mika made it to the guild and the red-headed elf hugged Jace and gave him a quick kiss. For some reason this made him feel guilty and he purposefully made himself not look at Mika.

"I heard you had a busy night!" Charlena said.

"You could say that." He nodded.

"I'm glad you came when you did," she said. "I can't play tonight. A bunch of my friends are getting together so I have to do the real world thing tonight. I just logged in quickly to let you know."

Jace was disappointed but he forced a smile. "That's okay, you go do the real world thing."

Charlena gave him a mischievous grin and for just a moment, he thought she glanced at Mika. "We can both do the real world thing when you wake up."

He knew she was referring to his body, at least he hoped it was his body, still in a coma. If Charlena was right, she'd found his body. They'd know for certain when she went on Friday to ID the body.

Once again Jace was reminded that his real body was probably in a long-term medical pod hooked up to the game to keep his mind stimulated. That brought back worries of what sort of shape his real body was in. He could think of a number of worse case scenarios like paralyzation, disfiguration and several others. He had to force himself to think of something else or he'd start becoming depressed.

"Well," Charlena said, breaking him back to the present moment. "I'm logging off now! You guys have fun!"

With that, she stepped forward and kissed Jace again. Like she'd done before, she logged out while they were still kissing, leaving Jace in an awkward pose for a moment until he felt her disappear.

Slightly embarrassed, Jace stood straight and looked at the other two girls. Mika's face was unreadable, but Diana just smirked.

The older woman just shook her head. "So, now what? Do we do solo quests all night?"

Jace shrugged. "We're not in a hurry and Mika and I have to wait until dark to do our quests. If you want, we can go to an inn or pub and have a nice slow meal for a change."

"Oh," Diana said and her arm into his. "It's been a while since a handsome man has asked me out to dinner. What do you say, Mika? Should we go out too?"

Mika seemed to brighten at his suggestion. She walked to Jace's other side and, mirroring Diana's move, slipped her arm in Jace's. "Yes, let's go out."

Chapter 33

They were already in a Merchant District and tried to find a tavern or inn nearby. Within a few minutes, they had stumbled upon a large, two story tavern…

"This is where the dwarf asked us to come," Mika said, pointing at the large sign in the shape of a tankard.

Diana and Jace looked up at the sign. In painted letters, it read: Twisted Tankard Tavern.

"Think you're right, dear one," Diana agreed.

"Let's go in!" Mika said excitedly.

Shrugging, Jace opened the door for them and chuckled as Luna went running in first. He guessed she was expecting to get some fish.

The girls went inside and Jace was about to follow them when he felt a sharp pain in his chest.

Twyla Harlande uses Surprise Attack on YOU for 213 damage.
You have died.

One moment, Jace was reaching for his chest, and the next moment he was in ghost form.

Insubstantial, he stared down as a woman clad in nondescript leathers withdrew the dagger from his back and quickly sliced off his right ear.

Involuntarily, he reached for his ghost ear, but he was a ghost now and couldn't even touch himself. Looking back down, he saw the woman take the gear, step back and vanish. Seconds later, Mika poked her head out the door and saw his body.

"Jace!" she screamed and rushed over to him.

He wanted to tell her he'd be respawning but as a ghost, he couldn't interact with the normal game world. He'd have to respawn and then explain things to them. He selected the option to respawn and the world shifted around him.

The next thing he knew, he was gasping for air as he appeared in the Whitecliff cemetery. He sat up and looked around, still dazed from the abrupt shift in scenery. Around, he saw other players respawning and running off.

He reached up to his right ear and, although he knew it should be there, was relieved to actually feel it back in place. Player's bodies couldn't be permanently disfigured and whenever you respawned, you received a brand-new body in perfect shape.

Jace stayed in the seated position and gritted his teeth as he re-summoned Luna. It had been a while since he'd had to, and the pain was sharper than he remembered. It still felt like someone had jabbing a hook into his guts and was slowly, painfully yanking it out. Ignoring the pain, he pushed all of the mana and health he could into her.

Luckily, it didn't last long and his familiar appeared nearby. Like him, Luna was momentarily confused by the abrupt change. For her, a moment ago she'd been in the tavern. Now she was in the graveyard. She looked disappointedly at Jace. "Fish?"

He chuckled despite himself. "Don't worry, we'll go get fish. It just looks like we'll be walking there naked. Well, not exactly naked. A player could only get truly naked if they initiated intimate contact with another player or NPC. Otherwise, male characters always received a loin cloth and female characters received a loin cloth and a chest wrap that covered their breasts.

Remembering his soulbound weapon, Jace checked his inventory. Sure enough, the Kraken's Claw was there. At least when he respawned, he wouldn't be completely defenseless.

Pushing himself to his feet, Jace padded towards the front gate with Luna trailing after him. He tried to ignore the stones and twigs that dug into his bare feet but at 100% sensation, it was difficult.

Jace jogged past the guards. Apparently, they were used to players running by in loincloths. Or possibility, part of the AI that controlled them were programmed to ignore mostly naked players. Either way, they ignored him.

As he jogged, Jace thought back to the person who had killed him. He'd never seen them before, but he knew who the person was. Or should he say, he knew WHAT she was. She was an assassin. And she'd assassinated Jace.

When he'd played Mordred, he'd been part of the assassin's guild. Whenever he took a contract, he was required to bring back their right ear to prove he'd fulfilled the contract. The assassin had cut off his ear, which meant she had been fulfilling a contract. Jace frowned. He started to wonder who would have taken a contract out on him but then realized who it must be. Drakkar.

The pirate must have hired the assassin's guild to kill Jace. Jace smiled as he jogged. He wished he could be there when Drakkar realized he was alive. He'd love to see the expression on the man's face.

Finally, Jace made it back to the Twisted Tankard Tavern. Mika was still kneeling over his body, but Diana just leaned against the wall nearby.

"About time you get back," Diana said. "This one's been worried you wouldn't come back."

Mika looked up, saw him, and dashed forward to wrap him in a tight embrace. Then, she stepped back. "I am glad you are alive! We didn't know what happened to you!"

Jace gave her a smile and then stepped to his body and looted it. As he did, he gave the girls a serious look. "It was an assassin. Apparently, someone took out a contract on me. Three guesses who that might be?"

"The evil captain!" Mika spat.

"Wait! You can take contracts out on players?" Diana asked. She seemed shocked at the very idea.

Nodding, Jace finished equipping his gear and stood up as his old body faded away. "You can. Obviously, it doesn't have lasting results like it would with an NPC, but we can be killed and that ends the contract."

"So, what's the point?" Diana asked.

"If it's a player who puts out the contract on another player, it's usually to annoy them," Jace said. "Plus, starting at level 10, we'll get a death debuff when we die. It gets steadily worse, the higher level you are. At 90+, it can prevent you from doing much of anything while you have it and it lasts almost a week. I've heard of high-level raiders taking out contracts on other raiders so they could get their spot."

"That sounds barbaric," Diana said, not bothering to hide her disdain.

Jace couldn't help but agree. "Yes, raids are a serious business - literally. If you loot the right item, you could literally make millions of gold by selling it to a buyer who really wants it."

"That almost makes it more crass," Diana said and then lapsed into silence.

"Let's hope that's the last assassin that comes after Jace," Mika cut in. "We must be on our guard!"

Jace nodded but he doubted being on their guard would have made any difference. Judging by the amount of damage the assassin had done with their Surprise Attack, he guessed the assassin had been at least level 30. None of them would have stood a chance. Even all of them working together wouldn't have been able to bring the assassin down.

"Do you still feel like eating?" Diana asked him.

"Fish!" Luna chimed in, causing them to chuckle.

"Yes," he replied, but then quickly added. "But I think I'll sit with my back against the wall."

They went inside the tavern and found a table against the wall. Jace tried to relax, but after the assassin, he was on his guard. He would have liked to downed a few meads or something even stronger, but he and Mika had jobs to do later and the effects of the game-induced intoxication could last for hours.

Once their food came, the three of them ate in silence for a long while. Finally, Mika spoke up. "Will there be more assassins?"

Jace finished chewing a bite of his steak and then shook his head. "I don't think so. Now that the assassin has killed me, technically the contract is complete. Drakkar will receive the ear and he'll assume I'm dead."

"But what if he finds out you're still alive?" she asked.

"He shouldn't," Jace replied. "Both he and his ship are banned from Whitecliff and branded as outlaws and pirates. With any luck, we'll never see him again."

"Because we've been so lucky so far," Diana added, her voice dripping with sarcasm.

"Even if he does find out, the most he could do is send another assassin after me and that would just mean respawning. At least, until I hit level 10. Even then, the death penalty at lower levels isn't so bad and it goes away fairly quickly."

"We must stay on our guard," Mika insisted.

"You're right, we should," Jace agreed.

They lapsed back into silence as they continued eating. Jace noticed that Luna had finished up her fish and had curled up in the chair next to him and fallen asleep. Absently, he reached over and stroked the cat's fur. She stirred a little but then began to purr.

"Have you made any progress on getting into the Noble District or the palace?" Diana asked after a few bites.

"Yes," Jace replied. He realized he hadn't told them about his deal with the guildmaster. "I made a deal with Webley. He'll use his contact to get us into the Noble District. But it's a one-time favor, so we can't use it until we know for certain how to get into the palace."

"What about the birthday party you told us about?" Diana said. "Is there a way we could get invited to it?"

Jace shook his head. "Parties in the Noble District, and especially the Royal Palace, are for nobles only. Those types of events are basically a reward for the players who have paid outrageous amounts of money to buy titles. Even in the game, there are have's and have not's."

"So, it's like a country club?" Diana suggested. "Buy a membership for an absurd price to get access to the golf course. Then, there's member only activities as well."

Having never been to a country club, Jace had no idea but it sounded like an apt analogy. "I guess so."

Diana looked wistful. "Once we get this all sorted out and I get my money back, maybe I'll buy a minor title. I've always wanted to be a countess."

Jace and Mika both stared at the woman. Jace wondered just how much money Diana had. If she could really buy a title, she must have millions of dollars. Or maybe she was just joking.

The little group lapsed back into silence then as each of them finished up their meals. Soon they were done, and they split up to do their nightly questing.

Chapter 34

Jace and Mika's job went well and they each earned an additional 300 gold in stolen loot that they pawned at the Black Market. Like Jace's previous breaking and entering quests, Luna had been their lookout.

The two of them had broken in, robbed the place blind and then quickly left. Working together, he'd quickly finished both jobs and turned them in back at the guild house. The experience from the quests pushed him into level 5 in Mage. It wasn't much of a gain, but he didn't want to outpace Charlena and have to switch to another class.

Mika earned level 3 in Rogue and received the *Backstab* ability. Jace thought it could be great to see her *Backstab* something with her katana but then remembered it could only be used with piercing weapons. Jace doubted he could talk her into using a pike or a spear.

Jace took the opportunity at the Black Market to pick up a replacement for his lost grapple and rope. At his suggestion, Mika picked up a grapple and some picks. She hadn't picked any locks before so he also found a large padlock, he could use to teach her.

They checked back in with Webley, but he had no other jobs for that evening and told them to come back tomorrow night. With nothing else to do in the guild house, they decided to head back to the inn.

After they left the thieves guild, he paid back the money he borrowed from Mika for the gnomish rockets. She'd tried to refuse but Jace was insistent. He showed her that he had plenty of money left from what he'd taken from Drakkar.

What finally convinced her was pointing out the fact that the more their money was spread out, the less they would lose if one of them lost their body. Jace sensed she was a practical person at heart and when he put in those terms, she had relented and accepted the money.

It was just after midnight when they reached the inn. The main dining room was closed so they slipped up the stairs and went into their room. Jace hadn't really spent any time in the room but found that it was actually decently sized and nicely furnished.

As Diana requested, there was only a single large, canopy bed in the center of the room. At the foot of the bed was an oversized chest to store belongings. To the right of the bed was a small table with two chairs. To the left was a large metal tub that looked large enough to fit two people. Then he remembered, this room was the honeymoon suite.

"Not bad," Jace commented as he walked in.

"Yes," Mika agreed. "Diana and I waited up here until breakfast a couple of days."

Nodding, Jace let himself fall onto the bed. He was surprised at just how soft the mattress. He closed his eyes for a moment but found that his brain didn't slow down nor did his body feel any need to sleep at all.

"I have tried to sleep," Mika told him. "Even as a monster. I would try to sleep, hoping I would wake up from this dream. It never worked. It still does not. Now I know it is because I am dead."

Jace opened his eyes and turned over to face Mika. She had seated herself in one of the chairs at the little table and was looking at him. "How do you feel about being dead?"

"It makes me sad," she said. "But I think I have accepted it."

Jace nodded and waited for her to continue. They hadn't really talked about much since they'd been reunited in Whitecliff and he hoped she'd open up to him.

"I had very few friends. I owned a small fashion shop where I made and sold my own clothing," Mika continued. "When I wasn't running the shop, I was making new clothes. Not time or money for going out."

"You're a fashion designer?" he asked. Other than programming and gaming skills, like lockpicking, Jace didn't possess any other real skills. He was intrigued that she could not only come up with the ideas for new clothes, but then make them as well.

"Seamstress," Mika corrected.

"But you designed your own clothes?"

"Yes."

"I think that makes you a fashion designer," he said and then remembering she was from Japan, he added. "At least in America you'd be a fashion designer. Here a seamstress is someone who sews clothes from a pattern and hems or repairs clothes."

Mika considered that for a moment and then smiled. "Yes, fashion designer sounds better than seamstress too! But I did not make much, like a real fashion designer. I made enough to pay the rent on my shop and to buy more cloth, supplies and groceries."

Jace nodded. "I was sort of in the same boat. I made enough to get by but that was it." Suddenly he remembered the armor she'd made him. "Wait. Is that why you worked on your crafting skills?"

"Yes," she replied. "It is not so different. Just much faster."

"That's really neat," he told her. Other than *Poisonmaking* as Mordred, he'd never bothered with the crafting skills. If she kept up with her skills, she could actually make some decent in-game money. Player crafted gear became more and more powerful at the end, but she'd need to learn enchanting to make the real money.

Jace realized they'd gotten off the topic of her former life and how she was dealing with being dead.

He was about to ask her another question when the door opened, and Diana walked in.

"Oh," Diana exclaimed, momentarily startled. "I didn't expect anyone else. Usually, you two show up around breakfast time."

"We finished early," Jace told her.

The older woman came and plopped down on the bed next to Jace. Her body was touching his and she turned, their faces only inches apart, to give him a seductive smile. She held his gaze for a moment before gracing Mika a far less flirtatious grin.

The closeness of her voluptuous body both made Jace uncomfortable and excited. Despite the fact that hcr mind might be in its 90s, her virtual body was that of an extremely well-proportioned 25-year-old and his own body was reacting to it. He wondered if she'd done that purposefully, just to play with him.

Regardless of the reason, he rolled over a bit to put a little space between them. With more distance between them, he looked over at Diana. "Did you get some quests done?"

"What did you do?" Mika asked.

Diana dismissed her question with a gesture. "More matchmaking. Apparently, that seems to be what her priests do. Matchmaking and relationship counselling. I thought there'd be more sex involved."

Mika's cheeks turned slightly pink but Jace just rolled his eyes. "They probably gave the quests parameters, knowing not everyone would be okay with virtual sex. Or maybe those are reserved for Moureva, the goddess of lust."

"Ohh," Diana purred. "Now that sounds more up my alley. Why didn't you tell me about her before?"

Jace grinned. "Because she's also the goddess of lies, betrayal and jealousy. She's considered an evil goddess and you won't find a temple in the good lands."

Dian pouted. "More's the pity. Sounds like fun."

"Probably not as much as you think," Jace shrugged. "It's probably just the opposite. You're probably breaking up relationships."

Diana looked wistful and lapsed into silence and Mika didn't seem to want to talk as openly with the other woman in the room. Instead, he reviewed their plan and tried to brainstorm with the girls on ideas to get into the Royal Palace. Unfortunately, none of them came up with anything new.

Hours later, Luna reminded them that it was breakfast time by asking for more fish. They decided to move their conversation down to the dining room and they all ordered waffles. Jace had just taken the first bite of his when a commotion by the door grabbed his attention.

There were three armored men just inside the door of the inn and they were speaking to the very nervous looking dwarf proprietor. As he took in their armor and their tabards, Jace realized they were knights.

"We are looking for Dedrurrurth," announced the leader of the knights and Jace exchanged a worried glance with Mika. Had the guard somehow found out they'd robbed the houses? The proprietor pointed at their table and Jace swore silently.

Under the table, he produced his sack of coins and shoved into Diana's hands. She took it but gave him a confused look.

"In case I get imprisoned," he told her, and she nodded. If this was about one of the jobs, he'd done for the thieves guild they might imprison him. If that happened, he might need to find a way to kill himself. He'd lose his corpse and all of his possessions, except for the Kraken's Claw, but at least his money would be safe.

The knights stopped in front of the table and looked down at Jace. "Dedrurrurth?"

Jace nodded. "I'm Dedrurrurth."

"I must ask you to come with me," the knight ordered him with a deadpan voice.

Jace stood up and scanned the guards. They were each level 40 and Jace realized he had no chance at all to overpower them. He saw Mika's face go grim and her hand drop down to her katana.

He gave her a slight shake of his head and mouthed the word "No." Her heart might be in a good place, but these knights were beyond any of them.

"This way," the knight gestured back towards the door.

"I'll be back," Jace told the girls and then turned towards the door. The knights neither contradicted him nor confirm his assertion, so Jace walked to the door. The other patrons stared at him, most likely wondering what he'd done to warrant attention from the Royal Guard.

When they got outside, the men formed up around him. The lead knight moved in front of him, while the other two knights went to either side.

"Where are you taking me?" he asked as they began marching to the south.

The knights didn't answer him, so Jace tried again. "Come on, don't I at least deserve to know where we're going?"

The lead knight stopped so abruptly, Jace almost walked into him but stopped himself just in time. The man spun around, his face inches from Jace's own. "We are taking you to the palace."

Jace gulped as he tried to imagine what they wanted from him. Did they need more information about the tiara? Had they found out his real involvement with it? Did they know he was a member of the thieves guild?

The questions hit Jace one after another in rapid fire. The knight spun back around and just before they started off again, he spoke again. "The king would like a word with you."

Chapter 35

Time seemed to slow down as the group marched towards the west entrance of the Noble District. After the knight had told Jace that the king wanted to have a word with Jace, his imagination began to run wild. He couldn't understand why the king would want to see him.

He racked his brain, trying to think of any other situation he'd heard of where a king had asked to see a player. Other than ceremonies where they received titles they had bought, he couldn't think of a single instance.

Jace tried to figure out what that meant for him. He suspected it wouldn't be anything good. Most likely, they'd uncovered some evidence that the thieves guild was involved and Jace was going to be the fall guy.

He considered using his *Vanish* skill to simply disappear and then get lost into the crown. At one point, he even equipped his Infiltrator's Hat, instantly willing it to look like the hood that had been there just a moment ago.

The problem was, if he did run, he'd be branded an outlaw and his faction would drop far into the negative with the guards. Then, even if he died, his faction would remain negative and they'd attack him on sight. His only way to avoid that was to accept whatever punishment they gave him.

If they executed him, he'd lose his corpse and all his possessions, but his faction would stay intact, and his crime would be wiped away. Then, when he respawned, he could pick up as if nothing happened. If they imprisoned him, he'd have to think of some other way to die so he could respawn.

He continued to mull around ideas and possibilities until suddenly they stopped in front of the palace doors. Jace swallowed reflexively as he realized they had arrived. It appeared his time had run out.

Doormen in the king's livery opened the double doors and the small procession entered a large chamber that was richly furnished. The polished marble floors and white pillars were a stark contrast to the buildings outside the Noble District. In addition, the walls were lined with paintings of what Jace guessed were either former kings or heroes of the realm.

But the large chamber wasn't empty. It was filled with people of all sorts. Some of the people were obviously nobility, judging by their fine dress. Others were more common looking and of those, many of them had knightly escorts like Jace. Were these the condemned? The people waiting for the king's judgement?

As Jace stared at the various people, a man walked by that he recognized. It was the captain of the Royal Guard, Captain Avolin. The man seemed to catch sight of Jace at the same time and he stopped in front of him.

The knights with Jace snapped to attention and saluted with their hand over their breast. "Captain!"

"At ease knights," the captain told them as he returned the salute. He turned to Jace.

Unable to help himself, Jace blurted out his question. "Do you know why I'm here?"

Avolin looked around and gestured to the people in the cavernous room. "His Majesty is holding court today. These people are suitors, like yourself, awaiting His Majesty's boon, favor or judgment."

"Do you know why I'm here?" he repeated.

The captain bowed his head. "I apologize, but I do not. You were summoned then, I take it?"

Jace nodded and eyed Avolin for a reaction but the man's face remained deadpan.

"You may wait here until your name is called," Avolin told him. "When it is, these good knights will escort you in through the far entrance." The captain turned to Jace. "And a word of advice, don't forget to bow."

Jace gulped as he looked at the large doors at the far end of the foyer. When he turned back around to thank Avolin, the man was gone.

Nervously, Jace waited with his escort. Then the knights had become like statues, not moving and saying nothing. That frayed Jace's nerves even more. He felt like he was the condemned man and they were his executioners.

The double doors at the far end would open every few minutes and a man would come out and announce a name. Someone would go inside, and the doors would be shut. Jace waited for his own name to be called. And he waited.

According to his timepiece, almost four hours had passed. He silently berated himself for not having the forethought to hand the gnomish timepiece to Diana, considering how much it was worth. He'd have no easy way to replace it if he lost it on his corpse.

Luna had stayed with the girls and he tried communicating with them through her, but it was difficult to convey his situation in a way that Luna could relate to them. Instead he sent quick simple messages to them as the time passed.

"Dedrurrurth," a man in silk livery called from the other end of the room and Jace's sense of dread jumped to new levels. For a second, he considered turning around and running, but then the knight next to him spoke.

"Your turn," the knight said, and the men stepped forward, forcing Jace to step forward as well.

The crowd parted to allow Jace and his escort to move to the double doors where the herald waited.

"Dedrurrurth?" the man asked as he approached.

Jace started to nod but the lead knight beat him to it. "This is Dedrurrurth."

The man in livery motioned him into the room. "You may enter."

The knights moved to the side, and Jace realized they would not be accompanying him into the throne room. He wasn't sure if that was a good thing or a bad thing. Trying to calm his pounding heart, he stepped into the throne room.

"Throne room," Jace sent to Luna.

The throne room appeared to be similar in size to the room he had just left. The walls and ceilings were the same white stone and the floor was similarly tiled in marble. Unlike the large open room, he'd just left, this one was divided by large, white columns that appeared every ten feet, creating a path to the throne.

The throne, or should Jace say thrones, were located on a raised dais and currently a serious-looking bearded man sat on the one throne while a beautiful but aloof woman sat on the other throne.

Glancing to either side, Jace saw that there were guards at each pillar, all the way up to the throne. On the far side of the pillars were richly dressed people who Jace guessed were noble court. He considered scanning the crowd with his HUD to see if there were any players but just then another herald in front of the dais called out.

"Dedrurrurth," he said in a strong, rich voice. "You may approach the throne."

Jace began walking towards the king. He kept repeating "don't forget to bow" in his head, over and over. He didn't want to offend the king if the man was going to decide Jace's fate. Ahead, he could see another attendant standing slight to the side of the walkway, about 15 feet from the dais. He walked over to the man and paused. The man gave him a slight nod and then a meaningful look at the floor.

Right! Don't forget to bow. Only, Jace had no idea how to bow. He thought back to what he had seen in the old vidstreams and the holostreams. He dropped to one knee and lowered his head.

A long moment of silence followed and Jace imagined the executioner coming up behind him and lopping his head off in front of the entire court.

Suddenly a new voice, rich and commanding authority, echoed through the chamber. "Rise Dedrurrurth, for you are the hero of the hour."

Jace wasn't sure if he had heard correctly. But he stood up and faced the throne.

The king stood up and walked down the dais. Now that he was no longer sitting, Jace could see he was a large, muscular man who was built and carried himself more like a warrior than a king. The king wore a deep purple robe that was lined with some sort of fur Jace didn't recognize. Under the robe he wore a golden vest over a tunic of shiny, extremely well-crafted chain mail. His high leather boots were exceptionally well-made, but had shiny, engraved plating. On his fingers, he wore a number of rings, including the royal signet ring.

He walked to stand in front of Jace and looked him up and down. Then clapped him on the shoulder. "I am told by Captain Avolin that you single handedly uncovered treason, bested an entire ship of pirates and retrieved my daughter's birthday present."

The king glanced to the side at a man and Jace turned slightly to see it was Captain Avolin himself, standing between two of the nearby pillars. The captain nodded at the king in confirmation and the king turned back Jace and raised an eyebrow. "Is this true?"

Jace gulped and shook his head. "Not exactly, Your Majesty."

"Oh?" The king looked at him quizzically.

"I had a friend who helped with the diversion and then I didn't really 'defeat' the entire pirate crew as much as set their ship on fire and got chased through the streets of Whitecliff until the good Captain and his soldiers sent them running," Jace told him. He wasn't sure if there was some truth detecting priest lurking around, but he guessed lying to the king wasn't a very good idea.

The king threw his head back and laughed. "So, you give credit for your success to a friend and the good Captain?"

Jace nodded.

"But I also hear that it was your plan that tricked a confession out of that traitorous Tiebaut," the king told him. "Is that true?"

"With the captain's help, Your Majesty," he replied. He wasn't about to take credit for the captain's work and make an enemy of the man.

"Dedrurrurth," said the king, "you appear to be a modest man. You could take the glory for yourself, but instead you share it with the captain and your friend."

The king turned to the crowd and gestured at Jace. "Modest and wise. Few of us ever accomplish anything of note without help from others. Recognizing that help, and acknowledging it, is a mark of a true hero."

The king turned, walked up the dais and sat back down on his throne. "Even though you had assistance, you were pivotal in uncovering the plot as well as retrieving my daughters present. For that, I wish to both thank and reward you."

Jace stayed silent, mostly because he was speechless. He had expected to be heading to a dungeon cell. Either that or have his head handed to the king - minus his body. Now he was about to be rewarded? He could hardly believe it.

"Since the traitor has been dealt with," the king said loudly, talking to the entire court now, not just Jace he realized. "I find myself with one less noble. Normally, this would not bother me."

The king paused and the court laughed at Jace guessing it was some sort of inside joke.

"However," the king continued. "I feel this particular vacancy should be filled. And who better to fill it than the person who uncovered the traitor, a true ally of Whitecliff…" The king paused, apparently for dramatic effect. "… Dedrurrurth."

There was scattered applause and Jace's eyes went wide. Did the king intend to knight him? Was this even possible? Could he really become a knight without buying a title?!

Once again, the king stood up but this time, an attendant rushed forward and offered the king a sword. The king held the sword up and walked down the dais to stand in front of him. The king smiled. "If you would be so kind as to take the knee again."

Jace did as he was told and lowered his head.

"By my power and right as King of Whitecliff," said the king and he touched each of Jace's shoulders with the flat of his sword. "I hereby convey to you the title of Baronet of Whitecliff, with all rights and responsibilities thereof. The former lands and properties of Tiebaut shall pass to you for so long as you continue to serve Whitecliff."

The king stepped back then. "Arise, Sir Dedrurrurth, Baronet."

Jace stood and once again, there was soft applause.

"Now," said the king. "As much as I would love to hear the full story of your exploits, I'm afraid I have a court to run. Would you join us at my daughter's birthday on the day after tomorrow? I shall have an invitation sent to you."

Jace opened his mouth to thank the king but no words came out. He closed his mouth and then tried again. "Thank you, your majesty."

He realized he was just standing there, rooted to the space he was in when an attendant came to him from behind a pillar and took Jace by the arm. The attendant bowed from the waist to the king, gently pushing on Jace's arm at the same time.

Jace got the hint and tried to mimic the attendant. They held the bow for a moment and then the attendant led him back out the room, the way he had come. As he stepped out into the crowd of people in the foyer, the crier stepped out and called another name but Jace was still so shocked he didn't hear it.

He had come in expecting to be thrown in the dungeons or killed. And now he was a noble or some kind? Had he understood that correctly? He wasn't even just a knight, he was a baronet, wherever that was. And if he heard correctly, he would receive the property of Sir Tiebaut. Did that mean the manor he broke into? Jace just stood there outside the double doors for long moments before making his way to the back of the room and out into the courtyard.

He needed to tell the girls.

Chapter 36

"Excuse me, Sir Dedrurrurth" said a man in the royal livery.

Jace had just stepped out of the palace and was still in a daze when the man before him repeated himself.

"Excuse me, Sir Dedrurrurth," the man said again.

His mind was still a whirlwind of thoughts and emotions at the unexpected turn of events. Forcing himself to focus, Jace looked at the man. "Yes?"

"Milord," the man began. "My name is Camdyn Cheshiree. If you would accompany me for a moment, we would like to record your patents of nobility and have your signet ring bound to you."

Jace nodded and followed the man through the courtyard, out of the palace grounds and into the Noble District. The man stopped in front of a long, three story building not far from the castle. Above the door was a polished copper sign in the shape of a quill and scroll. On the sign were the carefully painted words "Patents Office".

Following Camdyn inside, Jace was led to an office. He sat in a chair while the man scribbled down a bunch of information and then stamped the papers with several different seals. Finally, Camdyn produced a ring from within his desk and then called in a Mage.

A female fairy, a smaller humanoid the size of a gnome but with gossamer wings, floated in and landed next to Jace. Fairies were another playable race from the good faction that made excellent Mages. Despite their wings, they couldn't only fly 5-6 feet above the ground but, they were immune to fall damages and pits.

This particular fairy was clad in white robes that bore the royal crest on one breast and the scroll and quill on the other breast. She had short pink hair and two small antennas protruded from her forehead.

"We need to bind Sir Dedrurrurth's ring to him," the man told the fairy, offering her the ring.

The fairy nodded, flew over and took the ring from Camdyn. Then, she dipped down to be eye level with Jace. "Sir Dedrurrurth, my name is Magnolia Sunbuttonare and I will be binding your signet ring to you. Are you right-handed or left handed?"

"Right," Jace replied.

"Please hold out your left hand then," Magnolia told him in a high-pitched voice that had a sing-song quality to it. "I will place this on your left pinky finger and cast a spell. Don't worry, it won't hurt."

Jace nodded and obediently held out his left hand. The fairy Mage then placed a gold ring on his finger, made some gestures and spoke an incarnation. *"Ligat animam!"*

You receive Signet Ring (Baronet).

Jace saw the system message and it was immediately followed by a pop-up message.

Do you wish to permanently bind this item to your character? (Yes or No)
Warning: This action cannot be undone.

Since he didn't really have a choice if he wanted to keep the title, Jace chose Yes and bound the ring to him.

Signet Ring (Baronet) has been bound.

"There we go," Magnolia said. "All done."

"Thanks, Magnolia," Camdyn said.

"Milord," the little fairly inclined her head and then flew out of the room.

"That's all for the patents, Sir Dedrurrurth," the man said. "Your patents will be filed and if there should be any contestation, you can refer them to us. "Just a few more items of business."

Jace looked at Camdyn expectantly.

"Yes, well. It seems the king not only granted you the title of the former Sir Tiebaut, but also the lands and other assets," the man reached into a drawer and pulled out a ring of keys and several bundles of papers. "These are the keys to the estate, as well as his vineyards and farms to the south. And these are the titles for his holdings, careful some of the ink is quite fresh."

The man pushed the materials over to Jace who made them disappear into his inventory.

"Oh," Camdyn interjected. "I almost forgot. His bank accounts have all been moved to your name. You should be able to access your assets from any of the alliance banks."

"Thank you," Jace said numbly. All of this was overwhelming, and he needed time to process it.

"I believe that is all of the business we have for you," Camdyn said as he stood up. "It was a pleasure serving you, milord."

Recognizing the polite dismissal, Jace stood up and almost turned around to go but suddenly thought of a question. "What exactly is a baronet?"

Camdyn smiled and nodded. "A baronet is a title of recognition in the kingdom, with a standing between that of Knight and that of a true Baron."

"But I'm still nobility?" Jace asked.

A pained expression came over the man's face. "Your pardon, milord, but technically no. While you do enjoy many of the same privileges, you are not technically a noble."

Jace sighed. Jace didn't really know what that meant in game terms. He had a signet ring so that meant he should be able to come and go into the Noble District. Were there other things he couldn't do? Could he attend court? Did he have access to the Royal Palace?

"Do I have access to the Royal Palace?" He asked Camdyn excitedly.

Once more, the man put on a pained expression. "Alas, milord, only nobles have access to the Royal Palace, except by invitation."

His momentary excitement vanished in an instant. For a moment, he'd thought all of their problems were solved. With access to the palace, they could have searched at their leisure for the secret room that held the *Help Desk*. That reminded him of something else.

"Am I allowed to invite guests into the Noble District?" he asked.

Again, Camdyn put on the pained expression which Jace was beginning to believe must have practiced. "I'm afraid guests are not allowed for security reasons. However, if you have a spouse, she would - of course - be allowed be welcomed. If you require servants or craftsmen, we can supply you with some who have already been vetted."

Jace frowned. That meant Charlena, Diana and Mika wouldn't be allowed in.

"I'm sorry, milord," the man said, obviously seeing the disappointment on Jace's face. "Those are the king's laws, not mine."

"Thank you," Jace said.

"You're welcome, milord."

Retracing his steps through the building, Jace found the door and left the Patents Office. He began walking back toward the west entrance of the Noble District. He was half-tempted to go check out Tiebaut's home. Then he corrected himself. It was his home now. It still felt surreal. Even as Mordred, he'd seriously considered becoming a noble, or knight, or whatever Jace was now. Titles were ridiculously expensive. They started a million gold to buy, which was the real world equivalent of a million dollars. And that was just for a lowest rank of "nobility", which was Knight. Jace guessed Baronet was twice as much and the next level, true nobility, was much more expensive.

He wanted to go check out Tiebaut's home. No, not Tiebaut's. It was his home now. He hadn't gotten a good look at it the last time. Now he could remedy that and go explore his new house.

"Girls worried," came Luna's voice in his mind and he started.

Taking a moment to gather himself, he realized the house would need to wait. The girls had been worried, and he should meet them and explain what happened. "Coming back. I'll explain to them."

"Girls happy," his familiar replied.

Jace couldn't suppress a smile as he walked through the gates of the Noble District without challenge. After all that time of trying to figure out a way to get into the Noble District, now he could just walk freely in and out whenever he chose.

When he made it back to the inn, the girls were waiting for him. When Mika saw him, she practically tackled him as she threw herself onto him and embraced him in a tight hug. She seemed about to kiss him but then her eyes flicked to Diana and she hopped down.

"Good to see you're still alive, dear one," Diana said from her chair. "And not in prison, oh, I guess they call it the dungeon here."

"Yes," Mika agreed, obviously still excited. "We were worried about you!"

Jace motioned her to sit down and then did the same. Luna hopped up on his lap and began purring and he stroked his fur as he related his story. He started from when he'd left them to the moment he'd returned. When he finished his story, he sat back and continued to stroke Luna.

"So, it's Sir Jace now is it?" Diana teased.

Frowning, Jace shook his head. "Actually, it's Sir Dedrurrurth, since they took my character name."

"Oh my," Diana said. "That's a mouthful."

"I know," he agreed.

"I think it's wonderful!" Mika interjected, her eyes bright with excitement. "You are a brave knight in one of the stories now!"

"I don't know about that," he shrugged. Then he relented, giving into Mika's excitement, and grinned. "But it is pretty cool!"

"But we common folk can't come see your new château?" Diana pouted.

"Sorry," he apologized. "I did ask but apparently, that's not allowed. It makes sense from a game standpoint, if WorldCog allowed guests, it would lose its exclusivity and they wouldn't sell as many."

"I don't begrudge them making money," Diana agreed. "It's just inconvenient for us."

"Jace can get inside the Noble District," Mika said. "But we need a way in. And we both need a way into the palace."

"That about sums it up," he told them. "Although, Webley still owes me a favor, so I can get you into the Noble District, but you'd have to stay in my house or risk getting arrested and fined or imprisoned. That's something we'll need to wait to do until we have a way into the palace."

"I hate to be a Debbie Downer," Diana said. "But do we have ANY idea how we can get into the palace?"

They all looked at each other for a moment before Jace sighed. "No. But my thieves guild faction should be high enough that I can ask Webley about it next time we're there."

"What do we do in the meantime?" Diana asked.

"Kill monsters!" Mika said, her hand on her katana...

Checking his timepiece, he saw that it was almost 3pm. His little misadventure had taken up most of the day. There wasn't really time to do a quest before Charlena logged in. Jace struggled to think of what to do for only three hours.

Once again, he considered leaving the girls to do their own quests and going to visit Tiebaut's home. After all, it was his now and he'd only really seen in the dark the time he'd broken in. He felt like someone who had just received a Christmas present, but couldn't open it.

"We can kill beetles!" Mika offered.

Jace winced, remembering the last time they'd fought the Beetle Queen. He really didn't feel like losing more items. Maybe if they just stayed with the smaller beetles and avoided the queen. "Sure. We can kill beetles."

As they got up to leave, Mika touched his arm. She looked up brightly. "Don't worry, if you get dissolved again, I will make you more armor!"

Chapter 37

Whether it was because they were high-level, or the better weapons Jace and Diana had received, the beetles were much easier this time. It took them only 5 minutes to kill one and then recover. In two hours, they were able to kill a total of 19 of them.

Once they turned them in the beetle eyes for the repeatable Beetles quest, Jace was only a few hundred experience away from 6th level. Mika and Diana gained levels, bringing Mika up to level 4 in Rogue and Diana to level 5 in Priest.

They met Charlena at the adventurers guild and related the events to her. Jace told her about the visit to the castle, the encounter with the king and becoming a Baronet.

"Wow, your lordship," Charlena said playfully. "Do we curtsy for you now?"

Then she threw her arms around him and kissed him. "This is great! Now we can get into the Noble District."

Frowning, Jace shook his head. "No visitors apparently."

"That's not fair!" Charlena backed up and crossed her arms.

"I know," Jace agreed.

"Can we sneak in?" Charlena asked. "You did it right?"

"No," he told her. "I was only able to get in with the help of the thieves guild contact. I have another favor, but it's a one-time deal. I could get you in, but I couldn't get you back out."

"So, you have this cool house and stuff," she said. "But none of us can come visit?!"

"We're plebs, dear one," Diana said. "Sad but true."

"Grr!" Charlena growled. "That's too much like real life."

They were all silent for a time before Charlena let out a breath. "Well, whatever. Let's go kill something."

"I checked the board, there are no quests for our level," Mika chimed in.

Charlena glared at Mika, who looked down. Then she turned back to Jace and seemed about to say something, but Diana cut in.

"Can we kill more beetles?" the older woman said loudly. She glanced between the other two girls and then looked pointedly at Jace.

Charlena closed her mouth and then opened it but this time Jace spoke up with a different idea. "With Charlena, maybe we can handle some of those higher level orcs. What do you think?"

Jace wasn't experienced with much jealousy from women. It was rare enough that one woman had wanted him back in reality. Suddenly having two women who liked him felt good but also made him feel guilty. He felt like he was betraying both of them.

The worst part of it was, he didn't really have time for either of them. Not until they got things sorted out. He needed to get to WorldCog's support so they could fix the bug in the code. Now that he was about to get confirmation that he was alive and stuck in a medical pod, it was even more important to him. He needed to be able to wake up and exit the pod properly. If he didn't, then on top of whatever physical injuries he had sustained, he might end up with brain damage as well.

Jace hated to think about what injuries he had sustained in the car accident. He started to go crazy as he imagined the possibilities. He kept trying to put it out of his mind by thinking of anything else. He'd been doing it since he first appeared in the game. But now that Charlena was just days away from seeing his body, he found it harder and harder not to think about.

And now, having Charlena acting out at Mika, he wasn't sure what to do. He literally had zero experience with two girls interested in him at once. This was something Damian might have experienced - if he was to be believed.

Thinking of the senior programmer he worked with, Jace once more thought of the code and Damian's reaction. The more he remembered it, the more the programmer's reaction seemed extreme, even for Damian.

He'd known the senior programmer since he'd started working there. He was a jerk a lot of the time, but he'd also helped Jace out with various problems he'd run into. Could Damian be involved in this somehow? Or was he working to fix the issue before news of it hit the net?

"Orcs?" Charlena asked, snapping Jace back to the moment. The red-headed elf looked intrigued. "Like the ones we fought on the mountain?"

Jace shook his head, glad she was thinking about the game again. "No, these would be tougher. But then again, we're tougher too. Plus, they'd be much better experience and might drop some decent loot."

Now, all of the girls were considering the idea.

"I'm game," Diana said first. "Anything's better than those dreadful beetles."

"I am game as well," Mika said, hand on her katana. Jace saw her eyes flit to Charlena while the other girl wasn't looking.

Charlena nodded. "Sure, let's kill some orcs!"

The group marched on in mostly silence, other than the occasional outburst from Diana about something she'd see in a shop they passed.

Jace didn't speak either. He was wondering what Charlena would think of him when he woke up and they finally met in person. Would she still like him? Would they get together in real life? Would he even be able to get together with her? Or was his body too mangled from the accident?

Finally, the group reached the gate. Jace talked to the guards and received a repeatable quest to kill Ironfist orcs and collect their tribal gray sashes. He also received a quest to find and kill the Ironfist Warlord. Considering they'd barely managed to take down the Beetle Queen, he wasn't sure he wanted to run into a more powerful boss.

He and the girls followed the guard's directions past the beetle area, to that road that led north and south from Whitecliff. It was the road he'd traveled to reach Whitecliff as part of the caravan. He knew that was only a few days ago, but already it seemed like weeks. Much had happened in those few days.

From one of the hills looking down on the road, his group could see other players battling orcs. As they watched, Jace could see that the orcs were coming from the forest and would run towards the players on the road. Several players would fire arrows, crossbows, spells and, Jace thought he saw, stones and throwing stars at the creatures. They'd keep firing until the thing dropped and Jace knew whoever had done the most damage would get the experience and be able to loot the body.

"That's a lot of players down there," Charlena said.

"Are they all grouped?" Diana asked as another orc broke from the trees and was cut down before it had gotten halfway to the line of players.

"No," Jace shook his head. "They're camping the area and whoever gets in the most damage, gets the credit for the kill. They get the experience and the loot."

"No one is cooperating?" Mika asked.

Glancing down, he could see the chaotic storms of arrows and other missiles as they rapid-fired the incoming orcs. "No. They just burn it down as fast as they can and hope they get in more damage than everyone else."

"Is that really what we want to do?" Diana frowned.

Jace looked up and down the road. The northern branch of the road entered the woods about a half mile further up. He wondered if they would have better luck north. He almost thought of going south but his caravan hadn't encountered any orcs. Was that because of the sheer numbers of people in the caravan?

"I don't feel like competing with a bunch of other players," Charlena told the group. "We'll be expending a lot of effort for only a chance to get experience."

"No," Mika corrected. "We would get most of the kills. They are solo, we are a group. All of our damage would count for a group kill."

Charlena gave her a cool look but said nothing.

Jace shook his head. "It would work for a bit, until the people around us realized we were grouped. Once they do and see that we're getting all the kills, they'll PuG it and we'd be working against other groups."

"Pug?" Diana raised an eyebrow. "Like the dog?"

Jace chuckled. "No, as in 'Pick up group'. It's what they call a bunch of random people who get together to do something. They even have pick up raids. Both tend to end up in disaster since people aren't really working towards a common cause. They get greedy or jealous and then everything falls apart."

The mention of PuG reminded him of the dwarf, the rabbit-kin, and the succubus he'd grouped with to get the Sash of the Kobadera. It seemed a lifetime ago and maybe, in a way, it was. He'd thought he was dead. But with Charlena's help, he'd found out that he wasn't dead. He owed her a lot.

"So, what do we do, dear ones," Diana yawned.

It was obviously a fake yawn since neither he, Mika or Diana actually seemed to require sleep. She was just being melodramatic. But she did have a good point. He looked back to the north.

"Let's go north. Towards the forest. There doesn't seem to be many players over there," he suggested, pointing towards where the road met the forest. The girls followed his finger and glanced to the north.

"North is good," Mika grinned.

Charlena glanced at the Japanese girl and shrugged but Diana looked thoughtful. "Why is it that there are no players in that direction."

"Maybe they're lazy," Charlena muttered.

"They're loss is our gain," Jace said and started down the hill to the north. "Let's go hunt some orcs!"

His small band made their way the half mile where the forest overtook the hills. It was almost an unnatural division between green grass and then suddenly a dense line of trees. They followed the edge of the forest west to the road.

As the group approached the road, a huge orc burst from the forest on the far side of the road and bellowed a war cry. "You trespass on our lands! Die humans!"

This orc was two feet taller and about 50 pounds heavier than orcs Jace and Charlena had fought on the mountain, near Skystead. As the orc charged his group, it got close enough for Jace examined the huge thing in his HUD. Then he understood why no other groups were camping this area.

Chapter 38

"It's level 20!" Jace yelled and immediately cast his Air Armor, bumping up his *Defense* to 12. He looked at the stats again, just to make sure he hadn't misread them.

Ironfist Orc Brute
Level 20

Unfortunately, he had been right. The creature was level 20, making it a tier 3 monster. That meant its armor and weapons were 2 tiers above their own. And because it was a level 20 warrior, it had at least 200 health. It was formidable, but it was still only a solo monster and they were a group of four. Maybe they had a chance.

Jace unsheathed the Kraken's Claw and Ardmore's Bane, bathing the area in soft white light. With his magic and the items, he had, he had an amazing *Defense* for his level. But would it be enough to keep him alive from this hulking brute?

"Come get some!" Jace shouted his *Taunt* as the orc lumbering into range. The creature veered toward him and raised its huge, two-handed club over its head.

At that moment, the twang of a bowstring sounded, and an arrow soared at the approaching monster.

Almedha Pressalor Precisely shoots Ironfist Orc Brute for 0 damage.

The arrow glanced off the orc's breastplate but was immediately followed by a *Flame Bolt* that hit the creature's neck, sizzling the exposed skin.

Mizzlethain-galliegarde burns Ironfist Orc Brute with Flame Bolt for 8 fire damage.

The brute was on him and it brought its huge club down at Jace.

Ironfist Orc Brute crushes YOU for 12 damage.

He managed to deflect some of the blow with his buckler, but the massive club still took 15% of his health with one swipe. But now it was his turn. He sliced and stabbed with his weapons, aiming at the unprotected parts of the orc. At the same time, Mika moved to the side and slice at its thigh with her Bloodstained Katana.

You stab Ironfist Orc Brute for 3 damage and 3 acid damage.
You slash Ironfist Orc Brute for 6 damage.

Raajoget slashes Ironfist Orc Brute for 11 damage.
Ironfist Orc Brute is Bleeding.

Mika's magical katana was doing a good amount of damage, nearly as much as both of his weapons combined.

Charlena moved around back for her precise strike while Mika circled as well. Diana took several steps to the side, making sure she wasn't near the creature's front. No doubt, they'd all learned from the queen Beetle's acid attack that standing behind the tank wasn't a good idea.

Charlena disappeared and then snapped back into view as she let another arrow fly.

Almedha Pressalor Precisely shoots Ironfist Orc Brute for 19 damage.

The orc ignored the arrow that lodged itself in its back and brought his club around for a backhanded blow across Jace's body.

Ironfist Orc Brute crushes YOU for 17 damage.
Ironfist Orc Brute Bleeds for 3 damage.

Pain exploded in his left arm as the blow struck him and he grunted in pain. Mika and Diana struck at nearly the same time. The katana sliced across the back of the orc's leg even as a *Flame Bolt* burned its bare shoulder.

Mizzlethain-galliegarde burns Ironfist Orc Brute with Flame Bolt for 7 fire damage.
Raajoget slashes Ironfist Orc Brute for 6 damage.
Ironfist Orc Brute is Bleeding.

"I'm going to need some healing," Jace croaked and then it was Jace's turn. Using both blades, he attacked the brute's unarmored hip.

You stab Ironfist Orc Brute for 10 damage and 3 acid damage.
You slash Ironfist Orc Brute for 0 damage.

Kraken's Claw sank into the muscle of the creature's hip, causing it to snarl in pain. Unfortunately, it twisted, and the sword skidded along the bottom of the breastplate without doing any harm.

He couldn't see Charlena because of the hulking brute in front of him but he heard her arrow thud into him and saw it wince.

Almedha Pressalor Precisely shoots Ironfist Orc Brute for 18 damage.

Then the orc brought its club down again but Jace's left hand moved to deflect the blow with the buckler.

Ironfist Orc Brute crushes YOU but you Block.
Ironfist Orc Brute Bleeds for 3 damage.

Even as Jace deflected the blow, the glow of restorative magic surrounded him as Diana and Mika both cast their healing spells.

Raajoget heals YOU for 6 health.
Mizzlethain-galliegarde heals YOU for 7 health.

Feeling better, Jace retaliated at the creature, aiming one weapon high and the other low.

You stab Ironfist Orc Brute for 1 damage and 3 acid damage.
You slash Ironfist Orc Brute for 0 damage.

Unfortunately, that tactic didn't seem to work. The Kraken's Claw scored a burning line of acid across its breastplate and then across the thing's arm. His sword clanged into the brute's greaves without scratching them.

The red-headed elf loosed another arrow from *Stealth*. She was getting good at using her *Vanish* and following it up with a *Precise Shot*.

Almedha Pressalor Precisely shoots Ironfist Orc Brute for 3 damage.

Unfortunately, her shot merely grazed the orc and the thing raised its club for another strike.

Ironfist Orc Brute crushes YOU for 14 damage.
Ironfist Orc Brute Bleeds for 3 damage.

Jace deflected much of the force of the blow, but enough of it came through that it felt like the bones in his arm might break. The other girls got their own attacks in and Jace saw that Diana had switched to her wand. Hopefully, she was saving some mana for more healing.

Mizzlethain-galliegarde shoots Ironfist Orc Brute for 4 magic damage and 2 acid damage.
Raajoget slashes Ironfist Orc Brute for 6 damage.
Ironfist Orc Brute is Bleeding.

Jace got his own attacks in, going for the creature's left arm, above its vambraces.

You stab Ironfist Orc Brute for 8 damage and 3 acid damage.
You slash Ironfist Orc Brute for 7 damage.

This time, he blades found bare skin and the orc snarled. "I will kill you human!"

"Not, I think, today," Jace replied as Charlena's arrow thudded into its shoulder.

The orc's eyes opened wide for a second, but then narrowed. "Your head will decorate my belt little human!"

Almedha Pressalor Precisely shoots Ironfist Orc Brute for 11 damage.

Trying to make good on his promise, the huge creature wound back with a two-handed grip on his club as if about to hit Jace's head like a baseball and the club was his bat.

Ironfist Orc Brute crushes YOU for 12 damage.
Ironfist Orc Brute Bleeds for 3 damage.

Jace got his buckler up in time to deflect the blow over his head, mostly. The blow still rocked his head and he momentarily saw stars. In the back of his mind, he appreciated that level of detail the developers had added. At the same time, he wished some of them would have tried it at their sensory level set to 100%.

"Need more healing," Jace said, but even as he finished his sentence, the girls cast their spells and he was bathed in light. He grinned, impressed with how much progress they'd made playing together. That was especially true of Diana, who had never played the game before being inserted.

Raajoget heals YOU for 8 health.
Mizzlethain-galliegarde heals YOU for 9 health.

He didn't waste any time but retaliated with his own blades, trying to slice at the orc's right thigh, which was now exposed from its swing.

You stab Ironfist Orc Brute for 0 damage.
You slash Ironfist Orc Brute for 0 damage.

Unfortunately, he was still off-balance from the blow to the head and hit blades skidded off the creature's greaves again.

Almedha Pressalor Precisely shoots Ironfist Orc Brute for 8 damage.

"I'm out of mana," Charlena yelled out as her arrow struck the brute in the leg. Without mana, she couldn't use her *Vanish*. If she couldn't use her ability, Jace knew her damage would drop off. His mental count of damage should put them somewhere close to a quarter of the orc's health, so hopefully they didn't have much more to go.

Ironfist Orc Brute crushes YOU for 17 damage.
Ironfist Orc Brute Bleeds for 3 damage.

This time, Jace wasn't able to deflect as much of the blow and the impact against his shoulder rattled his entire body. He grunted in pain and forced himself to stay upright.

Mizzlethain-galliegarde shoots Ironfist Orc Brute for 5 magic damage and 2 acid damage.
Raajoget slashes Ironfist Orc Brute for 5 damage.
Ironfist Orc Brute is Bleeding.

A bolt from Diana's wand flew over his head to strike the orc in the cheek while at the same time he heard Mika yell as she sliced at the brute from behind. Bringing his own weapons up, Jace sliced at the creature's arm as it pulled back its club.

You stab Ironfist Orc Brute for 7 damage and 3 acid damage.
You slash Ironfist Orc Brute for 1 damage.

The orc grunted but otherwise didn't seem overly bothered. Still, Jace knew its health had to be low. A few more hits and it should go down - hopefully.

Almedha Pressalor shoots Ironfist Orc Brute for 5 damage.

Charlena's arrow scored a hit on the brute's shin but it didn't even flinch. It swung its club sideways again, like it wanted to knock Jace's head out of the park, but his body moved of its own volition.

Ironfist Orc Brute crushes YOU but you Dodge.
Ironfist Orc Brute Bleeds for 3 damage.

Jace dodged the attack and the orc was momentarily thrown off balance. Then a blast from Diana's wand hit square in the face, just a Mika's katana sliced it across the back of the neck.

Mizzlethain-galliegarde shoots Ironfist Orc Brute for 4 magic damage and 2 acid damage.
Raajoget slashes Ironfist Orc Brute for 7 damage.
Ironfist Orc Brute dies.
You gain 200 experience.

You have gained a level.
You are now level 6 in Mage.

Jace side stepped the brute's body as it collapsed onto the ground. They'd managed to do it. They'd killed a level 20 monster.

"Is that all the experience we get from that fight?" Diana scoffed.

Jace looked to the edge of the forest. "Let's back up really quick before another one appears!"

The others, who were out of mana or nearly out of mana, nodded and followed Jace back to the hill. There, they all collapsed on the ground.

"That was fun!" Mika said, bright eyed. "We killed a great foe!"

"With not much to show for it," Diana said sourly.

"I hit level 8!" Charlena said excitedly.

"Congratulations!" they all responded.

"Good job!" Jace added. "You did a great job! Thanks for the healing! You guys stayed on top of it!"

Mika beamed and even Diana offered a genuine smile.

"Now what?" Charlena asked. "I still have a couple of hours."

Looking back to the forest, Jace grinned. "I say we kill more orcs!"

Chapter 39

His group killed six more orcs before Charlena had to log out. They would have killed more but they were nearly party wiped when an Ironfist shaman appeared. The orc's magic blasts had ignored Jace's armor and he hadn't lasted long. Once Jace died, the shaman had turned on Charlena and killed her before Diana and Mika had finally brought it down.

Despite the deaths, his group had fun and were learning to work together better. Plus, they were earning decent experience without any competition with other players. Mika and Charlena seemed to be getting along better. At least Jace thought they were. He decided he'd ask Diana what he should do about the two girls. After all, she was a 90-something-year-old and romance writer. She should have some tips.

Charlena was now half-way to level 9, while Mika was level 5 in Rogue and Diana was level 6 in Priest. Jace had also leveled up again. Along with level 7 in Mage, he had gained a new special ability, *Enhance Familiar I*, that came with choices. He had seen it pop-up but had ignored it while they fought so he would have time to think about it. He brought up the ability again as they walked back to Whitecliff.

Enhance Familiar I
Range: N/A

Cost: N/A
**Description: As your arcane power grows, so does
your connection with your familiar. Your familiar
gains one of the following abilities.**

Available abilities:
Armored Familiar
Channel Spell
Remote Viewing
Resistant Familiar
Share Spell
Special Ability Enhancement

Jace looked at the abilities. *Armored Familiar*
didn't seem very practical since she wasn't a frontline
fighter. While it would grant her some protection, it
just didn't seem worthwhile at this point. Maybe later.

Channel Spell had possibilities. Being able to
cast spells through Luna could come in very handy.
Unfortunately, any aggro she gained would be
transferred to Jace, so he wasn't sure how useful it
would be except to pull creatures.

He looked at *Remote Viewing* as a candidate
too. Luna was small and could get into tight places.
Seeing through her eyes would make her the perfect
scout.

Resistant Familiar gave some decent resistance
to magic or elemental damage, but it only applied to
one type of energy. Jace wasn't sure he would have
chosen it even if it gave resistances to all energy. Not
at this low a level.

When he looked at *Share Spell*, he almost took it right away. It would allow any spell he cast on himself to be shared by Luna. At the moment, that only covered *Air Armor*, but that alone would give her more armor that *Armored Familiar*.

Special Ability Enhancement was a little vague, but it seemed to be intended to enhance the special abilities of the prestige familiars like Imp and Faerie Dragon. He wondered if it would enhance the ability Luna had gained from the ritual blood in the saurian village.

The saurians had made Jace their shaman and he had killed a huge alligator, enchanted its blood, and used the blood to anoint the new chief. He'd also been forced to drink the remainder of the blood, which had granted him 2 additional mana permanently.

What the villagers hadn't seen was that Jace had left some blood on his fingers. He smeared it on Luna, hoping it would make her stronger. Instead, it had given her the ability to grow many times her size but at the cost of burning through her mana in less than a minute. Would this improve that?

He looked down at the cat, trailing him. "Any ideas which of the abilities I should choose for you?"

Luna glanced up at him. "No."

"A lot of help you are," he said and went back to looking at his HUD. He debated on *Share Spell* and *Special Ability Enhancement*. In the end, his curiosity got the best of him and he chose *Special Ability*

Enhancement just as they reached the gates of Whitecliff.

"Alright," Charlena said. "I have to log for the night. Thanks for the fun. I'll see you tomorrow night."

She hugged Jace and kissed him. As was her habit, she disappeared in mid kiss, leaving him holding nothing. Luckily, he was used to it and the passing NPCs completely ignored players logging in and logging out. It was part of their programming.

"One second," he told Diana and Mika. He looked down to Luna. "Do you feel any different?"

Luna seemed to consider that question and then gave him an expression that Jace could only be the cat equivalent of a shrug. "No."

"Hmm," Jace said. He thought she might automatically know what the ability had done. Now, there was only one real way to find out. "Luna, turn into your big cat form and see how long you can hold it."

"Yes," the cat said and then suddenly transformed into a cat the size of a cougar, maybe even a lion.

Mika and Diana both jumped back with a start as the giant form Luna appeared.

"Since when can she do that?" Diana asked. It was only then that Jace realized they'd never seen her giant form before. Charlena had seen it a couple of times before they had reached Whitecliff but never the other two.

"I sort of gave her a special ability by smearing blood on her in a lizard man village," he replied.

Diana and Mika both gave him blank looks. Nearly at the same time, they both said, "What?!"

Jace relayed the story to them of the saurian village and how he had become the shaman. He told them about the alligator, enchanting the blood, marking the chief and then how he'd been expected to drink the blood. The girls looked a little squeamish about the blood drinking and he couldn't blame them - he'd been squeamish too. Then he relayed how he'd kept some of the blood to see if it would make Luna stronger.

He'd just finished the story when he noticed that Luna was still giant sized and still here. "You're still big?"

Luna seemed to raise her chin at the question. "Yes. Big."

"She can stay big!" Mika said brightly and began rubbing Luna's big head behind the ears.

"Do you know how long you can stay this size?" he asked her. Already it was minutes longer than before. If she could maintain this size for this long, she might be a real asset in a fight. Especially since she could have essentially the same amount of health he had, minus one.

His familiar was maneuvering her head to try to get Mika and scratch certain spots. The cat stopped for a moment and looked at him. "No."

"A giant orange tabby cat," Diana said, coming over to stroke Luna's fur. "Even I have to admit, that's pretty cool."

Jace had to agree. Of course, he was thinking of it from a purely tactical standpoint. But that was the way he had learned to think of the game. Some people called it meta-gaming, but he thought of it as good decision making and getting the most from what you had.

Looking at Luna, he had to admit Diana was right. Having a giant cat was pretty cool. "She is pretty cool."

His familiar looked from the girls to Jace, giving him a smug expression. "Yes."

As they walked to the inn, he watched the reactions of the people they passed. Most of them didn't give Luna more than a passing glance. Jace guessed that in a world of dragons, ogres, griffons and more, a cat the size of a tiger didn't really phase people much.

Once they got to the inn, that was a different story. Luna was still able to maintain her size but Jace didn't think having the equivalent of a tiger sitting at the table would be okay with the owner or the patrons. He turned to Luna. "Can you shrink back down?"

"Why?" Luna asked, causing Jace to raise an eyebrow. Did Luna actually like being larger? That was interesting.

Mika giggled. "I think she likes being big."

Jace glanced at Mika and guessed she was probably right. Somewhere in her code, she realized she was more formidable as a large cat. He'd need to give her some incentive. "Because I don't think they will let you in while you're so big. And that means we can't order you any fish."

That huge cat seemed to consider that and then suddenly shrunk down to her original size. "Fish!"

With Luna back to normal, they went inside and ordered waffles for them and fish for Luna. As they ate, they talked about ideas to get into the palace. It didn't take long for the conversation to devolve into some ridiculous ideas. At one point, one of them suggested a catapult and possibly even a trojan horse. The ideas went downhill quickly after that.

After dinner, if waffles could truly be called dinner, they split up to do their guild quests. Diana went off to the temple, while Jace and Mika went to the thieves guild.

When they talked to Webley, the guildmaster had congratulated him on becoming Baronet. Apparently, the man didn't miss anything that went on in the city.

"So, what does that make you?" the guildmaster asked. "The gentleman bandit?"

After a little talk about his new status, Weblety had given them the night's quests. The quests were simple breaking and entering jobs. Once again, because they were grouped, they were based on Mika's level instead of Jace's. He found that annoying, but at least they were able to do the same quests.

Jace made sure they took their time with the quests, giving Mika a chance to max out her *Stealth* skill and giving her access to the *Vanish* ability. With that, she could at least get in critical strikes. She'd still need to save some of her mana for healing, but with Diana also healing, Mika might be able to do some serious damage with her two-handed katana on a critical strike.

Despite the quests being at Mika's level, they were enough to push him to level 8 in Mage. Mika was only 50 experience away from 6th level in Rogue, so after they had gotten back with Diana, they killed two beetles before breakfast.

Luna had grown and helped them with the fight, though against the thick armor plating of the beetle's exoskeleton, her claws didn't do much damage. Even so, every little bit helped and given how long she was able to remain in the giant form, he guessed her ability was now toggleable. She could grow and shrink at will and stay in her giant form as long as she wanted. But he would test more later to be sure.

While they were eating breakfast, a man in the king's livery appeared. The man spoke briefly with the owner, who pointed towards their table. Jace began to get nervous. Now what?

The man in livery walked over to their table, cleared his throat, and then said in a loud, firm voice. "Sir Dedrurrurth, Baronet. You are cordially invited to attend the birthday party of Her Royal Highness, Princess Katerina, at the Royal Palace, this Weeksend at 7pm."

Reaching into his tunic, the man pulled out a sealed envelope and handed it to Jace. "Pray thee, what answer should I give His Majesty?"

Chapter 40

An invitation to the princess' birthday party? Jace wanted to facepalm himself as he suddenly remembered the king had mentioned that. At the time, he'd been too shocked by his sudden elevation to Baronet and the implication it carried. Now he remembered clearly the king had mentioned her birthday party.

Thoughts flooded his head. An invitation to the palace. Was this it? Was this his way in, his opportunity to look for the *Help Desk*? Would he be able to look for it? Or would there be too many people around? What if they all searched? Wait. Could the girls even come with him?

"Sir, what answer shall I relay back to the king?" the man in livery asked again.

"Am I allowed to bring a guest?" he asked.

The man put on a practiced smile but somehow managed sad looking eyes. "I'm sorry Baronet, invitees and spouses only. No other guests."

"Spouses only?" Diana chimed in.

The man bobbed his head towards Diana. "Correct, Madam. Spouses only."

Diana then jabbed him side with her elbow. She leaned toward him. "Tell him yes. Tell him you'll bring your spouses."

Jace looked at her confused. "What?"

"Tell him," she nudged him. "Tell him you'll be attending along with your spouses."

"My…" Jace started but Diana jabbed him again.

"TELL HIM!" she whispered louder. "You'll be going with your SPOUSES."

Jace turned to the man and smiled. "Yes, I will be attending with my spouses."

"Sir, your… SPOUSES?" The man looked slightly taken back and emphasized the "s" at the end of spouses.

"You did say invitees and spouses, right?" Diana asked sweetly.

"I... uh…" the man stuttered but then recovered. "Yes, of course. Um, may I tell the king how many spouses will attend?"

"At least two," Diana answered for Jace. "Possibly three."

"Three?" the man looked at Jace with a slightly impressed look on his face. "Very good. I shall relay your answer to the king."

"Thank you," Jace managed.

The man turned and left the inn. When he had gone, Jace spun and faced Diana. "My SPOUSES?!"

"It's perfect, dear one," Diana soothed. "You can marry us and then we can go to the party and, I'm guessing, get into the Noble District. Am I right?"

Jace opened his mouth to protest but then closed it. He remembered back to when he'd received his signet ring at the patents office. The man had talked about a spouse. A spouse. As in singular. "But the patents office only mentioned a spouse. Spouse. Singular!"

"Dear one," Diana laughed. "I may not have played this game before, but I have played the game of life for quite a while, not to mention contracts. Ugh! Too many contracts! One thing I learned is there are always loopholes."

"Yeah but…" Jace started.

"I'm not as familiar with this game as you are," Diana broke in. "But are you allowed to marry more than one person in the game?"

He thought about it for a moment and realized she was right. That was possible. In fact, he knew for a fact people paid good money to marry a lord or lady, so they had access to the Noble District and possibly the Royal Palace if the person had a high enough rank. "Yes."

"Can you marry three?" she asked. Her eyebrow was raised but she already had a look of triumph on her face.

Jace wasn't sure. It wasn't something that had ever been relevant for him. He started to tell her so, but she held up her hand.

"I happen to know that you can have at least four wives because I saw the ceremony at the temple last night… or was it the night before?" she grinned. "Some male pig, sorry, I meant player, and four women got married while I was getting my quest. I'm pretty sure he was just a knight."

Jace looked from Diana, who was smiling, to Mika, who was blushing. "Are you serious? You want me to marry all three of you?"

Diana brushed away his question with a gesture. "Three wives is nothing. I've had five husbands. Granted, not all at the same time, but I think it still counts for something. Besides, do you have any better ideas on how to get us all into the Royal Palace?"

Jace thought furiously. Unfortunately, she was right. They'd all been trying to think up ways to get into the palace since they'd arrived. This was the first and probably best opportunity they'd have. Possibly even the only opportunity. Then he thought of a way out.

"I can't, even if I wanted to," Jace told her. "A marriage is thousands of gold. There's no way we can earn that much in a day."

The older woman just grinned, apparently already having an answer. "Didn't you just inherit an entire estate? Doesn't that include a house, probably some servants and… some bank accounts?"

Trying to keep his mouth from falling open, Jace realized she was right. In the excitement of getting the title and the lands, he'd forgotten about the bank account. But how much money did Baronets get? Tiebaut had been willing to pay a million gold for the tiara. Maybe he had millions more.

"Yes," Jace said cautiously. "There was a bank account. I haven't checked it yet, so I don't know how much is in it."

"Perfect," Diana said. "You and Mika go check your account while I go pay a visit to the temple and see what the cost of marriage is." When neither Mika or Jace moved, she stood up and made a clapping gesture. "Come on! Chop! Chop! We haven't got all day!"

Then she pushed past Jace and started out the door. Over her shoulder Diana called, "Meet you back here in an hour or so!"

Jace watched her leave and then turned to Mika. There was still some color in her cheeks, but she looked resolved. "I will marry you."

Rubbing his forehead, Jace motioned Mika. "Come on, let's go to the bank."

Jace and Mika left the inn, followed by Luna. The cat immediately resumed her giant size the moment they left the inn, causing Jace to stop and look at her. "You like being big, I take it?"

Luna rubbed her enormous head against him, knocking him back a step and causing Mika to giggle. "Yes."

The three of them walked down to the Luxury District. Among the shops, Jace had also seen the Bank of Whitecliff. Even though it was called the Bank of Whitecliff, all of the banks were interconnected, and money and bank vaults could be accessed from any bank in the same alliance. It hadn't originally been that way and had been more realistic, where your money stayed in whatever bank you deposited it in. Eventually, pressure from the users had forced WorldCog to make the change and explained it away as the banks partnering with the mages guild or something like that.

He thought of his Mordred character again and the money he'd accumulated and stored in the bank. It was only a few hundred thousand gold, but he thought he'd have plenty of time to amass more wealth before becoming a permanent part of the game. Of course, once he woke up from the coma, he'd have a second chance.

They arrived at the bank and went in. The guards had started to object to Luna, but the cat seemed to understand that indoors, she needed to be small. Before they could even articulate their objections at the huge cat, Luna shrunk down to her former size and strutted past them as they gawked.

Unlike modern banks, the Whitecliff bank didn't have a line to see a teller. Instead, they talked to a receptionist who, after looking at Jace's signet ring, directed him to the office of a small gnomish woman.

"Hello," the small gnome said in a cheerful voice. She motioned them to sit in the chairs opposite her. "My name is Jiteyzz Copperchart, how may I help you, milord?"

Jiteyzz was about three feet tall with green and blue hair pulled back into a bun. She had a cute button nose and large orange eyes. She was wearing a plain grey dress but bright orange shoes that matched her eyes.

They both sat while Luna started wandering the room, sniffing everything. "I'd like to check the balance in my account."

Jiteyzz nodded. "What name is the account under, milord?"

Cringing inwardly, Jace told her his monster name. "Dedrurrurth."

"Thank you, milord," she said. "Just one second while I look that up."

The woman brought out a large, leather bound volume that she paged through. "Ah, yes, Sir Dedrurrurth. It appears you have 557,438 gold in your account, presently."

Jace's eyes bulged as she read off the number. A half a million gold. That was twice as much as he had on Mordred. He wondered if he could have it transferred over to Mordred once support resolved whatever bug had happened to him and the girls.

Mika leaned over to him. "You are rich!"

He nodded though he wondered how rich he actually was. He guessed that as a landowner, he had taxes to deal with and who knew what else. Tiebaut must have a clerk who kept track of his finances. He would need to see if the person had been transferred to Jace's employ and get an accurate idea of what money was coming in and going out. Provided he was in this character long enough to have to worry about it.

"Was there anything else?" the little gnome asked.

"Do you know anything else about my finances?" Jace asked.

"I'm afraid I only have access to your current balance, milord," she apologized.

"Thank you anyway," Jace said. "I think that will be it then."

Closing the book, the gnome stood up and came around to the other side of the desk. "If there's nothing else, milord, then I thank you for your patronage and wish you a good day."

Jace and Mika got up and left the bank with Luna following after them. The moment she was outside of the bank, she once again grew large.

"Does this mean we get married?" Mika asked.

Jace looked back at the bank. Obviously, money wasn't an issue, so he couldn't use that as an excuse. Despite his internal misgivings, he knew Diana was right. He needed the girls to come with him and marrying them seemed to be the only way.

He nodded at Mika. "It looks like we are."

At that, Mika jumped onto him, wrapping her legs around his waist, and encircling him with her arms. "I will make a good wife!" Then she kissed him.

Chapter 41

They met up with Diana later that morning. She was smiling wickedly as Mika and Jace slid into their chairs at the table.

"Good news," Diana said before either of them could speak. "The ceremonies will only cost 10,000 gold each, if we all get married at the same time. If we each want separate ceremonies, it will be twice that. And my temple can do it tonight."

"What?!" Jace sputtered. "Tonight?!"

"As soon as Charlena logs in," Diana nodded. "Don't tell me you're getting cold feet."

Jace realized it was only in-game marriage but part of him didn't like to be rushed into decisions like this. Plus, it was only temporary. Once support got him sorted out, he'd be Mordred again and he doubted the marriages would carry over.

When he really thought about it, he realized he was too practical to let this opportunity pass him by. It was what they'd been striving for this entire time. To get into the palace. Was he really going to let a little thing like matrimony get in his way?

He also knew divorce was easy in the game and didn't cost anything. Much like marriages in the real world, virtual marriage had a high divorce rate. Of course, that could be because so many people sold or traded marriages to nobility for money or favors. Just like in the real world, there were always people willing to sell or trade a piece of their soul for a little slice of the good life.

"No," he finally answered Diana. "It was just a bit sudden."

Diana waved her hand dismissively. "Not at all. I assume we'll need time tomorrow to make things official with the nobility police or whatever they are calling themselves."

Jace nodded. She had a good point. He assumed he'd need to take them to the patent office to get them signet rings or whatever type of passes spouses were given. "Good point."

"At least there isn't a lot of red tape or waiting in this world," Diana observed. "Imagine if there was a two-week waiting period or some such nonsense."

"Oh," Diana looked up. "I almost forgot. Do you have money? What did the bank say?"

"We have money," Jace sighed. "About a half million gold."

A wicked gleam came into Diana's eyes and she put her arm around Mika. "Girlfriend, I think you and I need to go shopping for wedding dresses!"

"Wedding dresses?" Jace gasped. "Are you serious?"

"Shopping?!" Mika repeated enthusiastically. Jace eyed both of them. They both grinned back at him. "Fine. But I need to go get money."

"We'll go with you," Diana said. "After all, we're both going to the Luxury District."

The three of them, plus an enlarged Luna, left the inn and went to the bank. While the girls waited outside with Luna, Jace withdrew the gold he needed for the ceremonies. He also took out another 10,000 gold for the dresses - he hoped they wouldn't be more than that, plus some money to get himself something to wear to the birthday party and he assumed he'd need to bring a gift. As an afterthought, he made sure he'd have enough to get the girls some wedding presents.

He also thought of certain magical items they would need once they got to the palace. Glasses of Revelation. The glasses were fairly rare and only useful in certain situations. Most people didn't even bother with them, but for their purposes they would be invaluable. The Glasses of Revelation revealed secret doors.

After taking enough money to buy one or two pairs of glasses, Jace gave the girls their money and told them to find something for the wedding and the birthday party.

"We'll see you tonight," Diana said and taking Mika's arm in her own, they took the money and hurried off, leaving Jace and Luna alone.

He looked to Luna. "Will you be coming along to the party?"

"Fish?" she asked and Jace suddenly had a vision of her pouncing on servers and devouring platters of any seafood dishes.

"Possibly," he told her. "But if you go, you have to remain small, okay?"

She seemed to consider his request and then sat back on her haunches. "Yes."

"Fine," Jace agreed. "You stay small and I'll see what treats we can find you at the party - assuming they let familiars in at all."

That seemed to appease the big cat and she got to her feet and rubbed herself against Jace, purring.

"Hey," said a nearby voice. "How'd you get a big cat?"

The speaker was obviously a player. He was a large, imposing werebear in golden plate mail armor. Across his back his back was strapped a large shield and at his hip hung a wicked looking spiked mace. Jace examined him.

Deegon Templarr
Level: 25

"A special quest," he told Deegon. "In a swamp south of Skystead. It gave my familiar the ability to grow."

Jace wasn't about to elaborate but he saw no reason to be rude. After all, if he saw someone with a giant cat, he'd probably ask about it too.

"Oh," the werebear replied, obviously disappointed. "It's a familiar. I thought maybe it was a pet or something. You must have gotten it a while ago."

"Why do you say that?" Jace asked curiously. It seemed an odd thing to say.

"The dragon, man," he said. "Haven't you heard? It controls the entire area around what used to be Skystead. It's crazy man. The thing's been destroying entire towns and now Crossroads. It must be some sort of new expansion."

"Wait! What?" Jace sputtered. "What was that about Crossroads?"

"It was destroyed yesterday," the werebear told him. "Dissolved into puddles of goop by the thing's acid breath."

"What about raiders?" Jace asked.

The werebear shrugged. "I read on the forums that three raids tried. Tried and failed. Not only that, but the thing dissolved their bodies man! That's insane! They lost hundreds of thousands of gold worth of gear and potions. Everyone's wondering if that's going to be the new normal. If so, raiding just got a lot more dangerous and a lot more expensive!"

Jace nodded. "Hopefully not."

The werebear grinned. "Hey, people will get their chance soon, raider or not."

"What do you mean?"

"A couple of players who have been shadowing the dragon reported that it's heading this way," the werebear said grimly. "It's coming to Whitecliff."

"Are you serious? When?" Jace managed to get out. The idea of a dragon laying waste to a city like Whitecliff didn't seem possible but a raid level monster in the hands of a player was a very dangerous and unpredictable thing.

Deegon nodded grimly. "It'll be here early next week unless it stops and destroys some villages along the way. At least, that's what the scouts are saying."

"Thanks," Jace told the player. He was trying to get his head around what this might mean for him. What if the dragon attacked and destroyed the castle? He'd never be able to use the *Help Desk*. At least, not in Whitecliff.

"No problem, man," Deegon said. "If I were you, I'd do what I'm doing. Get the heck out of dodge. I'm taking a ship on Saturday… uh… I mean, Weeksend. It cost a pretty penny and you always risk the pirates, but better than being a puddle of goo when the dragon gets here."

Jace nodded. "Good luck."

The werebear grinned again. "You too, man!"

After the player ambled off, Jace looked at Luna. "Did you hear that? The dragon's coming. Now we don't have a choice. We have to try during the party. We probably won't get a second chance."

"Dragon," Luna's ears went back at the mention of the dragon. "Bad Dragon."

He couldn't help but to agree. "Yes. Bad Dragon. We'd better go find the girls and let them know."

The two of them wandered around the Luxury District, trying to find the girls but didn't have any success. Most likely, they were in one of the shops, trying things on. Jace considered looking for an outfit for the party, but remembered he probably had an entire wardrobe of outfits at Tiebaut's house. And since all gear and clothing grew or shrank to fit the wearer, he should be able to find something for himself there.

Instead, Jace spent some time looking for gifts for the girls. Instead of the normal type, he figured he'd buy something somewhat useful. He went to the Central Market and found the player auction area.

The player auction area, sometimes called the Player Auction House, was a series of vendors where players could post items for sale or buy items other players had posted for sale. Normally, that only included items from your own faction, in this case, the good faction. Things from other factions could be bought as well, but only from the Black Market and at a 20% mark-up, unless you had a high thieves guild faction.

Sifting through the items was time consuming but he found two items he liked. The first was a magical quiver which would produce puncturing arrows. They'd allow Charlena to ignore up to 2 points of armor with her bow. He thought she'd appreciate that.

The second item was a magical bracelet which increased the magic damage of wand attacks by 2 points. It was gold, set with three pearls and looked kind of fancy. It would definitely be useful and hopefully nice enough that Diana will like it.

Though he was looking for gifts, he'd been keeping an eye out for the Glasses of Revelation. He'd found two pairs, but the price was more than he had anticipated. Unfortunately, he didn't have a choice. Those glasses would be the only fool proof way to reveal secret doors. Without them, they'd spend an hour just searching a single room. He purchased the two pairs of glasses and then went to look for Mika's gift.

The gift for Mika was more complicated and he had to go to the thieves guild. The Japanese girl loved being a samurai or ninja. He found a ninja hood in the Black Market that reduced the cost of *Vanish* by 1 mana. It would allow her to get more critical hits or allow her to save a little more mana for additional healing. Plus, she'd look like a ninja too.

He also found a collar that was obviously meant for a familiar or pet. It was a collar but resembled a black bow or bowtie. It gave the wearer 1 point of *Defense* and 1 resistance magic, fire, acid, ice, and lightning. For a low level item, it seemed powerful but Jace guessed that was because it was only usable by pets or familiars.

The Black Market also yielded one more pair of glasses and even though these were more than the others, he had to buy them. That gave him three pairs. One of them wouldn't get glasses which would cut their chances of finding the *Help Desk*.

Disappointed at not finding another pair of the magical glasses, he decided not to buy something for the princess until consulting the girls. Hopefully, they could give him some insight into what a princess might want.

With the girls' gifts in hand, he went to the Noble District. He passed the guards with no problems and went directly to Tiebaut's house. The same house he'd broken into just days ago and which now belonged to him.

He went to the front door and, retrieving his keyring, opened the door and went inside his new manor.

Chapter 42

Several people were lined up inside the foyer to greet him. The first was a portly, male halfling just inside the door, dressed in what Jace could only think of as butler regalia. He had a receding hairline and the hair he did have was cut short. Despite this, his sideburns came down low enough that they could almost be called mutton chops. The halfling smiled at Jace as he opened the door and inclined his head.

Just past the halfling was an older male gnome with a bald head and large gnomish spectacles that made his eyes appear twice as large. The gnome was dressed in a brightly colored suit that looked like something a tacky man might wear to an Easter party.

Across from the butler was a human woman who appeared to be the cook, though she was surprisingly slender for a cook. The woman was dressed in a white dress which had a stained apron over it.

Opposite the gnome was a female halfling who looked like a match for the butler. She was round, with an unruly mop of brown hair. She was dressed in a short tunic and breeches and, as was the tradition with many halflings, wore no shoes. Judging by the grass and dirt stains, Jace guessed she might be the gardener or groundskeeper.

The final person was a young, attractive blond woman with a very large chest who was dressed in a stereotypical, if very anachronistic, French maid style outfit. The outfit wasn't from the medieval period but Jace knew the developers had thrown things like this into the game, just for the fun of it. Given her curvaceous figure and vacant expression, Jace wondered if she'd provided other "services" that just being a maid for the previous Baronet.

The halfling inclined his head, which seemed to be a signal for the others to do the same. "Sir Dedrurrurth, we've been expecting you."

"Hello..." Jace said, and then looked at the halfling expectantly.

"Forgive me, milord," the butler looked apologetic. "I am Fimipp Wisesworn, your butler and head of household. Allow me to introduce the staff."

Fimipp gestured to the gnome next to him. "This is Mr. Kithkorn Lockwire, your clerk."

Kithkorn inclined his head again. "Milord."

"Across from me," the halfling gestured to the slender human woman, "is your chef, Mrs. Finnja Swail."

Finnja also inclined her head. When she spoke, her voice was much lower than Jace would have expected from so slender a woman. "Milord."

"And next to her is your groundskeeper, Miss Wathi Bladne."

"Just Wathi, milord," the halfling inclined.

"And finally," the butler said, and he noticed a tone of disapproval in the butler's voice. "Your maid, Miss Yvette Haley."

"Just Yvette," giggled the maid.

"Nice to meet you all," Jace told them. He remembered Luna, who was peeking inside, sniffing. "This is my familiar, Luna."

"Such a pretty kitty," Yvette cooed.

"Will she require a home to be built on the grounds?" his butler asked.

Jace looked down to Luna. Mentally, he asked her to shrink down in the house, and she did so. His servants all started, except for Fimipp. The halfling simple nodded. "Very good, milord. Does Miss Luna have any special dietary requirements?"

"Fish!" Luna sent mentally, though it came through more like a yell.

"If you could make sure that she has all the fresh fish she can eat," Jace replied. "She really loves fish."

"Very good sir," the halfling nodded.

Jace stood there awkwardly for a moment, unsure what to do or say next. Luckily, Fimipp seemed to sense this and turned to the others. "Off to your duties everyone. I'm sure if Sir Dedrurrurth wishes to discuss your individual duties with you, he will summon you to his study."

"I'll be looking forward to it," Yvette giggled. "Being summoned, that is."

Fimipp made a gesture and the rest of the staff rolled their eyes at the buxom woman and turned to leave. When they had started to walk away, he turned back to Jace. "What do you require, milord?"

"I… uh…" Jace started but momentarily forgot why he was here. Then he remembered. "I need to pick out an outfit to get married in."

The slightest expression of surprise passed over the butler's face, but he recovered so quickly Jace wondered if he had been mistaken. "Of course, milord. If you will follow me, I will show you to the master bedroom."

Jace had nearly said he already knew where it was but stopped himself just in time. There was no point in revealing he'd broken into the house. Though technically, he wasn't sure he could be charged with breaking into his house before it was actually his house. But it was still best to keep that part of his life to himself.

Yvette suddenly popped out from one of the side rooms. "I can show him the master bedroom."

"I wouldn't dream of taking you away from your cleaning duties," Fimipp told her and he gave her a stern look. "Off with you!"

The young maid winked at Jace but went back into the room she'd emerged from. It was a small living or entertaining room, if Jace remembered from his night time tour of the manor.

Upstairs, Fimipp opened the doors to the master bedroom. Jace was careful not to go right to the closets, but instead let the butler walk around the room and explain everything. When he was done, Jace explained that he was getting married and had been invited to the princess' birthday on Weeksend. He then went through several outfits that Fimipp set out. Tiebaut appeared to have spent vast sums of money on clothing that made him appear much higher in status than he was, giving Jace many options.

He settled on silk ruffled shirts under velvet coats. One of the jackets was trimmed in red, the other in green. With those, he would wear black breeches and high, leather boots that were polished so well he could see his reflection.

Putting both in his inventory, he turned to Fimipp. He could choose which outfit to wear for the wedding later. Right now, there was something else he needed to ask the halfling to do. "I'm getting married tonight and I assume some of these rooms up here are bedrooms, correct?"

Fimipp nodded. "This is correct, milord. Shall I have one prepared? And may I say, congratulations, milord."

"How many are there?" he asked.

"Besides the master bedroom," the butler replied. "There are three guest bedrooms."

"Perfect," Jace smiled. "Prepare them all."

"All, milord?" the halfling merely raised an eyebrow.

"If everything goes well, I'm marrying three women tonight."

"I see, milord. Shall I have Mrs. Swail prepare a wedding feast?" he asked.

When he thought about it, the answer was apparent. The girls would want to check out the house as soon as they got married. But he doubted any of them would have time for a sit down meal. Then an idea struck him. "No. Can you ask her if she can prepare some plates of little desserts, the kind you'd have at a party?"

"Of course, milord. Are there any desserts in particular you wish?"

Jace considered that for a moment. He really didn't know any fancy desserts, at least, not ones in the game. "Tell her to use her best judgement."

"And where will Miss Luna be staying?" the butler asked.

Looking down at Luna who just looked innocently back at him. "I suspect she will sleep wherever she wishes. She should be given free rein in the house." Thinking again, he amended his comment. "Within reason. I'd keep the larder locked."

"Very good, milord. Is there anything else?"

Thinking about it, Jace shook his head. "Not for the moment. I'm not sure what time we'll be back, but it will probably be after dinner time."

"We shall be ready, milord."

"Excellent," Jace told the halfling. "I need to get going so I can see what the girls have gotten."

He started to leave but then suddenly remembered his gifts. Spinning to face the butler, he smiled. "How are you at wrapping presents?"

Fimipp just raised an eyebrow. "I am manageable, milord. Do you have gifts you wish to have wrapped?"

Jace produces the items he'd picked up for the girls and handed them to the halfling. "Yes, can you wrap these?"

The butler simply nodded. "Of course, milord."

"Just label them what they are," he told the butler, so I know what to give to whom.

"As you wish, milord."

"Thank you, Fimipp," he told the halfling. "I'll be back later."

"Yes, milord."

Jace and Luna left the house then, with the cat reverting back to giant shape. She really enjoyed being in the larger form. He didn't blame her. If Jace could have magically changed his size back in the real world, he would be 6' 8" all the time as well.

He went to the patents office next and inquired about getting his soon-to-be wives access to the Noble District. It was surprisingly simple. He just needed to bring the marriage certificates and rings would be made for them. The man did warn that if they became divorced, her ring would stop granting access but Jace had known as much.

They would be open until 8pm, so if they got married shortly after Charlena logged in, they should be able to get the rings done tonight.

He thanked the man and then left to go find Mika and Diana. As he left the patents office, he checked the time. By habit he equipped the gnomish timepiece, glanced at the time. It was 5pm, Charlena would be logging in soon. He was about to unequip it when he stopped. Technically, he owned the timepiece now, it wasn't stolen property from Tiebaut any longer. It was his. Smiling, he left it on.

"Let's go find the girls and see if they're done shopping," he said to Luna.

The huge cat didn't bother looking at him, she just continued walking next to him. "Yes."

Chapter 43

It took a while to find the girls and, in the end, he had to ask Luna to track them. He found them in a pink building with a large window that displayed elegant gowns. A sign of thread and needle hung from the outside with the words, the Velvet Door in pink and powder blue. The two girls were coming out of the shop. When they saw Jace they smiled and waved.

"Find something to wear?" Jace asked.

"Oh yes, dear one," Diana replied. "We both found very nice gowns for tonight and for Saturday."

"Weeksend," Jace corrected. "It's called Weeksend in the game."

Diana dismissed him with a gesture. "Whatever it's called, we have dresses for it."

Mika was nearly vibrating with excitement. "Let's show him!"

"Show him?" the older woman looked aghast. "Absolutely not! He'd technically not even supposed to see us on the wedding day until the ceremony. At the bare minimum, we should at least keep the dresses as a surprise."

Mika looked crestfallen.

Noticing the energy drain from the other girl, Diana rolled her eyes. "You can at least show him the party dress."

At Diana's words, Mika beamed and in a moment's notice she was wearing a beautiful green velvet gown. The gown had an embroidered golden corset and golden embroidery on the sleeves, collars, and the hem of the dress. It looked stunning on her. She looked to him for his approval.

"Wow!" he managed. "You look amazing."

Mika beamed and did a small pirouette as he admired the view. When she finished, the dress disappeared, replaced by her normal gear. She looked at Diana. "Show him yours now!"

The older woman tsked. "Oh, I think I'll wait and surprise him. Besides, isn't it time we go find his third wife?"

Jace saw a shadow of something pass over Mika's face when Diana talked about a third wife but then he was checking his timepiece. "You're right. It's almost six. We need to get to the gate where we left her."

The three of them and the giant tabby cat arrived at the gate moments before Charlena appeared. One minute they were searching the people at the gate for any sign of her and the next she appeared.

"Hi guys," she said, as she appeared. "What's going on?"

Jace had tried to explain but Diana cut him off. She explained the invitation, their opportunity, and the only way to get in was for all of them to marry him. After she finished speaking, they looked to Charlena for her reaction.

"What?" Charlena said when she saw everyone's eyes on her. "Yeah. Of course, I'll marry him. I mean, it's just game marriage. It's not like it's real."

Whatever he had been expecting, her reaction wasn't it. Apparently, the other girls thought the same. Jace understood that to Charlena, this was all just a game she played. While it was the only life he, Diana, and Mika had known for months, this was just a few hours a day for the redhead. She had a real life to go back to when she logged out.

"That's very pragmatic," Diana said, breaking the silence. Jace wasn't quite sure, but the older woman's tone had changed. Maybe for her, this was real life. Being dead, it was the only life she'd ever get. The same with Mika.

"Are you going to buy a gown like us?" Mika asked. If she had taken offense to Charlena's words, it wasn't detectable in her tone.

Charlena brightened. "You bought gowns?"

"Yes," Mika said. "Jace gave us money."

The redhead looked at Jace. "Well, if Jace is buying, why not?"

"You'll need to make it quick," Jace told her. "The patents office closes at 8pm."

"Patents office?" Charlena asked.

"It's where we'll get your signet rings so you can enter the Noble District," he told them.

"Well then," she said. "Speed shopping time."

Charlena wasn't kidding either. They practically ran to the Luxury District and she found two gowns she liked in the second shop. Once they'd bought them, the group headed down to the Temple District to Diana's temple.

Chykela's temple was a large, stone building that reminded Jace of the old Greek pantheon. In fact, almost all of the temples he'd seen in the game were the same. The only ones that were different were the temples devoted to the non-human gods and goddesses.

"Now what?" Jace asked as they entered the temple.

"One minute," Diana told them. "Let me go talk to one of the high priests. But we may want to switch into our wedding clothes, so we're ready to go as soon as they are."

With that, Diana turned and hurried away, disappearing into one of the many corridors that lead away from the entrance chamber. Jace looked from Mika to Charlena and they all shrugged about the same time.

In moments, the three of them were dressed in their wedding garb. He hadn't been allowed to see Charlena's dress either. Diana had insisted. When he'd tried to come into the store, she'd stopped him with a stern look. He and Luna had been forced to wait out in the street while the women shopped for a dress for her. This was the first time he was seeing them in their gowns.

Charlena's gown was white in what Jace could only describe as a fairy tale style. It had a low, square necklace, a tight bodice but got bell shaped at the hips, spreading out several feet. That and the puffy, short sleeves made him think he should be fitting her for a glass slipper.

Mika's gown was almost the opposite. It was white as well but had a high "V" neckline and was very form fitting. The dress hugged her shape like a second skin until it got down to the knees. There, it spread out, but not nearly as much as Charlena's.

The two girls looked at each other appraisingly and then looked to Jace.

"Wow," Jace said, trying to find the right words. "You two look stunning."

That seemed to be the right thing to say, as both girls smiled radiantly.

Then Diana returned and Jace's mouth hung open. The wedding gown looked more like negligee. It was tight fitting enough to make Jace wonder if it were actually painted on. The fabric was sheer but had flowers embroidered into it that hid the most intimate parts. To say the neckline was low-cut was an understatement. It was a "V" that stretched down to her belly button, with the sheer fabric straining to contain her ample bosom.

Dian struck a sexy pose and glanced at Jace with bedroom eyes. "I take it by the huge puddle of drool on the floor that you approve?"

Jace snapped his mouth shut and nodded, not trusting himself to speak at that moment. The dress had obviously been created to be an attention getter and Jace was having a difficult time keeping his eyes off her. Luckily, the person who had come with her spoke up.

"I am high priestess Ortelia Bradly," the woman said. Her glowing eyes marked her as a half-angel nephilim. "And I would be happy to perform your ceremony Sir Dedrurrurth. Do you have the donations to the temple ready?"

Jace nodded and fished into his inventory. He brought out 40,000 gold in trade bars and handed the box to her. He found it oddly reminiscent of Tiebaut handing over the gold for the tiara. He resisted the urge to glance around the room to see if there were any hidden guardsman.

"Thank you, milord," the high priestess said. "If you'll follow me, we will perform the ceremony.

The group was taken to a large circular chamber with a twenty-five-foot-tall statue of the goddess standing inside a large, circular pool of water. Candles were floating on bowls or boats of some sort, casting flickering shadows across the room.

The high priestess took a few minutes to summarize the ceremony, which seemed very straightforward.

Ortelia stood in front of the goddess statue, just outside of the pool and the four of them formed a semi-circle around the high priestess. She gave a little speech about the goddess, love, and marriage. It was a little verbose and Jace considered just telling her to say, "Man and Wife!" but realized the girls would have killed him.

Finally, they got to the vows. They were very similar to the vows he'd heard on the vidstreams when people got married with maybe a little extra goddess stuff thrown in. They all repeated various parts when the priestess got to them and then, before he knew it, she was pronouncing them all married.

"You may kiss your spouses," the priestess said.

Before Jace could do anything, he heard Diana say, "Age before beauty, dear ones." The next thing he knew, Diana had pressed her lips, crushing his mouth into hers. And it was then he realized that there was something to be said for years of experience.

But then it was over and Charlena shoved her way to him and, giving the older woman a scornful look, kissed Jace just a fiercely. When she released him, she backed up and barely suppressed a glare as Mika came up to him.

She looked between the other two girls and planted a small, sweet kiss on his lips before retreating.

"Congratulations!" the high priestess said. "I'm afraid other duties call, but my clerk will see to your marriage certificates." The woman gestured to a robed acolyte in the back.

They thanked the nephilim priestess and she quickly disappeared through one of the doors just as a man in similar robes appeared.

The newcomer smiled at them. He was attractive and young and was dressed in the robes of a priest. "I'm Brocton Clapham, clerk of the temple. I will be filling out your marriage certificates."

The man sat down on a bench near the wall and motioned them to come to him. "Sorry, this is easier if I'm sitting down."

"Sir Dedrurrurth," he said. "It is customary sometimes to take a new last name or a new name entirely upon being wed. How do you wish to have your name recorded? And bear in mind, this will be legally binding, and you will be known by this name henceforth."

Jace almost laughed. The clerk was describing a character name change but in game terms. That must be part of the cost of the ceremony. Finally, he could get rid of Dedrurrurth. He was tired of being called by a kobold name. He wanted to hear people call him by his real name. "Jace Burton."

"Jace Burton," the clerk repeated. "Very good, milord."

"Lady Mizzlethain-galliegarde," he said. "What name shall I record on the official document."

"Diana," she responded and then hesitated for a moment before winking at Jace. "Diana Burton."

"Diana Burton," he repeated and then looked at Charlena.

Charlena was looking at Diana, who Jace knew she admired, with narrowed eyes. Then she nodded and looked back at the clerk. "Fine, since we're using real names. Charlena." She looked pointedly at Diana. "Charlena Burton."

"Mika Burton," Mika blurted out before the man could ask her. She looked around at everyone and smiled broadly. "It's like we are sisters now."

Momentarily taken off guard, the clerk quickly recovered. "Mika Burton, got it."

Her comment took the other girls off guard as well. Diana just raised an eyebrow. Charlena glanced at the girl and then her expression softened a bit.

After a few minutes, the papers were finished, and the clerk handed them each a copy. Once they had the papers, they wasted no time and made a beeline to the patent office to get their rings.

When they reached the gate to the Noble District, the guards addressed Jace by his new name. He found it amusing that they would magically know his name, but that was game logic. "Sir Jace Burton, how may we help you, milord."

"I was just married," he told the guard. "And my wives would like to get their signet rings."

He held out the marriage certificate and after glancing at it, the man backed. "Milord, I will have two of my men escort you to the patents office right away."

The newlyweds followed the guards and thirty minutes later they all were wearing matching signet rings.

"So," Charlena said, admiring her new ring. "Can we finally see your fancy new house now?"

They all chuckled and Jace nodded. "Absolutely. Let's go to our new home."

Chapter 44

The servants were all gathered again when Jace and the girls arrived, and he introduced all of them to his new wives. New wives. He had a hard time wrapping his head around the idea, even if it was just an in-game marriage.

As he had requested, Mrs. Swail had created numerous platters of desserts. Jace counted eight platters in all and guessed the poor woman must have been cooking since he'd left the manor earlier. Among the dishes, Jace saw fritters, something that looked like funnel cake, and several types of cookies. There were other things he wasn't sure about, but which looked equally delicious.

The servants started to leave but Jace asked them to stay and enjoy the desserts. They all seemed surprised and Fimipp tried to tell him about protocol. He just kept insisting and, in the end, had to pull rank until they all joined in.

He also found out he had a wine cellar and they brought up many bottles of wine and mead to share among them. After about an hour, everyone had relaxed and Jace asked Fimipp about the presents. The butler retrieved the now tastefully wrapped packages and handed them to Jace.

"What are those?" Charlena asked, finishing her wine.

"Wedding gifts," he told her. "They're on the practical side, but hopefully you'll like them."

He looked to the halfling as he held up the largest of the gifts and the butler mouthed, "Quiver."

"This is for you Charlena," he said and handed it to her.

She smiled broadly and took the package. She wasted no time and ripped into the package. "A quiver?"

"It allows your arrows to bypass two points of *Defense*," he told her.

"Nice!" she said, and the item disappeared into her inventory. She stood up and, after swaying a bit, walked over, and kissed him full on the mouth. "Thanks, Jace!"

He could tell she was intoxicated, at least in-game she was. The moment she logged off, she'd be sober, but the game would make her feel the effects of the alcohol until then. She backed away and went back to slump in her chair. Pouring herself another drink, she raised the glass to Jace. "Cheers!"

The smallest package was easy, and he gestured at his wrist as he looked at the halfling. The butler nodded. "This is for you, Diana."

Diana smiled and sauntered up to Jace. She took the offered package pouted. "A present for me. I didn't get you anything. Hmm. Maybe I can give you something later. After all, it is the wedding night."

Jace wasn't sure if he went pale or if the color rushed to his face but he was momentarily unable to formulate a response. "I… uh…"

Charlena and Mika had both perked up at her words and were glaring at both Jace and Diana. Diana waited for an answer for what seemed an eternity before she burst out in laughter. "Oh darling, you're so easy. No, I think I'd have a fight on my hands, even if you did say yes."

The older woman winked at him, turned, and walked back to her chair. Mika and Charlena both watched Diana the entire way and Jace half expected one of them to lunge at her. When she got back to her seat, she opened up her package to reveal the bracelet. "Very pretty. I assume it has some functional use too."

Jace swallowed. His mouth had gone dry as his mind had briefly entertained the idea of being with the raven-haired woman. The thoughts had come unbidden and as he looked at Charlena and Mika, he felt guilty for even having them.

He cleared his throat. "Yes… uh… it increases your wand damage."

Diana looked pleased and slipped the bracelet on. "That will certainly come in handy. Very thoughtful, Jace. And stylish."

Lastly, he took the remaining package and offered it towards Mika. "This is yours. I hope you like it."

Mika walked forward and took the package. She performed a small bow. "Thank you, Jace Burton."

Then she opened it up and turned it around in her hands until she saw what it was, then a huge grin formed on her face. "It is a ninja mask!"

Jace nodded. "It'll reduce the cost of your *Vanish* ability by 1 mana. Then you can do some serious ninja strikes."

She bolted forward and threw her arms around him. "Thank you Jace! It is perfect!"

Mika, who was still wearing her wedding dress, put the hood on and assumed what looked like a martial arts stance. "I am ninja!"

The group chuckled and Charlena, who had just down another glass of wine or mead, laughed. "Ninja Brides from VEIL! Sounds like a B-movie vidstream."

Jace laughed at the imaginary as well and bet if he searched hard enough in the archives, he'd find a ninja brides vidstream. "Yes, but it would probably be Ninja Brides from Outer Space!"

The buzzed women laughed, especially Charlena, who he knew also liked the older vidstreams from the late 20th century. She laughed and then added. "Or Undead Ninja Brides!"

At first, Diana's laugh surprised him, but he remembered she'd been 90-something years old when she died. Despite the 25-year-old body she now had, Jace realized she'd actually lived in the late 20th century. It was a sobering thought and made her previous "offer" seem a bit creepy.

Jace looked at the servants, who were all in chairs and couches on the opposite side of the room. They weren't laughing, but Jace understood that the constraints of the AI program wouldn't allow them to understand references to the outside world. At least they were eating and drinking.

As the laughter died down, Jace called Luna over to him. "And this is for you. It will make you harder for enemies to hit you."

He placed the bow collar on the cat who just looked at him. Then she used her rear leg to scratch at her neck before trotting back to the bowl of sardines Mrs. Swail had set out for her.

"She's secretly very thankful," Jace said as he watched the cat go and the girls burst out laughing. He smirked. Apparently, he was hilarious when everyone was drunk.

A sudden thought popped into his head as he remembered the werebear from earlier. He turned back to the girls. "I almost forgot! We may have some trouble in Whitecliff very soon."

The girls perked up and from the corner of his eye, he saw the servants become more attentive as well.

"I was talking with someone earlier," Jace told them. "He said the dragon wiped out Crossroads. They think it's heading here next."

He heard gasps from some of the servants and the girls sat up. Charlena focused on him. "As in, Crossroads is gone?"

Jace nodded. "Just like Skystead. My guess is, it's been systematically wiping out the outlying towns and villages to reduce spawn points. Now, it's coming here. Even if it doesn't wipe out the city, my guess is, it will start by taking out the graveyard."

"Can it wipe out the city?" Diana asked. "I mean, there are hundreds of soldiers and… wizards and stuff."

Shrugging, Jace took a sip of his mead. "I really don't know. But that acid breath is insanely potent. What would they do if it just flew high above the city and rained down acid until there was nothing left?"

"It would do that?" Mika asked.

"If I wanted to wipe out Whitecliff," he told them. "It's what I would do. I'd keep out of spell range and just rain acid down. Let's face it, if the person is smart, and he seems to be, he already realizes that the dragon is only really vulnerable when it's on the ground. So why would it land or even come in close enough."

He thought about it. "For that matter, he could just fly around grabbing huge stones and drop them on the city without any risk to himself. It's a raid level boss. I don't know what can stop it."

"That's terrifying," Diana said. "When is it supposed to be here?"

"Early next week," he replied. "As far as I know. And it could start off by laying waste to the palace."

"The palace?" Charlena exclaimed, a little too loudly. "Isn't that where the help-thingamabob is?"

"The *Help Desk*," Jace nodded. "It is. That means, we might not get another chance at this. Saturday, er, Weeksend, might well be our one and only chance to contact support unless we want to go to a different capital and try to get into their palace."

"A different capital?" Mika asked. "There is more than one *Help Desk*?"

"Yes. Supposedly, there was one in each capital. But we'd run into a similar problem there as we originally had here."

"Getting into the palace," Diana offered.

"Exactly," he told them. "And we have a decent amount of money, but I think even knighthoods cost about a million gold."

"Then we will find the *Help Desk* at the party," Mika declared.

Jace chuckled. "We'd better."

"Then what?" Diana said. "What happens once we find the *Help Desk*? I assume things don't just magically get fixed."

"You're right. They'll log a ticket. I'll give them all the specifics and hopefully, with the information I can provide, they'll be able to find the bug and identify the people who were affected. They should be able to put you back into regular game characters with all of your assets."

"That would be nice," Diana mused. She looked around at the manor. "I am totally buying myself a noble title and getting a manor. And a vineyard. You all will be welcome of course. Party at my house!"

The group chuckled or smiled, and the conversation died down.

"Oh shoot," Charlena said suddenly as she tried to stand, fell back into her chair, and then pushed herself up. "What time is it?"

"10pm," he told her after checking his timepiece.

"I have to go," she slurred. "I have work tomorrow. I'm taking a half day so I can go identify you tomorrow at 5pm. I'm not sure how long it will take me there but it's a two-hour train ride back plus the walk to and from the station, so figure three plus hours. I should be able to log in around 9pm or so to tell you the good news."

She had been slowly moving towards Jace as she spoke and then collapsed into his lap. She smiled up at him, her cheeks flushed. "I'll give you a proper wedding kiss when you wake up."

It looked like Charlena might kiss him but then suddenly she was gone and Jace was left with his arms out in an awkward pose. He dropped his arms to his sides.

Jace turned to the servants. "Thanks for being a part of the party, but if any of you need to go to bed, please don't feel obligated to stay."

Several of the servants looked relieved and even the ones who didn't stood up. They thanked him and said their goodnights before disappearing back towards the kitchen. As Yvette went past him, she stopped and whispered. "If you want your room cleaned later tonight or early this morning, there is a bell on the side of your bed. I will be up to tend to your needs at any time of the day."

Jace must have blushed because he heard Diana snickering. "Let me guess, the maid wanted to...clean your chambers?"

He nodded. Even though he hadn't drunk as much as Charlena, he was still feeling buzzed and thoughts of the busty maid were still lingering in his mind. Part of him still had a hard time with the difference between how things had been in the real world versus now.

In reality, he had been average looking at best and awkward around girls. Plus, being a nerd didn't exactly endear you to women either. The idea of being married to three beautiful women and having an attractive maid practically throw herself at him was a foreign concept.

Jace was tempted to take advantage of the offer, he was a guy after all. But part of him resisted. Even if he was interested in Diana, he doubted the older woman would say anything. Well, he might get teased about it, but she didn't seem the judgmental type.

Charlena would not understand nor easily forgive him, despite the fact that they'd never really said they were even boyfriend and girlfriend and she'd made her thoughts on game marriage clear. To her, it was just that: something she did in the game.

Mika was different. He was attracted to her physically. But that wasn't all. She had a sweet innocence and a silent strength that spoke to him. Together, they made her hard to resist. Still, he knew she would wait for him to make the first move. Maybe. Sometimes, her boldness surprised him.

"So, now what do we do?" Diana asked in a sultry voice. "Or is this going to be the most boring wedding night ever?"

Chapter 45

Since none of them actually required sleep, the trio decided to go murder some more beetles. Once they killed a dozen of the things, they realized the beetles were no longer a challenge for them - especially with Luna helping. Despite this, the experience had elevated Diana to 7th level in Priest. She was now higher than Mika in the class. One more level of Priest and the older woman could switch back to Mage.

Pleasantly surprised, Jace noticed immediately that the system messages were using their new names and it made it infinitely easier to read them. If for no other reason, the marriage was worth it just for the name change!

Since the beetles hadn't proven to be a challenge, they went to the lower level orc area. It was now past midnight on the east coast, so they hoped there wouldn't be as many players this late. They were right. His group was able to easily find a spot to pull and kill the orcs.

Unlike the other orcs they'd fought, these orcs were only level 15. They were one tier below the level 20 orcs, and it made a huge difference. They quickly adopted a strategy of letting Mika be main damage dealer, while Diana saved her mana for healing and attacked with her bracelet enhanced wand. Combined with Luna's damage and Jace's own DPS, they were easily able to kill the lower level orcs.

As they were resting in between kills, Diana looked around. "What will happen to all of this if the dragon comes?"

Jace glanced around the area and to the palace, visible off in the distance. "I don't know. There's a very real possibility the dragon could raze the city and everything around it."

"So, your house and title…" she trailed off.

"Will be worth nothing," he sighed. He'd thought about that too since the werebear had told him about the dragon. If the city was destroyed, all the stuff he had would be gone. Maybe not the money, but he needed to get clarification on that.

A few hours into their camping the orcs, Jace reached 9th level in Mage and Mika gained her 7th level in Rogue. Only a few thousand more experience until he was level 10 and had access to the next tier of weapons and armor. That would make fighting and tanking the monsters much easier.

He was thinking about where he could get next level armor and weapons when a huge orc stepped out of the forest and let out a deafening bellow. The thing came running towards his group and Jace quickly examined it in his HUD.

Ironfist Orc Warlord
Level 17

It was the orc warlord from their quest, and it was huge. It was eight or more feet tall and built like a bodybuilder. Worse, Jace could see the thing was waving two huge axes through the air. They were large enough to be two-handed weapons, but this thing was wielding them like they were normal axes.

Jace cast his *Air Armor* and prepared to meet it when a shout came from his left. It was a taunt and the orc veered sharply towards a group of four players that had come running over when the thing appeared.

"Did they just steal our orc?" Diana huffed.

"They did," Jace growled. "But whoever does the most damage gets the experience. Let's go."

His group didn't hesitate but followed him to wear the orc had reached the other group. There was a dwarf, a nephilim, a halfling and a gnome - the stereotypical good faction party. Jace brought them up in his HUD, so he could see their levels.

Jurguth Goldenguard
Race: Dwarf
Class: Paladin
Level: 11

Alalad Spiritgazer
Race: Nephilim
Class: Cleric
Level: 12

Bixur Richtrack
Race: Halfling
Class: Scout

Level: 12

Mumkan Shortmaster
Race: Gnome
Class: Wizard
Level: 13

Their levels were all in the teens, which meant Jace and his group would have a difficult time out damaging them. Difficult, but not impossible. Especially since Jace wouldn't be tanking and could use his backstab ability.

His group reached the orc just as it got to the other group. They fanned out in semi-circle around the back of the orc, mixing in with the members of the other group who were moving into place.

"Hey," snarled the dwarf. "This is our mob!"

"Because you stole it from us," Mika snarled.

The gnome laughed. "What are you all, human? And you're not even level 10."

"Yeah," chuckled the halfling. "Go back to the baby area and kill beetles or something."

The orc growled and attacked the dwarf, bringing both axes down at the much smaller dwarf. They bounced off the paladin's armor, but the player had a worried look on his face. "Geez! They're both two-handed axes!"

"I got you," the cleric told him and cast a healing spell.

The halfling slashed a dagger at the thing's back while their wizard casted a larger *Flame Bolt* at the orc that set the thing on fire. No doubt the gnome's attacks gave him the *Burning* quality, which would continue to do fire damage for a few seconds.

"What the heck?" the halfling spat. "This thing's *Defense* is high. My dagger didn't do anything."

"My *Flame Bolt* hurt it," the gnome grinned.

Of course, since none of the opposing group was part of his group, he couldn't see their damage, or the damage inflicted on them by the orc warlord. But he did see his own group's damage.

Mika Burton slashes Ironfist Orc Warlord for 5 damage.
Ironfist Orc Warlord is Bleeding.
Diana Burton shoots Ironfist Orc Brute for 4 magic damage and 2 acid damage.
Luna claws Ironfist Orc Warlord for 0 damage.
Luna claws Ironfist Orc Warlord for 0 damage.
Luna bites Ironfist Orc Warlord for 2 damage.

Jace frowned at the damage his group was doing. The halfling had been right. This thing's *Defense* must be high, and it would be a struggle to damage it, except by magical means. Then he stepped forward and drove his saber into the things back while slicing across the back of its leg.

You backstab Ironfist Orc Warlord for 22 damage and 9 acid damage.
You slash Ironfist Orc Warlord for 1 damage.

Jace grinned when he saw his backstab damage. He'd been the tank for some time now and it had been a while since he'd been able to backstab a monster. And with the Kraken's Claw, he could do some serious damage. Maybe they had a chance after all.

The orc cried out when Jace stabbed him, but it focused its hatred on the dwarf because of his *Taunt*. The thing sliced both of its enormous axes at the dwarf's head. Both blades bounced off the dwarf's shield or his helmeted head.

"Ouch," the dwarf said but there was no real pain behind his words. Jace guessed, like most players, his sensory level was set low for combat. He probably got 10% of the pain, if that.

A little jealous of the dwarf's ability to take a blow without feeling every little muscle fiber being severed, Jace and his group attacked.

Ironfist Orc Warlord Bleeds for 3 damage.

Mika Burton slashes Ironfist Orc Warlord for 0 damage.
Diana Burton shoots Ironfist Orc Brute for 5 magic damage and 2 acid damage.
Luna claws Ironfist Orc Warlord for 0 damage.
Luna claws Ironfist Orc Warlord for 0 damage.
Luna bites Ironfist Orc Warlord for 0 damage.

You backstab Ironfist Orc Warlord for 11 damage and 6 acid damage.
You slash Ironfist Orc Warlord for 0 damage.

Jace cringed as he saw how poorly his group had done. He could only hope the other group was doing just as poorly, but judging by their comments, they weren't.

"Hey," the gnome said, as he noticed Luna. "How do they have a giant cat helping them? Is that even fair?"

"Maybe it's a pet?" the cleric yelled.

The orc didn't care about pets or how much damage each group was doing. It only seemed interested in killing the dwarf. It attacked again with both axes as if it were trying to hammer the paladin into the ground.

The dwarf grunted as he caught the first blow on his shield but then the second one struck his shoulder and whistled. "That was a good hit… 16 damage. And that's through my 11 *Defense*."

The paladin and the rest of his group attacked the warlord and then Jace and his group attacked.

Ironfist Orc Warlord Bleeds for 3 damage.

Mika Burton slashes Ironfist Orc Warlord for 2 damage.
Ironfist Orc Warlord is Bleeding.
Diana Burton shoots Ironfist Orc Brute for 7 magic damage and 2 acid damage.
Luna claws Ironfist Orc Warlord for 0 damage.
Luna claws Ironfist Orc Warlord for 0 damage.
Luna bites Ironfist Orc Warlord for 3 damage.

You backstab Ironfist Orc Warlord for 13 damage and 6 acid damage.
You slash Ironfist Orc Warlord for 0 damage.

Once again, his group didn't do as much damage as he was hoping. Even Mika's critical strikes were only occasionally making it through the warlord's armor. Of course, those thoughts fled his mind as the creature suddenly reared back and screamed.

Ironfist Orc Warlord goes Berserk.

"I've got a bad feeling about this," he managed before the thing spun and attacked him.

Ironfist Orc Warlord Bleeds for 3 damage.
Ironfist Orc Warlord slashes at YOU for 6 damage.
Ironfist Orc Warlord slashes at YOU for 4 damage.

He caught the blows on his buckler and his shoulder, but they hurt. Jace grimaced and wished he could adjust his own sensory input.

"Haha!" the dwarf laughed. "It's attacking them now!"

"Is he roleplaying the pain or something?" the cleric asked.

"Weirdo," the halfling chuckled.

The group was trying to position themselves behind the orc when it spun again. This time, the axes came down on Mika.

Ironfist Orc Warlord Bleeds for 3 damage.
Ironfist Orc Warlord slashes at Mika Burton for 12 damage.
Ironfist Orc Warlord slashes at Mika Burton for 13 damage.

Mika screamed behind her ninja mask as the blades cut into her. Jace wanted to rush over to help her but he knew there was nothing he could do except try to *Taunt* it.

"Fight me!" he cried out, but the orc ignored him.

"Did he just try to *taunt* the orc? Duh, Mages can't do that," the gnome snickered.

It became clear that the *Berserk* ability of this orc was causing him to attack random targets, so everyone stopped trying to position themselves and just continued attacking. Except for Jace. He rolled behind the creature, came up and backstabbed it again.

Mika Burton slashes Ironfist Orc Warlord for 4 damage.
Ironfist Orc Warlord is Bleeding.
Diana Burton shoots Ironfist Orc Brute for 6 magic damage and 2 acid damage.
Luna claws Ironfist Orc Warlord for 0 damage.
Luna claws Ironfist Orc Warlord for 0 damage.
Luna bites Ironfist Orc Warlord for 0 damage.

You backstab Ironfist Orc Warlord for 4 damage and 9 acid damage.
You slash Ironfist Orc Warlord for 0 damage.

"Keep attacking newbies," the dwarf yelled. "You're just helping us kill it quicker."

Jace ignored the dwarf but guessed the paladin was probably right. But Jace hated to give up.

"Pour it on!" Jace encouraged but then the orc spun again and came down on Mika again.

Ironfist Orc Warlord Bleeds for 3 damage.
Ironfist Orc Warlord slashes at Mika Burton for 8 damage.
Ironfist Orc Warlord slashes at Mika Burton for 4 damage.

The blows weren't nearly as bad, and this time Mika didn't cry out. Instead she *Vanished* and attacked the creature even as the other group attacked.

Mika Burton slashes Ironfist Orc Warlord for 5 damage.
Ironfist Orc Warlord is Bleeding.
Diana Burton shoots Ironfist Orc Brute for 7 magic damage and 2 acid damage.
Luna claws Ironfist Orc Warlord for 0 damage.
Luna claws Ironfist Orc Warlord for 0 damage.
Luna bites Ironfist Orc Warlord for 1 damage.

You backstab Ironfist Orc Warlord for 12 damage and 9 acid damage.
You slash Ironfist Orc Warlord for 2 damage.

His entire group at least did some damage and judging by the sour faces from the other group, only the dwarf and wizard did any real damage. But before he could celebrate, the warlord spun again.

This time, the axes came down on the gnome, who flinched but otherwise didn't react to the blows. Then his eyes went big. "Oh man! It just took out half my health. Healer! Medic!"

His group and the other group attacked at relatively the same time and the creature went down. As it fell, to his great surprise, Jace received a system message.

Ironfist Orc Warlord dies.
You gain 900 experience.

The other group seemed to all pause, possibly waiting for their own system message. After a moment, they realized it wasn't coming.

"You cheaters!" yelled the halfling. "How the hell did you outdamage us?"

"What the -?" muttered the dwarf.

The gnome was still yelling for a medic and didn't seem to even realize the warlord was dead.

"Freaking noobs," the cleric muttered.

"Sorry gentlemen," Diana purred. "We beat you fair and square."

"Hah," barked the dwarf. "None of you are even level 10! And what's with the same last name? What are you, like brother and sisters?"

"We are his wives!" Mika said proudly.

The other party went quiet.

"Wives?" asked the halfling.

"Yes, dearie," Diana cooed as she went over to Jace and draped herself over him. "We're two of his wives. The third one had to logoff or she'd be here too."

Mika seemed to catch on to what Diana was doing and threw her arms around Jace. "Yes, he is a very good man."

"Three wives?" the gnome said, giving Jace an appraising look.

Diana pulled on Jace's arm, leading him back towards Whitecliff. She looked back towards the other party. "All this fighting has gotten me a bit... hot. I think we should go back to the house. What about you Mika?"

Mika bobbed her head but Jace could see some color in her cheeks. "Yes, let's go back to the house!"

The girls were leading him away and he suddenly remembered something. Momentarily untangling himself from the women, he ran back to the orc's body and looted it. Then he waved to the other group who was looking at him with unabashed admiration.

"Sorry, I gotta go," he smiled. "The girls are waiting."

As he rejoined the girls, he heard the cleric behind him. "Three wives?"

Then another voice just as he walked out range. "Must be a rich son of a…"

Chapter 46

The trio headed back to the gates, where they turned in the repeatable quests for the orc sashes, as well as the quest to kill the warlord.

You have completed the quest, "End The Warlord's Rage"
You gain 450 experience. Experience to next level 1,480.
You gain +50 faction with Whitecliff City Guard

It wasn't as much experience as Jace would have liked, but every little bit counted. He had hoped he might reach 10th level before morning, but it didn't seem to be in the cards. It was only 3am, a little too early for breakfast. They walked past the Dwarvish Fork Inn and Jace paused.

"I guess we should continue eating breakfast here," he said as his two wives followed his gaze. He glanced at his timepiece. "Once it's breakfast time."

"Well," Diana said. "This is where you told us all to meet. Whether or not the others you freed will make it here is another thing."

"Yes," Jace agreed. "I'm guessing there are no caravans from the west since that's the direction the

441

dragon is coming from. I doubt any caravans from the east want to come here right now."

"Because we have an acid breathing dragon about to destroy the entire city!" Mika agreed.

"There's that," Jace smirked. "I think I'd postpone my travel plans if the itinerary involved becoming dragon bait."

"What are we going to do about it?" Diana asked. "Please don't tell me we're going to sit here hoping that support helps us before the dragon gets here."

Jace shook his head. He knew from experience how long fixing a complex issue could take. It could be days or even a couple of weeks. Hopefully, they'd put as many people as possible on the problem, but you never knew with WorldCog. No, they couldn't just wait here like lambs to the slaughter. "After the party, regardless of whether or not we find the *Help Desk*, we should leave. We have enough money, we can board a ship and sail for one of the other capitals."

"How?" Mika asked. "There are no caravans."

Jace smiled. "We can afford a teleport now, but we'd have to do two teleports to get our entire group and that'll be at least 20,000 gold, probably more since we're not in a guild. Then there's the servants. I know they're just NPCs, but I don't feel right leaving them behind."

Mika nodded. "No. That would be wrong."

"Maybe we could just leave Yvette to mind the store," Diana offered with a wink.

Mika seemed to consider it but shook her head. "We can't do that."

"Oh, I know. I know," Diana said. "Jace is the hero in this little story and heroes don't leave big chested bimbos to be eaten by dragons. They rescue them."

"Are you sure?" Mika asked.

"Look at him," Diana gestured to Jace. "Do you really think he'd leave her behind?"

Mika and Diana stared at Jace for a moment, then Mika shook her head. "No, he is too nice."

Jace looked from one girl to the other. "Do I get any input in this?"

"No," they both said and then, realizing they spoke the same thing at the same time, they both giggled.

"Fine, fine," Jace said, holding his hands up. "You two talk about me all you want."

"Wait," Mika chimed in. "You didn't say. How are we all going to get out of here?"

"A ship," Jace said. "We have more than enough money to commission one and I'll find one with enough rooms for all of us. But I need to do it at first light. Once word of the dragon gets around, I suspect the ships will get full very fast."

"That sounds exciting," Mika grinned. "We will sail the seas!"

"Where will we go?" Diana asked.

"I'm not sure," he shrugged. "I'm thinking it will depend on what ship we get passage on. I definitely want to make sure it's one of the capitals though. Or at least, close to one of the capitals. I don't know the good faction cities as well as I know the evil."

"In the meantime," Jace said. "Mika and I need to make a quick run to the thieves guild. I'd like to try and get a quest in before dawn. Maybe I can make level 10."

"Yes!" Mika agreed enthusiastically.

"Hmm," Diana pursed her lips. "Actually, I need Mika. She and I need to go shopping in the Central Market. They're open, right?"

"Shopping?" Mika gave the older woman a quizzical look. The older woman favored her with a pointed look, and something seemed to pass between them. "Oh yes… shopping!"

"Most of the shops should be open," he told them, looking between the two women suspiciously. They were obviously up to something. "It's one of the few places in the city that never sleeps."

"Excellent," Diana replied and held out her hand. "If only I knew a handsome, young lord with lots of money, who could help out two penniless women."

Jace rolled his eyes and looked into his inventory. "How much?"

"5,000 should do it," Diana said.

"5,000!" he exclaimed. "What are you planning to buy?"

"Women things," Diana said, waving his objection way.

"Yes," Mika giggled. "Women things."

He waited for her to elaborate but she continued to look at him expectantly. "Fine."

Jace took the remainder of his money, just under 7,000 gold and handed it to her. "There's some extra in there. Can you see if you can find a nice present for the princess? It is her birthday and I suspect they'll expect us to bring something."

"Oh," Diana purred. "A present for a princess… on a budget. That's quite a challenge."

"If you find something that you think is suitable," Jace sighed. "And you need more money, just let me know. But try to keep it reasonable. This place could be gone in a few days and that money will be all we have to live off of."

"I am the epitome of reason," Diana said with not even a touch of sarcasm.

"Okay," Jace said. "You two go shopping and then meet me back here for breakfast, okay?"

"Yes, yes," Diana said, putting her arm through Mika's. "Ta-ta! Run along!"

"Come on," Jace said to Luna, who had been cleaning herself.

He left the girls to go shopping. He knew he didn't have much time left so he jogged all the way to the thieves guild. When he arrived, he was greeted by Thom and Gerry at the door and then immediately went looking for Webley. He found the guildmaster at one of the tables and the man looked up as he approached.

"If it isn't our own Baronet," Webley grinned. "Still associating with your friends in low places?"

"You know it," Jace returned the smile.

"Taking a little break from the noble life to do some honest labor," Webley asked, then amended himself. "Or should I say, some dishonest labor?"

"I'd like to get two jobs if possible," Jace told him.

The guildmaster chuckled. "Had least the soft noble life hasn't curbed your enthusiasm." Webley waxed thoughtful for a moment and then looked back at Jace. "I think I have just the thing."

The jobs were both easy. First, he had to plant a crate of forbidden dark elf wine on a ship docked at the docks. Next, he needed to sneak into the harbor master's office and place a note on the desk of one of the customs agents to search the ship.

In the morning, someone would find the note and the ship would be searched. Once they found an illegal crate of dark elf wine, the captain would be fined and or imprisoned and the ship would be impounded. Idly, Jace wondered what the guild was getting out of it, but he knew not to ask too many questions.

He made it back to the guild as dawn was breaking and turned in the quest, earning himself level 10 in Mage. This meant he was now in the next tier of play and had access to tier 2 weapons and armor, which would make him much more formidable. Because he had crossed the tier, he was also given a new thieves guild jerkin but this one was level 10!

He checked his stats to see what else he gained but there was nothing. Jace thought he would have earned new spells but then he remembered that after 1st level, all spells had to be bought from the mages guild. He smirked. Yet another expense.

He thanked the guildmaster and headed back to meet the girls. As he walked, he became curious about how his new level affected the Kraken's Claw, since it was a scaling weapon. He brought the weapon out and examined it.

Kraken's Claw
Type: Saber

Level: (10)
Damage: (15) + (6) (Legendary) + (2) (Sharp)
Wt: 3 lb
Special: This item is Legendary and scales to the wielder's level. In addition to normal damage, blows from this weapon inflict an additional (6) Acid damage. This weapon also carries the Puncturing quality and ignores 3 Defense.
Description: Forged in the heart of a volcano, the smith who created this blade is rumored to have embedded it with a fragment of the soul from the legendary Kraken.
Soulbound: This item has been soulbound. It cannot be sold or traded and appears in the wielder's inventory when they respawn.

Sheathing his weapon, he couldn't help but grin. It was an awesome weapon and he really hoped they'd let him keep it when they put him back in Mordred.

Feeling good, he made it back to the Dwarvish Fork. Technically, he was still a guest since he had the room until midday. It didn't really matter since the dining room was open and he found the girls waiting for him at the table.

When they spotted him, Mika waved enthusiastically with the big grin on her face. Jace walked over and saw they had a package on the table between them.

"We have something for you!" Mika blurted out the moment Jace sat down. "You will like it so much!"

Diana rolled her eyes. "So much for the surprise." She waved her hand in a dismissive gesture. "Go on, go on. Open it before she bursts."

"This is for me?" Jace asked.

"Yes," Mika said. The almond-eyed girl was practically vibrating with excitement. "It's a wedding present."

Grinning, Jace pulled the package to him. "Thank you. You didn't have to get me anything."

"Of course, we did, darling," Diana said. "Personally, I wanted to get you the diamond studded codpiece."

Jace stopped unwrapping as he felt the heat in his cheeks. "You got me a codpiece?"

Diana waved away his worries. "I said that's what I wanted to get you. But Mika insisted on something practical. As it is, I think it's stylish and practical."

A little more wary, Jace finished unwrapping it to find a bundle of red cloth. As he unfurled it, Mika couldn't seem to resist and blurted out, "It's a cloak of invisibility!"

Chapter 47

"A cloak of invisibility?" Jace asked incredulously. He pulled the bright red cloak free of the wrappings and held it up. It was definitely a cloak.

"Well, as close as we could find and afford," Diana admitted. "And the lowest level we could find was level 10, but it looks like that's not a problem any longer."

Bringing up his HUD, Jace examined the item.

Mountebank's Cloak
Type: Cloak
Level: 10
Wt: 3 lb
Special: +10 Stealth. When outside of combat, Stealth checks automatically succeed. Any effect that normally cancels Stealth, causes the cloak's magic to fail.
Description: Worn by the famous cat-kin Rogue, Qroccar Meminoh, it was lost when he climbed into a bedroom window to woo a maiden, only to find her father waiting with a crossbow.

Jace whistled. For a level 10 item, it was amazing. Diana was right, it was the closest thing he'd find to an invisibility cloak at this level. With the boost in his *Stealth* and checks automatically succeeding, even against higher level creatures. "Wow! This is awesome!"

"I told you he'd like it," Diana said. "Especially with his proclivity towards the practical."

Smirking, Jace swapped the cloak out with his armored cloak. His *Defense* went down, but if the cloak did its job, he shouldn't need to fight.

Now that he was level 10, his skill rank maximum was 20. If he could reach rank 20 before they went to the party, his effective score would be 30. With his *Stealth* checks automatically succeeding, he would be invisible to all but the highest-level characters. It truly was a powerful gift. "Thank you. And you were able to afford this with the money I gave you?"

Mika and Diana exchanged looks but it was Mika who spoke. "We sold our wedding dresses to get the extra money."

Jace wasn't sure how much virtual wedding dresses meant to the girls, but he appreciated their sacrifice. "Really? You sold your dresses? Thank you."

Mika beamed but Diana just waved it off. The older woman cleared away the wrappings and beckoned him to sit down. "Since you are now level 10, I take it your nightly activities were a success?"

Nodding, Jace slid into the chair across from the two girls. "Yup, level 10 in Mage now. I guess that means I can switch classes again but I'm not even sure what to switch to. Should I switch to Rogue now and get that to 11 and then go back to Fighter?"

The waitress showed up then and they all ordered waffles, except for Luna. The little cat was in the chair next to Jace, looking up expectantly. "And fish for my cat."

The waitress nodded and headed back to the kitchen. Once she was out of earshot, Diana spoke up. "Why are you even worried about switching classes? Won't the WorldCog people just zap us back to the way we should be once you find the thingamabob?"

Jace grinned. "It doesn't work quite that fast. It could take them a while to set things right, so we could be stuck in these bodies for a few weeks."

"So?" Diana asked. "You'll still end up losing anything you do or gain here, right? Not to mention, you'll be waking up any day now and will be back in the real world."

There was no bitterness in Diana's voice, just a statement of fact. She didn't seem to resent the fact that Jace was alive and he was glad. Mika, Diana and Charlena were really the only real friends he had.

"What will you do when you wake up?" Diana asked and Mika perked up at the question.

"I don't really know," Jace told them. "Hopefully, I'll still have a job. Otherwise, that'll be the first thing I have to do."

"What about WorldCog?" Mika asked. "They are bad."

He shrugged. "Maybe. We don't know for certain. I definitely need to blow the whistle on them, even if they fix the issue. Their process needs some oversight and accountability, so this type of thing doesn't happen again."

"Do you think anyone will listen?" Diana asked. "After all, aren't they like the biggest company in the world now?"

"There's that," Jace frowned. "I don't even know who - if anyone - would listen. I'll take my case to the Department of Justice if I have to."

"Will you visit us in the game?" Mika asked, her voice suddenly very small.

"Oh, darling," Diana told him. "You must come back and visit. I plan to have a huge manor house once I get my fortune."

Jace raised an eyebrow. "How much money do you have?"

The older woman gave him a wicked smile. "That would be telling. But suffice it to say, I shouldn't be lacking for anything."

"That much, huh?" Jace said wistfully.

"Oh, dear one," Diana smiled. "You married well. When you come visit, I'll take good care of you."

"He married two rich wives," Mika broke in, smiling. "I am worth a lot too. I would have left it to charity, but I never got a chance to update my will after I inherited my grandmother's estate."

"He's obviously a gold digger," Diana said.

"Wait a minute," Jace objected, keeping a deadpan face. "Right now, I'm the one with the money. Doesn't that make you two gold diggers?"

Diana rolled her eyes. "No, but it does make you one heck of a lucky man."

Mika seemed to consider and then nodded. "That's right. You are a lucky man Jace."

Luna looked up at that moment, made eye contact and meowed one word. "Yes."

Jace held his hands up in surrender. "Fine! Fine! I'm a lucky man."

Diana reached out and took his hand and squeezed it. When she spoke, there was no hint of teasing in her voice. "Jace, I mean it when I said I hope you come and visit. You will always be welcome in whatever manor I end up with. If it weren't for you, I really don't know what I would have done. I'd probably still be in the body of that mechanical-spider-thing."

Not knowing what to say, he didn't say anything and held her gaze for a long moment as she squeezed his hand. Finally, she released it and sat back.

"I don't know if I will buy a house," Mika said, breaking the silence. "But you can come on an adventure with me. We will have a good time together."

"That sounds fun," Jace said, but then added in a playful tone. "But you'll have to gain some levels. Mordred is 95 and he's ready to be a raider."

Mika pouted. "That's right. We are too many levels apart."

Jace smiled. "I'll be waiting for you and besides, it won't take you that long. We… mean you, won't sleep. You'll be able to catch up while I'm working and sleeping."

She brightened at his words. "Yes, I will catch up and then we will go on adventures!"

"We're talking like this is all over," Diana said. "And we haven't even found the *Help Desk* thingy. Maybe we shouldn't count of chicks before they're hatched."

"Jace will find it," Mika said confidently. "You said it before. He is a hero."

He hoped she was right. Even with the cloak, searching the palace would be a risky endeavor. There were bound to be high level guards all over. Even with the magical cloak, there was no guarantee any one of them - or all of them - wouldn't be caught.

The worst part was, they could search the entire night and still not find the *Help Desk*. If that happened,

Jace wasn't sure what they'd do. With the dragon closing on Whitecliff, they'd be hard-pressed to find another opportunity to get into the castle before the dragon arrived. And if the dragon destroyed Whitecliff, then what? He'd have to start over in a new capital and figure out how to get into their palace.

"Why so morose?" Diana asked. "Married life got you down so quickly?"

Jace smirked. "Just thinking about tomorrow night."

"We'll find it!" Mika said with confidence.

"Is that all?" Diana asked. "Thinking about this evening and Charlena's little visit to the hospital?"

Part of him had been thinking about that. No, not thinking about it. Dreading it. What shape was his body in? What would Charlena come back and report? He hated to admit it, but he was afraid. He was afraid of what she would tell him and what he'd have to live with for the rest of his life. Was he crippled? Was he missing a limb? An eye?

He knew it was silly to speculate and that his imagination was running away with him. Still, he had this gnawing dread in the pit of his stomach about it. It was irrational, he knew, but it was there, nonetheless. And the only way he could deal with it was to shove it to the back of his mind.

"Sorry," Jace forced a smile. "I just don't know what to expect."

"She'll say it is you and that you are still alive," Mika assured him.

But Diana seemed to be reading his mind. "You're worried about what state your body is in, aren't you?"

Jace nodded.

"Darling," she said. "I'm sure everything is fine. There's no use in worrying about it until she gets back."

"I know," Jace sighed. "It's still hard… not knowing what to expect."

Diana nodded, her face taking on a more motherly expression. "I lived for a long time. Almost a century. In my years, I have had a myriad of health issues and I know the dread that comes with waiting for the results of a test that can irrevocably change your life. It's a feeling like few others."

He remained quiet. Diana may be an incorrigible flirt, but she had a lifetime of experience and writer's insight. She was right on the money with the way he felt. It was a feeling unlike anything he'd felt. And the closer he came to finding out, the worse it became.

"You will be fine," Mika told him. "And no matter what. You will have us."

Jace smiled at her words, though he didn't even know if that were true. It had been months since his accident. He didn't even know if he had a job, let alone an apartment. His rent was automatically deducted from his account, but he wasn't sure whether or not he had any money left in his account. It had to be close.

When the money ran out, and it would soon, he'd be evicted. The landlord would sell all of his stuff and rent out his apartment. Not only would he not have a place to go back to, he wouldn't have a pod to play the game. Without a pod, there would be no game for him.

He needed to wake up and he needed to get out of the game. If he didn't, he'd have no life to go back to.

Chapter 48

Mika and Diana also showed Jace the present they'd gotten for the princess. It was a gorgeous golden bracelet that looked like vines. On the tips of the vines were small diamonds. It was elegant yet simple and then he noticed that there were exactly eighteen diamonds.

"Eighteen diamonds," Jace commented. "And she's turning eighteen. Nice touch."

"I thought so," Diana agreed, and Mika just nodded.

After breakfast, Jace told the girls that he needed work on his *Stealth* before tomorrow night. It was still early in the morning, and he suggested the lower level orc area where he could sneak into the forest and pull the orcs to the group.

The girls agreed and they returned to the orc area, but a little further south along the road. Here the orcs were only level 10. This played nicely into Jace's ulterior motive. Being level 10, his old gear was outdated. By killing some level 10 orcs, he might be able to replace his gear without having to spend more money.

He had money. He had more money that he'd ever had before in the game. But if they didn't find the *Help Desk* tomorrow night and then the dragon destroyed Whitecliff, he'd need every penny and probably much, more to get into another palace. He needed to conserve.

The other reason Jace wanted to be out here, fighting orcs, was to keep his mind off of Charlena's visit to the hospital today. In eight hours or so, she would be looking at someone in a coma - hopefully, him. Then she could come back and tell him that he really was alive. And tell him what shape his body was in.

The waiting was driving him nuts and if he didn't have a distraction, he thought he might lose his mind. Or drink himself into a virtual stupor with virtual mead. He didn't think the latter was a good idea since he had things to do.

Before leaving the inn, Jace went up to the room they'd rented and unsummoned and resummon Luna. It had been a while and the pain surprised him momentarily, but he pushed through it and dumped all his mana and as much health as it would let him.

"Feel any different?" Jace asked the little cat after she'd appeared.

His familiar stretched, walked over to him and rubbed up against his leg. "No."

He had wondered if she would be any stronger, now that he was a level 10 Mage, but apparently not. She looked exactly the same as before. When Jace thought about it, that made sense. He'd seen level 90+ familiars and they looked exactly like their smaller counterparts.

"Let's go," he told the orange tabby and went downstairs to gather up the girls.

When they reached the spot Jace wanted, the two girls and Luna set up near the road as Jace got ready to go pull an orc. Jace slipped on his magic cloak and made sure all of his armor and weapons were equipped.

Then, he opened his HUD. Jace was level 10 in Mage now, making it his highest class. Once again, he could switch classes. He brought up his character sheet and looked at his class list.

Mage: 10
Rogue: 9
Fighter: 4

He was the party's tank. The logical choice would be to return to Fighter. Despite this, Jace wanted to get level 10 in Rogue first. It was less than 3000 experience away and it would give him *Critical Eye II*, increasing his damage on critical strikes to x3 instead of x2. With the *Kraken's Claw* and his *Feint*, he'd be able to do a lot more damage.

He debated for a long moment before deciding to trust his instincts and go with Rogue. He made the switch, smiled at the girls, and went into *Stealth*. It was time to kill orcs and chew bubble gum. And he was all out of bubble gum.

His group did exactly that until just after noon. The orcs weren't much of a match for his team. They didn't have nearly the armor that the warlord had, nor the health. Plus, Luna's combat abilities did seem to improve slightly as well.

During the fighting, Mika reached level 8 in Rogue. Shortly afterwards, Diana reached level 9 in Priest. Jace was now less than 800 experience away from level 10 in Rogue but as much as he wanted to finish up, there were more important matters.

"Let's head down to the docks," Jace told them, as he checked his timepiece.

"Booking our passage out of here?" Diana raised an eyebrow.

"Yes," he nodded. "Before the ships are all taken - assuming they aren't already."

The group returned to the gates where they decided to let Mika turn in all the sashes. She was further behind in experience than Jace or Diana and they agreed she should get the experience from the repeatable quest. She objected at first but eventually relented.

From the gate, they went directly to the docks. When they reached the docks, they found them packed with people and Jace had a bad feeling they might be too late. His group split up and began asking the various ships about passage.

Jace soon feared he may have waited too long. Every captain he talked to was either already full, were leaving before the princess' birthday party or weren't equipped to handle passengers. It wasn't looking good.

After an hour, he met up with Mika and Diana. By the expressions on their faces, they didn't not bring good news. "No luck?"

"Well I did get several offers of passage - in the captain's bed," Diana chuckled mirthlessly. "But other than that, no luck."

They looked to Mika, but she shook her head. "I had no luck. The ships are already booked, leaving too soon or impounded."

Impounded? Jace had planted evidence on a ship for Webley. Was it the same ship? Had the guildmaster managed to secure himself a ship to escape the dragon?

He gave the girls a lopsided grin. "I may know a guy."

The two girls gave him curious looks but Jace just smiled. "Diana, can you meet us back at the gates. Mika and I need to go talk to a certain guildmaster."

"Oh?" the older woman raised an eyebrow. "Are you sure you don't want me to tag along?"

"Not unless you want to switch classes again," Jace told her.

Diana seemed to consider that but then shook her head. "Tempting, but as I understand it, I'll be more powerful once I hit level 10. I don't want to start all over again with a different class."

"Yes," Mika answered before Jace could. "Level 10 means better weapons and armor. And better spells."

Jace nodded towards Mika. "What she said."

"I'll stick to Priest for now," Diana said, "and meet you at the gates."

After Diana left, Jace and Mika went to the thieves guild. Jace wasn't used to going in broad daylight, but he didn't think it could wait. They knocked on the door and an unfamiliar werebear and sourly looking dwarf opened the door and let them in.

Neither of the door guards said anything as Jace and Mika walked past them and into what was now the guild's "tavern". Jace looked around but didn't see Webley around and thought the man might be sleeping. Then he heard a whistle from the top of the steps and all noise in the place stopped. On the stairs was the guildmaster.

"You two," Webley pointed at them. "Up here."

He and Mika pushed through the tavern to the steps and climbed up to Webley. The guildmaster took them to his office and shut the door once they'd entered.

The man was unreadable and Jace was beginning to wonder if they'd done something wrong or were in trouble with the guild in some way. But as the guildmaster sat down, a broad grin split his face. "I hear congratulations are in order."

Jace and Mika shared a look but the guildmaster just laughed. "Surprised, I know? I pay a lot of money to be informed of what goes on in my city and a Baronet marrying three young ladies is newsworthy information."

"If they were here, I'd congratulate the other two, Charlena and Diana, right?" he smiled, obviously showing off his intelligence gathering.

"Impressive," Jace admitted.

The guildmaster's smile faded as he took in the couple's expressions. "It looks like you're not here to share the good news. What do you need?"

"Just curious if there's a certain boat in impound that might be reserved for a fast escape from a city with a very large black dragon coming towards it," Jace said.

The guildmaster's eyes narrowed but then he smiled, and he looked over to Mika. "He's a bright one."

Mika grinned and looked at Jace. "Yes, he is."

Webley sat back. "And what if it were?"

"How much for passage for me, my wives and a few servants?" he asked.

"Right to business. I do like that about you,"
Webley said. The guildmaster considered the question
for a full minute before coming to a decision.

"I like your style," the guildmaster told him.
"And your instincts. You're partly right. I had you
plant that evidence so the ship would be impounded
before it could leave. It'll stay that way until tomorrow
night, when it will take some passengers out of
Whitecliff and head North..."

"Does that include you?" Jace asked. He had a
feeling he already knew the answer, but he wanted to
hear the guildmaster say it.

"No. I'll stay here until the last minute and see
what opportunities arise. Once the dragon is here, I
have a one way ride out of here," Webley replied.
"And before you ask, no, I can't take you."

"Teleport?" Jace asked.

The guildmaster nodded. "Exactly right. It's a
scroll and it will only take me."

Jace realized that was a possibility as well but a
scroll would cost 10,000 gold each and was a personal
one time use item. It would instantly transport the
person reading the scroll to a predetermined
destination. If he wanted to save himself, the girls, and
his servants, that would cost almost 100,000 gold.

"What about the ship?" Jace asked. "Is there
room on it for us?"

"There might be," Webley told him. "I already have a few handpicked people from the guild. But…"

"It wouldn't be free," Jace finished for him. "How much?

"For you, 2,000 apiece," he said. "And I'm guessing you've already checked the other ships and know that's a bargain."

Normally, passage would be no more than a 1,000 gold each, but 2,000 was still significantly less than what the ships were charging now. But that made Jace suspicious. "Not that I don't appreciate it but why so little?"

The guildmaster chuckled and brought out a bottle of mead and three glasses. He poured a half a glass of mead in each glass. Then, give one glass to Jace and another to Mika. He held his glass up like he was making a toast. "Consider the rest a wedding gift. Cheers."

Chapter 49

After talking over the details with Webley, Jace and Mika left the guild and went back to the inn to meet Diana. She was waiting for them at their usual table and they told her of Webley's offer of passage on the ship.

"So, we have a way out of the city now onboard a thieves' ship," Diana commented. "Are we sure it's safe?"

Jace shrugged. "Probably a lot safer than staying here and taking our chances with the dragon."

"He was very nice," Mika said. "He said it was a wedding present for us."

"Hmm," Diana bit her lip. "Does that seem a bit out of character for him?"

"What do you mean?" Jace questioned. He'd been so happy to get passage that he didn't question the guildmaster's motive.

Diana turned to him. "He's got a ship that probably is a money maker for him with passage away from Whitecliff at a premium. He could probably make five or six times the money selling it to someone else.

So why take a loss like that for, let's face it, a minor player in the thieves guild."

Jace just stared at her. It was nice to believe that Jace had earned enough faction with the guild to be valuable to Webley, but Diana was right. He was just a small player. And if that was the case, then why had the guildmaster given him cheap passage.

"Why do you think he did it?" Jace asked.

"Personally," Diana chuckled. "I suspect that when that ship tries to leave dock, having a Baronet onboard is going to grease the wheels, so to speak. Not only a baronet, but the man who returned the princess' crown. I can't imagine any harbormaster in their right mind would want to detain you and risk the ire of the king."

"That's sneaky," Mika said and narrowed her eyes. "Like a ninja."

Jace considered Diana's explanation. He'd taken Webley's actions at face value. Maybe part of him wanted to think that the guildmaster and he were like friends. But Webley was looking out for his own interests. He didn't care about Jace or the girls. Or was he killing two birds with one stone - helping them out and helping himself out.

"So, he's using us," Jace smirked. "But we have a ride out of here."

"True enough," the older woman said. "Just be careful about being so trusting. It's an endearing quality but there are too many people in the real world and this world, presumably, who will take advantage of it."

He didn't think he was really naive, but he nodded anyway. Was she right? Was he too trusting? His parents had, before they died, taught him to always do unto others as you'd want them to do to you. He thought he was honoring them by treating people the way he wanted to be treated and trusting people the way he wanted to be trusted. Was that so wrong?

Diana seemed to sense where his thoughts were taking him, and she reached out and took his hand. "Dear one, I think your innocence is charming, but there are very bad people in the world and count yourself lucky if you haven't run into them yet. But taken from an old woman who had people coming out of the woodwork to get a piece of her, there are some very bad people out there. Greed can corrupt even the best of people."

"Not Jace," Mika smiled and put an arm around him. "He is a good guy. He is a hero like you said."

The older woman chuckled. "You might be right. But that doesn't mean the people around him can't be corrupt. And let's face it, this guy Webley IS the guildmaster of a thieves guild. He's basically Al Capone."

Mika looked at her blankly but Jace knew the reference from old gangster vidstreams. He turned to the Japanese girl and thought of a comparison. "Like a Yukaza boss."

She smiled and nodded.

"So, what are you saying?" Jace asked Diana.

"I'm saying you need to be careful," the older woman replied. "Be careful with who you trust."

Jace nodded. He knew he was too trusting but that's the way he'd always been. He trusted quickly and easily until someone burned him, then it was almost impossible for him to trust that person again. But he didn't know any other way to be.

Checking his watch, he swallowed as the timepiece showed 5:02pm. At this very moment, in the real world, Charlena was probably looking at his body. He felt himself getting nervous as, once again, his mind started playing different scenarios.

Mika seemed to notice the shadow come over his face after looking at his timepiece and she gently turned his head towards her and smiled. "Everything will be fine."

He forced himself to smile, but he knew it wasn't genuine. His mind was now on the possibilities of what Charlena would find in that hospital.

"Why don't we go kill some more orcs," Diana suggested, in an obvious ploy to get his mind off what was going on in the real world.

"Sure," Jace muttered, though his heart wasn't in it.

The group left the inn and traveled back to the orc area, only to find it overrun with other players. It was early evening and the masses were starting to login for the evening. Even so, over the course of the next few hours, they were able to kill the eight orcs he needed to get to level 10 in Rogue. That earned him *Critical Eye II.*

Critical Eye II
Rogue Ability
Description: You are trained to spot weakness in others. When you strike from stealth or opportunity, your strikes are always critical hits. Critical hits now do x3 damage.
Note: This replaces Critical Eye I. This does not stack with Backstab.

Jace wanted to be excited but the feeling in the pit of his stomach wouldn't let him. He couldn't really summon up any enthusiasm for Mika when she reached level 9 in Rogue, though he did at least put a smile on and congratulate her.

Mika and Diana were now level 9 and he was 10. Charlena was only level 8, so they'd need to sit out while she did quests and caught up. Either that, or they'd all need to change classes again.

"Let's go back to the inn," Jace told the girls. "I need a drink."

"Actually, should we go back to the manor?" Diana asked. "After all, that's where she'll log in."

They did exactly that. The three of them returned to the manor and plopped down on the couches. He asked Fimipp to bring him mead and wine and he began drinking. As the time passed, Jace became more nervous and more agitated. At one point, he began pacing.

Apparently, that was too much for Diana and she finally snapped at him. "Jace, I know you're worried, but you're driving us nuts. You need to do something to take your mind off of it."

"Like what?" Jace demanded. No matter what he did, his mind kept coming back to whether or not he was okay in the real world.

Diana gave him a sly look that made both Jace and Mika blush, but the older woman just stared at him in open invitation.

Jace was half tempted to take her up on the offer. He desperately needed a distraction from his thoughts. But he doubted Charlena or Mika would like it very much and he wasn't even sure it really would take his mind off it.

He checked his timepiece. It was only 9pm. Still another hour to go. He looked and saw Diana still looking at him with a raised eyebrow.

"Even if you were serious," Jace told the older woman. "I can't."

"Well, never say I didn't offer," Diana said, fluttering her eyelids at him. Then a playful smile crossed her face. He couldn't tell if that meant she had just been teasing him or if it had been a genuine offer.

They all grew quiet as the time slowly ticked by and they continued to drink the wine and mead.

Jace continued his pacing, desperately trying to get his mind on anything but what Charlena was going to say.

Finally, at almost 10pm, the tell-tale swirl of color appeared in the chair where Charlena had logged off. A moment later, the red-headed elf's body formed in the exact spot where she had disappeared the previous night.

Charlena blinked and looked around the room until her eyes found Jace's. She didn't move from the chair but stared at him for nearly a minute without saying a word.

Finally, Jace couldn't take it any longer. "Was it me? What shape am I in?"

The red-head didn't say anything at first but then she narrowed her eyes. "I did see a body today and it looks like you - except not quite as heroic."

So, it was his body in a coma. He was alive after all. He felt part of him relax but the other part of him was still tied in a knot. "Am I okay? I mean, what shape is my body in?"

"The body I saw looks fine," she told him. "The doctor said there were some hairline fractures to the legs where the car hit but the main trauma was to the head. Severe concussion."

"So, my arms and legs work?" Jace asked, feeling a little more tension drain away. Hairline fractures weren't bad. In fact, given how long it had been since the accident, they were probably already healed. He smiled but noticed that Charlena wasn't returning his smile. In fact, she didn't look happy at all.

"What? What's wrong?" Jace asked.

"What's wrong is," she replied, "you're not Jace Burton."

Jace couldn't keep the confusion out of his mind and off his Jace. "What? What do you mean? You said it's me."

"No," she interrupted. "The body I saw today was Jace Burton. I did a quick search and found some pictures online to verify and show the doctors. He came in as a John Doe because apparently your wallet got lost somewhere after the accident. The problem is, you're not him."

Now Jace was really confused. The body was his. She'd said it. It looked like him. She'd found pictures online of him to confirm. "I don't understand. The body's mine. I'm in a coma inside a medical FEVRE pod."

Charlena shook her head. "That's the thing. Jace Burton, the real Jace Burton, isn't in a medical pod. He's not hooked up to the internet at all. He's on a bed, in a hospital, hooked up to a respirator."

"Wait? What? That doesn't make any sense," he said. "How can I be in the game if my body isn't in a pod?"

"Exactly," Charlena said. "So, who are you really? And why are you impersonating Jace Burton?"

Jace could feel the eyes of all three girls on him, waiting for an answer. The problem was, he had no idea what to tell them.

Chapter 50

Jace didn't understand Charlena's revelation. It made no sense. If he was in a coma, that meant he was alive. If he were alive, then he wasn't a brain backup loaded into the system. That only happened when a person died.

But she said he wasn't in a medical pod. So, how was he in the game? None of this made any sense. He couldn't just magically be in the game. He had to be hooked up to the game somehow. Charlena must be mistaken. "Are you sure I'm not in a medical pod? I mean, they probably look different."

Her face was hard. "I'm positive. I even asked the doctor. He showed me an actual medical pod. You're not in one. I told him I'd been talking with you in the game and he said that he didn't know who I was talking to, but it wasn't you."

Jace just stared at her. This wasn't possible. He was Jace Burton. How could he not be in a medical pod? He opened his mouth to say something else but closed it. He couldn't think of anything he could say just then.

"I'm not sure what your game is but I'm tired and this is too much for me to handle right now,"

Charlena said abruptly and then disappeared as she logged out.

Mika and Diana glanced at where the other girl disappeared, and then looked back at him. Jace fell back into one of the chairs, his mind whirling.

"Are you Jace?" Mika asked in a quiet voice. "It's okay if you're not. You helped me get out of the monster bodies. You helped Diana too and the man in the groll. You are a good person, it doesn't matter what your name is."

Jace looked at her and forced a smile. "As far as I know, I'm Jace Burton. I remember my childhood, my parents…" He paused as he remembered the moment, he'd been told about the accident that killed his parents and sister. "I remember their death. I remember college, all the odd jobs I worked and then working for WorldCog. I am Jace Burton."

Mika smiled. "I believe you."

"I believe that you believe you are," Diana shrugged. "A rose by any other name and all that. Unless you're a ghost in the machine."

His smile faltered. A ghost in the machine. Is that what he was? Had his consciousness somehow entered the game? No. That was ridiculous. It might make for good fiction, but it was impossible.

He was Jace Burton. He was a programmer. A troubleshooter. He needed to think logically, like the programmer he was. He needed to troubleshoot the issue as if he were troubleshooting bad code. Yes, that was it. But where to start.

Sometimes it helped him if he talked aloud like he would with his co-workers. He stood up and began pacing.

"I'm Jace Burton. Fact," he said aloud and noticed that the girls were watching him. "My body is in the hospital and in a coma. Fact. Assuming Charlena is right, my body is not in a medical pod. Fact. But my consciousness is in the game. Fact."

He turned a paced the other direction. Mika and Diana were looking at him curiously. "If I am not in the game using a pod, I must be in the game some other method. There are only two methods I know for getting into the game. One, using a pod. Two, having a backup of your consciousness uploaded. But… That only happens when you're dead. And I'm not dead."

He turned again, resumed pacing, and continued his thoughts. "So, how am I in the game? I was in a car accident. I was taken to the hospital. I've been in a coma. I'm not hooked up to a medical pod. It doesn't make sense. Unless there's some new technology that transfers a person's mind into the game and leaves the body in a vegetative state."

Jace realized how impossible that sounded. It was like something from a bad science fiction book. And who would have done that to him? WorldCog? Why do that if they could have just killed him? And hadn't they tried to kill him with the car accident? No, that didn't make sense.

"Occam's Razor," Diana said and Jace turned to look at the older woman. "All things being equal, the simplest explanation is probably the most correct."

"I know what Occam's Razor is, I'm a programmer," he smiled. "What do you mean?"

"Well, dear one," the older woman said. "To paraphrase a great detective, when you rule out the impossible, whatever is left, however improbable, must be the solution. Go back to your first two solutions."

"What? That there are only two ways to be in the game?" he asked.

"Right," Diana nodded. "You said there are only two ways. Either using a pod or having your consciousness uploaded."

"That we know of," Jace countered.

"Well, let's go with what we know," she replied. "There are only two ways."

"Okay," Jace agreed.

"Let's assume Charlena is right and that she did talk to a doctor who knows what he's talking about and you are not in a medical pod or connected to the internet in any way. That means, you are not directly connected. Right?"

"Right."

"So, what does that leave you?"

Jace frowned. "It leaves an upload. Only that can't happen unless you're dead. It's regulated by the government."

Diana raised an eyebrow. "And mistakes never happen?"

That tickled something in the back of his mind. Something from a very early conversation he'd had with Charlena. "When I first met Charlena, I thought I was dead and had been uploaded. When I told her, she'd looked me up in the newsfeeds."

"That seems morbid," Diana interrupted, making a face.

Ignoring her, he continued. "She told me about the blurb that mentioned me being hit by a truck. And that… I had been pronounced dead at the scene."

"So, you are dead?" Mika asked. "Like us?"

Jace shook his head. "Not quite. The paramedics must have pronounced me dead and notified WorldCog since it would have been in my file."

"But then he'd been revived, maybe on the way to the hospital," Mika offered.

"Or at the hospital. Charlena did say you arrived at the hospital without identification, so you were treated as a John Doe," Diana added. "What do you want to bet one of the paramedics stole your wallet since they thought you were dead."

"That means, I'm not the real Jace," he sighed. "I am his last brain backup."

Walking back over to the chair, Jace collapsed into it as he considered what this meant.

Mika started to open her mouth to say something, but Diana shook her head and Mika clamped her mouth closed. He couldn't help but see the concern on her face, but he didn't know what to say.

When he first arrived in the game, inside the body of a monster, he'd thought he was dead. Now, he didn't know what to think. The real him was alive and he was just an out of date copy. It was a lot to come to grips with again.

As he was thinking about it, something suddenly struck him. He was a copy of the real Jace's brain uploaded into the game WHILE the real Jace was still alive. What would happen to him when WorldCog or the government found out? Would they delete him like old programming code?

That was a terrifying thought. Being deleted. Ceasing to exist. Dying. It didn't matter that the real him would keep on living. He, copy or not, didn't want to die. "I don't want to die."

Mika looked at him with alarm. "Die?"

Diana made a dismissive gesture. "Darling, you can't die. You're inserted into the game, like us."

"No," Jace said bitterly. "Not like you. You were inserted when you died. You willed yourself into the game. It was all legal and above board."

"Yes, but you did too…" Mika started but he shook his head.

"No. I was put in here by accident," Jace said. "And the real me is out in the real world, alive."

"So, there's two of you," Diana said. "So what?"

"So," Jace replied. "When WorldCog finds out about me, an accident, they'll want to correct that accident. They'll purge me from the system."

"No," Mika said. "They can't do that!"

"They can and they will. Insertion is heavily regulated by the government," he told them. "Once the mistake is discovered, they'll delete me. They have to by law."

"Then we don't tell them," Mika said fiercely.

"We're going into the palace to talk with the *Help Desk* and tell them about our situation," he said. "Once they start investigating and troubleshooting the issue, they're bound to find out."

They were all silent for several minutes until Diana smiled. "Darling, why not just lie."

"What?" he asked.

"Lie," she told him. "Tell them you're Jace Burton's twin brother or something."

"His twin brother?" he looked at her skeptically.

"That would explain the DNA match, right?" she smiled.

Jace thought about her suggestion. He didn't know enough about twins to know if they shared the same DNA, but it was worth a try. After all, what were they going to do to him if they caught him lying? Delete him? That would be the end result if he told the truth.

He nodded. "That might work. MIGHT. It's worth a shot at least."

"Maybe we shouldn't go to the *Help Desk*," Mika said.

Jace looked at her. "But then you and Diana and the others won't have your money. And anyone else still in a monster body will be trapped. I don't know if I can live with myself knowing I could help them and not giving it a try."

Mika smiled, but her eyes were sad. "See, you are a good person."

"And just for the record, if it meant keeping you around," Diana said. "I'd forgo my money. But you're right. There are other people out there trapped in monster bodies and I don't wish that on anyone."

"Me either," Mika agreed. "It is a terrible way to live."

"Then we find the *Help Desk* tomorrow night and contact support," he told them.

He tried to make his voice sound brave but inside he wasn't convinced that lying would work. WorldCog had access to all sorts of data. The chance of them finding out that he, or the real Jace, didn't have a brother was high.

On the other hand, maybe they'd be more worried about the bug than with his real identity. Plus, he realized, he did have a trump card. He could tell them why a dragon was about to destroy one of the largest cities in the game. That might earn him some good will.

Who knew, maybe he'd get out of this situation alive after all. He smirked inwardly. That was the strangest thing. Jace was alive, at least, his real body was alive. But would he, the uploaded Jace, survive. That was the question that concerned him.

Chapter 51

After telling the girls he needed some time alone, Jace retired up to the master bedroom with Luna. The cat hopped up on the bed and found a comfortable spot near the pillows as Jace considered everything. The revelation that he wasn't the real Jace or even the only Jace had rattled him more than he cared to show the girls.

It was that he wasn't the real Jace, or even the only Jace. It was also the very real possibility that he would die. Well, maybe not die, but at least cease to exist. And that's what would happen if they pulled the plug on him.

He didn't really think that support would believe he was Jace's twin brother. Even the most minimal research would prove that he wasn't. He'd have no birth certificate, no school history, no foster history, nothing. Then, once they discover he was just a copy of the real Jace Burton, they'd delete him. They'd have to. After all, there were federal regulations and all sorts of laws governing the insertion of people into the game.

Jace laid back on the bed and sighed. If he found the *Help Desk* and contacted support, he was screwed. It was as good as signing his own death warrant. It might not happen right away. They'd probably look into the bug first. But eventually, they'd get around to "fixing" him, only to find out he wasn't supposed to be there in the first place. And then… death. Or oblivion. Or whatever happened when a person's consciousness was pulled out of the game.

What if he decided not to find the *Help Desk* at all? If support didn't know about him, they wouldn't delete him. Except, if he didn't talk to support and tell them about the bug, Mika and Diana would never get their assets back.

The girls had told him they'd rather give up their money if he lived. He hadn't told them but that was probably the nicest thing anyone had ever said or offered to do for him. Jace had never really asked anyone for anything since his family had died, nor had any accepted any charity. But just the fact that they were willing to give up who knew how much money to keep him around really touched him.

But even if he could accept their decision, that didn't help the poor souls who were, even now, trapped in monster bodies with no chance of rescue unless Jace happened to stumble upon them. They would be forever doomed to an endless cycle of death and rebirth as different monsters. Mika had thought she was in hell. How many others were there in the game right now, trapped in monster bodies who might be thinking the same thing?

No. As much as he wanted to live, to go on existing, he couldn't do that at the cost of other people suffering some sort of eternal torment. If he did, what kind of person would that make him? Certainly not the kind person his parents had wanted him to be. Not the kind of person he wanted to be.

He'd always wanted to be a hero. Jace had wanted to be the kind of person who would push someone out of the way of a moving car or rush into a burning building to save a child. He had thought he would be brave in that moment and just do the right thing. Now, as he was faced with the very real prospect of giving up his own existence to help others, he found it wasn't as easy as he thought it would be.

Maybe that was because he had too much time to think about it. To mull the decision over in his mind and contemplate the consequences. Or maybe he wasn't as brave or heroic as he really hoped he would be.

Jace struggled with these thoughts until light shone through the bedroom windows. Morning had come and with it, his resolve to go through with finding the *Help Desk*. He knew it had to be done, even if it meant he had to die.

Getting out of the bed, Jace left the bedroom and went downstairs. Luna trailed after him and he suspected she was hoping for some fish.

They found Mika and Diana chatting in the same room he'd left them in. They both stopped talking as he came down and looked up at him. When neither of the girls said anything, Jace realized they were waiting for him. Waiting for him to tell them what he had decided.

"We go on as planned," Jace said, trying to sound more enthusiastic than he really was.

"But…" Mika said. "They might delete you. You said so."

Jace smiled at her. "I know. But if we don't get to the *Help Desk* and tell them what's going on, other people will be trapped in that hell that you were in - going from monster body to monster body. I can't live with that."

Mika nodded, but he saw her eyes moisten.

"You're the noble hero after all, dear one," Diana smiled. "I knew you were the type."

"Hardly," Jace smiled despite himself. "I'm scared they will end up deleting me."

"And yet you're doing it anyway," Diana said. "Sounds heroic to me."

Mika was smiling. "Jace is a hero."

Jace didn't know what to say to that so he changed the subject. "I don't suppose Charlena logged back in?"

Mika frowned but said nothing.

Diana was silent for a second as she looked to Mika but finally replied. "No, she hasn't logged back on."

He was disappointed but not surprised. Charlena had actually seen his body and been told by a doctor that there was no way he was the real Jace. He wasn't sure what she'd thought he was, but he had an explanation now. Unfortunately, that would have to wait.

Fimipp appeared then and brought with him a platter of waffles and a small saucer of salmon. "Some breakfast, sir?"

****

Jace, Mika and Diana ate waffles while Luna devoured the salmon. As they ate, they discussed plans on how to go about the search. It didn't take them long to realize they couldn't really make a plan since none of them had any idea of the interior of the building, other than Jace's brief visit to the throne room.

"I doubt the party will be held in the throne room," Diana said. "Most likely they have some sort of ballroom."

"Good point," Jace agreed. "So, we have absolutely no idea where we'll be."

"We'll have to sneak out and explore," Mika offered.

"Like a ninja," Jace smiled.

"Yes," Mika gave him a big grin. "Like ninja."

"I can try to charm one of the nobles or guards to give me a tour," Diana suggested. "Of course, that will most likely only involve the publicly accessible areas."

"True, but it's a start," Jace said. "And it won't get you thrown in the dungeon. In the meantime, Mika and I will need to try and sneak out and do some snooping around."

"Yes," Mika nodded. "With the cloak we got you, you will be invisible."

"To a certain degree," he told her. "A very high-level NPC or character can still see through my *Stealth*. I'll still need to be careful."

"What do we say if we get caught?" Mika asked suddenly.

Jace thought for a moment and, remembering some of the old vidstreams he loved, came up with the answer. "Tell them you're looking for the bathroom."

The three of them waited the rest of the morning and Jace stayed all afternoon, as well. Diana and Mika left to get their hair and make-up done. There were no cosmetics kits that players could buy themselves. Instead, if a player wanted to change their appearance, they went to a salon and paid in-game money and they could change just about everything - for a price.

The two girls were gone all afternoon and when they finally returned, both women were dressed in their gowns and completely made up. He had to admit, they looked incredible.

Both women had their hair done up in intricate braids and yet both were different. Diana's hair was braided and then pulled up onto the top of her head, with a few curls on either side of her head. The braids were intricate and were done with beads of silver that matched the silver trim of her blue and silver gown.

The gown itself was gorgeous. It appeared to Jace to be two pieces. The first was an outer, burgundy colored dress trimmed in silver. It had a plunging neckline and was slit down the middle on the bottom. Under the outer dress was a shiny silver dress. The ensemble was cinched tight around her thin waist, giving her a very womanly hourglass figure.

Mika's hair was braided too but the front of her long, straight hair was braided and pulled around to the back of her head where the braids met. Interspersed with the braids were tiny green flowers that matched her dress.

Even though Jace had previously seen Mika's green velvet gown, the effect of the women's make-up, hair and the little green flowers in her hair made her look incredible.

"You both look amazing," Jace managed to get out. In truth, dressed the way they were, they both looked like models, especially Mika. He was actually having a hard time keeping his mind off her.

Both girls beamed but then Mika's lips formed a pout. "Where is your outfit?"

Jace quickly equipped his own party clothes. He had chosen a white silk shirt with an ascot. Over the shirt, he wore an embroidered black jacket trimmed in silver. Matching black pants and high black leather boots completed the ensemble.

"You look very handsome," Mika smiled.

"Thanks," he replied.

"Are you going to do anything with your hair?" Diana asked as she gave him a critical look.

"My hair?" he asked.

"Yes," she nodded. "It needs to be slicked back. That's the style for nobles."

"Too late now," Jace shrugged. Then he remembered the hat. He put it on and willed his hair to be slicked back and to make the hat as unobtrusive as possible, he made the hat appear as a thin silver braided circlet.

"Very nice," Diana approved. "The circlet is a nice touch. Very noble."

Jace grinned. "Thanks."

Seeing the girls made him think of Charlena and he looked over to the chair where she had disappeared.

"Sorry, dear one," Diana said as she smoothed out a wrinkle in her gown. "It doesn't look like Charlena is coming."

"We can do this without her," Mika said, folding her arms over her chest. "We don't need her."

Jace nodded. "We can. But I wish we didn't have to. The more of us searching, the more chance we have of finding the *Help Desk*. We're only going to get one shot at this. Who knows if I'll ever get invited back? Or for that matter, who knows if the city will be here at the end of next week."

"We will find it," Mika smiled and Jace envied her confidence.

"Of course, we will," Diana said, though the older woman showed much less enthusiasm.

Fimipp appeared then in the doorway and cleared his throat. "Sir, the party at the palace begins in one hour. It would be prudent to leave now."

Jace looked at the halfling. "It won't take an hour to get there. It's not even a mile."

"Yes, sir," the butler agreed. "But you will be expected to arrive by carriage and the line for carriages will stretch for some distance."

He and the girls exchanged looks. Jace had thought they'd just walk to the palace, but he guessed Fimipp was correct. This was an official event and the nobility would be expected to observe protocol.

"I guess we're going by carriage," he told the girls. He turned to the halfling. "Where can we get a carriage?"

"I took the liberty of reserving one for you," the halfling said, inclining his head. "It has just arrived."

Jace chuckled and the girls all looked impressed. "Well done, Fimipp."

Fimipp nodded his head in acceptance of the compliment and then looked around the room. "Will Lady Charlena not be joining you?"

"Apparently not," Jace looked to the chair where she had disappeared and sighed. He was hoping she would have logged in so he could explain things to her. He'd hoped she would have at least given him that chance. And now they were going to have to head off to the party without her.

"Very good, sir," the butler said. "Whenever you are ready, you can follow me. The carriage is ready to depart."

He looked at the girls. "Time for us to go. You girls ready?"

Mika and Diana looked themselves over and then nodded. "We were born ready."

"Yes," Mika agreed with the grin.

"Indeed," Jace smiled. "But there's one other thing we need to do before we leave. Take any equipment you don't want to lose and leave it in your bedroom. It should be safe in this house, at least until we get back."

"Why?" Mika asked as she fingered her katana.

"If we get caught," he told her. "Try to make sure you die somehow so you respawn. That way you don't get stuck in a prison cell. If you do die, you would normally lose your body since we can't exactly stroll back into the palace and get it. But if you leave your gear here, you won't lose much."

"That makes sense," Diana said. "But won't they be on to us? Won't they just confiscate the house if we commit a crime? Like they did with that other noble fellow?"

"No," Jace shook his head. "It doesn't work that way with players. Once we have a title, we have it for good. It's part of the coding. Otherwise, people would never spend millions of dollars on something that could be easily taken away."

"And they're all about money," Diana mused.

"Exactly," Jace nodded.

The girls did as he said and he went upstairs as well and emptied his inventory until he was only carrying his lock picks, his Infiltrator's Hat, the Kraken's Claw, and a few hundred gold - in case he had to bribe someone he ran into. When they were done, they met in the foyer.

"Let's go to the ball," he said and offered his arms to them. The girls took his arms and they followed the halfling out the front door to where the carriage waited.

Luna padded after them and he idly wondered if it was appropriate to bring a cat to a noble event. Then again, she was his familiar. If it were a problem, he could always dismiss her and resummon her after the party.

Jace stopped and turned to Fimipp. "If Lady Charlena does appear, tell her we had to leave but that we would love it if she joined us."

"I will, Sir," the halfling said.

The three of them, and Luna, crowded into the carriage and then, with a word from Fimipp to the driver, they were off to the princess' birthday party.

Chapter 52

Fimipp had been right. The carriages were lined up all the way to the entrance of the Noble District and then curved around to the north. As they drove past the line to take their place, Jace checked out the other party-goers.

While many of them were NPC nobles, Jace thought almost half of them must be players. And judging by the levels he was seeing, his group just may be the lowest level players at the party tonight.

"I can't believe all of these people are nobles," Mika said, as their driver maneuvered them into their spot.

Jace turned from the window and looked at the stunning Japanese girl. "That's what happens when WorldCog allows people to buy noble titles. You get a ton of nobles."

"In Japan," Mika mused. "There are only four noble clans. Not that they have noble titles any longer. Only the Imperial family has titles now." She looked out the window at the long line of carriages. "There must be hundreds of carriages. Does that mean there are hundreds of noble families?"

Shrugging, Jace glanced out the window as well. "Probably. WorldCog made this an exclusive club that people pay big bucks to join. Most of that money comes from the real world, which is why they're the most valuable company on the planet. People pay for an eternity of pampering and parties."

"Sounds boring," Mika said.

"Sounds wonderful," Diana chimed in. "You youngsters don't know it yet, but after a certain point in life, you really have had enough of working your fingers to the knuckles. You begin to enjoy the little, and not so little, luxuries in life."

Jace and Mika turned to the older woman. Diana looked wistfully out the window. "That's what I thought I was signing up for when I had my attorney change my will. An eternity of luxury and pampering. It sounded divine."

"Once support fixes everyone," Jace told her. "You'll get your life of luxury."

Diana turned back to them and smiled. "Yes. That does sound nice. But I do have to admit that playing the game with you three over the last week has been... invigorating."

"You had fun," Mika smiled.

"Yes, dear one," Diana agreed. "I had fun. There's a certain thrill to the game that I had not expected. I think I will miss it when things get fixed."

"Why?" Mika furrowed her brow. "You can keep playing."

"Right," Jace agreed. "Why do you have to stop? Once they put you in whatever character you originally asked for, you can start playing again."

Diana waved her hand dismissively. "I don't know. I doubt it will be the same without you two, and Charlena, of course…"

"It's not like we can't play together," Jace told her.

"We will be thrust into different parts of the world," Diana shook her head. "I was supposed to be an elf with a huge vineyard in the elven lands. Our Jace here, will be all the way up here. You, I'm not sure where you will be. Didn't you tell me you were one of those cat people?"

"Cat-kin," Mika confirmed and then frowned. "You are right. If the company will put me back in my cat-kin, I will not be on this continent. I will not be able to see any of you."

"See what I mean, dear," Diana said. "It's a bit depressing when you think about it."

The girls lapsed into silence but Jace spoke up. "You two forget that you both have money now. Life insurance, royalties or any money that transferred in from the real world. You COULD pay for passage to some place where we can meet up."

"But then what?" Diana asked. "It might take me a couple of weeks to catch up to you if you didn't do anything, but what level is your cat-kin, Mika?"

Mika looked pained. "Almost level 50. It took me almost a year to make it to that level."

Jace sighed and nodded. "Once you get past level 30, things really slow down. That's the way they designed it. It's the most time-consuming game there is, but it's the only game you can be uploaded into when you die, so they have a monopoly. It gets even worse at 50 and then again at 70."

"You're not exactly inspiring hope," Diana told him.

"It wouldn't be easy to catch up to her," Jace explained. "But it's not impossible either. Especially considering we don't sleep."

"That is true," Diana and she looked at them wistfully. "I do miss sleep. I miss dreaming too."

"Yes," Mika nodded. "I miss sleep too. I wish there was a way for us to do that."

Jace shrugged. "Maybe there is. Right now, none of us have access to the real HUD of an upload. For all we know, there's a sleep function."

"That would be nice," Diana said. She looked between the two of them. "So, what are we saying. That we want to get together once this whole thing is resolved?"

"Yes!" Mika said enthusiastically. "You are my friends. Friends should stick together."

Smiling, Jace nodded as well. "I hope we do. I'd like to see you both again."

"Both of us," Diana teased. "Or one of us in particular."

Jace caught Mika's eyes for a moment before she looked away, her cheeks red. He knew she liked him. And he liked her. Part of him also liked Charlena but her recent abandonment had made him reconsider what feelings he might have had.

Charlena had helped him. She'd helped him a lot and discovered his body. Well, she'd discovered the real Jace's body. But he also had the feeling that she wasn't interested in a virtual relationship. At least, that's the impression he'd gotten from some of the things she'd said and done.

Now, she had logged off and hadn't come back to help them in the most important thing they could do. Find the *Help Desk* and contacting support. Part of him wanted to understand her point of view, but the other part felt betrayed. And hurt.

They'd never said they were anything. Not boyfriend/girlfriend. Certainly not lovers. But still, he'd thought they had developed at least a friendship. What kind of friend would turn their back on a friend during an important mission?

He tried not to think of it as the carriage moved up another space. They'd made it to the corner and were now on a straight shot to the palace. But at the speed the line was moving, they wouldn't get there until a little after 6pm.

"Let's go over this plan of ours again," Diana broke the silence. "If we can even call it a plan."

Jace gave the older woman a lop-sided grin. "It's mostly a plan."

"It's more like 12% of a plan," Diana scoffed. "Barely even a concept."

Jace waved off her dismissal. "It's the best plan we can come up with given we have no idea what we're walking into, where we'll be or where to look."

"You know," Mika said, making a sour face. "When you say it that way, it kind of sounds like we are doomed to fail."

"Et tu, Brute?" Jace said, looking at the Asian girl.

Mika just looked back at him and grinned. "At least we all have glasses."

"There's that," Jace rolled his eyes. "I did ask for suggestions. We really don't know what we're walking into and that makes it impossible to really plan. We have to play it by ear."

"And what do we do if we get caught?" Mika asked.

"Like I said earlier," Jace explained. "Escape if you can. If you can't, try to make sure you die. It doesn't matter how. Just die so that you respawn."

"And you're sure you won't lose your title or anything if one of us gets caught?" Diana asked.

"I'm not 100% sure," he admitted. "But I've heard of nobles doing some pretty crazy things and they still retained their titles."

"It won't matter anyway if that dragon comes," Mika said soberly. "If the whole city is destroyed, you won't have a title or house, right?"

They all went quiet at her words but Jace nodded soberly. "True. If the dragon destroys the city, I assume all titles will be null and void, though I may be wrong. The title may remain unless every city in the country is destroyed. But I doubt we'd be that lucky."

"You never know," Mika smiled.

"True," he agreed. "You never know."

They each retreated into their own thoughts as the line of carriages slowly progressed towards the palace gates. He wasn't sure what the girls were thinking about, but he began going over scenarios in his mind of the conversation he was going to have with support about their situation.

The most important thing was to explain the bug that was happening to the people being inserted into the system. If he accomplished nothing else, if he could get them to fix that issue, then he would feel good.

His second priority had been to get their help in getting access to the medical pod's HUD so he could wake himself, but that wasn't an issue anymore since he now knew he was an uploaded consciousness.

Now his second priority was to explain that the dragon was a player and that there wasn't a bug into NPC AI routines. He guessed they were probably going through that AI code with a fine toothed comb, or at least a high powered debugger. But they wouldn't find anything since the flaw wasn't with the AI.

One of the keys to his interactions was now for him to say as little about himself as possible. Originally, he was going to tell them all about himself and working as a programmer for WorldCog. But given the recent revelations, he needed to bring as little attention to himself as possible.

The time seemed to pass quickly and soon they were close to the gates. Looking out the windows, Jace could see men in royal livery standing at attention alongside the road. Each one of them held a torch on a long pole, essentially acting as human lampposts.

The gate, which Jace hadn't paid much attention to on his previous visits was also lit up with candles and torches that gave off a warm, inviting glow. Before they knew it, it was their turn to through the gates and then another ten minutes before they reached the castle itself.

The sun was just dipping towards the western horizon, but the castle was already lit with what Jace guessed were either magical spotlights or gnomish mirror lights. That magical castle in the mouse park in Orlando had gone out of business decades ago, but he'd seen pictures of it in some of the vintage retro vidstreams and books he'd collected. As he looked up at the light illuminating the various towers of the Royal Palace, he thought it might give the mouse castle a run for its money.

Then their carriage stopped in front of the Royal Palace and he and the girls exchanged excited glances. Finally, it was their turn to join the party.

Chapter 53

A man in livery opened the door and placed steps in front of the carriage door. "Milord, miladies."

One by one, they exited the carriage and then, offering his arms to Diana and Mika, he escorted them up the walkway to what appeared to be the entrance. This was a different entrance than he'd used during his audience with the king, so everything was unfamiliar.

Jace looked around and saw that this side of the palace was some sort of garden or lawn, or possibly some combination of both. There were tastefully arranged shrubbery, flowers and small trees positioned about the area along with numerous stone fountains.

The fountains were dimly illuminated with some sort of magic, allowing them to be easily seen from anywhere in the lawn. Even from the walkway, Jace could see that the fountains had been enhanced with illusions to make it appear that watery creatures swam around the fountains. He looked down at Luna who seemed captivated by the illusions of fish, dolphins and even sea nymphs.

"It's not real," he sent to her through their mental link.

"Fishes," she sent back longingly. "Not real?"

"Not real," he emphasized but guessed that before the night was over, Luna would slip away and try catching one.

He could see couples and small groups of people scattered about the garden, but he was too far away to tell if they were players or NPCs. Even as he watched, he saw servants moving around the garden, serving food and drinks on silver and gold platters.

His group continued down the walkway, which was lined with statues of lions. In the mouth of each lion was a glowing orb of light. The magical light danced and flickered, almost like it was a torch. They bathed the entire walkway in a soft illumination.

"They really went all out," Diana murmured.

Jace couldn't help to agree. "Yes, but this is probably how every function is. That's why people pay millions of dollars for a noble title."

"Too much extravagance," Mika breathed.

Looking around at all the opulence, Jace couldn't help but to agree. Having lived his entire adult life scraping by, he found the entire thing excessive. If he'd had a tiny fraction of the wealth being displayed, he wouldn't have had to hold down multiple jobs to get through school.

They were following a line of people who had disembarked from their own carriages. They'd step forward a little, then they heard a herald yell out a name and title, then the line advanced. Finally, it was their turn and a herald took their invitation and then announced in a loud voice. "Sir Jace Burton, Lady Diana Burton and Lady Mika Burton."

A few heads turned their way but for the most part, they were ignored. Jace might very well be the only knight or baronet in attendance and his announcement did not attract any attention. In a room full of counts and barons, no one cared about a lowly baronet.

The entrance ballroom they'd entered was enormous but was nearly packed. It was also much more lavish than Jace had expected. The floors were polished white and gray marble. They were so shiny that the entire floor looked like a mirror. It was actually a little disconcerting.

The walls were a white stone, most likely marble, but inset with gold trim designs. The walls were also rippled, creating small alcoves that held various statues or simply a place for two or three people to withdraw from the crowd.

Looking up, Jace could see that the center of the ceiling had been painted to resemble a summer's sky, complete with clouds. It wasn't until he stared for a moment that he saw the clouds were moving. More illusions. Outer part of the ceiling was gilded carvings.

Every ten or twenty feet, large chandeliers seemed to be suspended in midair, about 10 feet above the heads of the party goers. Jace squinted at the chandeliers but could not find anything holding them up. More magic, no doubt.

All the good races of the realm were represented. Jace could see multiple fairies hovering around the room, as well as gnomes, dwarves and even a werebear in a very large and tight-fitting gold trimmed jacket. That was in addition to the humans, elves and halflings that littered the room.

One thing Jace was glad to see was that most of the wizard players had their little faerie dragon familiars with them, either flying near them or sitting on their shoulders. It made Jace feel slightly less conspicuous having his own familiar nearby. Even as he thought of her, the orange tabby moved between his legs, to avoid the people moving around.

"Stay close," he told her.

"Yes," she replied, keeping a wary eye on all the moving people.

He began systematically scanning the crowd in his HUD to see who the players were and who the NPCs were. To his surprise, it seemed the vast majority of them were players. When he thought about it, that didn't really surprise him. The nobility really had been designed in a way to entice real people (or their brain backups) to spend lots of money.

"Mmm," moaned Diana as she bit into something which appeared to be a chocolate covered jelly treat with red fruit filling. "This is so good."

Mika perked up and snatched one from the tray of the servant who had just passed. She bit into it and grinned. "Very good. Cherry."

Seeing how much the girls enjoyed the candies, Jace looked around for another tray of them. As he was scanning the crowd, he saw flashes of what he thought was red hair. And they were getting closer. Could it be Charlena?

Out of the crowd came a broad, red-headed dwarf. He was dressed in a ruffled shirt with a bright red surcoat and his beard was exquisitely braided. The dwarf looked very familiar but Jace struggled for a minute until he realized who the dwarf was. "Thedrir?"

The dwarf grinned broadly and held out his hand. "Milord Jace, I didn't realize I had been fighting with a count! Or is it an earl? Maybe a baron? Surely not a duke?"

"Baronet," Jace corrected, smiling. "And I wasn't one then. I was just given my title. You clean up well."

"Aye," the dwarf said, fingering his braided beard. "I might say the same for you. And the lasses!"

"And you brought both of the lovely lasses," the dwarf looked at him questioning. "How'd you manage that? I'm the manager of the band and I barely got in." He leaned it close. "It's all the big wigs. Normally they don't like my lot but apparently quite a few nobles recommended our band."

"Your band is here?" Mika asked excitedly.

"Oh yeah," Thedrir nodded. "By special invitation. Very hoighty-toighty!"

"I can't wait to hear them!" Mika told him, her eyes bright with enthusiasm.

"So, you bought a title?" the dwarf said, looking Jace up and down. "No offense, but I didn't figure you for the type."

Jace shrugged. "I'm not and I didn't. The king gave me the old Baronet's title after, I suspect, he beheaded him."

The dwarf's eyes opened wide. "Really? For what?"

"Apparently, arranging the theft of the princess' tiara," he told the dwarf. "I recovered it and helped the guard apprehend him."

"Whoa!" exclaimed the dwarf and then lowered his voice. "Sounds like quite an adventure! And he made you royalty. That's crazy!"

"I'm not technically royalty," Jace smirked. "Basically, on step above a knight. I'm only here because I recovered the crown... Er… tiara."

"Still. That's cool! I think knights get some special privileges and stuff too, right?" Thedrir asked.

Jace shrugged. "Maybe. Anyway, it's good to see you. And it's very cool that your band got invited to play here." He dropped his voice. "Are they paying you well?"

The dwarf smiled and winked. "And then some!" The dwarf looked over to an ornate clock that stood in one of the alcoves. "Time to get back to the band. We start playing soon! See you later!"

The dwarf turned and disappeared back into the sea of people. Looking around, Jace pulled the girls in tight. "There's a lot more people than I thought. It should be easy to get lost in this crowd and then find our way to some other part of the palace."

"There are also a lot more guards than I thought," Diana said, gesturing with her chin to the armor clad guards than stood at intervals on the far side of the wall."

Jace glanced around the room and saw the guards were almost exclusively at the far wall. "I'm guessing that's where the king will appear. For now, we should fan out and at least search the room. For all we know, the *Help Desk* is hidden in a secret compartment somewhere in the ballroom.

"How do we get into the room if we do find it?" Diana asked, looking at the throngs of royalty.

"Very carefully," Jace told her. "But first we have to find it. Split up and meet back by the entrance in say… half an hour."

Mika gave him a long glance before turning and disappearing into the crowd. Turning away, he blended into the crowd and made his way to one of the walls. Luna had followed him, and he looked down at her. Mentally, he sent her a message. "If you smell a secret passage, let me know."

The cat looked up at him. "Yes."

Slipping on the Glasses of Revelation, Jace scanned the wall. Slowly and methodically, worked his way around, looking for any sign that there was a secret door or some sort of secret passage.

Every now and then, he'd look down to Luna to see if she had picked up and smells that might indicate a passage behind the wall. But each time she showed no indication that she had found anything. While he trusted the glasses, Luna's nose had saved him too many times to discount.

They made the slow circuit around the room until he got close to the line of guards. He'd seen a few other people try to get close to them, but each time the guards rebuffed them. They were keeping the area free of players and NPCs alike.

Jace was about to turn to go back to the entrance when the crowd suddenly began to grow quiet. In only a few breaths, the whole place had grown silent as they'd prearranged it. That's when he noticed the herald coming through the crowd to the line of soldiers.

The herald was dressed in silk livery, similar but much more expensive than what the servants wore. He walked right through the line of guards and up to a raised dais before turning around. By now, everyone was quiet and when he spoke, he wasn't shouting.

"My lords and ladies, may I present," the herald called out. "His Highness, King Roulant, and her Highness, Queen Ariella. And, my lords and ladies, it is my great honor to present, her highness, Princess Emma-Rose."

Everyone in the room, including Jace, took a knee as the royal family appeared from behind a curtain and walked regally to the dais. The king was dressed in a fine, deep purple velvet coat with gold and silver trim. Under the coat, he wore white silk shirt and ascot with a sparkling gold sash around his waist. He wore the same crown Jace had seen on him the last time.

The queen was a middle aged woman but very beautiful. She had honey blond hair that was piled on top of her head in an elaborate style. Just above her hairline, she wore a slender tiara of gold decorated with diamonds and sapphires. Her dress was pale blue and looked like something straight out of a fairy tale book. It was layers of transparent blue mesh fabrics that must have been extremely thin. Even though they were transparent, there were so many layers that you could only make out the outline of the shapely legs underneath. On her feet were blue crystal slippers that could have given Cinderella's a run for their money.

The princess looked much like her mother, but her hair was fairer and her complexion paler. Her hair was piled on top of her hair, similar to her mothers, but had the addition of small blue flowers in her hair. Also like her mother, she wore a blue dress, but much more conservative. It was a more traditional off the shoulder blue and white gown with a low V-cut necklace - but not too low - and a thin waist. The bottom of the gown was blue and white silk layers.

The king surveyed his subjects and after a moment gestured with his hands. "Arise, all of you! Welcome to my daughter's birthday party! Everyone eats, drink and enjoy!" He looked to the very back of the room, where now Jace saw was another dais. On the opposite dais were several well-dressed and well-groomed dwarves and with various musical instruments. The king gestured to them. "Let the party begin!"

With that signal, the band known as Dwarven Thunder, began to play.

Chapter 54

Everyone turned to the band as they began playing a fast paced, upbeat Celtic song. At first, no one moved as everyone seemed to be entranced by the music. Then one or two couples walked onto the floor. They began to do some sort of couples dance that looked like a polka as far as Jace could tell. But they looked like they were having fun and soon more and more couples joined them.

Jace wasn't a huge fan of Celtic music, but he did find the energy of the song infectious and looked down to see his foot tapping in time with the beat. While he was looking, he saw Luna next to his leg with her ears back. Apparently, she didn't like Celtic music. Or perhaps it was simply too loud for her.

The royal family had taken seats on their thrones and very wealthy looking people were starting to come forward, one at a time and talk to the king or queen. Jace guessed they must be the upper tier of nobility. Was that Dukes and Duchesses? If they were players, he couldn't even fathom how much money they must have paid to get their titles. Ten million? Twenty million? Whatever it was, it was far beyond what Jace could ever hope to have.

As the first song ended, the band weaved one song into another song with a similar tempo and the dancing continued. Jace resumed his examination of the wall and alcoves but found nothing. He made his way back to meet the girls. By the time he got to their meeting spot, the band had ended its second song and started a new one.

This new song was slow, and some dancers left the floor, while new ones took their places to slow dance with their partners. Jace was looking for the girls when suddenly Mika appeared out of the crowd and grabbed his hand.

"Come on," she grinned. "Slow dance!"

Mika pulled him onto the dance floor and pulled him close. Her arms went around his neck and his arms dropped instinctively around her slim waist. She seemed to have a natural rhythm and her hips and feet moved to the slow beat. Jace on the other hand struggled to keep up with her.

He was looking down at his feet, trying not to step on hers when she spoke. "You look very distinguished with your glasses."

Jace looked up and saw that she had taken hers off before deciding to pull him onto the dance floor. "Thanks… I think. Isn't distinguished just another word for old."

"You are not old Jace Burton," she said. "Neither of us are. We are like spirits now. Without age."

"I guess that's true," he admitted. "Assuming they don't kill me off."

Her face grew pained, but she seemed to master it quickly and smiled up at him. "They will not. You will live in the game with us."

Jace didn't know what to say to that, so they danced the rest of the song in silence. Her big brown eyes stared up into his and he found it hard to match their intensity. He'd probably feel much more flattered - and much more nervous - if his mind wasn't preoccupied with their mission tonight. He needed to stay focused. But it was hard with a beautiful girl in his arms.

The music ended and they stepped apart and applauded the band with the rest of the dancers. Dwarven Thunder broke into another spirited Celtic song and Jace took Mika's hand and quickly led her off the dance floor.

"You two enjoy your dance?" came a voice from behind them and Jace turned to see Diana pushing through the crowd with a knowing look on her face. She still wore her glasses which gave her a very "sexy librarian" look.

"Yes," answered Mika with a huge grin. All three of them moved closer together so they could speak more softly.

"Any luck?" he asked the two girls, but both shook their heads.

"Nothing," Diana frowned. "Are you sure these glasses work?"

"I've used them before," Jace told her. "And one of the nice things about the game is, there are no counterfeit magic items. If you look at any secret door while wearing the glasses, you'll see a bright glow around it. It's really hard to miss."

"Are you sure they won't have some counter charm or whatever it's called that might block them?"

"I don't see how. NPCs can't see the *Help Desk* or the door that leads to it. I don't see how they put any sort of anti-magic spell around it."

Diana seemed to consider that. "That makes sense - in the real world. Let's hope it makes sense in this game world."

"Did you find someone to give you a tour?" Mika asked.

"No, dear one," Diana replied. "Though I may have identified a few prospects. If we're done with this room, I can go see if I can charm any of them."

"Yes…" Jace began but then looked down and didn't see Luna. He scanned the room but there were too many people to see where she might be.

Reaching out with his mind, he spoke to her. "Where are you?"

"Fishes!" came Luna's response.

"Oh no," Jace sighed and the girls looked at him in alarm.

"What?" Mika demanded, her eyes darting around the room, looking for danger.

"I think Luna is going to attack one of the fountains," he told them.

The three of them rushed outside and looked around the gardens, trying to spot the wayward feline. But there were at least a half dozen fountains and not all of them were visible.

"There she is!" Diana pointed. Jace followed her finger and saw Luna just as she pounced onto a tiny dolphin illusion. His familiar passed right through the dolphin and disappeared into the fountain with a splash. A moment later, she scrambled out of the water like it was boiling lava and came running towards them.

As Luna reached them, she stopped and shook herself off. The soaked cat looked up at him mournfully. "Bad fish!"

Jace chuckled. "Yes, bad fish. Are you done chasing things in the fountains now?"

His familiar looked chastised and began to lick herself dry. Jace turned and began to head back to the room when an odd figure caught his eye. It was a dark elf male and a tall one at that. Dark elves were one of the evil races and generally killed on sight in any of the good lands. And yet, the guards paid him no more attention that they paid anyone else.

"Do you guys see that…" Jace started to say to the girls but then stopped as he got a closer look at the elf. There was something very familiar about the elf. The long pointed ears and ebony skin weren't familiar, but the face was. It was slimmer than it should be, because it was an elf, but it was a dead ringer for someone he knew. Someone he worked with. Damian Sangrey.

He took a hard look and really scrutinized the face as the dark elf stepped up to the entrance to the ballroom. The face was a little different because it had the dark elf template applied to it, but Jace was sure that had to be Damian.

They'd talked about their characters at work and Jace knew Damian had a dark elf warlock who was a couple of levels above Jace, something Shadetalker or Shade-eater or something like that. It couldn't be a coincidence. But then, what was he doing on this side of the continent? He must have spent weeks building up the faction to be able to walk into Whitecliff, let alone in the Royal Palace. Funny he'd never mentioned that.

"What is it?" Diana asked.

Jace ignored them as his excitement grew. If it was Damian, he could help them! Maybe he could help them find the *Help Desk*. Maybe he could even speak with support in person and escalate the issue!

A whole world of possibilities opened up. Suddenly, things didn't feel quite as hopeless. Jace took a step towards the elf and then heard the herald as he announced the dark elf.

"Ambassador from Shiedrigish, Duke Alalorn Shadegazer," the herald bellowed, and the dark elf stepped through the door and paused, as if giving everyone a chance to gaze upon him. Even from here, Jace could see the haughty airs the player put on, so similar to the real Damian.

Then Jace's step faltered as he registered the titles he'd just heard. Ambassador?! Duke?! Jace brought up his HUD and scanned the elf right before he disappeared in the crowd.

Name: Alalorn Shadegazer
Race: Dark Elf
Class: Warlock
Level: 97

Shadegazer. That had to be Damian. But how could it? Ambassador was a lot like a title in that you could purchase it for a specific country and gain immediate faction with them. But it cost a ton of money. And Duke? That was the highest noble title there was in the game. It cost tens of millions of dollars. How could Damian possibly afford it?

The answer hit him like a freight train. Damian couldn't afford it. Not on his salary. There was no possible way. And if the senior programmer really had that sort of money, there was no way he wouldn't be throwing it in everyone's face every day.

"Holy -" Jace gasped but Mika suddenly gripped his chin and twisted his face to look at her.

"Jace," she said slowly. "Are you okay? We've asked you three times."

Jace blinked. Three times? He hadn't even been paying attention. And now his brain was reeling from this new realization. Pieces were falling into place in his mind. Suddenly, things made sense.

"I think," he muttered, trying to think it through. Trying to connect all the dots. "I think… I just figured out who is responsible for all of this."

The girls shared concerned looks. Diana waved a hand in front of his face. "Are you okay Jace? What did you figure out? Responsible for what?"

Shaking his head to clear it, he took the girls by the arms and led them through the garden until they were out of sight of the ballroom. Finally, he let go of their arms and then turned to face them.

"Jace," Mika looked worried. "You are acting very strangely. Are you alright?"

Diana's hands were on her hips and she was giving him a motherly look. "She's right. Is there something wrong with you?"

"That dark elf Duke," he started. "I think it's my co-worker, Damian. And I think he might be responsible for all of this."

Chapter 55

"Wait? What? Who is responsible for what?" Diana asked, clearly not understanding what Jace had meant. Even Mika looked confused.

"That's what I thought," Jace explained, taking a sideways glance back at the ballroom where Damian had disappeared. "I thought it was a bug and that WorldCog was covering it up while they were trying to quietly get it fixed."

"But now you don't think that?" Diana asked.

Jace shook his head. "No. I just saw one of my co-workers, a senior programmer on my team, go into the ballroom."

"Can he help us?" Mika asked hopefully.

Again, Jace shook his head. "No. In fact, I think he's the one who created the 'bug' that sent us all here."

The two girls glanced towards the ballroom and then back to Jace. Diana cocked an eyebrow. "And how do you know that?"

"Because they just introduced him as Duke and Ambassador," he told them. "Duke is the highest royal title you can buy. I'm guessing it's in the tens of millions of gold range."

Mika whistled softly and even Diana looked concerned. "And I take it this…"

"Damian," Jace supplied.

"I take it this, Damian, doesn't have that sort of money?" Diana finished.

"No way," he explained. "He's a bit of a jerk and really loves to flaunt anything he does better or something more he has. If he had that much money, even in-game, he would have bragged about it every chance he had."

"And you suddenly think this Damian fellow is the cause for all our troubles?" Diana asked skeptically. "How is that even possible?"

Jace took a deep breath. His mind was still catching up with his theory and he was struggling to put it into words. It was hard for him to believe, but it all made sense. The last memory he had of the real world was finding that obfuscated code. Damian had acted really strange and even hostile. At the time, Jace just thought that it had just been Damian being Damian and just acting like a self-important jerk. That was before Jace had seen him in-game.

Damian was a Duke. That would have cost millions and millions of gold that Damian didn't have. And the likelihood of him having stumbled into the title like Jace did was unlikely - especially the highest and most valuable title in the game. It just didn't seem possible. And even if he had, there was no chance he wouldn't have bragged about it to everyone on the team.

The only way Damian could have gotten that much gold was to have stolen it. And while Jace might have thought it was possible that he could have somehow done it inside the game, it was too coincidental.

Damian just happened to have the insertion code signed out. And the code he had signed out just happened to have obfuscated code that hid its true purpose. And the people being inserted into the game just happened to be inserted into monster bodies - without any of their money. And Jace just happened to have tried to be killed the same day he discovered the code? That seemed like too many coincidences. He remembered hearing that there were no coincidences, only the illusion of coincidence.

Is that what Damian was doing? Taking the assets of people who were inserted into the game when they died? And then covering his tracks by somehow changing their entity type to be an AI, forever trapped in a monster body and unable to communicate with anyone?

And when Jace had discovered it and told Damian that he was going to bring it to Phil's attention, suddenly he'd been hit by a car and "killed". Problem eliminated. And then Damian must have known or guessed that Jace would have been willed into the game - Jace was sure he'd mentioned it in some of their conversations. Damian must have done something to flag Jace's account for the same treatment.

It all made sense now. The code. Damian's actions. Jace's near death. His being marked as a monster AI. It made sense to him.

And as he thought about, he realized that every single person he'd saved had been rich to some degree. Mika had just inherited money. Diana was a successful author with who knew how much in royalties. Even Duglas and Yosyp had talked about having money. And who knew how many other people had the same thing happen to them.

"Jace… earth to Jace," Diana said, waving her hand in front of his face. "I asked you three times about this Damian fellow."

"Sorry," Jace said. He'd been so wrapped up in his own thoughts he hadn't even heard her.

"You think this man is the cause of all of our problems?" Mika asked with a fierce depression.

Nodding, Jace cast a glance back at the last spot he'd seen the dark elf. He'd thought Damian had been his friend, or at least, friendly. Well, at least, as friendly as Damian could get. They'd even gone out after work a few times.

"I think he killed me," Jace told them. "Or, I mean, tried to kill the real Jace. And I think he believes he succeeded."

"And all this because he has a title?" Diana asked, again showing her skepticism.

"Right before I 'died'," he started. "I discovered some hidden code in the insertion routine. That's the routine that takes people who have died and 'inserts' them into the game. It also transfers all of their marked assets into the game so they can start a new life."

"Damian got really upset when I brought it to his attention," he told them. "Damian can be really moody, and I didn't think much about it. Then, the next thing I know, I'm dead. Or at least, I thought I was dead."

"Not only am I dead," he continued. "But I'm in a monster body where I can't communicate to anyone else about what I found. Then I find other people who are in monster bodies who, as far as I can tell, were all rich before they died."

Diana's eyebrow went up at that. "Everyone was rich?"

"I'm not sure how much money you had, but Mika inherited money just before she died. Douglas was some sort of investor and even Yosyp mentioned money and million dollar life insurance policy."

Mika was nodding. "He is right, I had just inherited several million US dollars before I died, plus a sizable estate in Tokyo."

"Hmm," Diana muttered. "Maybe you have something there. After all, greed is a powerful motivator."

"He is a graverobber," Mika spat. "He is despicable."

Diana turned to Mika. "Technically, you're right. He's robbing from the dead - which happens to be us. That's an apt analogy."

"Except it's worse," Jace cut in. "Not only is Damian robbing graves, but he's bulldozing the grave so no one knows the grave was robbed. And he's killing to cover it up."

Diana put a hand on his shoulder. "I'm sorry, dear one."

"Except he didn't quite kill me," Jace smirked. "At least, not the real me. I'm alive and in a coma back in the real world. Or… he is… geez… I don't even know what I am anymore!"

Mika took his hand, "You are our Jace."

Diana smiled and nodded. "It's true. You're ours. After all, we're married." The older woman held up her hand and wiggled her signet ring and then gave him a seductive smile. "Or did you forget."

He chuckled despite himself. "How could I forget?"

"If Damian is the cause of all of this," Mika narrowed her eyes. "Can we just kill him?"

Jace chuckled again but shook his head. "He's level 97. I doubt we'd be able to damage him, even if we tried. Plus, it wouldn't do any good. It's just his character. If he somehow managed to kill him, he'd just respawn. The only difference would be, he'd know about us."

"He already knows about us," Diana said bitterly, her mouth twisting into a mask of disgust. "He stole our money and trapped us in monsters."

"I don't think so," Jace said. "I mean, the knowing part. My guess is he has it automated. He must have programmed some criteria into the routine to pull out certain people with a certain amount of money. I don't know. But I doubt he's picking people specifically. That would take too much time and probably expose him to more risk."

"But he singled you out," Mika pointed out.

"You're right. But I think that was because he was trying to silence me after I saw the code," he reminded them. "I wasn't rich, so he probably manually added me to the code so I would be affected."

"So, then what do we do?" Mika asked, clenching and unclenching her fists. "We can't let him get away with it."

"We won't," Jace said. "We stick to the plan. We find the *Help Desk* and contact support and tell them what's going on. With what we know, they should hopefully be able to do something about Damian and fix you guys."

"And what about you?" Mika furrowed her brows. "What if they delete you?"

"I have to take that chance." He tried to sound brave, but the thought terrified Jace. He didn't want to die. He wanted to keep living. He tried to take solace in the fact that he was really alive and that his real self would keep living. Provided his real self actually woke up from the coma.

"So, back to the original plan," Diana said.

"With one exception," Jace said. "We need to avoid Damian at all costs."

"But why…" Diana started.

"Because if he sees me," Jace replied. "He'll recognize me. Not only do I look like the real Jace, but I was stupid enough to change my character name to my real name. I don't know exactly what he could do to us, but let's not risk it."

"He hasn't seen either of us," Mika said, gesturing to Diana.

"But we changed our last name to Burton," the older woman sighed.

Jace nodded. "Best if he doesn't see any of us. Hopefully, that won't be too difficult, considering he's the only dark elf in attendance."

"That should make it easier," Diana agreed.

Mika nodded too, but Jace could see the anger painted on her face.

"Mika," he told her. "The best revenge we can get is to contact support and report him. He'll face real consequences in the real world that will be much worse than what we could do here."

That seemed to pacify her, and she nodded curtly. "Then let's find the *Help Desk.*"

"Yes," he told them. "And we need to do it as soon as possible and then leave before we accidentally bump into Damian."

They turned to go but Mika put a hand on his shoulder. "He knows what you look like, right?"

"Yeah."

"You have the hat that changes your appearance," she pointed to the circlet he wore. "You can disguise your appearance."

"Good idea," Jace said and with a thought, he was a plain looking elf, wearing the same outfit he'd been wearing. He held up his finger to make sure the signet ring was still showing. "Hopefully, none of the NPCs question me about the change in appearance."

"We should stagger our entrances," Diana said. "So it doesn't look like we're together. Then, meet back here in an hour unless you manage to find a way past the guards or manage to get a tour. We'll plan to meet back here or, if we see Damian anywhere outside, we meet on the opposite side. Agreed?"

Jace and Mika both agreed.

"Good luck," Jace told them as they began to spread out. He waited until the girls were out of earshot before he finished. "We're going to need it."

Chapter 56

Jace held back and waited until the two girls had entered the ballroom. Once they had disappeared inside, he entered. He immediately scanned the crowd to try and determine where Damian was. At first, he didn't see him but eventually spotted him talking with the king.

That was good. If Damian was busy talking with the king, then he wouldn't spot Jace. But he needed to take advantage of the situation and try to sneak out of this room into the palace proper and start searching for the *Help Desk*. It was more important than ever that he talked to support.

Having previously scoped out the ballroom, he knew there were two exits on the south wall that led into the rest of the palace. There was also an exit on the west wall. There were also exits to the east, but that was where the king was and there was no way to get to them. Unfortunately, all three of the exits he had access to were blocked off by guards.

He'd need to use his cloak and risk sneaking by them. If he could get past the guards at the doorway, it should be much easier. At least, he hoped any guards inside wouldn't be nearly as alert.

Taking a moment to examine all of the doorways, Jace chose the west most door on the south. That doorway was further away from the floating chandeliers, so it was the most dimly lit. Hopefully, that would enhance his chances of sneaking by.

With his attention on the door, Jace wasn't fully watching where he was going and bumped into one of the guests.

"Sorry," he muttered but then looked down to see that it was Thedrir, and the dwarf was with the rest of the band. It was then that Jace realized that there was no music. The band had obviously stopped playing.

The dwarf looked at him for a moment, his eyes going glassy, before a look of confusion crossed his face. "Jace? Burton? Did you change your appearance or are there two of you?"

Jace sighed. Obviously, Thedrir had looked at him in his HUD. Despite the hat's magic masking his appearance, it couldn't mask his name. At least, not to a player who examined him. He nodded to the dwarf. "It's me Thedrir. I'm... incognito."

"Jace," Thedrir grinned. "Imagine bumping into you again." The dwarf winked. "Pun intended. Incognito, huh? Some sort of cloak and dagger stuff? Very cool. My lips are sealed." The dwarf made a gesture with his fingers over his lips. "While I have you here, let me introduce you around."

Thedrir motioned to each dwarf in turn and introduced them. "Jace, this is Valatum Flinthead, who plays the flute, Khoukreag Flaskmaster on the mandolin, Thadmurim Oakenthane on the bagpipes, and that sourly looking dwarf sized orc is my brother, Utolir Ironbelly. He's on drums."

"Nice to meet you all," Jace said. He noticed they all wore similar outfits, a dark green shirt over which they wore a short, brown leather tunic. They also all wore kilts with an orange, blue and tan or brown tartan. They looked very Celtic.

"How did you like the music?" Utolir asked. He looked similar to his brother but had sandy blonde hair and beard.

"It's good," Jace smiled. "I'm not a big celtic music person, but maybe Dwarven Thunder will convert me."

The dwarves grinned. "We have a lot of converts, both in the game and out."

Jace was intrigued. "Do you play outside the game too?"

"Aye," Khoukreag answered. He was an inch or two taller than Thedrir and Utolir and had a shorter, more trimmed beard. "We were playing in the real world long before we thought of doing it in the game. We have our songs on all the major online stores."

"Right," grunted Thadmurim. The bagpipe player was shorter than the other dwarves with a larger belly and jet black hair. "The hard part is dividing our time among both worlds. The women want us in both worlds."

The other dwarves chuckled at his joke. But then Utolir nudged Thedrir and gave him a meaningful look. His friend nodded and he looked at Jace. "Sorry, we have to go while they're on break. We're about to get the grand tour."

Jace did a double-take and he cleared his throat. "Grand tour?"

"Yeah," Khoukreag bobbed his head. "Part of the doing the show was a tour of the palace in between sets. And we're not going to have much time if we don't hurry." The dwarf motioned for them to move along.

"WAIT!" Jace said, more loudly than he had intended and lowered his voice. "Wait. You're going on a tour of the palace?"

"That's what he just told you," grumbled Thadmurim. "And we're running late."

"Thedrir," Jace pleaded with his dwarven friend. "Can you take me on the tour too?"

Thedrir looked skeptical, as did the other dwarves.

"Please. It's important. REALLY important," he told him. "One could say, it's a matter of life or death."

The dwarves' expressions went from skeptical to disbelief. It was obvious they weren't buying his story.

Jace tried to think of something to convince them but without taking the time to explain everything but came up blank.

"I think you've been hitting the mead too hard, friend," Utolir said and gave his brother a stern look.

Then an idea hit Jace. He took off his gnomish timepiece, which was worth thousands of gold. He held it out to Thedrir. "If you take me with you, I'll give you this. It's a…"

Thedrir held up his hand, his eyes wide as he stared at the gnomish timepiece. "I know what it is. And you'll just give it to me if we take you with us?"

Dwarven Thunder was looking from Thedrir to Jace, their eyes wide as well. Jace wondered exactly how much the timepiece was worth and then decided it was better if he didn't know. "Yes. If you get me on the tour. It's yours, no strings attached."

Thedrir considered that for a second, his eyes darting from the watch to Jace's face and then back. He looked at other dwarves, who motioned him to take the deal. The dwarf sighed. "If you're offering me that thing, you must believe this is really important."

"I wasn't exaggerating," Jace told him.

"Fine," Thedrir said and just pushed the timepiece at him. The dwarf waved it off and shook his head. "I'll try. I can't guarantee I can get you on the tour. It was really just for the band members."

"Too bad you ain't a dwarf," Khoukreag chuckled. "No one ever counts the dwarves!"

Jace gave him a lopsided grin and a thought later, he was a dwarf, complete with dark, braided beard, green shirt, leather tunic and kilt. The dwarves started for just a moment and then Thedrir smiled. "That might work. Fine. Get in the middle of us and if anyone asks, you're the uh…"

"Harper," Thadmurim snickered. The other dwarves shrugged and that seemed to be decided.

"Okay, okay," Utolir gestured for them to move along. "Let's go, before none of us go on a tour."

His merry band of dwarves marched back the way he had come, towards the first entrance on the south wall. When they reached the double door, they halted and Thedrir stepped forward to talk with one of the guards.

The conversation went on several minutes, with Thedrir gesturing at the dwarves and then the palace before finally walking back to the group. He had a grin on his face. "They're going to get the chamberlain." He lowered his voice and nudged Jace with his elbow. "And you're in."

Jace let out a breath he hadn't known he'd been holding in and returned the dwarf's grin. "Thanks, Thedrir, I owe you one."

"You owe me a gnomish timepiece," the dwarf winked. The dwarf looked around, presumably to see if anyone was watching, and then held out his hand.

Jace handed it over to him. It was a lot to lose but if he found the *Help Desk*, it would be worth it. Besides, he grinned inwardly, he had a second one back at the manor.

A middle-aged man in fine livery appeared on the other side of the guards and spoke to them for a few minutes before the guards parted and he stepped through. The man had brown hair, streaked with gray but he wore a floppy hat with a feather that hid most of his hair. The chamberlain wore a sleeveless velvet tunic in the king's colors, under which he wore a plain, white shirt made of silk. On his legs, he wore dark hose and tall, black leather boots completed his ensemble.

The chamberlain looked over the dwarfs and smiled, but it didn't reach his eyes. "Master dwarves, I am Parlan Geadasach, palace chamberlain. I was informed that you wish to conduct your tour now?"

"That is correct, Master Parlan," Thedrir replied. "If it's not too inconvenient."

The chamberlain's practiced smile didn't falter as he replied. "Of course not, it would be my great pleasure to guide you on your tour of the palace and educate you on its marvelous history."

"Excellent," Thadmurim muttered. "Let's get moving so I can get some mead before we have to get started again."

The dwarves chuckled at Thadmurim's comment, but the chamberlain didn't share their mirth. He simply nodded and maintained the same fake smile he'd put on in the beginning, reminding Jace of an oily salesman. He had a feeling none of them were going to enjoy the tour very much.

Thedrir looked at the chamberlain and nodded. "He's right about hurrying it along. We need to be back to start the next set."

"Yes, yes," the chamberlain nodded. "As you wish. We will begin in just a moment. We're waiting for one more person who wished to see the palace and was given permission to do so by His Majesty."

"Another person?" the dwarves muttered. "I thought it was just us."

"Originally it was," the chamberlain nodded. "But when a visiting Ambassador asks for a tour, it's rude to decline."

Jace's blood went cold at the mention of an ambassador. But then again, there had to be many ambassadors at the party. It didn't mean Damian. He couldn't.

"Ah," smiled the chamberlain and Jace noticed this time it was a genuine smile. "Here he is now. Duke Alalorn Shadegazer, thank you for joining us."

Unable to breathe, Jace turned to see the dark elf he'd seen earlier. His old co-worker, and the one that had betrayed him. It was Damian. And he was coming on the tour as well.

Chapter 57

Damian smiled at the dwarves. Even though it was a different face, the face of a dark elf, Jace recognized the cocky grin as belonging to his co-worker. There was no doubt this close up.

"Nice playing," Damian told the dwarves.

"Thank you, your Grace," Thedrir inclined his head. "We'd be happy to play at your manor some time, for the right price."

Damian smirked. "I'll keep that in mind."

"Ahem," the chamberlain cleared his throat. "Shall we begin the tour?"

Despite Damian's proximity, Jace had the presence of mind to pull out his glasses again and put them on. He still needed to find the *Help Desk* and he wasn't going to do that if he couldn't find the secret room that held it.

Assuming he did find it, he'd have to work out how to slip the group and Damian so he could contact support. Moving with the line of dwarves, he followed the chamberlain as the man began to talk about the different rooms, paintings, and statues.

They'd been going through rooms for about five minutes when Damian's dark elf walked alongside him. The dark elf looked down at him, eyes narrowed. "Jace Burton, huh?"

Jace swallowed involuntarily. Damian must have scanned all of them with his HUD. Why, Jace didn't know, but he'd seen the one thing Jace couldn't disguise. His name. Forcing himself to remain common. "Yes," and then belatedly added. "Your Grace."

"All of the other dwarves have names that I might expect from dwarves," the dark elf continued. "All except you. You have a more… curious… name."

"Thank you, your Grace," Jace muttered and tried not to look at Damian. He was afraid his face would betray him and that his former co-worker would see how nervous he was.

"I knew a Jace Burton once," Damian said. "Terrible programmer. Couldn't tell a for...next loop from a multidimensional array."

Jace swore internally. Damian suspected. He wished he'd never changed his name. Now that he knew Damian was the culprit, his name felt like a giant neon sign that pointed him out. Still, maybe he'd just think it was a coincidence. "Programmer? Like a computer programmer? Huh, I'm a musician. I don't know anything about programming."

"Really?" Damian said. "That's interesting. It's also interesting that you are a rogue and yet you have a familiar."

Jace looked down at Luna and Jace swore under his breath again. Damian might be a jerk, and if Jace was right, a criminal, but he was still sharp. Still, it wasn't completely unheard of for other races to multiclass. They just had to deal with the 25% experience penalty. But they'd do it to get a special prestige class and Jace suddenly remembered one that might just save his butt.

"I multiclassed to Mage," Jace replied. "So, I can get the Runemaster prestige class."

Damian was quiet for a few paces but then retorted. "If I remember correctly, Runemaster requires a Fighter based class and a Mage based class. And yet you have Rogue and Mage. Curious, don't you think?"

He felt like Damian was toying with him, but maybe he was just testing him. Jace needed to keep his cool. Damian loved word games and trying to trip people up. He needed to think before he responded. "Yeah, I didn't realize that until I had changed. But now it's too late. Unless I want to delete the character and start a new one. I'm still considering that."

"Hmm," Damian responded and then went quiet for several more steps.

Jace hoped his former co-worker was satisfied. Maybe his answers had at least put some doubt in Damian's mind. Of course, that hope was completely crushed by Damian's next words.

"I know who you are, Jace," Damian whispered. "I don't know how you got out of where I put you, but I know what you're trying to find."

"And what's that?" Jace whispered back, doing his best to feign ignorance.

"It's what you're using those glasses to locate," Damian replied. "You're looking for the *Help Desk*."

Jace felt the blood drain from his face. Damian knew.

"Nice try," his former co-worker said smugly. "But it won't do you any good. I'm going to log off, go into the work and move the *Help Desk* some place where you'll never find it. Or, at least, some place you'll never get to. Maybe… the king's bedchamber or… better yet, the princess' bedchamber. Maybe I'll do that and then tell you where it is and watch your pathetic little attempts to get to it."

Jace clenched his teeth. He wanted to punch Damian or throttle him, anything to wipe that smug expression of his face. "I'll make it."

Damian actually laughed at that. "No, you won't. You're nothing. You're less than nothing. You're dead and there's nothing you can do to change that. And after I move the *Help Desk*, I think I'll come back in and see what trouble I can get you into. I'm sure I can think of something creative."

"You…" Jace was so angry he couldn't even finish his words.

"See you soon, Jace," Damian grinned evilly. "And when I get back, I'll find you. It shouldn't be so hard with you using your real name. Idiot." And then, Damian disappeared.

Jace felt the icy grip of despair pulling at him. Damian was right. The developers had a way of changing the location of the *Help Desk* whenever it was discovered. Damian shouldn't have access to it, but there were a lot of things Damian shouldn't have access to. At the moment, he had to assume that his former co-worker could move the *Help Desk*.

"Did that guy just log out?" one of the dwarves said, but they all turned back to the chamberlain who was explaining a painting of two dragons.

If that were the case, Jace had very limited time. It was late. Damian had to be at home. To move the *Help Desk*, he'd need to go into work. He'd need to be at his work computer. He couldn't just do it from his home computer or from a FEVRE pod.

Jace racked his brain. How far was Damian from work? A half hour? He took the train, didn't he? Or did he have a car? Jace remembered the car accident that Charlena had said he'd been in. Had it been Damian driving the car? Had he tried to kill him?

He had to assume Damian had a car. That meant, there wouldn't be any extra time while he waited for a train. So maybe he had 30 minutes. Maybe a little more, maybe a little less.

That meant he had no time to spare. As the group began to head into the next room, Jace bent down on the pretense of adjusting his boot. Luna stayed with him and they let the other dwarves go into the next room before Jace pulled out the cloak and equipped it. Immediately, he went into *Stealth*.

Jace looked down and saw Luna. She'd be a dead giveaway. He doubted there were many orange tabby cats in the palace. Anyone who saw her would know something was out of place and they might investigate.

"Luna," he told her mentally. "I need to carry you under the cloak, so you're hidden. It's really important."

The cat looked up at him but seemed to hear the fear and desperation in his voice. "Yes."

With that, he reached down, picked her up and then cradled her under the cloak. "Sorry Luna, but we have to move quickly."

"Yes," the tabby replied.

With Luna tucked under the cloak, Jace moved as quickly as he could while remaining in *Stealth*. There were surprisingly few guards around and he went from room to room. With each new room, he paused only long enough to scan the room with the glasses and then he was off again.

He quickly lost track of time and wished he hadn't given away the gnomish timepiece. Or that he'd brought the second one with him. It didn't really matter though. He had to keep looking. He had to find the *Help Desk*.

He wasn't sure exactly how long it had been, but he was pretty sure he'd covered the entire downstairs. He'd even poked his head into the throne room, which was currently empty. There was no sign of any secret room on the first floor. It was time to move up.

He retraced his steps to one of the staircases. There was a guard at the base of the stairs, but he managed to slip by. At least the cloak was working better than he'd expected. So far, no twitched an eye at him as he'd passed. He hoped it stayed that way. He didn't have any time for any distractions.

On the second floor, he began going from room to room. There were many guest bedrooms and sitting rooms and all sorts of other rooms. Then he reached a different wing and saw that there were guards at the entrances.

As quickly and quietly as he could, he slipped right between the two guards and began searching the rooms. He immediately realized that these must be the royal quarters, judging by the sheer opulence of the rooms.

Then he ran into a problem. There was a wide hallway that led to three sets of double doors. There were doors on either side of the hallway, about halfway down. The final set of double doors was at the end of the hallway. And there were two guards in front of the doors.

The problem was the doors were all shut. If he opened any of them, the guards would be able to see. Even in a world of magic, a door opening seemingly by itself would get the guards attention and they'd come to investigate.

He looked at the three doors again. As he looked harder, he could make out crowns above each door. These were the royal bedrooms. They had to be. And that would explain the guards. The room they guarded was probably the king's bedroom.

He backtracked and looked to see if there was access to a balcony he could use to try and climb over to any of the rooms. Unfortunately, there was nothing accessible from any of the rooms he found.

If he wanted access to those bedrooms, he'd need to think of some way to distract the guards so he could peek into the rooms. And Jace would need to do it soon. Damian could already be at WorldCog, trying to move the *Help Desk*.

But how could he distract the guards without giving himself away or causing an alarm. He'd been very lucky so far, but he wouldn't want to test his luck. The last thing he needed was for someone to raise an alarm and have the place swarming with guards.

He looked through his equipment, but he'd left most of it back at the manor. He didn't have much that could cause a distraction. Then Luna shifted in his arms and he looked down at the cat hidden under his cloak.

Luna might be able to create a diversion. But how? What was the best way to use her? As he thought about it, a plan began to emerge. And it just might work.

Chapter 58

Jace strode around the corner and into the hallway containing the royal bedchambers. As he did, the two guards stood up straighter and eyed him. Making sure he looked extremely obvious, he looked up and down the hallway.

Jace took a moment to examine both of them in his HUD to get their names. Then, he called out to the guards. "Zachary. Braiden. Have you seen an orange tabby cat?"

The two guards looked at him in confusion. So far, his plan was working. He'd used the hat to disguise himself in the same uniform he'd seen on the other guards. At the moment, he looked like a nondescript royal guardsman. And by using their names, he had created a false sense of familiarity.

"A cat?" asked the taller of the two guards, the one named Zachary.

Jace let out a sigh of frustration. "Yeah, some Duke or Earl or something gave the princess a cat for her birthday. She went crazy over it. But the thing ran off and now she's downstairs in the ballroom bailing her eyes out. Captain said he'd give whoever finds it a week of paid leave."

Just as he hoped, both guards perked up. The shorter one, Braiden, looked skeptical. "The captain's going to give a week of leave. That doesn't sound like him."

"I know," Jace shrugged. "But the queen is upset because the princess is crying at her birthday and you know how the king gets when the queen's upset."

The two guards gave him knowing nods. It had been a guess, a gamble based on how the king had acted when they'd met. Jace figured that he was the type of many who would get anxious or upset when his wife was upset. The guards seemed to have just confirmed it.

"Well," Jace said. "I'm going to keep looking. I want that week of leave!"

With that, he turned and went back down the hall and turned the corner. As soon as he did, he put the cloak back on and went into *Stealth*. He looked down at Luna, who had been waiting for him just around the corner.

"Remember," he told her mentally. "Wait until I give you the signal. Then casually walk down the hall until they chase you. I need you to lead them into a few rooms and stay away from them as long as you can. If they catch you, let me know and I'll dismiss you."

Luna looked up at him and cocked her head. "Yes."

"Wait for my signal," he told her and then slipped back around the corner, concealed by his cloak.

He walked to the first set of double doors and got as close to the wall as possible. Then he gave Luna the signal. A few moments later, she walked around the corner and began coming down the hallway.

It seemed to take the guards a few seconds to register what they were seeing, but then the taller guard elbowed the other one. "Hey Braiden, is that the orange cat? The one the princess is looking for?"

The other guard's eyes went. "How many orange cats do you think there are in the palace?"

"Come on," Zachary said. "Let's get it."

"We're not supposed to leave our post. You know that," Braiden argued, though Jace could see the conflict on his face.

"You stay then," Zachary smiled. "I'll get the week of leave."

"Oh no you won't," the other guard said and they both started towards Luna. "Here kitty, kitty."

Luna played her part perfectly. She sat down and looked at them approach. Just as they came within a few feet of her, she bounded off down the hallway and the guards ran past Jace as they gave chase.

"Come here kitty!" he heard one of them yell as they turned the corner.

Wasting no time, Jace opened the closest door, the one on the right, and ducked into the room. He scanned the room but saw no secret doors. He did see that this room had several other rooms attached to it and he quickly searched them as well.

Judging by the decorations and the paintings, Jace guessed this was the queen's room. That meant the room across the hall was the princess' bedroom. He cracked the door open and made sure the hallway was still clear and then moved across to the princess' room.

The princess' room was nearly identical in setup to the queen's room, but it definitely had a younger motif to it. There were horses, unicorns, and other creatures a teenager might like. There was also a flyer of Dwarven Thunder next to her dressing table. He'd have to tell Thedrir - if he ever saw the dwarf again.

Unfortunately, he saw no secret doors in her room either. He checked the bath chamber, a sitting room and finally, he checked her walk in closet. That's when he saw it. The far wall of the walk-in closet was glowing. Could that be it?

Excitedly, Jace went to the back wall and began searching for a way to open the secret door. It took him a moment, but he found a stud that clicked when he pushed it. The secret door opened up into a small room round with only one furnishing.

In the middle of the room was a small, oak desk with a stack of parchment and a quill. He'd done it. Jace had found the *Help Desk*.

Rushing over to the desk, Jace sat down and picked up the quill. He grabbed one of the pieces of parchment and began writing.

"I need to speak to someone in support."

He waited. And waited. Several minutes went by and Jace began to think that perhaps the *Help Desk* had finally been decommissioned permanently. Then, letters appeared underneath his.

"This is Paige with VEIL support." The writing stopped momentarily and then resumed. "How are you accessing this chat?"

Impatiently, Jace replied. "I found the *Help Desk* in the Royal Palace in Whitecliff. I need your help. This is urgent."

There was a long pause.

"One moment. I am getting a supervisor."

Jace tapped his fingers on the desk as he waited several more minutes.

"This is Ethan. I am a supervisor here at VEIL support. You said you have an urgent issue. Can you please describe the problem you are having? But please be aware, we no longer support this channel so any further communications will have to be done on the support site."

"There is a man named Damian Morfran who works for WorldCog. He has modified the insertion routine so that people with money are being inserted into the game as monster AIs while he gets all of their assets. He's on his way to the office right now to move this *Help Desk*."

There was a pregnant pause before Ethan responded.

"Is this some sort of joke?"

"No, the dragon that is headed to Whitecliff is being controlled by a player. That's why no one has been able to stop it. They're not bound by the normal rules. They don't have to use special abilities and special attacks at certain intervals."

There was a long pause.

"Who is this and how do you know this?"

"This is J…." Jace started to write but realized he'd almost told them his real name. He remembered just in time that he needed to be Jace's twin brother. He tried to come up with a name that began with J and wrote the first thing that came to his mind.

"This is Jynx Burton," he wrote. "I am Jace Burton's twin brother. Damian tried to kill Jace and he's in a coma. He worked with Damian on a WorldCog troubleshooting team and found out about the code. That's when Damian tried to kill him."

Jace paused and thought about what else he could write. "There are lots of people trapped in monster bodies. Every time they die, they get put into a new random body. And they're set at 100% sensory feedback. It's hell for them. I think it's driven some of them crazy."

"How do you know this?" came the response.

Thinking only briefly, he decided to go all in with his lie. "My brother was trying to get evidence against Damian before he was put in a coma. I was helping him. He explained it all to me."

"And you said Jace Burton works for WorldCog?"

"Yes, he works or worked for them," Jace wrote back. "As a junior programmer on one of the troubleshooting teams. It's the same team as Damian Morfran. Damian has stolen millions of dollars - including the money from an author named Anika Holden who writes romance novels under the pen name Diana Stewart."

There was another long pause. Then something started to happen. The room started to stretch, and he felt a wrenching sensation. He managed to keep hold of the quill. "Help. Something is wrong with the room."

"Someone is trying to move the *Help Desk*," Ethan wrote back. "We're trying to lock it into place. If we get disconnected, we'll look into this. You're inserted?"

"Yes."

"Can you make it back to this *Help Desk* or another?"

"I don't know."

"We'll try to have someone contact you in-game…."

And then suddenly Jace felt a wrenching sensation and he was flying out of the room. Things seemed to whirl around him for a moment. Then he blinked and found himself on the floor of the walk-in closet, lying on his back. Painfully, he pushed himself up and looking around, he found his glasses.

He put the glasses back on and wasn't surprised to see that the back of the closet no longer glowed. The secret door was gone. The *Help Desk* had been moved.

Damian must have gotten into the WorldCog building and managed to move the *Help Desk*, just as he said he'd do. But Jace had actually gotten to it first. He'd talked with support. He'd told them about the people and about Damian's thefts. Jace grinned. Damian had been too late.

But would support believe him? Would they look into Damian? Hopefully, they'd at least look into the insertion routine. Once they found the obfuscated code, they'd have to do a full investigation.

How long would that take? And how did Jace avoid Damian until they figure out what was going on? He was contemplating those questions when he heard voices outside the princess' room.

"Where are Zach and Braiden?" a gruff voice demanded. "Why did they leave their posts? You two, search the queen's chambers and the princess'."

Jace began to panic. If there were guards out there, he may not have a way out. He needed to think of something quickly. And then, like a thunderbolt hitting him, he came up with the perfect idea.

Thinking back to what Damian's dark elf had looked like, Jace willed himself to look as close to him as possible - all the way down to the clothes. He heard the door open and he stepped out of the closet and startled two guards who were just coming in. He reached over to the princess' dressing table and grabbed a pearl necklace that was laying out.

"A souvenir of the evening," he said. "Something to take back to Shiedrigish."

Then he rushed forward and darted between the two guards, doing a somersault between them, and coming up in the hallway. He looked down the hallway and saw Captain Avolin at the door to the king's bedroom. Just as the captain looked his way, Jace used his *Vanish* skill and disappeared.

He ran down the hall and around the corner. As he rounded the corner, Jace equipped the cloak and dropped into *Stealth*. He disappeared and threw himself against the wall as the captain and two guards rushed past him.

"Was that the ambassador?" the captain was saying.

"Yeah," said one of the guards. "I think it was. He said something about Shiedrigish."

"Where did he go?" the other guard asked.

"Sound the alarm," the captain yelled. "We have an intruder!"

Jace let them go around the next corner and then slipped into a side room. It was a guest bedroom and Jace remembered it had a small balcony. He went out to the balcony and, after making sure there were no guards below, he jumped down to the ground.

The moment he hit the ground, he entered *Stealth* again and started to make his way back around the garden. As he crept along, he remembered to dismiss Luna. Apparently, she was still leading the guards on a merry chase.

As he saw the message, letting him know that she had been dismissed, alarm bells began ringing around the courtyard.

Chapter 59

Willing the visage of the dark elf to vanish, Jace reverted back to his normal appearance. He entered *Stealth* and moved out to the wall which surrounded the palace. He followed the wall around to the gardens. When he reached them, he halted.

Ducking behind some large shrubs, he removed his cloak and stowed it back into his inventory. He started to leave the cover of the foliage when he had a thought. If he was questioned and they had that high-level truth detecting priest, Jace needed some plausible version of the truth he could tell them.

He removed the hat and stuffed that into his inventory as well. His hair no longer looked slicked back, but he was fine with that. Jace had done what he'd needed to do. He'd contacted support and told them about the insertion routine and Damian's illegal activities. Now, he just needed to get out of here.

Damian would be coming after him. He was sure of it. Whether to cover his tracks or just out of revenge, the older programmer would want to find him and eliminate him. Jace didn't know exactly how Damian might do that, but considering what he'd done to the insertion routine, Jace had to assume Damian would have something nasty in the game.

He and the girls needed to disappear. And they needed to do it tonight. Damian knew his character name now. With that information, he could easily trace Jace and possibly the girls as well. They'd need to change their names and they'd need to do it now.

Taking a deep breath, Jace emerged from behind the shrubs. He'd barely taken two steps when a gruff voice called out. "You there. What are you doing?"

Jace turned to see a guard who had been standing on the other side of a tree. He'd missed spotting the guard and now he needed to think quickly. Luckily, an idea came to him quickly.

"I'm looking for my familiar," he told the guard and made a show of looking around. "It's an orange tabby cat and I can't find it anywhere."

"An orange tabby, you say?" the guard said suspiciously. "Come with me."

Jace sighed and followed the guard. He realized that using Luna as his excuse had been a bad idea considering he'd used her as the distraction in the palace. He was undoubtedly being taken to be questioned. Mentally, he went over his story and began to formulate the most truthful version of events he could tell, without actually telling the entire truth.

The guard took him back the way he'd come and around to a different side entrance where a group of guards waited. They approached and the guards suddenly became more alert.

"Wyatt, who's that?" said one of the group, a sort skinny fellow.

"He was in the garden, Sergeant" the guard accompanying him, who Jace now knew was named Wyatt, replied. "Said he's looking for an orange tabby cat?"

The guards exchanged grim glances. The sergeant motioned for one of the other guards. "Parker, go fetch the captain."

The sergeant stepped closer to Jace and looked him up and down. "And who are you, sir?"

"Sir Jace Burton, Baronet," Jace replied. There was no use in lying since the captain would know him. Plus, if they brought one of those truth priests, he wouldn't get away with any lies anyway.

"And what were you doing in the garden? Away from the other guests?" the sergeant asked.

"I was looking for my familiar," he told them. "I noticed she was missing. Earlier she had attacked one of the fish illusions in the fountains and I thought she might be trying to go after another one."

"I see," the sergeant said. The man seemed about to ask another question when the door behind them opened and the captain and two more guards appeared.

Captain Avolin looked at Jace and rolled his eyes. "Why do you always seem to be in the middle of some sort of trouble?"

Jace smiled at the captain and shrugged. "I didn't realize I was in the middle of any trouble this time. I was just looking for Luna, my familiar."

"An orange tabby cat?" the captain said.

"Yes," Jace nodded. "I haven't seen her for some time."

"When was the last time you saw your familiar?" Avolin asked.

Jace thought about his answer. No one here looked like a truth priest, but just in case, he needed to make sure whatever he said was the truth. "I'm not sure exactly."

That was true. He didn't have his timepiece, so he wasn't exactly sure when he'd seen Luna last. Was it five minutes ago? Six minutes ago? Ten minutes ago?

"But I definitely remember seeing her when that dark elf was talking to me," Jace continued. That was true as well. Luna was next to him when Damian had been talking to him.

"Dark elf?" Captain Avolin raised an eyebrow. "You were talking with a dark elf?"

"Yes," Jace nodded. "I think he was an Ambassador or something. He was very unpleasant. He actually threatened me."

"Threatened you?" The captain looked surprised. "How?"

Jace thought back to Damian's words. "He said he had to do something and then afterwards he was going to come back and see what trouble he could get me into."

"Why?" the captain demanded. "Why would he threaten you? Do you two know each other?"

Jace thought how he could answer that question truthfully and still stick with his narrative. Then it came to him. "I had never seen that dark elf before tonight. As to why he threatened me, I think he was afraid I would reveal his plans. I heard him say something about the princess' bedchamber."

The captain gave him a hard look. "You heard someone mentioned the princess' bedchamber and you didn't report this?"

Jace shook his head. "Captain, I wasn't sure exactly what he meant or if he were even serious. For all I knew, they could be lovers and I wasn't about to be the one to make a false accusation to the king about his daughter and a dark elf."

Captain Avolin looked at him grimly but nodded. "Yes, I can see where you might not want to be embroiled with that sort of thing. But, in the future, you should bring it up with me. I can assure you I will conduct a discrete investigation."

"Sorry," Jace said. "What's this all about anyway? I mean, I was a little far from the other guests, but I don't think that warrants being interrogated. I mean, I was invited to the party."

"Let's just say that an orange tabby cat was spotted in the palace earlier," he said. "And may have been used as a distraction."

"A distraction?" Jace asked as innocently as he could. "For what?"

The captain pursed his lips. "I'm not at liberty to discuss that. But thank you for the information, Sir Burton. It was most helpful. Wyatt, return Sir Burton back to the party."

"And Sir Burton," the captain said. "Be careful not to stray too far from the party. And if you see the dark elf again, inform one of the guards."

"I will," Jace assured him.

The captain spun and went back into the palace. Once he was gone, Wyatt escorted him back to the gardens and then left him to resume his post.

No sooner was the guard out of sight when Diana and Mika came rushing over to him.

"We saw the guard take you away," Mika said breathlessly. "We thought you were in trouble."

Jace held up his hands to forestall any questions. "Right now, we need to leave. I'll explain everything in the carriage. But we need to leave now."

Whether it was his expression or his tone of voice, both girls nodded, and they quickly made their way back to the entrance. They found a woman in the king's livery by the driveway where they had been dropped off.

"Ready to leave, milord and ladies?" the woman asked.

"Yes," Jace told her. "We need to find our carriage."

"I will summon it for you," the woman said. "You're name?"

"Sir Jace Burton," he told her.

"Very good, Sir Burton," she said and then gestured. A young man who looked barely eighteen came running over from some hidden spot between the shrubs. "Fetch Sir Burton's coach straightaway."

"Yes, Mum," the boy said and then rushed off.

"It will be just a few moments," the woman said.

His group stood in silence until the carriage appeared, though Jace could tell both Diana and Mika were anxious and obviously wanted to ask him questions. He appreciated their patience and once they were inside the coach and on their way home, he tapped on the outside of the carriage.

The driver stopped the carriage and leaned down. "Yes, Sir?"

"We're not going to manor," he told the man. "Take us to patents office, right now."

"Yes sir," the man replied, and in a moment, the carriage was on its way.

"Patents office?" Diana asked with a raised eyebrow.

"We're changing our names," he told them. "Tonight."

"Why?" Mika asked, her face a mask of confusion.

Jace took a deep breath and then related what had happened to him. He told them about the dwarves and the tour. And how he'd bribed Thedrir to be part of the tour. Then he mentioned how Damian had joined the tour as well.

"You ran into him?" Mika asked, wide-eyed. "Did he recognize you?"

Jace nodded solemnly. "He did."

He quickly related the rest of the story. How he'd found the *Help Desk* and contacted support and then made his escape and hopefully implicated Damian in the theft of the pearl necklace.

"That was very good," Mika beamed. "You are clever."

Diana was more practical. "So, now what? You've contacted support. What do we do now? And do you think they bought your story about being Jace's twin brother?"

Jace shrugged. "I don't know whether they bought it. I assume they'll take what I said at face value but they'll no doubt do some research. Hopefully, they'll focus on Damian first."

"So, your name is Jynx now?" Diana said, giving him a disapproving look.

He shrugged again. "It's the first thing that popped into my head. And I WAS a little preoccupied at the time. And under a time crunch."

"I'm not judging," Diana grinned, though it was clear by her expression that she was.

"I like it," Mika smiled.

"So, we need to change our names so Damian can't track us?" Diana asked.

"Yes," he replied. "There are tools he has access to that can locate players. Mostly they're used by support, but Damian has access to them too. They can search by character name and then it gives their exact coordinates in the game."

"That is very bad," Mika said. "He can find us anywhere!"

"Exactly," Jace told her. "That's why we need to change our names right now."

The coach came to a halt and they all shuffled out. The patents office was still open and Jace guessed it was to allow players to buy titles at any time of the day. Considering how much money WorldCog made each transaction, he wasn't surprised.

His group went inside and found a gnome who was working the graveyard shift. The gnome came over to them and smiled. "How may I help you, milord and ladies?"

"How much does it cost to change your name?" he asked.

"A name change, sir?" the gnome repeated. "Fifty thousand gold."

"FIFTY THOUSAND GOLD?!" he repeated incredulously. They'd gotten a marriage certificate and a name change for 10,000 gold each. How did they remotely make sense? "Why is it so much? And how come I can change my name when I get married and it only costs 10,000 gold?"

The gnome seemed a little taken back by his outburst but smiled apologetically. "I'm sorry, milord. I don't understand the reasoning for all of the laws, I merely obey them."

Jace turned to the girls who were looking equally incredulous. He's thought it would only be a few thousand, maybe five thousand. Fifty thousand was an outrageous sum. Just another way for WorldCog to extract their thirty pieces of silver.

"I'll be back," he told the man and then left with the girls. It appeared he would need to make another stop first.

"To the bank," he called to the driver once they were back inside the carriage.

Chapter 60

They went to the bank, retrieved the money and then returned to the patents office. On the journey from the bank back to the patents office, they discussed last names. The girls offered many suggestions, from the Japanese word for ghost to references to classical literature. None of them really stood out to Jace.

Just before they arrived back at the patent office, they decided on Knightly. After all, for the time being he was a Baronet, which was one step up from a knight.

"Jynx Knightly?" he asked, mulling over the sound of it.

"I like that one best so far," Mika told him.

"I'm fine with it," Diana said as the carriage came to a halt. "And it looks like we're out of time anyway."

They paid the patents office the 150,000 gold for all three of their name changes. Jace became Jynx Knightly, while the two girls kept their first names but changed their last names to Knightly. Once the name changes were complete, they returned to the manor.

It was after midnight when they walked in and none of the servants were up. They each returned to their rooms and gathered up all of their weapons and equipment. In addition to his regular equipment, Jace retrieved the second gnomish timepiece and strapped it to his wrist. In a world with few clocks, a wristwatch was very useful.

As he was putting items back into his inventory, he came across the log books he'd taken from Drakkar. He made a mental note to read them at some point to find out what he could about the man.

Once they had collected all of their belongings, they gathered back downstairs in the main living room to discuss their next plans.

"Now what do we do?" Mika asked.

"Yes," Diana added. "How long before Damian comes looking for us? And can he really do anything to us in the game?"

"I'm not sure," Jace told them. "Assuming he left the office right after he moved the *Help Desk*, he would be home now and logging back in. I'm hoping the situation at the palace will either get him kicked out of Whitecliff, or at the very least, have him questioned for some time."

"How long?" Mika asked.

"I don't know," Jace admitted. "But we have a ship to catch tomorrow and I think we should be on it early."

"You think the dragon will still attack the city?" Mika asked. "Won't the *Help Desk* stop it?"

"No," he shook his head. "The dragon will be here Monday. There's no way they'll be able to troubleshoot it that quickly."

"That's a pity. How early do you plan to go to the ship?" Diana asked.

"I think we should wake the servants up right now," he told them. "And go down there now. It means spending the rest of the night on the ship, but I think it's safer than staying here."

"Can he really hurt us?" Mika asked.

"I don't know Mika," Jace replied. "But I wouldn't put it past him. Look what he's done so far. There should be safeties in the system to prevent him from actually doing permanent harm to us, but he may have put code into other routines that allow him to bypass it. A backdoor, so to speak."

"I, for one, don't feel like taking that chance," Diana said.

"Then we go now?" Mika asked.

"As soon as everyone is ready," he told them. "I'll go wake them."

Hours later, they were standing on the deck of the deck of the *Sea Tyrant*. Webley had been good to his word and the captain, a female raccoon-kin named

Tehra Yehmee, had welcomed them aboard and shown them to their cabins.

Now Jace, Mika and Diana stood up on the upper deck as the sun peeked over the eastern ocean. The other passengers had boarded a few minutes ago and soon they'd be leaving for the gnomish capital of Nynymmost to the north.

Jace glanced back at the city of Whitecliff, wondering if it might be the last time, he saw it. It had been his home for the last week. He chuckled to himself. This past had been tumultuous and felt more like a month. But somehow, they'd managed to find a way into the palace and contact support.

Now, they just needed to stay off of Damian's radar and survive long enough for support to do their work. Then the girls would be restored and hopefully, he'd still be around too.

He thought about Charlena then. She'd been such a help when he'd first arrived and now, she had abandoned them just when they could have used her help the most. Not that he really blamed her. Finding out the real him was in a coma had thrown him for a loop too.

He'd thought about leaving a note for her at the manor but couldn't risk it falling into the hands of Damian. He knew it was only a matter of time before his old co-worker tracked him down to the manor and then he'd undoubtedly search it for clues to where they'd gone. No, she was on her own now and he wished her well.

"Let loose the moorings," he heard the captain bellow. "And prepare to set sail."

Jace took a last look at Whitecliff as the ship started to move. He hoped it wasn't the last time he'd see it. Walking to the bow of the ship with Mika and Diana, they all stared towards the horizon and whatever adventure lay ahead of them.

Epilogue

Jace opened up his eyes. At least, that's what he intended to do. The moment he cracked them, pain flooded into his brain like someone was pouring molten lead into his skull. He quickly closed his eyes and moaned.

He waited what seemed like a minute and then tried to open his eyes again, this time just a fraction. He blinked as his eyes adjusted to the light and then, just moving his eyes, looked around the room.

To his shock, he realized he wasn't in his bedroom. In fact, nothing looked familiar. As things came more into focus, his addled brain started putting things together. It looked like he was in a hospital.

He tried to remember how he'd gotten here but his head hurt, and he felt foggy, like he'd been drinking the night before and this was just some really bad hangover. Only it felt worse than any hangover he'd ever had.

He glanced to the back of the room and saw a red-headed girl sprawled out in the chairs across from his head. From what he could see, she was cute in a girl-next-door sort of way, but he didn't know who she was. She appeared to have fallen asleep on the chairs. Had she been waiting for him? Did she know him?

His mouth was dry and had a funny taste in it. When he tried to wet his lips, he found them dried and cracked. He tried to move his hand but found that he was too weak. His hand moved slightly but only came up an inch off the bed.

Frustrated, Jace tried to get the sleeping red-head's attention. "Hello."

He'd meant it to be a greeting, to get her attention, but it came out as a barely audible hiss. He tried wetting his mouth again, but he had no saliva. His mouth was dry.

He tried again. "Hello!"

This time, the girl stirred. She looked up with sleep filled eyes and blinked several times. The red-head looked around the room and then stopped when she came across Jace. Her eyes went wide, and she jumped out of the chair. "Nurse! Nurse! He's awake."

Moments later, several people in white jackets appeared and he was subjected to all sorts of poking, prodding and questions.

Someone shone a small flashlight in his eyes as someone was holding onto his wrist - probably taking his pulse. Another person was listening to his heart with a stethoscope. He seemed extremely popular at the moment.

"Do you know your name?" asked one of the people in the white jackets. It was a stocky woman with short blond hair. She was looking at him and when he didn't answer, she repeated the question. "Do you know who you are?"

"Jace," he croaked. "Jace Burton."

The woman nodded, smiling. "Good Jace. Do you know where you are?"

He tried to shake his head, but the molten lava returned to his skull and he quickly stopped. "Hospital?"

"That's right," the nurse said and smiled. "You're in a hospital."

"Vitals are normal. Reactions and reflexes are normal," said another person in a white jacket, this one a middle aged man. "I'll go get the doctor."

"My name is Nurse Dakota," the blond nurse said. "You've been in a coma for several months. You were in a car accident. Do you remember?"

Jace started to shake his head but then remembered the molten lava and changed his mind. The pain in his head wasn't quite as bad now, but any movement brought back that feeling of molten metal poured into his skull. "No."

He said no, but he vaguely remembered something. A bright light and then lots of pain. He closed his eyes as he remembered the pain.

"The doctor will be here soon," she said. "I'll leave you with your sister until the doctor gets here."

"Sister?" Jace asked. He knew he was out of it, but his sister was dead. She'd died with his parents on the day he'd graduated high school. Luna. That had been her name.

The blond nurse disappeared from his field of view and he heard her footsteps leaving the room. Then, the pretty red-head face came into his view.

"Hi," she said. "You...uh… don't remember me, do you?"

Jace forgot and tried to shake his head and instantly regretted it. He stopped immediately and tried to reply. "No."

"I didn't think you would," she frowned.

"I'm sorry," Jace apologized. She was so pretty, he wanted to remember her. "Head hurts."

"You've been through quite a bit," the girl gave him a sympathetic expression. The girl moved her head down to his ear and he could feel her warm breath as she whispered the next words. "You and I need to talk alone after the doctor sees you. It's really important. Until then, don't tell them I'm not your sister."

She raised her head and smiled at him, then turned towards someone entering the room. Jace didn't know what to make of her words. His mind was still addled, and thinking was hard.

In a moment, another face appeared in his view. The man was Indian and smiled down at him. "Welcome back to the land of living Mr. Burton.

Join the Adventure

To learn more about the adventures of
Jace, Mika, Diana, Charlena, and
Luna, or to learn of John Cressman's
other books and projects, visit his
website at:

https://www.johnecressman.com

Or visit him on Facebook:

https://www.facebook.com/authorjohn
cressman/

Acknowledgements

I'd like to acknowledge all the members
of the LitRPG Authors' Guild who
helped me in so many ways! Without
your help, I could never have gotten this
far!

About the Author

John E. Cressman is an author, magician, mentalist, hypnotist, programmer, and longtime lover of roleplaying games and fantasy/sci-fi books.

As a teen, he wasted long hours creating D&D fantasy campaigns for his friends to play. He has tried several pen and paper roleplaying games from the original Dungeons and Dragons, Traveler and Star Frontiers to the new Pathfinder games.

He still enjoys computer RPGs and MMORPGs, with his current favorite being Elder Scrolls Online. He used to play Skyrim, but then he took an arrow to the knee.

John has published two books on hypnosis and is now trying his hand at the fantasy LitRPG genre with his new LitRPG trilogy, VEIL Online.